INQUISITION

Also by Anselm Audley

Heresy
Book One of the Aquasilva Trilogy

Available from Pocket Books

INQUISITION

Book Two of
THE AQUASILVA TRILOGY

ANSELM AUDLEY

POCKET BOOKS
New York   London   Toronto   Sydney   Singapore

POCKET BOOKS, a division of Simon & Schuster, Inc.
1230 Avenue of the Americas, New York, NY 10020

Copyright © 2002 by Anselm Audley

Originally published in Great Britain in 2002 by Earthlight,
an imprint of Simon & Schuster U.K. Ltd

Published by arrangement with Simon & Schuster U.K. Ltd

ISBN: 0-7434-2740-8

First Pocket Books hardcover printing October 2002

10   9   8   7   6   5   4   3   2   1

POCKET and colophon are registered trademarks of
Simon & Schuster, Inc.

For information regarding special discounts for bulk purchases,
please contact Simon & Schuster Special Sales at 1-800-456-6798
or business@simonandschuster.com

Printed in the U.S.A.

For my sister

Acknowledgments

I'd like to thank, again, all the people who originally contributed to *Aquasilva*, but for *Inquisition* especially to: my parents and my sister, Fred Dulwich, Naomi Harries, John Roe and Ben Taylor. Also to my friends from Somerset and Oxford who put up with my unholy interest in heretics, Inquisitors and the like. Finally, and most importantly, to my brilliant agent, James Hale, and to Rosie Buckman. Many, many thanks to both of you.

Equatorial circumference
as calculated by the Oceanographic Guild
65,397 miles

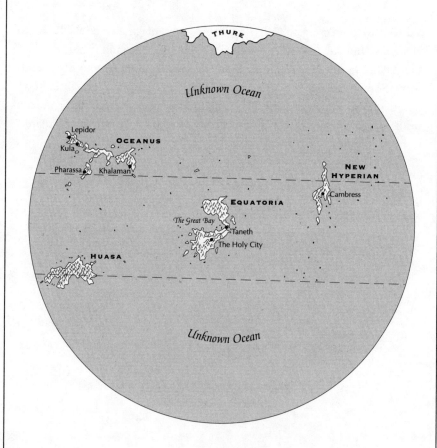

THURE

Unknown Ocean

Lepidor
OCEANUS
Kula
Pharassa Khalaman

NEW
HYPERIAN

Cambress

EQUATORIA

The Great Bay
Taneth
The Holy City

HUASA

Unknown Ocean

Continents

NOTE: Aquasilva is a much bigger world than Earth, with a diameter of about 20,000 miles; the continents are therefore drawn larger than life for legibility.

Kreon Eirillia
Cartographer to His Imperial Majesty
Orosius Tar'Conantur

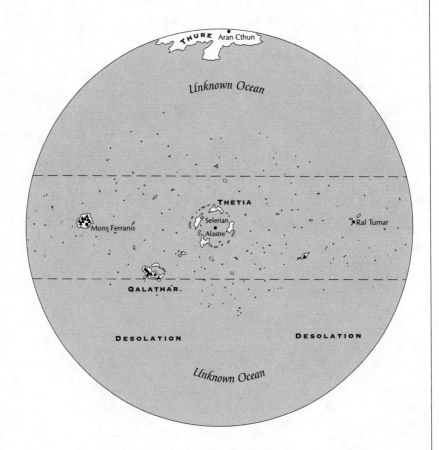

Archipelago

NOTE: Aquasilva is a much bigger world than Earth, with a diameter of about 20,000 miles; the continents are therefore drawn larger than life for legibility.

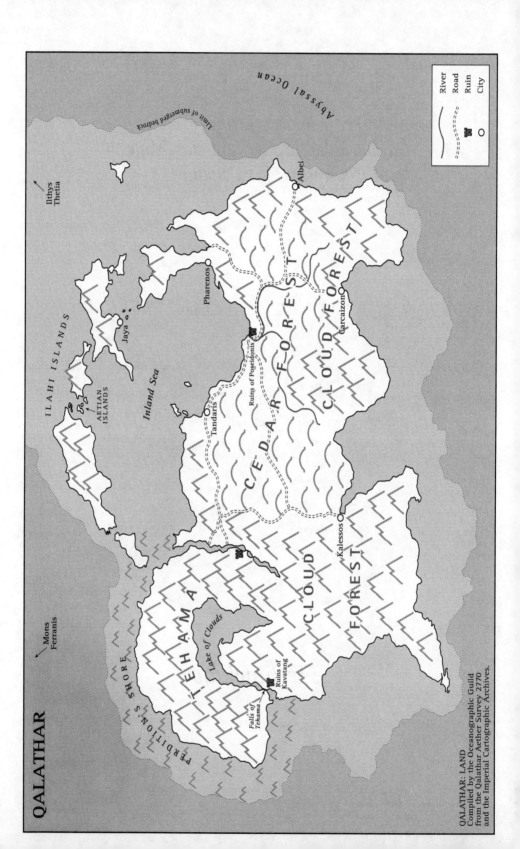

QALATHAR

Ilthys Thetia

Mons Ferranis

Limit of submerged bedrock

Abyssal Ocean

Albei

ILAHI ISLANDS

Pharenos

Jaya

AETIAN ISLANDS

Inland Sea

Ruins of Poseidonis

Tandaris

CLOUD FOREST

Carcalzon

CEDAR FOREST

PERDITION'S SHORE

TEHAMA

Lake of Clouds

CLOUD FOREST

Kalessos

Ruins of Kavatang

Falls of Tehama

~~	River
- - - -	Road
⊞	Ruin
○	City

QALATHAR: LAND
Compiled by the Oceanographic Guild
from the Qalathar Aether Survey 2770
and the Imperial Cartographic Archives.

As Things Stand . . .

The Domain has been defeated in Lepidor, with the two survivors, Midian and Sarhaddon, sent back to Equatoria in disgrace. Cathan stands in for his convalescing father as Count of Lepidor, enjoying with his friends an Indian summer at the end of the year.

Hamilcar returns to Taneth, later to be joined by Elassel. He has his feud against Foryth to pursue and a new opportunity of alliance with House Canadrath, who were brought into the picture by Cathan's call for help after Elnibal's poisoning.

The Archipelago is still suffering under the Domain's yoke, and it is there that Cathan, with the impatient Palatine and Ravenna, whose identity as the Pharaoh only the three of them know, turns his attention. He also has the ancient flagship, *Aeon*, to find.

Sagantha and his crew have gone on their way to more devious plots.

And in Selerian Alastre, the Emperor spins his webs of intrigue in the Imperial Palace . . .

INQUISITION

Prologue

"Is everything closed down?"

"Every last system, Admiral. I'm just about to take the reactor off-line."

Deep, pulsing blue light illuminated the four people standing there, casting uneven shadows on to the walls. *Almost like wraiths standing behind them*, Admiral Cidelis thought, with a shudder.

"Check that we have enough power in the reserves."

Centurion Minos nodded and walked forward to the huge glowing sphere that sat in the middle of the bridge, his face cast into sharp relief by the light. Beyond the little pool of radiance, the rest of the huge room was in gray darkness, its interfaces and displays still and dead.

There was utter silence for a moment as Cidelis looked for one last time around the bridge of his flagship. It was many centuries older than him and, with any luck, would outlive him by as long. But he would never see it again. He tried to imprint every last detail on his mind: Minos sliding his hands into the interface; Erista fumbling to light the torch, a look of fatigue and resignation on her face. And Hecateus, the master-at-arms, standing to Erista's left and holding her precious instrument case, his eye fixed on the sphere.

All of them knew that they were saying goodbye, to each other as well as to the ship. The Emperor had put an astronomical price on their heads, making it too dangerous even to flee together. There was a whole world out there, a diminished one perhaps, but with plenty of places to make a new life. For some.

"More than enough," Minos reported. "Shall I shut it down now?"

Cidelis shook his head. "Your task here is done. I will finish it—I will take the ship to her final resting place."

"You're staying, aren't you?" Erista said, as white flames leaped from the end of the torch, driving the shadows wild.

"Where else is there for me?" Cidelis said, smiling at her. The young scientist was a catch for someone, and thirty years ago he might have considered trying to be that someone. It would be a hard life for one in her profession now, what with the pogroms and the fanatics denouncing everything that looked remotely *unnatural*. But she was more than clever enough to find a place somewhere, perhaps as an oceanographer. Not even the priests could do without them.

She didn't protest, which surprised him. Nor did Centurion Minos, whose idealism still seemed to be intact despite everything that had happened.

Hecateus stepped forward, slinging the instrument case casually over one muscled shoulder. He was still wearing the remnants of a naval uniform, with the badge of his rank set proudly on a fraying collar.

"Goodbye, sir. It's been an honor to know you."

There was no one Cidelis would rather have heard it from. Not even from his wife, butchered by the enemy in the fall of Selerian Alastre. Hecateus had been ship's boy on Cidelis's first command, nearly a quarter of a century ago, and since then had kept every crew together for him. He'd even turned down the post of Deputy Quartermaster-General for this last assignment. Just a few short months ago.

"Thank you, Hecateus. Good luck in New Hyperian."

They'd intercepted a message a few weeks ago before the SkyEyes went off-line, a broadcast from an ex-Imperial flagship urging all surviving naval ships to join a colonizing expedition to the ravaged continent of New Hyperian, free from the tyranny of the Emperor. Hecateus, never having known another life than the Navy, had decided to give it a try.

Minos and Erista, whom he hardly knew, bid their farewells and then followed Hecateus out of the bridge, taking the torch with them.

Standing alone on the bridge, Cidelis waited until the echoes of their footsteps had died away before he sat down in his admiral's chair again to guide the ship her final few miles. Then, when she finally came to a halt, he gathered up the carrying bag lying on the floor, lit a torch of his own, and set off in the other direction. As if on cue, the deep blue light pulsed one last time, then died, leaving the sphere a black ball in its gimbals. It was so dark that nothing was even reflected from its surface.

It was a quarter of an hour's walk through the hollow, empty central passageway of the ship to the place where he was going. The huge double doors opened soundlessly in front of him, and he walked up the central aisle, seeming like a tiny speck of torchlight in the immensity of the hall. The walls were transparent and looked out into the ocean, but down here in the abyss there was nothing to see except blackness.

Even before he reached the steps, Cidelis saw the figure on the throne at the aisle's end, a shadowy presence in the gloom. When he came to the foot of the stairway, he stopped, unslung the bag, and propped the torch up in a flagstaff socket on the floor.

Then, slowly and unhurriedly, Cidelis changed into his dress uniform, correct in every last detail down to the rank stars and the fastening of the belt, as he had worn it for thirty-five years. Finally he strapped on his ceremonial sword, the silver chasing on its hilt glittering coldly.

Punctilious to the last, Cidelis took the bag with his other clothes and stowed it away in a cabinet behind and to one side of the throne, then went back to the center of the hall and walked up the steps to kneel solemnly before the corpse who occupied the throne. Tiberius Galadrin Tar'Conantur, Emperor of Thetia, stared unseeingly back at him, the deep gray eyes above his finely chiseled cheekbones untouched by decay, looking exactly as he had when he'd been alive. There was a faint, sad smile on his lips, and the robe he wore—the same royal blue as Cidelis's uniform—covered the fatal wound in his chest. There was a sealed wax tablet at his feet, a last message that Cidelis had already written to the next true heir to set foot on the ship.

There was only one thing wrong, but not even Cidelis had been able to remedy that. The crown that rested on the dead Emperor's raven-black hair was the Hierarch's diadem, not the Crown of Stars. That was on the head of the usurper, the traitor . . .

An immense sadness swept through Cidelis as he drew his sword, a sword that had never tasted blood, and reversed it. For a moment he almost hesitated, but then he looked up at Tiberius again, seeing the father instead of the son.

"Oh, Aetius, why? Why did you have to leave us? Why couldn't one of us have gone in your place?"

There was no answer, as he'd known there would be. He had made his farewells.

Then Cleomenes Cidelis, First Admiral of the Thetian Empire, drove his sword unerringly into his own heart. As the mist clouded his mind he thought he heard his Emperor's voice calling.

Part One
The City of Meetings

Chapter I

"It's winter! The Guild's confirmed it."

I sat up, squinting in the glare of the afternoon sun, to see where the voice was coming from. After a moment I heard footsteps on the path below, and then a head appeared behind the rocks.

"For sure this time?" somebody sitting on my right asked.

"When aren't they sure?" The original speaker clambered up the last few feet and came around to sit down on a threadbare path of grass.

"The priests were two weeks out last year." Her questioner shifted position and inspected her lute critically, brushing a stray seed-pod off the fingerboard.

"That was the priests. They haven't got a clue."

"They certainly ought to have—they're the only ones who can forecast it properly."

I looked up into the cloudless blue sky, as if somewhere up there I could see the same signs as the priests, to tell us the temperature was about to plummet and the storms redouble their efforts.

"The Guild would be far better at predicting winter if only the priests gave it a chance."

"Let's not get into that argument again, Cathan," the newcomer said, leaning back against the trunk of the lone cedar tree set apart from the forest near the cliff edge. "We've got a few more days of it being warm enough to sit outside, and there's no need to waste it. We'll have all the time in the world to argue when winter does come."

"When's that going to be?"

"When this unnatural hot spell finishes." She wore only a thin tunic and sandals despite the fact it was well into autumn. "Two or three days at most."

Two or three days. Well, nothing lasted forever, and we certainly hadn't expected this sudden return to summer temperatures so late in the year. It would have been even better if I hadn't had to spend so much time working, attending to clan business while my father was convalescing. He might have taken his title back, but he still wasn't fit to cope with all the paperwork, so I ended up doing it. It was a job I loathed, but it didn't seem quite so bad as it had been. Perhaps that was because I'd been through a lot worse now.

"Have you done anything useful?"

"Depends what *useful* means, Palatine," said Ravenna, who was sitting next to me with her back against the tree trunk. There was a book lying face down next to her, which she hadn't been reading for some time—at least, not since before the last time I bothered to look.

"Useful as in what you said you were going to do." Palatine's grasp of Archipelagan grammar was still a little sketchy sometimes, even after eighteen months away from the convoluted language of her homeland.

"Look through this book for something that obviously isn't there, you mean."

"If it isn't there, why are you bothering? Why not actually go and look for it somewhere?"

"Just as soon as you tell us where to start."

Palatine rolled her eyes and absently began twisting a green shoot around her fingers, unable as ever to keep still. She was the only one of us who hadn't welcomed the heat and the chance to do very little.

Sighing before picking the book up once more, the other woman started reading again. I had a copy too, but not the faintest idea where I'd put it. I couldn't remember having brought it out here . . . no, it was at the bottom of the chest in my room, where nobody would accidentally come across it and investigate its contents.

I moved back a little, trying to find a more comfortable position for my head on the broad tree-root. It really was too hot to do anything except lie around in the shade. Besides, there was no need to do anything. I'd done all the paperwork for today—the rest of the clan was feeling just as enervated, and people were reluctant to get down to tiresome ledgers or petitions. I banished from my mind the thought that there would be a sudden excess of such work with the onset of winter.

I closed my eyes again and slipped back into a contented doze, able to ignore the inconvenient projection on the root that was digging into my back, and even the highly irritating cooing from some doves in the woods behind us. Doves were fine in small doses, but the noise they made got on my nerves very quickly. The muffled sound of the surf on the beach below was much better, and served as an excellent accompaniment when the lutenist started playing an air a few minutes later.

"Palatine, how on earth did the Thetians win this war?" asked the reader suddenly.

"What do you mean?"

"They were drunk all the time. Look, the man who wrote this was their high priest, but in one week he goes to more parties than a regiment of socialites."

"We enjoy life," Palatine said. "When we have time free, we don't lie around under the trees staring dreamily out to sea."

"If it's so good, why don't you want to go back?"

I could almost feel the glare Palatine gave her, but didn't bother to open my eyes. Palatine had been irritable for at least a week, if not longer, and I was used to it by now.

"Stop arguing," the lutenist said without interrupting the flow of her melody. "You're disturbing my concentration."

"My apologies, Elassel," Palatine said, not sounding as though she meant it.

There was no answer, and my mind drifted off again, far away from the sun-dappled shores of Lepidor.

I knew the reasons for Palatine's short temper; all of us did. But it was what I was doing, or rather not doing, that was to blame. While she fretted, anxious for us to leave, I was content to wait—and do nothing. Not that I didn't have some support, because none of the others seemed in any hurry.

I hadn't told anybody why we were still here, why we were lingering so long when staying here for good obviously wasn't an option. I had pleaded clan duties, and for more than a month, as my father slowly recovered from the effects of his poisoning, it had been enough. But all of them knew that wasn't the real reason, that no dull paperwork, however necessary to the clan, required my personal presence. My mother and the First Adviser were just as capable and infinitely more patient.

"I suppose it's too much to ask if we'll be moving once winter's here?" Palatine said, jabbing her finger into my side. I looked at her indignantly, the bright sunlight momentarily dazzling me.

"I'm not going to leave just because the weather changes."

"Then when will it be? When the stars fall and the oceans rise to cover us all? When a priest opens his mouth without mentioning heresy? Or when everyone else has died of old age?"

"We've already told you. I'm not setting out until I have an idea where I'm going."

"So how does staying in Lepidor help you? There's nothing here that could possibly aid you, except that wretched book."

"And where else can we go?"

"You might consider a library. They have lots and lots of books in them, even old scrolls with cobwebs on that I'm sure might tell you what you're looking for."

"So the people who have gone to ridiculous lengths to hide the thing are then going to leave messages everywhere saying, *We are here.* Palatine, I know you hate doing nothing, but we can't just rush into this. And what happens if the Inquisition find out? If they get hold of it, that'll be the end of disagreement with them."

"Don't I deserve to be told just what you're waiting for? Don't we all?" She looked to the other two for support, and so did I. Elassel was concentrating on her lute playing, seemingly absorbed in the music.

Beside me Ravenna put the book down again and fixed her serious gray gaze first on me, then on Palatine.

"You're waiting for someone, aren't you? Someone in particular," she said.

I bit back an annoyed retort and nodded. Perhaps I hadn't been as clever as I thought.

Palatine buried her face in her hands, exaggerating as always.

"We could be here forever. Why didn't I see this earlier? I could have gone off on one of the other ships when they left. Cathan, Tanais takes months to turn up, and never where you want him."

"He said he'd be back when Lepidor was secure."

"But meanwhile he'll have been dealing with some clan rebellion or troublesome priest or somebody's agent, and he'll be stuck in a backwater for weeks at a time."

"Would you set out on a sea journey knowing you hadn't consulted an oceanographer? Tanais may not turn up when we want, but he was there when it disappeared. If anyone knows where it is, it'll be him."

"I wish you luck." Palatine stood up and headed off along the shoreline, disappearing after a moment behind the trunk of another cedar.

"She's only going to get worse," Ravenna said, staring after her. "And she does know Tanais better than you."

"That doesn't change anything. We still have to wait for him."

"I know, I know. But what if he doesn't come? Do you want to stay here all through the winter while the Inquisition schemes and plots? We may have won a victory here, but they're very bad losers, and by staying here we're certain to draw their attention again. It's best to keep moving."

Something rustled in the branches of the cedar tree above us, perhaps one of those wretched doves. Elassel's lute went on, accompanied by a chorus of cicadas.

"If they move against us, they're admitting that what happened wasn't just the work of a few renegades, and people will begin to wonder what they're up to."

"It's old news by now, Cathan. And a fundamentalist never forgets a setback."

"Nor does anyone else, it seems."

"If that includes our allies, then why so morose?" She took my hand and reached for the book again, but at that moment there was a sharp crack. A second bundle of cedar fronds fell on both of us, accompanied by a shower of cones.

"Jerian!" I shook my head, trying to clear bits of tree out of my hair as Ravenna brushed twigs off herself. I looked up to see my brother's grinning face looking down at us.

"I thought so!" he said triumphantly.

He was well out of reach, three or four branches above us, but before he could say anything else there was a strangled cry over to my right.

"Krreh! You little . . . it'll take forever to get all that dust out of my lute!" Pausing only to make sure her precious instrument was safe, Elassel jumped to her feet and ran around to the other side of the tree, and in short order my brother's triumphant grin gave way to a wail of outrage as Elassel clambered up toward him as easily as if she was walking along the beach. I'd never been sure where Elassel had learned to pick locks or scale walls and trees like ordinary mortals climbed steps, but her skills had proved useful more than once.

"As far as Jerian's concerned, grown-ups can't climb trees," I whispered to Ravenna. "With any luck he won't try this one again."

"I hope not," she said, dusting herself down. "You look a fright."

"Look who's talking. I think the primitive look suits you, especially that twig in your hair."

Ravenna's hands flew up to her mass of curly black hair before she saw my grin and realized there was no such twig.

"If I didn't know better, I'd say you really were related to Jerian." There was a sadness in her eyes suddenly, and I remembered her mention of a younger brother who'd been killed by the Inquisition's companion organization, the murderous holy warriors who called themselves Sacri, the Sacred Ones. Whether or not they were sacred, they were certainly devout. Devout in their zealous dedication to the religion of shedding blood.

A steady stream of protests and apologies was now coming from somewhere in the branches of the cedar tree, a noise which intensified as

Elassel reappeared from behind the trunk, her hand clamped round my brother's wrist.

"What do you want done with him?" she asked me, trying to stifle a smile. Elassel seemed to be constitutionally incapable of anything more than momentary anger—except where Halettites were concerned. She hated their entire people with a passion, which I thought might have some bearing on her escape-artist abilities. But she'd never said anything about it, and none of us wanted to ask.

"We could always give him a dunking," I suggested, gesturing down at the beach a few feet below us.

"I've got a better idea," Ravenna said, and went over to whisper in Elassel's ear. There was a howl of protest from the eavesdropping Jerian.

"I've got news," he said, shouting to make sure he got everybody's attention. "I won't tell you unless you let me go."

"Fine, then we will," Elassel said, bending down and gathering a handful of bark and twig ends. Having scattered them over Jerian's hair, she let go of his arm. "Now, what's the news?"

Jerian shot her a black look and drew himself up, shaking his head.

"Some important people have arrived from an important place with an important message."

"The sea's still just down there," Elassel said, but Jerian had got her measure by now.

"A huge manta," Jerian announced. "From Pharassa, with that big blond Canadrath man on board. He says there's news from Taneth, and he didn't look very happy. Oh, and Courtières is with him."

"The Halettites," Elassel said instantly, and slipped her lute into its leather traveling case. Ravenna and I looked at one another, and she nodded slightly. Both of us had had the same thought.

"Now you'll be gloomy all the way back," Jerian said, with a seven-year-old's intolerance for problems that didn't concern him.

"No, we won't," I said, forcing a smile.

Jerian chattered cheerfully as we made our way down the path and on to the beach, the quickest way back to Lepidor. There was a proper track through the forest to the logging road, but it meandered to avoid obstacles and wound round the side of a small hill, and none of us wanted to waste any time. I assumed Palatine had gone back into the city, because there was no sign of her sitting on the edge of the ten-foot rock cliff—in fact a sea wall—that separated the forest from the beach.

The city soon came into sight, across the broad curving sweep of the bay from where we were. Some of the stone buildings within the walls still had scaffolding around them, and many roof gardens were missing. This was the legacy of the storm we'd unleashed more than a month ago, ironically enough to try to protect the city. But most of the damage had been repaired: the walls had been bolstered, and construction of a new gatehouse between the Palace Quarter and the Harbor Quarter was well under way.

As we approached the city, though, my thoughts kept straying back to Jerian's news, especially the bit about the presence of Oltan Canadrath. We only knew him and his House slightly, since a month ago when they had led the relief force, and although we'd rewarded them for their help, they were still more or less an unknown quantity. So why had the son of Lord Canadrath come all the way out here to deliver bad news?

We entered the city through a small postern gate in the Palace Quarter, accessible only along a wooden walkway that ran under the walls. It was forever being damaged by waves and storms, but no one had ever proposed replacing it with a stone path: that would give enemies a clear route into the city.

The marines guarding the postern looked at us curiously as we approached.

"Been taking a dust-bath, Escount?" one of them said to me, his eyes straying to Ravenna's hair.

"My brother's taken up tree surgery," I said, before he could say anything suggestive. "Unfortunately he didn't take the trouble to check which tree he was operating on."

"You can come and prune my olive tree, then. Huge thing it is, keep you occupied for a week or so," the other guard said to Jerian, his bearded face split by a broad grin. "Good day to you."

The postern led into a narrow street only a short walk from the palace. The doors of the houses were all open because of the heat, and two old men playing cards in the shadows of a narrow colonnade greeted us as we went past. It was cooler here in the city, shielded from the sun by three- and four-story buildings and washing hung across the street on lines and poles. There was a gentle splashing sound everywhere, too, made by the little fountains that stood in alcoves and at street corners. Once these fountains had been the city's main source of water, but since the concept—quickly followed by the reality—of piped water inside houses had reached Lepidor about fifty years ago, their main purpose now was to keep the air fresh in summer.

Two more marines on duty at the gate of the palace waved us through and into the small whitewashed courtyard beyond; even with the tighter security since the invasion, they didn't need to check my identity. Like the houses, the palace gate was covered in scaffolding and the doors weren't yet finished. Wooden barricades were erected and taken down noisily at dusk and dawn.

"There you are!" came Palatine's voice. I looked up to see her standing on the balcony at the top of the flight of steps running up the right-hand wall. "What on earth have you been up to, Ravenna? Were you trying to dye your hair?"

"That was Jerian," I said, as my brother rushed up the stairs ahead of us.

My father and his guests were in the reception room, Palatine told us, looking more animated than she had in days despite the worried frown on her face. Ravenna and I brushed the dust out of our hair as best we could, using a polished bronze plate as a mirror.

"Come on, it'll have to do," Palatine said eventually. "If they appear without warning, they can't expect you to look immaculate."

I wouldn't have worried if it had just been Courtières, my father's oldest friend, but I'd only met Canadrath once before. I hadn't made a good impression then, either, hollow-eyed and bruised as I'd been, wearing a long robe to hide the livid marks on my arms and legs. This would be a definite improvement.

There was a servant waiting by the door to the reception room, and he announced us without formality.

"Ah, there you are," my father said, turning from his conversation with the other two men.

"Escount Cathan," the second man said, making the customary stiff bow to one of equal station. "I'm glad to see you in good health."

I bowed back, absurdly conscious that all three of them were quite a bit taller than me. Oltan Canadrath, who'd greeted me, had a fair coloring and blond hair rare on any continent, let alone equatorial Taneth. My second meeting with him only confirmed my impression of a man who was in the wrong business. With his straight beard and moustache, not to mention his impressive build, he should have been one of those northern pirates who'd roamed the Archipelago in the old days, making their home in the now-vanished primeval forests of Thure.

"He's right, Cathan," said Courtières, a friendly smile on his face. "You looked dreadful last time you met."

The greetings over, Palatine handed out drinks and Oltan told me and Ravenna his news.

"The Halettites have taken Ukhaa and seized the Delta," he said bluntly. "We've now lost all the mainland territories, and thirty thousand Halettite troops are camped under our noses."

"This being Taneth, the Merchant Lords are all rushing around trying to find things the Halettites want to buy," Courtières said acerbically. He might have looked like a bear, but he had a keen mind and was usually a lot more tactful than my father.

Oltan didn't take umbrage at this insult. "I fear the Count is right. Lord Barca and I have been pressing for military action, but the other Houses are reluctant to upset what they see as the new status quo."

There was silence for a moment. Anyone with any sense at all knew what bad news it was. Taneth might be a mercantile city built on islands, but it was still very close to the mainland, and the Halettite army had so far proved invincible. Lepidor's future, and that of most other clans, depended on a free Taneth ruled by the Merchant Lords. It couldn't stay as a trade center under Halettite military rule, especially not if they followed their normal policy of sacking captured cities. I felt my good mood drain away.

"They're not doing anything at all?" Ravenna asked.

Oltan shook his head. "Nothing whatsoever. Oh, the Council of Ten sent a protest to the King of Kings, but they might as well have saved themselves the ink."

"Are the Halettites preparing to attack the city?"

"Not yet," Oltan said. "They still don't have a fleet. They can make life difficult for us, but nothing more. As yet."

Then I realized why the heir to Canadrath, one of the largest Houses in Taneth, had come all the way out here. Lepidor had the biggest iron deposits in Oceanus, and we'd soon be the biggest weapons manufacturer as well. Oltan wanted to make sure our weapons wouldn't be going to the Halettites.

"Does this change anything?" I asked my father, who was wearing a loose green robe that had once been formal but had seen better days. He was concerned that the clan shouldn't see how much damage the poison had done, and was wearing the robe to give the appearance that he wasn't emaciated. Most people knew otherwise, but nobody said anything. Courtières's renowned healers had assured us he'd recover the lost weight in time.

"It makes our sale of weapons rather questionable," he said. "In view of the fact that weapons sent to Taneth will probably end up where we don't want them, shipping them there may not be such a good idea."

Where we don't want them. He wasn't talking only about the Halettites. They were the immediate menace, true, but behind them was the priesthood—the Domain, with its dreams of crusades and blood. They had tried to seize Lepidor for that very reason, to manufacture the weapons for a crusade. After everything we'd gone through, simply to sell the weapons to their allies was unthinkable.

And, as it happened, House Canadrath had made its fortune selling weapons in the Archipelago, the very place that the Domain wanted to cleanse with holy fire and Inquisitors.

"You want to sell the weapons somewhere else, then?" Ravenna asked.

"We'll have to talk to Hamilcar about this, because he's making his profit carrying our iron and weapons to Taneth." Hamilcar was our official Tanethan partner, with whom we'd signed the iron contract. And the man who'd saved all our lives in the invasion. "But if there's a market in the Archipelago . . ."

Selling weapons to kill Sacri—that was a different matter. I saw Ravenna's slight smile. For her, they were the butchers who'd destroyed her family. Sacri were not even human beings.

"I have some more information that you might find useful," Oltan said. "Concerning the two priests who survived the attempted coup here. Avarch Midian and . . . Sarhaddon, I think his name was."

My ears pricked up. They had been the only two survivors of the Domain force that had tried to take over Lepidor, and their fate would be a good indicator of how the Domain had reacted.

"Go on," my father said levelly.

"They went back to the Holy City, where apparently Prime Lachazzar saw them in person." That couldn't have been a pleasant experience; nicknamed "Hell's Cook," Lachazzar was apparently given to accusing subordinates of being in league with heretics when they failed. But Oltan's next words gave the lie to that. "Sarhaddon's been promoted to full Inquisitor and sent out to the Archipelago. The Inquisitor-General is already there, with orders to crush any thoughts of independence in Qalathar."

"They never give up," Ravenna said sadly. "They killed a generation and that wasn't enough. They took over the country and that wasn't enough. You know, the people they torture and burn are the ones who learn Qalathari, or who keep the dynastic histories."

"I'm sorry, I didn't realize," Oltan said sympathetically. "I took you for a Thetian last time we met, but I should have realized my mistake, seeing you now. There isn't a Thetian born who could look like you."

Canadrath was right, I thought as Ravenna smiled wanly, her good mood of a few minutes before destroyed by his news. For years she'd straightened her naturally curly black hair, endured the irritation of changed eyes, and spent as much time outdoors as possible to accentuate her coloring, pale for a Qalathari. She'd almost looked like a Thetian, but with brown eyes and a mass of black curls, nobody could mistake her any longer.

"What about Midian?" Courtières asked.

"He's been given a posting in the Archipelago, I'm not sure what. I don't think it's anywhere important, but it does mean he's at the center of things."

"So why does Lachazzar give them another chance?" Palatine said. "He's got plenty more where they came from."

"I don't think he has, actually," my father said. "Sarhaddon is exceptionally clever, although he rarely showed it when he was an acolyte here. He must be extremely loyal, too, and Lachazzar isn't stupid. Their defeat here wasn't Sarhaddon's fault. As for Midian, he comes from a powerful Halettite family. He's almost indestructible, a member of the old nobility in the Domain. This might have set his career back a bit, but he'll still make Exarch someday."

The thought of that arrogant boor one day rising to almost the highest post in the service of Ranthas was sickening. Even if I had agreed with their teachings, I had no time for the Domain with men like Midian and Lachazzar at the top.

"We know he wanted a Crusade," Palatine said, toying with a glass. "Since we've disrupted his plans, he's got to hit at the Archipelago some other way, and the Inquisition is the best answer. For him," she added, seeing the look on Ravenna's face. I couldn't imagine what she must have gone through, seeing her country systematically ripped apart by the Sacri who'd been running it ever since the Archipelagan Crusade, nearly a quarter of a century ago.

Ravenna had been born a couple of years afterward, and had never known a free Qalathar. She had inherited the title of Pharaoh from her grandfather, burned during the Crusade, but it had been nothing more than a hollow, mocking reminder of what they'd lost. I sympathized with her. Being an heir was bad enough anyway, as far as I was concerned, without having had to endure the agony Qalathar had gone through.

"We're in a position to help," my father said, fixing his gaze on Oltan. "If we can agree on a route for these weapons that bypasses Taneth and goes straight to the Archipelago, we might be able to slip people out on the return run."

The Canadrath heir looked doubtful. "Great Houses have to be careful not to get involved in smuggling," he began, but Courtières cut him off.

"If all the people you want to sell weapons to are moldering in

Domain prisons, nobody's going to give you money. If there's an organized resistance outside, you might have a chance."

"I suppose so," Oltan said, still looking doubtful. "It could ruin our commercial reputation if we're caught, though. It's illegal to import weapons into Qalathar, on pain of excommunication, so we'll have to find a third country to ship to. I think the first step, though, is to put a proposal to Lord Barca."

Chapter II

A whole day spent haggling over commercial minutiae had better have
been worth it, I thought, standing in the reception room of Lepidor's
undersea harbor as the Canadrath manta carrying our two visitors
detached itself from the docking gantry. It would be at least three weeks
before we could get an answer, or more likely an altered proposal with
more to discuss.

The day after Oltan arrived, the last day of summer, I had spent in my
father's sweltering office, trying to grapple with the intricacies of Great
House trade. I'd never had a head for figures, and by the time my father
called in his First Adviser, the portly Atek, to help calculate profit
margins and bribe percentages, I was almost asleep.

Still, I would be Count of Lepidor one day, and so I kept my
wavering attention on the numbers Atek scribbled on scraps of
parchment, struggling to stop myself looking out at the flat, invitingly
blue sea. This was what being a Count—or any kind of ruler—was really
about, and I had to admit I detested it almost as much as I hated the
feeling that everybody else was looking to me for leadership. Of course
it was a good feeling when everything was going well and there weren't
any hard choices, but I had experienced the worst aspects of the position
during the Domain invasion, and I never wanted to do so again.

Although my father was improving fast, he hadn't been able to sustain
Oltan's pace for a whole day, and so by the afternoon I'd been handling
Lepidor's end of the negotiations. And for my clan's sake, I couldn't give
up until everyone was happy with what we'd agreed. By sunset, with the
western sky tinted an abnormal reddish gold from horizon to horizon, I
knew that winter was here, and pleaded clan duties for a chance to swim
one last time in a sea still warm from the day's heat. It wasn't the action
of a clan leader, and I felt I was letting my father down, but who knew
when I'd have the chance again?

There wasn't time to go very far from the city or I'd have to come back in the dark, so I went a little way along the shoreline, to the beach below where we'd been sitting.

As I slipped out of my tunic in the strange, eerie light, the forest behind me almost silent, I looked out to sea. The sun was a burning orange ball against that astonishing coppery sky, bathing the city and the shoreline in a ghostly, almost apocalyptic light. My own shadow was a grotesque distension, like some gaunt wraith against the line of trees and the golden sand.

But strangest of all was the sea. Amid the colors of this spectacular sunset, the rippled surface of the ocean was stained a deep blood-red.

"The wine-dark sea," I said, not realizing I'd spoken aloud until someone answered.

"I was thinking the same thing," Ravenna said, standing up from where she'd been sitting in the shadow of a rock. We studiously avoided looking at anything except each other's faces.

The Thetian poet Ethelos had lived nearly six hundred years ago, but *he* must have seen a sunset like this one on some ancient island, before mankind had even set foot on the shores of Oceanus.

"I've never seen it like this before," I said, gesturing out at the panorama of sky and sea.

"Nor have I." Ravenna walked down the beach to stand nearby, another tall shadow-form. "Not even at the beginning of winter, when there are always wonderful sunsets. It's strange, really, how all these colors that the Domain like so much can seem so beautiful. They tarnish everything they touch, so why not the sunsets as well?"

"The sunsets have been here a lot longer than the Domain, and they'll be here a long time after it's been forgotten."

"I envy the people who'll watch something like this one day and never even have heard of heresy, or Inquisitors."

"We'll never be able to do that," I said, "but I'll promise this, as far as I can. One day we'll watch a sunset like this from the Palace of the Sea in Sanction, like the old Hierarchs used to."

She caught her breath and stared at me for a moment, then shook her head in puzzlement.

"There were so many things you nearly said just then."

In fact, there were, and some of them I didn't even realize until much later. It sounded a strange thing to promise, but both of us knew what it meant. Sanction, Aquasilva's ancient sacred city, had vanished when the Domain rose to power. Neither of us would be able to enter it until the Domain were gone, if the story of its disappearance was true. Two hundred years without sound or sight of it was the clearest indicator that the account was correct.

But there was more, and if I'd known what was to come I'd never have said it. Ravenna was wiser than me, and had already grasped things that I was too blind to see. And what neither of us mentioned, not then at any rate, was what the ritual of watching the sunset had meant to the Hierarchs personally.

"Shall we swim?" Ravenna said, after a few moments' silence.

We did, enjoying the warmth of the dark water until the ball of the sun finally disappeared and only a purplish afterglow was left in the western sky, with indigo cloud silhouettes against it. We didn't refer to the moment again as we pulled tunics over still-wet bodies and went back to the Palace.

The next morning, an impenetrable layer of low cloud covered the mountain tops, and there was a bitter chill in the air. Winter was like that now, although it hadn't always been. There was an absolute cut-off between winter and summer, a boundary we passed at the end of each year. After that date, the first storm system that blew up would last for months. A third of each year, give or take a few weeks. Only the Domain, with their ability to control and "see" the weather from above, knew why this was, and of course it wasn't in their interests to tell anyone.

I watched from the undersea harbor's reception room for a few moments as the Canadrath manta glided off into the gloom with slight, leisurely beats of its huge wings. Only when the water had completely swallowed it up did I turn and dismiss the two marines who'd served as an escort. I had work to do in the palace, but there really wasn't any need for them now.

The one good thing about winter, I reflected as I climbed the stairs to my study in the Palace, was that the hours spent inside weren't as bad. There was nothing to do outside except when it was snowing, and that novelty soon wore off as the cold seeped through my clothes. I wasn't an Oceanian by birth and I was never really happy in the cold, as much as I wanted to be. A year in the Archipelago, where it never snowed, had been enough to convince me that I didn't really miss it very much.

My father had given me the study years ago, and I'd used it on and off since then. In the last few weeks, though, it had begun to feel like my tortoise's shell. One of the servants had already lit the fire, and the room was pleasantly warm and welcoming—more than could be said for the documents on the desk.

I sat down in the chair and picked up the top sheet, my interest sparking when I saw Palatine's wild handwriting on it. For a moment I was puzzled, then I remembered what it would be. I'd mentioned to her during a break in negotiations yesterday that we'd need to pick her brains about Thetia. She'd evidently taken the idea to heart, because there were two pages entitled *Business in Thetia*. The first point, underlined several times for emphasis, was, *Thetia is ruled by the Emperor*, following that was an equally emphatic *Thetians hate Tanethans*.

Some of her words needed the services of a codebreaker to decipher them, but I guessed at the ones I couldn't immediately identify. After I'd finished, I leaned back in the chair and stared at the paper for a moment, wondering whether our proposal had been such a good idea after all. There had been no other logical place to sell weapons on to the Qalathari dissidents: Thetia was central, neutral and, as in Taneth, you could buy or sell absolutely anything there.

On the other hand, Palatine had pointed out several glaring disadvantages. The Thetian clans made life as difficult as possible for Tanethans trying to trade. A lot of them were very inward-looking, protectionist and given to wasting their strength on infighting. At the other end of the spectrum, clans like Palatine's own were fierce fighters and imperialists, despite their belief in republicanism.

And as for Selerian Alastre, the fabled Thetian capital . . . gods above! Some of the things she'd written had to be exaggerated, for whatever reason. I mean, *surely* no one could be a clan president and go to parties three nights out of every four? And as for the orgies she mentioned, it read more like the *Book of Ranthas*'s description of the evil city of Malyra, supposedly destroyed by the wrath of the gods hundreds of years ago.

I had to ask her about this directly. I tugged on the bell pull, and a few minutes later one of my younger cousins who was on running duty appeared at the door.

"Could you find Palatine and ask her to come as soon as it's convenient?"

He nodded and disappeared again. I would have preferred to find her myself; it seemed somehow rude to send a messenger. But I knew that if I went to find her it would be hours before I got back to work again.

Palatine came up half an hour or so later, as I considered a request for extra clan funds from the town of Gesraden: the Clan Tenth there wanted to put in a new water system because the old pipes were falling apart. From the sound of it, the Pharassan contractors who'd installed them in the first place had done a shoddy job. No point in hiring the same lot—I'd have to find out which group had done it. Elements, this was tedious.

"Cathan?"

I looked up, sighing with relief, and shoved Gesraden's petition to one side. It could wait; nobody was going to be putting in a new water system in winter. "I hope I haven't dragged you away from anything important; you're probably doing something much more vital than I am."

"You want to talk about Thetia," she said, coming around to my side of the desk. She didn't look chilled, so she hadn't been outside. Almost certainly she'd come now because she was bored, and I didn't blame her.

"I read your report, but some of it—"

"—is a little hard to believe. Unfortunately, it's all true." She dragged up a chair from the corner and I pushed mine away from the table to give more room, kicking it savagely in the process.

"You can't be serious! Even the President of Decaris and his brothel?"

"Cathan, as far as all this is concerned you're still a naïve provincial. Thetia is a wreck, and when things go as wrong as they have there, people start acting very strangely."

"But if all this—" I took her report from the pile "—is true, then how come the Thetian Empire is still so powerful?"

She didn't answer for a moment, staring thoughtfully off into the distance.

"There are two sides to Thetia. Yes, there are the things I wrote that worry you. The clans don't care about anything much, except prestige and the good life. Not all of them, of course," she added, meaning her own clan, the warrior Canteni. "All of this is what you see of Thetia, in the big cities and Selerian Alastre. But you forget that the Thetians are the best sailors in the world. We're both Thetians, you and I, and neither of us is happy away from the sea. For you, the sea is even more than that, but everyone knows that, when it comes to ships, Thetians are the best."

And that, despite assertions to the contrary by Tanethan merchant captains and Cambressian admirals, was certainly true. The rest of the world viewed the ocean as a highway and a route for trade, as well as a vast natural fish farm, but it seemed that, for Thetians, it was something more. Not a god or goddess, or, as the semi-mythical Exiles believed, a vast living organism, but more than just a place to travel through and harvest food from. And the Thetians had founded the Oceanographic Guild.

"So you're saying that it's their fleet that keeps them powerful."

"That, and the Emperor."

The one subject she'd avoided so far. There'd been no mention of him in the report, which had intrigued me. How could you write about doing business in Thetia without mentioning the man who, in name at least, held more authority than anyone else on Aquasilva? Even the Cambressians were afraid to cross the Emperor openly, though they wanted more than anything else to be free of even the illusion of Thetian overlordship.

"You've left him until last."

She nodded. "He's more dangerous than all the rest put together."

"What's he like? As a person, I mean."

"He's probably the most brilliant Emperor we've ever had. You feel, when you talk to him, that he's always several steps ahead of you. Of course, he plays chess, and he never loses. But he's heartless, cold, ruthless— anything in that line you can think of. He's not a good ruler for Thetia, because he wants to be an absolute monarch and we won't let him."

"I thought that was the point of an Emperor?"

"Not *our* Emperor." Palatine said, with a touch of pride. "In Thetia the Emperor—or the Empress, and we've had a few of them—isn't like, say, the Halettite King of Kings. He can't order someone executed without a trial, or issue edicts when he feels like it. In fact—" she paused, fists clenched as if she was concentrating on something just out of reach "—he's not really an Emperor at all. He leads the fleet and the Clan Assembly. But they actually pass the laws—he's just the balance. Without him the clans would fight all the time. With him, we just fight some of the time. Orosius wants more than that. He wants to rule on his own—and he wants the old Empire back. But because most of the clans are so disorganized, he can't get anywhere, and so he turns to the Domain for help."

Which was the worst problem. A megalomaniac on the Thetian throne wasn't too much trouble, given the Empire's weakened state, but if he was hand in glove with the Domain, that was a different matter.

"My father told me he was under the Exarch's thumb, and said something about an illness."

Exarchs were the Domain's potentates, owing obedience only to the four Primes—and, in some cases, not even to them. The Exarch of the Archipelago, invariably a nasty piece of work, had ruled his vast spiritual territories as a secular empire ever since the Archipelagan Crusade left a power vacuum there. The Exarch of Thetia, although less powerful, still wielded immense influence, equal to that of the King of my own continent of Oceanus.

"That's sort of true," she said. "He was very ill when he was thirteen, and it changed him. Sometimes he gets headaches, which make him pass out, and you don't see him for days. You should count yourself lucky you aren't in his place, because you'd have exactly the same problem."

That was something I didn't want her to remind me of. Both of us shared Orosius's bloodline; Palatine was his first cousin, and I was probably the same, although I wasn't certain yet. And though I'd never have admitted it, the thought terrified me. If either the Emperor or the Domain ever found out, I'd be tied to the stake again before I could blink, and this time there would be no Merchant Lords on hand to help. Orosius had already tried to kill Palatine, and as a woman she was much less of a threat in the Domain's eyes. And as for the illness—I could remember that, because I'd been ill at exactly the same time.

"But how much under the Exarch's influence is he?"

"Depends." She sat back in the chair, pulling a fold of her heavy winter tunic straight. "When he's ill, the Exarch's virtually in charge, and the rest of the time Orosius relies on him as First Adviser. There's a man called Zarathec, too, who's in charge of the secret service. Those two and Tanais are the only people he trusts."

We were nowhere near the original subject—doing business in Thetia—but I didn't mind. Tanais had promised to reveal my identity when he returned, and it was as much to be sure of that as for information that I'd delayed our departure. With any luck the Domain was unaware of the existence of another of Orosius's cousins.

What puzzled me was how anyone could have lost track of me originally. I knew I'd been born a Tar'Conantur, one of the imperial clan, in Thetia, and that for some reason the then Chancellor of the Empire had abducted me when I'd been a few hours old. There had been nothing about a hunt, so presumably the whole incident had been somehow hushed up or written off. But why go to all the trouble in the first place?

"If we sell the weapons in Selerian Alastre, is the Empire going to find out?" I asked, abruptly changing the subject. For some reason I didn't feel like talking about the Emperor anymore.

"Selerian Alastre's a very cosmopolitan city," Palatine said. "Not as many people as Taneth, but on a bigger island. Very hard to track down who's doing what, so unless they're looking for us . . ."

"Tanethan merchants selling weapons in the Thetian capital? It's not as if we'll be noticeable."

She ignored the sarcasm. A gust of wind rattled the windows slightly. I looked outside to see the previously unbroken gray cloud now scudding westward out to sea. It had taken on a darker overtone, almost purple; a storm, then. Ranthas only knew how long this one would last.

"I think you'll have to sign an agreement with a Thetian clan. Not one of the ambitious ones, like mine, but a small one. Not that many commercial interests, and probably on the fringe. Better with a major clan, but they all hate Tanethans too much. It's the only thing they agree about."

"Is that a normal thing to do?" I scribbled a few words on the bottom of her report to remind myself.

"It's been known to happen."

"Anyone you can recommend?"

"I can give you some idea," she said, shivering. "But Canadrath will be more useful, things must have changed since I left. And why is it so cold in here?"

With an exaggerated sigh, I got up and went over to the heater valve. In winter and during storms the palace was heated by hot water piped around the edge of each room. There was a flamewood furnace in the cellar that did the heating; it was expensive to maintain but necessary, given the icy temperatures in midwinter.

What would it be like, I thought, opening the valve some more and going back to my seat, to live somewhere warmer? The Archipelago and Thetia didn't have winters like this, Elements only knew why. Oh, it was colder, and there was very little sun. But in the Archipelago this was the monsoon season, when it rained every day, sometimes for weeks at a time. As far as I was concerned, that was infinitely preferable to freezing temperatures and building-size snowdrifts.

"You come and live in Thetia for a while and you'll see what a civilized climate's like," Palatine said.

"Getting drowned by rain, you mean." I leaped to the defense of Lepidor despite my personal feelings. This was home, and while I felt the cold more keenly because of my Thetian blood, I was used to the climate.

"I thought you liked being wet."

"There's a slight difference between swimming in the sea and swimming down the street," I said. Palatine grinned.

"You'd love it. I'm sure you're part seal—no one else has this thing about the ocean."

"And there you were, telling me about how all Thetians have a bond with the sea. If you're not careful, you'll end up sounding like a Tanethan."

"I prefer Taneth," she said, suddenly serious again. I could tell because she started fiddling with a stylus, running it up and down the edge of the desk. "Taneth is growing, it's going somewhere. You can tell that just by

listening to Oltan talking. Canadrath is a big House, with secure trade
routes and lots of money. They could be sitting on their backsides letting
the money flow in, and concentrating on getting on to the Council of
Ten. But instead, because they've had the sense to see a problem early on,
they're planning to launch a risky new venture. And with House Barca,
who they hardly know. If this was Thetia, they wouldn't be doing that.
They'd be knifing their rivals in the back, not bothering to go out and try
anything new. Thetia's living off past glories, and nobody seems to care."

Palatine twisted the stylus viciously, and it flipped out of her fingers to
fly across the room, hitting the heavy winter curtains. There was a guilty
look on her face as she got up to retrieve it.

"But why?" She'd only spoken about Thetia a few times, and I'd never
really understood what had begun the decline.

"You don't pay enough attention to anything that's not science." She
was right there, I had to admit. I'd been given a noble's upbringing,
schooled and tutored thoroughly by my father, who believed in as much
education as possible. But I'd only ever *worked* at anything scientific.
History, theology, law, grammar—all those subjects bored me intensely,
especially theology. And as for the writings of the Thetian philosophers
. . . for a time I'd hated Thetia simply for producing so many of them.

"Every country has its day," Palatine went on. "Two hundred years
ago Thetia won the Tuonetar War, and had a chance to develop. But
then the Domain came along, and the Hierarch murdered his cousin and
became Emperor, and it all fell to pieces. And you've seen how the
Domain rewrote history to make us the villains of the War."

"But why did you let them? I know you weren't there, of course, but
why?"

"Who knows?" She gestured expressively with the stylus. "It
happened, and the clans gradually surrendered everything to Taneth.
Two hundred years ago, Taneth didn't even exist."

That, at least, I had remembered, along with fragments of other
continents' histories. Taneth had been founded by refugees fleeing the
devastation of the War, who'd seen the islands in the divide of the
shattered Equatorian continent as a safe place to settle, protected by a few
miles of water from the internecine struggles on the mainland.

"What one man has done, another can undo."

"Now you quote Thetian poets at me, and I always thought you hated
them."

"I don't understand nine out of ten things they say, but I can use them
here and there."

"You'd never get by in Thetia. They argue about poetry in the Assembly—all the clan leaders have read everything. I remember watching a session once, when my father was still alive. The President of Mandrugor and the President of Nalassel fought on the floor of the Assembly about whether Severian was sympathetic to war in his epics." Palatine smiled faintly. "Trivial, really—it shows you how far we've sunk. But at least we still have something left: our poetry and our music. We can even argue about philosophy sometimes."

"But the Domain closed all the academies, didn't they?"

"There's something you have to understand about Thetia if you're going to get involved with Ravenna. I say Thetia, but it's the same for Qalathar and the rest of the islands. You didn't see it so much when you were there, because we were off the beaten track. In Thetia, people live outdoors. Our cities are built round plazas, our houses and palaces are built round courtyards and gardens, even the Emperor holds court outside a lot of the time. And even when we're indoors, there are as many large open spaces as possible.

"What it means is that we talk. We spend hours in cafés, parks, colonnades, spending time with groups of friends. We don't sit inside in ones and twos and scheme. Nothing ever stays secret, and there is no way to stop ideas from circulating. The Domain closed down the academies, banned demonstrations as heretical, and introduced a religious police to make sure heresy wasn't being discussed.

"But in spite of all that, they failed. You cannot stop people talking in the Archipelago, any more than you can stop the sun from rising. That's really why they hate Qalathar—and all Archipelagans. They can't control us like they do everyone else."

"But the Tanethans too spend all their time outdoors," I protested.

Palatine shook her head. "Not in the same way. They base everything around their Houses, and all the important people only go outside in order to go from one building to another. In Thetia, everything important is done out of doors, and you can't be a clan president if people can't see you. You can't hide. And that is why the Domain and the Archipelago cannot coexist forever. Sooner or later, however long it takes, one of them will destroy the other."

Chapter III

We waited for two more weeks, and still Tanais didn't come. The skies over Lepidor remained unrelentingly gray and bleak, broken only by a five-day winter storm that came from the south. A freak cyclone cutting across three storm bands, it inflicted serious damage on the town of Gesraden and Courtières's land farther down the coast.

Eighteen days after Oltan left, the Barcan manta making the bimonthly iron run arrived in Lepidor with a sealed message from Hamilcar.

Thankfully, my father had resumed most of his responsibilities, I thought as I took the letter upstairs. I was still taking care of more clan business than I had before, but it was only out of a sense of duty.

"Come in," my father said when I knocked.

He was sitting behind the desk, as I'd seen him so many times before, and looking almost the same. There were lines around his eyes that would never go away, though, and I felt a momentary stab of hatred for the dead Prime who'd tried to seize Lepidor from us. I hoped she was floating in the void beyond, cut off forever from the gods she'd pretended to worship.

I handed him the letter, wrapped in a waterproof cloth bag with weights sewn into it. He raised his eyebrows expressively.

"There are things here he definitely doesn't want anyone to see." He stood up and went over to the blue globe, a lovingly crafted model of Aquasilva in miniature, that stood on its pedestal in the corner. A tiny aether generator in the base swathed the model of our world in constantly changing cloud patterns. My father gave the mounting a very slight twist and withdrew a thin sliver of metal from the globe's north pole.

"Dangerous for him to stick his neck out in writing."

"You didn't look closely enough," my father said, as he returned to the desk. "Look at the seal on the bag. It's got a Domain impression on it and a Prime's mark. Almost certainly a gift from his guardian."

His guardian, who just happened to be Lachazzar, I thought, irritated that I hadn't spotted the tiny leaping-flames symbol. Hamilcar had already proved his loyalty during the invasion of Lepidor, but Ravenna still didn't trust him entirely because of his link with Lachazzar. He was a Tanethan merchant, after all, and there were some things it was safer for him not to know about.

The metal sliver had tiny irregular serrations on it, a particular pattern that would open the seal on this package and nothing else. Hamilcar had given it to us before he left, in case he ever needed to send confidential messages. I hadn't expected it to be used so soon.

The bag was actually made of a fine metal mesh that was covered in oiled cloth and secured at the neck by a cylindrical lock, with four keyholes to further confuse matters. It must have cost a fortune, because the workmanship was exquisite. Only kings, Exarchs and Merchant Lords could afford this kind of security, and no money could have bought the primarchial insignia on the seal.

My father slipped the key into the lock, turned it and then pushed it in a little more, before opening the bag and taking out a letter written on several pages of expensive parchment.

There was a silence while we both read it through, a silence broken only by shouts from the garden below where some of my cousins and their friends were taking advantage of a day of patchy sunlight.

"What do you think?" my father asked when I finished the last page and looked up.

"He isn't taking any chances. Assurances from the dissidents that they're interested, confirmation that they can pay, third-party communication. Even the letter doesn't mention anyone specifically."

My father nodded. "He's a lot more cautious than House Canadrath, but, given his position, I'm not surprised. They can afford a lot of new ventures; he can't. But he's looking to expand business in the Archipelago once he gets going and diversify to other fields than weapons. At a guess, I'd say he's not confident about Taneth's chances of survival."

I hadn't got any of that, and he must have seen my chagrin.

"Don't worry, I've been reading political letters for thirty years. You have to read dozens before you can recognize a lie, or something that isn't being said, and even then you still miss them sometimes."

"He wants us to make contact with the heretic leaders in Qalathar," I said, hoping that I hadn't missed anything else.

"Through Ravenna, but he says nothing about Palatine and Thetia. She was a clan president's daughter—I'd have thought he'd want to use her contacts."

I couldn't for the life of me see where that had come from, but even when I reread the passage I failed to see what my father was pointing out. Hamilcar did want us, through Ravenna, to contact the leaders of the heretic dissident movement in Qalathar. Principally to see whether they had enough money to do business with, I thought.

"I'll have to ask Palatine and Ravenna if they'll come," I said.

"Of course you must. Qalathar's dangerous, though. For the three of you to go there now, after what happened here, would be tempting fate. The Domain keeps a close eye on arrivals and departures."

"What about arranging another meeting point, somewhere neutral like Ral Tumar?" I suggested. "It would take longer to set up, but be better for everyone."

"It sounds a good idea, but I think you'd have problems. It'll be easier for you to get into Qalathar than for them to get out. We could have asked Sagantha, but in the meantime Ravenna should be able to help. You're in her hands here; it's her country and her people who'll suffer if things go wrong."

At that moment the aether communicator on my father's desk buzzed into glowing life.

"Who is it?" he asked, sounding annoyed.

"Oceanographic Guild." It was Tetricus, an oceanographer I'd known as long as I could remember. I could hear his excited tone even through the slight distortion of the communicator. "My lord Count, I'm sorry to disturb you, but we've just found a recording of a kraken on one of the ocean probes. The Master said you might want to see. We couldn't get through to Cathan, but if you could tell him . . ."

"He's here, and we'll be down right away." He cut the link.

I'd already jumped to my feet, hardly believing what Tetricus had reported. A kraken this close to land? It was unheard of. And the chance to *see* one . . .

My father smiled faintly as he stowed Hamilcar's message away in his desk and picked up his cloak. The recording would be there any time, of course, but kraken sightings were so rare even in the deep ocean that many people never saw one. My father had, once before, but I hadn't.

We couldn't find my mother, Ravenna or Palatine, but my father left a message with the guards telling them to come down to the oceanographer's building as soon as they appeared.

For all that the sun was shining, it was a blustery day, and the wind kept tugging at the hems of our cloaks. There seemed to be a rain of dead leaves coming down from the roof gardens that hadn't yet been sealed in for the winter. Gusts of wind whirled them around like miniature ocean currents. There were people in the streets, although the market stalls that stayed up for the rest of the year had been dismantled and the town seemed empty without them.

People waved to us as we passed them, and I endured a five-minute wait as a marine captain at one of the gatehouses conferred with my father about relaxing the guard so that more marines could be sent to help ravaged Gesraden. Elnibal seemed to have an almost superhuman patience for delays, and though I concealed my impatience as best I could, he could see it well enough.

Word obviously hadn't got around yet, because there wasn't a crowd of people on the steps of the oceanographic building. Built in the same style as the rest of Lepidor, it had a turquoise-tiled dome rather than a roof garden, and a large equipment yard around it. Underneath, I knew, there were bays for the Guild's official sea-ray and my personal one, *Walrus*, which they'd given to me rather than mothballing it when it got too old. I was rarely around these days, so the Guild was making use of it when they needed a second ship.

Once we were inside the building, it was easy to know where to go. A babble of voices was coming from the imaging room on the left side, and we found the entire Guild staff squeezed into the small room, their eyes fixed on a blurred aether screen about two cubits square mounted on one wall, above a mountain of recording and enhancing equipment.

"This is too much to believe," one of the Master's assistants was saying.

"Run it through the filter again," said the Master, sitting in one of the two chairs. "Too much blue still, can't make out any details."

"What if we change the contrast as well?" someone else suggested, their face hidden behind an apprentice's craning head.

The Master nodded, his walrus moustache twitching up and down. "Good idea. Come on, can't be here all day."

Tetricus, standing at the back, moved aside to make room for us, then looked around.

"Here's the Count and the Escount," he said, and attention was momentarily diverted from the screen.

"Don't worry about us," my father said. "We can see."

It wasn't strictly true. Being so short, I couldn't see the screen because of Tetricus's head in the way, but he made enough room for me to slip in and get a clear view.

"That's better," the Master rapped. "Stop there."

"Without a doubt!" the assistant said gleefully, a look of amazement on her normally staid face. There was an almost tangible air of excitement in the room, not at all spoiled by the general lack of space. "Look at those fins!"

My eyes were riveted on the screen as I watched a patch of ocean suddenly get darker as something appeared through the gloom. It was still indistinct, but I could make out the movement of a pair of flippers . . . surely they couldn't be that big, though? Then it began to turn side-on, and I gasped. Sweet Thetis, it was huge! I'd thought plesiosaurs were big, but this . . . the neck had to be ten yards long if it was an inch, and those jaws could have swallowed a shark.

I watched in stunned silence as a vast, pitted body passed in front of the recorder, dominating the field of view even though it was several hundred yards away. The body was entirely black, because at that distance and depth the recorder could only pick up shapes and movement, but that didn't matter to me. It was the most awe-inspiring creature I'd ever seen—no wonder the Domain regarded kraken as the spawn of chaos. Beside a creature like this, Lachazzar and the whole Domain paled into insignificance.

"Look at that skin," Tetricus said. "Must be six inches thick."

"Have you got a length measurement yet?" the Master asked somebody else I couldn't see who was crouched down in the corner beside one of the machines. "It's got to be seventy yards at least."

"How on earth does it feed itself?" the assistant said. "It must need to eat about a whale's weight every day."

"I think they eat anything," said the animal expert, Phraates, launching into a detailed account of strainers and shrimp. His exposition faded into silence when the tail came into view.

"Maybe a bit longer," the Master said, banging his fist on the table. "Eighty, I make it—better go and check on previous sightings."

With a few more flicks of its sinuous, elongated tail, the monster disappeared into the gloom again, and someone froze the recording.

"Holy Ranthas!" Tetricus said. "How on earth can anything be that big?"

"What's it doing up here, more to the point?" the Master asked rhetorically. "It's a deep-ocean creature, you can tell. No light down there, and that armor should be able to take it eight miles under or more."

"I wonder why it didn't attack?" Phraates mused, frowning. "That probe's more than a yard across—the beast must have noticed it."

"It probably can't see very well," the Master said. "And maybe it's like a dolphin—you know, uses those strange clicks."

It seemed bizarre, comparing the titan that had just swum across our streams to a dolphin—but then, not as bizarre as the idea that something so big could exist at all. We watched the recording again, this time to the accompaniment of a spirited argument between Phraates and the assistant about why the creature might have come up to the surface from its lightless home.

"What's the deepest any ship's ever gone?" Tetricus asked, as the Master delegated the two apprentices to set up another screen in the colonnaded front porch for all the people who'd be along once the news got out.

"Nine miles, I think," Phraates said, breaking off from his argument for a second.

"Thirteen," I said, at the same time.

"When was that?" Phraates demanded. "If you're thinking of the *Revelation*, the deepest they recorded was nine miles."

"We don't know how far they got on the last expedition, though," Tetricus pointed out. "It could have been much deeper, even if we don't have the record. But I don't remember anyone claiming to have got as far as thirteen."

"During the Tuonetar war, the Thetian flagship went to thirteen," I said. It was a calculated risk, telling them about that, but it was a matter only of interest to oceanographers. And besides, they might be able to help.

"I don't remember reading about that," Phraates said belligerently. Tetricus shrugged, but looked intrigued.

I didn't have time to say anything else, because at that moment the Master's cane jabbed me in the ribs. I swung around to see a fierce expression on his face.

"Why didn't you write up your last check in the logbook?" he demanded. "Water temperature's down two marks at the edge of the bay, and you don't tell me? Come into my office and give me a verbal report. You may be the Escount, but while you're a member of my guild I'm not having that sort of sloppiness."

I bridled; there was no need for him to berate me over something like that, but I caught an almost imperceptible jerk of his head. I was smarting as I followed him into the office, and he closed the door, cutting off the noise from the lobby.

"Sorry about that," the Master said gruffly, sitting down at the small, cluttered desk in one corner. There were nine oceanographers in Lepidor, a big staff for somewhere this size, and the building wasn't big enough to accommodate them all properly. "You were about to say something you'd regret."

"What do you mean?" I perched on the edge of a chair that was occupied by the oceanographic station's cat, Flipperless. Most stations had one, for luck, but Flipperless was, like most cats in Lepidor, half wildcat. And fairly savage if disturbed, so I was careful.

"It's not a good idea to mention that ship," he said. "Especially not where people can listen in."

"Are you talking about *Aeon*?"

"What else?" he demanded. "Thetian flagship in the War—of course I'm talking about the *Aeon*. But anyone with any sense keeps their mouth shut about that ship."

"Do you know where it is, then?"

"Don't be stupid. I know it exists, and so do some of the other Masters. If we knew where it was, we wouldn't be having this discussion. But for everyone's sake, the Domains are better off not knowing. What I want to know is: why are you looking for it?"

"The storms," I said. "The *Aeon* had access to the SkyEye system—it could see the weather from above. If we could predict the storms, it would take away a lot of the Domain's advantage."

The Master's face hardened. "So you can do to other cities what you did here? I don't like the sound of that."

"If you think I would, then you obviously don't know me very well."

"Why bother, then?" he demanded. "Command of the weather can only help you if you prove the Domain can't protect people against it. And the only way to do that is unleash a storm on some city that happens to have an Inquisitor in it."

"You'd rather I left the Inquisitors to their work? After what they did here?"

"You're not even denying what I'm saying, Cathan. Here in Lepidor you saved all of us from that mad Prime and her schemes. Using the storms the way you did to protect your clan, your girl, your friends, there's nothing wrong with that. But if you use the *Aeon* to work with the storms somewhere else, you're the one on the offensive, and you will cause people's deaths."

He wasn't going to see it my way, which saddened me; I'd hoped the Guild could be some help, but the Master was about as typical a senior oceanographer as you'd find.

"If the Domain didn't behave the way they did, I wouldn't need to use the storms at all."

"That's the way of the world, Cathan. There is only one god and they are His followers. They're dangerous at the moment, yes, but that's no reason to risk your life to forsake the true religion. Your father doesn't believe, but he was always content to fight his corner. You're not your father's son, though, so I shouldn't be surprised."

I stared at him for a moment. I'd known the Master since I was seven, and though he'd always been gruff and strict, he'd never been anything but fair. Now he seemed to have turned against me suddenly, become someone other than the Master I knew. I felt as if he'd just stabbed me.

"So if you won't tell me about the *Aeon*, who will?"

"Nobody. As far as the Guild is concerned, the ship is lost for good, and no oceanographer except me will tell you otherwise. The planet doesn't like being interfered with, Cathan, and you've already done it once." His weathered face creased into a smile, but to me it just seemed like a mockery. "You'd make a brilliant oceanographer. It's a pity, really."

Bitter, I stood up and stroked the sleeping cat one last time. I doubted I'd see it again. "My real father is dead, Master Domitius, but I'm sure he was no worse than the Count."

"Cathan!" the Master barked, as I left the room as quickly as possible. "What do you—" The door closed and cut off the sound of his voice, and I brushed my hand savagely across my eyes. There were still a lot of people in the lobby, but thankfully my father seemed to have gone, and Palatine and Ravenna were nowhere to be seen. I collected my cloak and almost ran out into the street, heading away from the Palace.

I felt terribly hurt as I walked blindly along toward the New Quarter, unable to believe what the Master had said to me. Why had he been so hostile? Was it the ship, or the whole idea of heresy? But as I went along, the feeling of rejection was gradually replaced by a cold rage. If the oceanographers weren't going to help me, if all they could see was their own small corner of the world, then I didn't need them. Maybe in Qalathar, where the Inquisitors were torturing people every day, they would be more willing to help. And if not, then I would find and use the *Aeon* with Palatine and Ravenna, and my Archipelagan friends. I didn't want to unleash the full force of a storm on anyone, but after what the Domain had tried to do—to me and the others—I couldn't let such considerations get in the way.

It wasn't until the evening that I had a chance to talk to Ravenna and Palatine about what my father and I had discussed earlier. Rather than use my study, which was too big ever to be comfortably warm, I lit a fire in the cramped storeroom I'd converted into a sitting room. The tapestries on the walls made it uncomfortably hot in summer, but in winter they kept the chill out very effectively.

"Where were you earlier?" Palatine said, throwing herself down in the chair opposite the fire. "When we got to the oceanographers' place, no one knew where you'd gone, and the Master was looking for you."

"He can look all he likes," I said, sitting beside Ravenna on the cushioned bench-seat. Then I changed the subject. "We had a letter from Hamilcar this morning. He agrees with House Canadrath but he's not going to commit himself until he's sure the dissidents can pay their way."

"You mean he wants us to go to Qalathar," Palatine said immediately. I nodded.

"How thoughtful," Ravenna said acidly. "I get a chance to go home again and help him in the process. Very convenient."

"Just Qalathar?" Palatine asked, her expression alight at the prospect of doing something at last. "Not Thetia too?"

"He's got his own contacts in Thetia," Ravenna said. "It's safe to work there, but he can't be seen getting involved with Qalathar—his guardian might get upset."

"That's unfair. You wouldn't sign a business agreement with an organization you knew nothing about. And besides, Ravenna, you are their leader by descent."

"How many people in my home country have ever seen me? If I go in there and tell them I'm the Pharaoh, first they'll lock me up while they check, and then they'll keep me locked up so I don't get away again. That's if the Domain don't find out, and offer me the use of their prisons instead. Bigger rats, but warmer." She wasn't smiling.

I'd discovered in the last six weeks just how tenuous Ravenna's claim to the throne of Qalathar was. It derived mostly from the assumption that the rest of her family—whom she hadn't seen in thirteen years—were all dead. And even if that was so, she would only be the second Pharaoh of her dynasty. Her grandfather, Orethura, who had died in the Archipelagan Crusade, had taken the throne after a fifty-year interregnum, with no prior claim at all. Perhaps more worryingly, if somebody chose to challenge it, was the fact that no one alive seemed to be able to prove her kinship to Orethura.

On the other hand, as far as the Qalatharis were concerned, the Pharaoh was female and approximately Ravenna's age, so perhaps they knew something she didn't. And the Domain seemed to have been very thorough in butchering her family.

"You have to go back sometime," Palatine said softly. "They believe in you, but they can't sustain that belief forever. The longer you wait, the more they'll build you up in their minds. And if they make you into a messiah, it'll cause as much trouble as it solves."

"It might be enough to drive the Domain out, though," I said. "The Archipelago's suffered enough."

"You're probably right," Palatine said musingly. "I think the Domain can only push so far. If they go over the edge they may find themselves with another uprising."

"And the last one ended in the Archipelagan Crusade," Ravenna cut in. "If you've quite finished planning my country's future, you haven't yet convinced me that we have any safe way to go to Qalathar."

"Nothing's ever safe, you should know that. But we know enough heretics in the Archipelago to have an introduction. How many people know who you are?"

"About six," Ravenna admitted.

"Who?"

"Does it matter?"

"Yes, most certainly. Sagantha is one, of course, and who else?"

"My two guardians before him—who live in Worldsend and Ilthys— my father's sister in Tehama, President Alidrisi and Fernando Barrati."

I didn't recognize either name, but evidently Palatine did. "President," if I remembered rightly, was the Thetian and Archipelagan equivalent of "Count," only Presidents were usually elective rather than hereditary.

"Alidrisi might be a problem, because he's still in Qalathar pretending to be a devout and faithful clan leader. Fernando Barrati—how does he know? He's just a playboy, spends his whole time chasing girls just like the Emperor does."

"His elder brother got me out of the Domain's clutches when I was a baby, and Fernando paid for one of my changes of wardship."

"You'll have to explain sometime how Clan Barrati got involved. But if Alidrisi's the only one we have to deal with, it should be possible to pass you off as a dissident living in exile, with the right connections."

It took another half-hour of argument before Ravenna was persuaded to see Palatine's point of view. I helped where I could, but mostly let Palatine do the talking, explaining the whole thing as one of her convoluted and usually successful plans. The trouble was, this time it had to be successful. During the invasion of Lepidor, her plan had only been salvaged by Hamilcar's intervention, and in Qalathar there would be no such safeguards.

Palatine looked very pleased when we finally got up to go to bed, almost certainly because we were finally doing something. I had wanted to wait a while longer, but we were going to leave for Oceanus's capital, Pharassa, in two days' time, on the coastal trader *Parasur*. From Pharassa we could catch a ship for Ral Tumar, the biggest Archipelagan city outside Qalathar, and from there on to Qalathar itself.

But I had no more time to wait for Tanais. I didn't want to find out just how closely related to the Emperor I was, because somewhere deep down I already knew the answer. And I was more frightened of that truth than I had been, six weeks ago, of being burned at the stake.

That night I had one of the terrible nightmares that had plagued me as a child, and that not even the healer had ever managed to wake me from. Most of it was too terrifying to remember, but when I woke up Orosius's cold, insane laughter was still echoing through my head.

Chapter IV

Ral Tumar was the first Archipelagan city I'd visited, and it was unlike any other I'd ever seen. Among the buildings that sprawled up the side of a hill among lush tropical forests, dozens of domes glittered as they caught a momentary shaft of sunlight. For a moment the white paint on all the houses was dazzling, then gray clouds rolled over the gap again. Despite the glowering sky, the capital of the Archipelagan province of Tumarian was an unbelievable sight.

Even the smell was different, I thought, breathing in warm, humid air that was a welcome relief after the dry sterility of the manta and the chill wetness of Lepidor. And even in winter, with Aquasilva blanketed by clouds, Ral Tumar was still comfortably warm, kept heated by the North Tropic Current.

"So good to be at the right temperature again," Palatine said, looking up the city's broad main street from where we stood at the surface entrance to the undersea harbor. It wasn't built on the Tanethan pattern of avenues; the street curved around a spur of slightly higher ground, meandering its way up to the palace at the top of the hill.

"What are those little towers everywhere?" I asked, puzzled, as we headed uphill between market stalls whose traders didn't seem in the least affected by the weather.

"Minarets," Palatine said. "Every house will have one—some are big enough to have rooms in. Like that one over there." I followed her arm and saw a circular tower with an onion dome on top, a balcony with plants on each of its two stories. There were roof gardens here, too, but a lot more greenery in the streets, and seemingly a park every couple of dozen yards.

"It gets so hot here in summer, they need the parks to keep cool," Palatine explained. "And we'd better get out of the way."

"Why?"

The answer was a loud trumpeting sound from behind us, and I followed Palatine and Ravenna, squashing into a narrow gap between two temporary stalls. I looked around to see what was making the noise, and my eyes widened as I saw two elephants making their stately way up the road. Rather than a howdah, each one had a kind of harness strapped to its back, with packing cases and boxes of goods fastened on to them.

"Never seen an elephant before, Cathan?" Ravenna said, giving me one of her increasingly rare smiles.

I shook my head, then blanched as the elephants' smell hit us. It was unpleasant mostly because of the sheer amount of elephant going past.

Archipelagans used elephants extensively, someone had told me once, but no one on the continents ever did. Something to do with lack of forests—the animals didn't like cooler, drier climates. Like Palatine, they belonged in the steamy heat of the islands, which I had to admit I'd never found too unpleasant. Perhaps it was because I was Thetian born, and the climate suited me.

That was another reason I liked Ral Tumar. I was small even for an Archipelagan, but at least here most people weren't much taller than me, and I blended in rather than stuck out. Compared to the locals, that was. The crowded streets were thronged with people ranging from blond men like Oltan Canadrath to a party of tall black-skinned men wearing suits of scale armor as if they weighed no more than silk tunics. They could have been Mons Ferratans, but somehow I doubted it. Mons Ferranis, on the western route into the Archipelago, was a prosperous trading city whose people didn't train for war if they could possibly help it. The warriors could be from anywhere in the unknown reaches of the Archipelago, which were much more extensive than the charted areas. Somewhere in the South, perhaps from the edge of the equatorial Desolation where the heat was too much for anyone to survive.

"Where's the shipping exchange, do you think?" I asked Palatine, as we set off up the hill again in the elephants' wake, careful to avoid the occasional pile of dung that hadn't yet been sluiced away.

"Your father said it was somewhere unusual, not by the waterfront or the palace. At least Ral Tumar is a decent size, not a bloated monstrosity like Taneth."

Which was quite true, I thought as we rounded the corner and came to a wide square with palm trees and the city temple on the far side. It looked glaringly out of place, with its red-painted walls and Halettite architecture, among the whitewashed, domed houses of Ral Tumar.

"Excuse me, where's the shipping exchange?" Palatine said, stopping a passing woman dressed in green silk, a merchant from her businesslike air.

"Over the square and left, you go in around the side." The Tumarian dialect was harsher than standard Archipelagan, but still perfectly comprehensible to someone who'd been raised in Oceanus. Most of the known world spoke Archipelagan of one kind or another, with the occasional notable exception like Thetia, whose language bore no resemblance to any other.

"Thank you," Palatine said. The merchant nodded graciously and walked off across the square, heading for a taverna with palm trees outside it.

"Good to be back in a civilized part of the world, at least," Ravenna said as we followed the merchant's directions.

"Makes a difference from Taneth, certainly."

The shipping exchange was a palatial building, evidently built with the proceeds from Tumarian's lucrative customs duties. Ral Tumar had managed to survive the Crusade, even though it had been on the Crusaders' path, by immediately capitulating. It was a tried and tested plan for Ral Tumar, a city that had always been a poor third in the Archipelago behind Selerian Alastre and Poseidonis, Qalathar's ruined capital. Now Mons Ferranis, on the western route from Thetia to Taneth, was beginning to overtake it as well.

"They can't even make up their mind who they belong to," Palatine said in disgust, pointing above the closed main gateway of the exchange. The flag of Tumarian hung between the Imperial dolphin and the golden scales of Taneth.

"Where's the Archipelagan flag, as if I didn't know?" Ravenna asked. It was a rhetorical question, because although Tumarian was nominally part of the Archipelago, an equally nominal dominion of Thetia, the Archipelago's flag had been banned.

The entrance to the exchange led into a courtyard with tamarisk trees and a lion-headed fountain gushing water into a long channel that ran around the edge. The city might be a rival of Thetia, but the pointed arches and geometric designs belonged to the same style of architecture I'd seen in pictures of Selerian Alastre.

This was the Archipelago, of course, so it was the courtyard itself that was the focus of activity. There were offices hidden in the shadows behind the arches of the colonnade, protected from the weather, but that wasn't where the real business was being done. Small groups of people were dotted around the courtyard, talking intensely, while a few men stood singly or in pairs, waiting for potential clients to come into range.

Poor quarry though we probably looked, a large woman swathed in voluminous silks descended on us before we'd even decided who to try first.

"Peace be upon you," she said; it was one of the many traditional Archipelagan greetings.

"And upon you be peace," Palatine replied.

"Passengers or freight?" the merchant demanded. The sharp, alert expression on her face belied her motherly appearance.

"Passengers, to Qalathar."

The other's eyebrows shot up, but the look of interest faded somewhat. "Got money, have you? That's an expensive trip from here, unless you're planning to go by slow boats."

"That could take a while."

"Yes, but nobody checks the slow boats. Ral Tumar to Qalathar is a very long journey, and not one you'd make without a good reason. It's never good to go to Qalathar without a reason."

I glanced at Ravenna, who shrugged very slightly and looked to Palatine. Our reason was supposed to be secret, and the Sacri monitored all traffic into and out of Qalathar. Three Archipelagans like us arriving without any particular reason by manta might well arouse suspicions.

"Does anyone do a run to Ilthys?" Palatine asked.

"Deck passengers on a manta?"

Palatine nodded, and the woman called over to a moustachioed man conferring with a colleague at the edge of the crowd.

"I owe you a good turn, Demaratus," she said, as the man came over. Despite his moustache, which gave him the air of a robber chieftain, he had a military bearing, and a walk that was more of a march than a swagger. His belt was worked with the gray-and-green swirl emblem of Clan Tumarian.

"Trying to buy me off cheaply, Atossa?" Demaratus demanded, but his tone was friendly.

"It must have happened to you before," Palatine said amicably.

"They want passage to Calatos," said Atossa. Calatos, I hoped, was the capital of Clan Ilthys.

"Just the three of you?" Demaratus asked. "No cargo?"

Palatine shook her head.

"Three hundred corons," he said, after a moment's pause. "Each."

"Who are you trying to rob? That's ridiculous. A hundred and fifty."

"You've got a nerve! A hundred and fifty wouldn't even get you to Thetia. Do you want me to drive myself out of business?"

"How much will it cost you to have us along, then? Next to nothing."

"I can fill my cabins with people who'd be glad to make the crossing for under four hundred."

"Where are they all?" Palatine spread her hands wide to indicate the empty space around us. Atossa smiled approvingly, then saw some more likely targets coming through the gateway behind us and bore down on them.

"They'll come by the time I sail. But I'll go down to two hundred and fifty, and I hope you're not expecting a cabin each."

"Two hundred, and two of us can share." Every manta, whether clan- or Tanethan-operated, had a few spare cabins for paying passengers. The clan authorities would decide the cargo to be carried, but the captain and crew were allowed their own small-scale enterprises; in the captain's case, that included taking passengers.

"Depends on how full I am. You're traveling as deck passengers, remember—you want comfort you'll have to pay. Two-forty."

"Deck will be fine. Two-twenty."

"Two-thirty," Demaratus said, grudgingly. "Any more and I'll wait for some other people."

"Done." They slapped palms, sealing the contract.

"Half before we sail, half in Calatos," Demaratus said immediately. "Those are clan rules, and I can't change them. My manta's the *Sforza*, gantry eleven of the clan harbor. She sails in four days' time, at the seventh hour. We're stopping off in Mare Alastre and Urimmu, should reach Calatos in twelve or thirteen days. It's winter, so there'll be the odd storm."

The two of them said the polite words of farewell and then we left the exchange. Atossa was bargaining furiously with a group of short, stocky men who sounded as if they weren't at home speaking Archipelagan, and she didn't notice us going past.

"We did quite well there, I think," Palatine said. "Four days isn't that long to wait, and he's taking a fairly direct route. The question now is what we're going to do until then. Somewhere to stay should be easy, and we might as well make the most of our time here. Was there anyone from Ral Tumar at the Citadel, do you know?"

I cast my mind back to the people I'd known during my year at the Citadel, a heretic stronghold in an uninhabited island group on the fringe of the known world. Mikas Rufele, Palatine's rival, and his friends had been Cambressians, Ghanthi a subject of the Halettites, Persea, my companion for most of the year, from Clan Ilthys . . . but no one I could remember had come from Ral Tumar.

"You remember that friend of Ghanthi's, the one who used to box Mikas sometimes?" Ravenna said, as we crossed the square again, heading nowhere in particular. "I can't remember what his name was, but I think he was from here."

"I know who you mean." There was a fierce look of concentration on Palatine's face for a moment, then she gave up. "Can't recall, either. If we do, we'll look in on him. But first, somewhere to stay. And something to eat, more importantly. You may both be as thin as rakes, but some of us have stomachs to feed."

"Who are you calling a rake?" Ravenna said indignantly. "You've been too long away, forgotten how hot it is here."

"In winter? You must be joking. Any colder and I'll freeze."

"*This* is cold? Would you rather go back to Lepidor?"

It was precisely because it was winter that we managed to find a fairly respectable hostel for a good price. My father had given me what funds he could spare, but he'd had to spend a lot on rebuilding the parts of the city that Ravenna and I had demolished during the invasion. And while Palatine and Ravenna had earned some money working for him in Lepidor, and I had a credit note from House Canadrath, we were going to have to be careful to make it last.

Especially since we still didn't know where we were going in the end. It could take a while to establish links with the dissidents in Qalathar, and after that we still had to find Tanais. And the *Aeon*, the mention of whose name seemed to have turned the Master against me back in Lepidor. The ship that I had to find.

The *Aeon* seemed a long way away the next day, as we ate lunch in a bar in Ral Tumar. Even in winter, it was warm enough for there to be tables outside under an awning, surrounded by a few small palm trees in earthenware pots. The bar was on a small square near the top of the hill, away from the hubbub of the main street and the marketplace.

"Mare Alastre could be a dangerous place to be," Palatine said, finishing off a stuffed vine leaf, one of the local delicacies. Clan Tumarian were major wine producers, shipping red and white wine to Taneth and Selerian Alastre, and the surplus of grapes meant that most of the food was in some way connected with them. It was spicier than I was used to in Lepidor, but delicious nonetheless. Only Ravenna had found any problem with it, something she'd been too polite to complain about in Lepidor: there wasn't anything like enough seasoning.

"Why?" Ravenna scattered something across her plate, almost certainly a spice that I didn't want to know about. "It's not your part of Thetia."

"It's still one of the biggest cities, capital of Clan Estarrin. The Estarrin may be fairly small and insignificant otherwise, but some of them will know what I look like."

"They think you're dead," Ravenna said, sitting back to enjoy her red-hot vine leaf.

"Yes, but if they see me walking down the street they might just notice, and wonder who I am. Wouldn't you do the same?"

"If Mare Alastre is as big as you say it is, we won't have a problem," she replied. "We can just hide in the crowd whenever anyone important goes past, or you can stay on the ship. And where is Urimmu? I've never heard of the place."

"It's the only town of Clan Qalishi," Palatine said, shrugging. "They're a strange lot, more interested in fighting than in trade. There are a couple of other clans like them around the place—mostly they hire themselves out as mercenaries. Don't know why he's stopping there, really. I've never been there, but from what I've heard it's not a very impressive place."

"We might have a problem once we arrive in Ilthys, though. It's a five-day passage to Qalathar by sail, and not many people will be risking the trip. They'll probably charge the earth for it."

"Meaning it could be difficult to get out?" I said, idly watching a cat stalking a stray twig out in the square.

"Yes. What if we have to leave in a hurry, and there's a storm? This whole plan depends on everything going right—and it won't, it never does. The nearer we get, the less I like the idea."

"But you've agreed to come along, and we have to do it for ourselves as well as for Hamilcar."

"He just wants to make sure of his profit."

"He's planning to give up his safe profit so as not to sell weapons to the Domain, Ravenna. You're too harsh on him, especially after he saved your life."

"For which I am more grateful than I can say. But he still has his own agenda, and who knows what he'll do if the Domain find out? If there's one thing a Tanethan can't bear, it's the thought of his precious skin being in danger. It's almost as bad as the idea of making a loss."

"If you think it'll help, we can stop in Ilthys and find Persea. She definitely has connections with the dissidents, and we know her house name. And she knows what's been going on."

"That makes sense, I suppose," Ravenna conceded, brushing her hair away from her eyes. "But you know how traitors spring up wherever the Domain is, and if they get one word that I'm in Ilthys, they might seal off the whole country."

"That's impossible," Palatine said, dismissing the idea with a wave of her hand. "Not even they can cut off a whole country, there are always fishing villages and smugglers to hand. And they can't do it for long without getting everyone annoyed."

"The Exarch has such a thick skin, he's almost impossible to divert from his scheme of the moment. But when we're there, I'm in charge," Ravenna said, fixing an intense brown gaze on each of us in turn. "I know my way around, and neither of you have ever been there. We do things differently from everyone else."

"I noticed. Do at least accept advice from time to time."

"As often as I need it." Ravenna went back to scattering spice on her food, but her behavior concerned me slightly. She seemed resentful of Palatine always taking the lead, as she had been at the Citadel, before she'd known either of us that well. Sometimes I felt as if I didn't know Ravenna at all.

After lunch we walked down toward the docks again. There was a large oceanographic station in Ral Tumar and I had my credentials as a member of the Guild, which would allow me to look in their library. And while there would certainly be no reference to the *Aeon*, or at least none that I would be able to find on such short notice, there might be something else useful. Everything I could read on deep ocean conditions could help to narrow the search, especially if I knew the lower limit at which mantas and sea-rays could operate. The *Aeon* had been capable of diving to unheard-of depths, and the crew could have done a lot worse than conceal their titanic ship too deep for anyone to stumble on it accidentally.

"Do the oceanographers have any big stations in Qalathar?" I asked Ravenna, who was less touchy now that we'd got off the subject of what we were going to do.

"None very significant. I don't remember very well, but I think their headquarters are in Saetu, on the south coast. They never replaced the station they lost when Poseidonis was burned. They keep a low profile."

"Saetu's nowhere near where we'll be. I'll have a look in Calatos when we go through." That was irritating, because it meant I probably wouldn't be able to continue the search while we were in Qalathar. On the other hand, it was one risk less that we might come to the Domain's attention.

"Mare Alastre too, if you've got time," Palatine said, unexpectedly. "They always have much bigger oceanographic stations in Thetia, because more people want to join the Guild."

"I thought you wanted to keep out of sight in Mare Alastre."

"I do, but you don't need to. You don't look too much like a

Tar'Conantur, at least not that anyone would notice. People will think you're Thetian."

"That's comforting."

We went around a corner past a shop selling coffee beans, the sharp smell of their roasting wafting out into the air, and into a short, wide avenue with mansions on either side set back from the road. Dominating the road was a huge building with at least ten towers and more than a dozen minarets, its center crowned by a turquoise onion dome that seemed to glow with color even under the gray sky. The aroma of coffee and the sound of grinding was replaced by the smell of plants and the noise of clipping shears.

We set off along the street, keeping well away from the elephant that was approaching from the other direction in an otherwise empty street. We'd almost drawn level with the front of the big building when the iron gates opened.

"Oh dear," Palatine said, as the elephant stopped just ahead. A small group of people emerged from inside and stood talking as the mahout brought the elephant to its knees. Two guards positioned a block to enable the passengers to climb into the howdah.

"It's the Thetian High Commission," Ravenna said. "You accuse me of hiding from my responsibilities, and you can't even go past a Thetian building."

"I'm not so stupid. But look at the elephant—only someone with money could afford those decorations. And red with silver is Scartaris colors. One of those people there might know me."

"Keep on walking, then."

As we walked past, pretending to have nothing to do with the other group, I found my gaze straying over to the people by the elephant. A tall, distinguished-looking man in a white robe was talking to a striking shorter man in a functional dark red tunic and light cloak. There were three men looking on; two of them, I could tell, were Imperial Navy, in royal blue, while the other might have been someone's aide. He didn't look like a Thetian, in fact, not with a skin that was almost copper-colored and those slightly slanted eyes.

The aide didn't seem to be concentrating exclusively on the conversation, and a second or two later his gaze met mine, too quickly for me to look away. Barely ten yards away, I could see a brief look of puzzlement on his impassive features before he turned back to the conversation. My heart started beating again, and three or four steps later the elephant blocked our line of sight. I didn't dare look back, even when we'd gone around the next corner.

"What did you do, Cathan, you fool?" Palatine said angrily. "Wave to him?"

"So he wouldn't have noticed us otherwise? Was he a friend of yours?"

"I've never seen him before in my life. But maybe he's seen me, because he obviously recognized one of us. So perhaps he tells that man in white, who just happens to be the Viceroy. Or maybe Mauriz Scartaris, who is the Scartaris High Commissioner for the Archipelago. Or even Admiral Charidemus there, in his blue uniform."

"What, that he's seen a dead revolutionary walking down the street?" Ravenna said fiercely. "You say I think I'm too important, then you flare up the moment some minor functionary looks at you. You're dead, Palatine, as far as they're concerned. They won't see what they don't expect to, and you can't blame Cathan."

My surprise at her coming to my defense eclipsed my annoyance at being blamed by Palatine. "Even if he saw you, and reports it, how many people would believe him?"

"Mauriz for a start. And then the Emperor's people who tried to kill me in the first place . . ."

"Palatine, you're talking complete nonsense," Ravenna cut in. "All of Thetia heard about your funeral, and every clan leader will have seen the body they thought was yours. You might be someone who looks like Palatine Canteni, but nothing more. Do you look like a clan president's daughter now? Not in the slightest. Now stop being paranoid and we'll head for the oceanographers."

Palatine stared at her for a moment, seemingly amazed.

"You have no idea what you're talking about. This isn't Qalathar, where the Domain rules by fear and you all have to keep in line. Thetia runs on secrets. That aide will be an agent for someone: maybe his own clan, maybe the Navy, maybe even the Emperor. Somebody will find out and then you'll know what I'm talking about. We're not play-acting in the Archipelago anymore, or have you forgotten those chains and that stake so soon?"

"I've been hiding from the Domain all my life, and they're far more insidious than the Thetians can ever be."

"If you want to ignore everything I say, go ahead, but don't expect anything good to come of it."

"You're a true Thetian if you can't believe I can get anything done on my own. Always have to manage everyone else's affairs too, don't you?"

"Go on, then. Forget we ever saw any of those people, and don't ask for my help in Thetia. You're as bad as your grandfather was, all stubbornness and no give." Before Ravenna could fling another reply at her, Palatine put on speed and walked ahead, disappearing down a narrow alleyway a little farther on. There were few people in the wide, crooked street, and nobody seemed to have noticed our altercation. No windows were thrown open in the house whose wall we'd been arguing beside, and the party of children in the garden opposite were too engrossed in their ball game to pay us any attention.

"Let her go and hide somewhere, in case the Thetian agents come down on her," Ravenna said scornfully. "Who is she to talk about grandfathers, anyway? Look at hers—what did he ever do for Thetia?"

Her smoldering temper lasted all the way down to the harbor, as we cut through into the main street again and through the bustle of the market in the main square, much busier than it had been yesterday. She didn't turn on me, though, because I managed to stop myself from rising to the choice insults she flung at my—admittedly deserving—Tar'Conantur family. The truth was that to me they represented very little, and I rarely thought of Palatine as a cousin.

As we approached the shoreline the throng of people thickened, and there seemed to be more people along the wharves and entering the undersea harbor.

"The oceanographers are along there, I think," Ravenna volunteered, pointing eastward. "In the building with the blue glass dome and the balcony."

We'd only gone a little way along the beach when the normal bustle of the wharves fell very quiet suddenly, and almost all that could be heard was the screech of the seagulls circling over the harbor. Wondering what had happened, I caught Ravenna's hand before she could go any farther, and turned around to see what was happening.

"What are you—" she said, and stopped. Even though neither of us was very tall, we were slightly above the level of the main wharves and both of us could see enough. Ravenna's hand suddenly went very tense, squeezing mine in a vicelike grip, but I was too distracted by a sudden gut-wrenching fear.

As the red-helmeted forms of a double line of Sacri emerged from the undersea harbor, their boots making almost no sound on the stone, the crowds parted enough for me to see the hooded men who walked in a barely audible rustle of robes behind them. I felt a sudden surge of helpless anger, remembering the last time I had seen them.

The Inquisition was here in Ral Tumar.

Chapter V

The crowd stood in sullen silence, as if turned to stone by the Sacri presence. No one wanted to draw attention to themselves by leaving the quay or slipping away in the opposite direction. They just watched, moving aside as the Sacri walked slowly out across the esplanade and stopped, forming a double line. More of them followed, coming down the steps to join their comrades and forming a complete semicircle around the entrance.

Behind them came Inquisitors, all almost identical in their white-lined black robes and pointed cowls that covered most of their faces. They seemed to glide rather than walk, the hems of their robes just brushing along the ground. It was their near-silence that was most daunting, though; they hardly seemed to make any sound at all as they moved. And the line seemed to go on and on, with, in the end, at least forty Inquisitors arrayed on the lower steps behind the Sacri.

As in almost every building in Ral Tumar, the entrance to the undersea harbor was set back slightly into a decorative archway, in this case at the top of a short flight of marble steps. Finally the last Inquisitor took his place. Then the senior Inquisitor, who was standing in front of the doorway, hands folded within the sleeves of his black robes, stepped aside to allow somebody else to emerge from the shadowy interior.

A moment later I saw exactly who it was, as a powerfully built, bearded Halettite came out and stopped at the top of the steps. Gems glittered on his robe, red-and-orange patterned in a flame motif.

"*Him*," Ravenna hissed, barely loudly enough for me to hear. "How could they send *him*?"

A third man, in the scarlet robes of a mage, took his place on the bearded man's right-hand side, as more priests, one in the robes of an Avarch, and at least a dozen more Inquisitors, filed out and surrounded them. I guessed the Avarch was Ral Tumar's; he had an obsequious expression that he no doubt reserved for superiors honoring him with a visit.

"In the name of Ranthas, He who is Fire, who brings light to the world, and of His Holiness, Lachazzar, Vice-Gerent of God and Prime of the Domain," the mage began, reading from a heavy, impressive-looking scroll, his amplified voice echoing off the buildings of the seafront. "Let it be known that, in defiance of the law of Ranthas and the teachings of His Domain, the world is sorely afflicted with the plague of heresy. That there are those who deny the teachings of the Faith, who defy the authority of Ranthas. That, though few in number, they preach their heresy, contaminating the minds of those pure in heart. That they have forsaken the True Lord, the Maker of Creation, and His servant Lachazzar, who by the right of succession is the only arbiter of the Faith on Aquasilva. That in rejecting the true faith they have condemned their souls to eternal exile from His life-giving flames and have spread their contamination throughout the world."

It was an Edict Universal, a general decree of the Faith issued by the Prime himself, an ordinance that no power of earth or heaven could disobey. While Edicts Specific were quite common, and given out whenever the Prime passed judgment in a matter, years sometimes went by without the passing of Edicts Universal. Acutely conscious that we were raised slightly above the crowd, I didn't dare move, terrified of doing anything that would attract the attention of the men on the steps. Ravenna was completely rigid, her clenched hand painfully crushing my fingers. I tugged slightly, and she relaxed her grip enough to let me move them.

"It is therefore decreed by His Holiness, Vice-Gerent of Ranthas, that there shall be an inquisition throughout the lands and the oceans. That agents of the Holy Office of the Inquisition may act, in accordance with the will of Ranthas, to root out the plague of heresy from the face of the waters. That they act with the holy and sanctioned support of Ranthas and of this Domain universal. That none shall obstruct, delay, impede or seek to confound this sacred duty, and that any who shall so seek be treated as sinners and heretics. That every man and woman, great and small, shall prove their true faith to the agents of the Holy Office of the Inquisition, and that all those who hold authority shall render to the Holy Office every assistance and aid.

"In accordance with this, it is set forth by His Holiness that any who shall come forward and freely confess their sins within the period of three days, admitting their guilt and being truly desirous of repentance, shall be absolved and punished leniently, so that they may never again lapse from the truth or stray from the path of righteousness. That any man or woman who has information regarding the heresy of another set it forth before the Holy Office, or by hiding it be considered a heretic. That on those heretics who do not freely repent their sins the Holy Office may use whatever methods it finds suitable within the law of Ranthas, constrained by no law of man. That for those whose sin is judged too grave the Holy Office is hereby authorized to purify them with holy fire according to the doctrine of Ranthas, and that any who seek to intervene shall be judged guilty by their actions.

"For the execution of this most holy and sacred task in the lands of the Archipelago, His Holiness hereby names and decrees as Inquisitor-General Midian, who shall in the course of his duty be answerable to none save His Holiness himself, and who shall be co-equal with His Reverence Talios Felar, Exarch of the Holy Office of the Inquisition. Let all acknowledge his authority or be cast out from the protection of God.

"Sealed by the hand of His Holiness, Lachazzar, Vice-Gerent of Ranthas, this first day of winter in the blessed year two thousand, seven hundred and seventy-four."

The silence as the mage rolled up the scroll and bowed to the bearded man, newly promoted Inquisitor-General Midian, was absolute. Then Midian raised his left hand and, like a breaking wave, the crowd collectively sank to its knees. Two rather short dark-haired people among a whole crowd of very similar Archipelagans, we nevertheless dropped to our knees as quickly as we could and bowed our heads, not daring to look up at the Inquisitors. Hitting the hard stone so quickly sent a jolt through my whole body.

I hardly heard Midian's prayer, blessing, or whatever it was, only the odd standard familiar line exhorting everyone to walk in the path of Ranthas and not to question the teachings of the Domain.

I would never have admitted that I was terrified of the Inquisition, because to do so was the next thing to heresy. But I wouldn't have been ashamed to admit it. Unlike virtually everyone else on Aquasilva, I had seen Inquisitors die, shot full of arrows by Lepidor marines and Hamilcar's men. But this was the first time I'd seen them since, and for some reason that made it much worse.

I had been entirely at their mercy then, not that mercy meant anything to Inquisitors, but they had only been playing supporting roles. There had been no question of my or Ravenna's guilt, so no need for them to put us to the question. Here in Ral Tumar I was free and in a position to escape. But if Sarhaddon got the slightest hint that we were in the Archipelago . . .

Midian finished his prayer and dismissed the crowd. For a moment nobody moved, then a clump of people nearby stood up tentatively and bowed to the new Inquisitor-General. The ranks of priests on the steps moved out of their careful formation and into a line of march. Six or eight carrying-chairs were brought around from the side of the library, each one a thronelike wooden seat carried by two burly Halettites. No one dared move away until all of the senior priests had got into their chairs and the procession set off, like a black and red snake moving into the heart of the city.

Then, finally, as the last crimson-armored Sacri disappeared from sight, the crowd found its voice again and began to disperse. Ravenna released her grip on my hand and stood for a moment without moving.

"Come on, we'd better get back," she said, in her old clipped, toneless voice. "There's not time to go on to the library now."

We went with the flow of the crowd along the shoreline for a while, then by mutual consent headed up a steep, narrow street between a chandler's and a bar. I looked nervously back over my shoulder when we reached the next intersection, with a slightly wider but strangely empty back street running parallel to the harbor. There was nobody following us—why should there have been?

"I feel," Ravenna said finally, her face devoid of its usual life and energy, "like a mouse being chased by a tiger. Because it's a cat, it's playing with me before it kills me, but because it's so big, it steps on everyone else while it's having its fun."

"They're not doing this because of you," I said, rather lamely.

"Don't be stupid," she said, with a momentary flash of temper that vanished as fast as it had come. "I know they're not hunting me, they're hunting heretics. They're a tiger in a whole roomful of mice, and that's not an exaggeration. They're telling us, and everyone else, that Lepidor was nothing. That we didn't make any kind of impression on them at all."

"We didn't. We pulled out a whisker, but the whisker will grow back, and now the tiger's angry."

"No, it isn't. It's implacable. It doesn't care about that. If it tramples enough people, we won't matter anymore. Oh, if it catches us it'll take more time killing us, but other than that we're just statistics. Lachazzar has issued an Edict Universal, and *no one* on Aquasilva will dare to defy any of it. It's aimed straight at the Archipelago, and not even Orosius himself will question a single word. Under Thetian law virtually the whole edict is illegal, but the Domain is too powerful for him."

"Ravenna, they won't last for ever. Nothing does. After the fall of

Aran Cthun the Thetians didn't face resistance anywhere on Aquasilva. But they collapsed, and look at what they are now."

"Still here, and inspiring fear. I know you're trying to help, Cathan, but you don't need to. You'll do what you can, and so will I, but in the end it won't matter. There's nothing we can do against this edict, because they can crush us without even thinking about it."

"What about the storms?" I persisted. "Perhaps we're not stronger than all the mages of the Domain, but there really is no one more powerful than the two of us together."

"There isn't, but even when we destroyed half of Lepidor with that storm, we were still helpless against that mind-mage. All we can do is anger them enough to make them turn on us—and please don't say there's anything we could do then."

There was nothing I could say, because I knew she was right. Neither of us was used to feeling insignificant but, compared to the power we'd just seen, we were. The knowledge hurt as badly as if it was physically gnawing at me, but there was nothing I could come up with to counter it.

"We'll have to change our plans, I think," she said, a few minutes later, as we reached the street below the embassy avenue and cut across toward our lodgings near the city wall. "Qalathar won't be safe. One traitor among the dissidents, one person who has a grudge against any of us, and we'll be arrested. And even if we're lucky, they may still take in someone we know and question them."

"What about the weapons? Do we just keep on selling to the Halettites?"

"You don't give up, do you? Almost as bad as Palatine. Listen, if we go to Qalathar now, we probably won't make it back. This is a huge tribunal they've got here, and most of the Inquisitors will be heading farther in. There will be more ships going to other island groups, but at the moment Midian's heading for Qalathar as slowly as possible. He'll stop everywhere he can, get his Edict read out, and stay for a few days to receive a few people back into the fold.

"His people will be in Qalathar quite soon now. They'll want to impress him, so that he'll arrive the day before they've planned a huge ceremony in which they'll burn fifty or a hundred people. Their dungeons will be bursting with suspects, and they'll be checking everyone trying to leave."

"The Edict was encouraging people to come forward and denounce each other."

"That's standard, and there's sometimes a reward. You know how they work?"

"In principle," I said, trying to remember what they'd told us at the Citadel.

"It's a good thing Palatine isn't here, because she hates even thinking about it. It's the way they work that annoys her most, not what they do; you know how much she believes in Thetian law."

"As opposed to the Inquisition's interpretation of law."

"Guilty until proven guilty, yes. They accuse you, and you have to prove your innocence in a secret court without any witnesses to back you up. Not surprising that nearly everyone is condemned."

"What did that *punished leniently* bit mean? They knock them out before burning them?"

"You have to wear a mark on your clothes, go to the temple barefoot every week, and be ritually flagellated each year at the Festival of Ranthas. That's the standard one. For commoners. For nobles it can be different, better or worse."

I was appalled. I should have known, of course, from my previous encounters with the Domain, but for that to be called lenient . . . "For how long?"

"Five, ten years or the rest of your life, depending on how genuine they feel your confession is."

"And people actually come forward and confess?"

She nodded sadly. "For something like this, they will, because if somebody else denounces them afterward, things are a lot worse. Not that many are burned, of course, but there are things almost as bad." Almost absently, she put her arm around my waist, and I hugged her shoulders. We both had friends in Qalathar and the rest of the Archipelago who were known heretics, tolerated and even welcomed by the faithful of their clans. But when the Inquisition arrived, clan loyalties began to break down. Persea, like me, had already escaped the stake once, but how long would her luck, or that of any of the others, fare with this edict?

It was small consolation to know that only the Archipelago was targeted, that Lepidor wouldn't suffer, or Mikas in Cambress, or even Ghanthi under the Halettites. They wanted to destroy the Archipelago, because it was too alien to everything they believed in, too different to accept their orthodoxy.

We came out into the small courtyard where our lodgings were, a two-story annex of the building next door, run by the House who lived there. Built in traditional Archipelagan style, like the rest of the city, it was plain, but meticulously clean as dictated by the Archipelagan clan codes. Hospitality was very important in the Archipelago, something the Domain seemed to abuse shamelessly.

We climbed the narrow wooden stairway to our rooms, and Ravenna knocked on the door of the room she shared with Palatine. There was no answer.

"She's gone off to prove that she was right," Ravenna said in resignation. "I just hope she stays out of Sarhaddon's way. How could they send those two, especially Midian? He's an evil old goat." She rammed the key into an inoffensive keyhole and twisted it savagely, pushing the door hard for good measure.

I hoped nobody had been listening to that. It didn't look as though Palatine had been back here since we'd argued with her, because there was no sign of anything different. I was in a cubbyhole next door, so this was the only place large enough to talk. I drew up the rattan blind on the window to let some light in; it wasn't hot enough for the shutters to be drawn.

"You want us not to go on to Qalathar?" I said, sitting down on Palatine's bed, its patterned blanket turned down neatly. "I know it's risky, but . . ."

"But I never want to be captured by them again. They didn't torture us that time, as they will if they capture us here. You've read the Thetian *Histories*, so you remember how Hierarch Carausius was so crippled by torture and magic he could hardly walk."

"But there's no guarantee they will capture us."

"Do you want to risk it? Don't tell me you aren't as scared of them as I am."

"They won't kill us, though, will they? Not if they know who we are?"

She sat down next to me, a weary expression on her face.

"Cathan, for all that—" She broke off and went on, skipping whatever she'd been about to say. "You can be terribly dense sometimes. I know you're trying to convince me it'll be all right, but you know that's not true."

"But they won't kill us—why were you trying to convince me they will?" To be sure, I wasn't certain why I was still arguing for going to Qalathar, because I *was* afraid and I didn't want to go anywhere I might fall into the hands of the Inquisition again.

"In Lepidor," she said softly, "I chose the stake rather than become their puppet. I can't really tell you why, because I'm not sure. But doesn't that tell you something?" The other thing I couldn't understand was why she seemed to be so calm, when usually we'd have been shouting at each other by now.

"You never wanted to go home," I persisted. "Even back in Lepidor, when we had no idea this was going to happen, you made as many objections as you could. You don't want to go there, and it's nothing to do with the Inquisition."

"You really think so? As if there haven't been Inquisitors there for the last quarter of a century."

"How are you ever going to go back, then, if you're afraid of them as well? What we're doing isn't safe, and you should know that better than any of us."

"I do," she said, more heatedly this time. Perhaps I'd been wrong about her calm. "Which is why I'm the one who's been trying to persuade you and Palatine not to go. Only your heads are so thick I need a sledgehammer to get through to you."

"*Why?* You aren't a coward by anyone's standards, and you've never shrunk from anything like this before. You even wanted to go to Tehama, which you said was the worst place in the . . ."

I looked at her sharply, my voice trailing off. Ravenna had told me at the Citadel that she was from Tehama, the plateau above Qalathar whose people had fought on the Black Sun's side in the War, and been cut off from the world by the Thetian reprisals. Tehama sounded dreadful, by all accounts, but something didn't fit.

"You said the other day that you hadn't been to Qalathar for thirteen years, since you were seven or so. But I thought you were born and grew up in Tehama."

"I was. I spent a year in Qalathar, because the Barrati brothers wanted me to know what my country looked like. The Prime back then was quite harmless, and things were more relaxed for a while. Didn't you believe me?"

"I'm sorry," I said, cursing myself for having doubted her, and cursing the Inquisitors for seeding mistrust everywhere. "Am I forgiven?"

She smiled faintly. "Of course. I'm so used to keeping everything secret that I forget to tell things to people I trust."

I seized on her last words, unwilling to let a chance go.

"Then don't I deserve to know why you don't want to go to Qalathar?"

"Very neat," she said angrily. "I say something I mean and you just fasten on it to try and win the argument. I won't make *that* mistake again."

"Why is it so difficult for you to admit it, Ravenna? I'm only asking, because if it's something we haven't thought of . . ."

"It's something that you'll just label as me being emotional again," she snapped. "You want to go to Qalathar, arrange a deal for Hamilcar and see if anyone there knows anything about the *Aeon*. Fine, on the *Aeon* I agree with you. But we don't have to go to Qalathar. We *shouldn't* go to Qalathar."

We were getting nowhere, like two equally matched duelists fighting with sticks. Every time I said something, she just replied that she didn't want to go, and all I could do was keep asking why. I felt as if I was pushing futilely at a locked and bolted door.

"I get your message. But if we don't go there, how are we ever going to make this deal with Hamilcar? If we're going to sell to the di— these people," I said, suddenly aware that the window was open and our voices were getting louder and louder. I jumped up from the bed and went over to the window, looking out first into the square and then down below. There was nobody standing below us, and the only other people visible in the square were in the fruit shop opposite, haggling over some melons. "Before Hamilcar can sign any deals, he has to be sure that they can pay, and that they are who they claim to be. They're based in Qalathar, so where else can we go?"

"There are other places in the Archipelago—Ilthys, for example. Qalathar may be the center, but we can just as well contact them somewhere else and arrange a meeting in an out-of-the-way location."

"What, so that they can put their lives in danger instead of us? We can defend ourselves, at least, but risk exposing them just to save our own skins? They're as much afraid of the Inquisition as we are, and they're Qalathari citizens."

"Exactly my point," she said. "If we go to Qalathar we're strangers, without any very good reason for being there. They know how to get around the Inquisition, and they'll have good reasons for traveling to Ilthys or wherever. The Domain can't stop people traveling or monitor everyone who goes in and out. For all that I come from there, it's not our home ground."

"So you want us to go and sit around in Ilthys while they do all the running back and forth."

"How stubborn can you be, Cathan? We don't put them at any more risk by doing this, whereas if we go to Qalathar itself while the Inquisition are there in force we'll definitely be putting ourselves at risk. You're not being considerate, just stupid. And of course the Inquisition won't kill us if they catch us—what a waste that would be. I'll be made to work as their puppet ruler here while you're shipped back to the Holy City in chains to be kept on a leash until they need a water-mage. Palatine will probably be burned. Do you want that to happen?" She finished on a commanding note, her stare boring into me.

For a moment we glared at each other, both of us angry and unwilling to concede anything. If I gave in, I'd never find out why she didn't want to go, and we'd probably never get there. She was exaggerating, I was sure of that. Exaggerating the danger, the likelihood of being caught, how safe it was for the dissidents. Which meant that she still had a deeper reason for not going, something probably not connected with the Inquisition.

And the fact that she'd delivered an ultimatum probably meant she was on the verge of giving up. If I could just keep on for a little longer, I thought as we faced each other like mules on a mountain path, she might give up. But I couldn't fail to see that she didn't trust me, which hurt bitterly. I'd hoped, after everything that had happened in Lepidor, that we would be past this. But we weren't. And, I had to admit, I still wasn't certain of her. Of anything about her. There were too many unanswered questions, too many things left unsaid.

But as uncomfortable seconds passed, my resolve crumbled, worn down by the one thing that had betrayed me before and would betray me again. Something that I always felt I should have been able to resist, but never could, not when I would be putting her in danger.

"No," I said, looking down despite myself. It felt like a surrender, which in a way it was. "We'll have to talk to Palatine, though." And Palatine would blame me for giving in. I sometimes wished there were two of us, or four. Three was an awkward number, always two against one.

Ravenna didn't look pleased, though. Rather, she seemed saddened. I hoped that was a good thing, but there was no way to tell.

I stood up, not wanting to be near her, and went over to the window again. Somewhere over to the right, across the domes, Midian and Sarhaddon were sitting in the Temple, probably planning their strategy for the purging of the Archipelago. They would win if they killed enough people, managed to rip the heart out of the heresy. And they had already made us concede something simply by arriving here. I was no better than all those who put up with the Domain and turned a blind eye to its doings simply out of fear. They had stopped us going to Qalathar by fear; whether it was my fear, Ravenna's or anybody else's didn't matter. The promise of a time when this would be forgotten—the promise I'd made to Ravenna on that beach, and on another beach before—suddenly seemed empty and meaningless.

Chapter VI

In need of a break from Ravenna, I decided to make my delayed visit to the oceanographers. Now that I knew where their station was and more or less how to get there, it didn't take me very long to work my way down through the side streets. It was still only mid-afternoon, and most people were still working, so the city felt rather empty. Possibly emptier than usual, because of the arrival of Midian and his tribunal of Inquisitors.

Thankfully I didn't see any Sacri on my way down, but when I reached the busier seafront, there was an air of gloom and menace that hadn't been there before. People didn't seem quite as open, and I saw more than a few suspicious glances, some directed at me, some not. I wondered how bad things would get in Ral Tumar. They would probably be better than farther in, because Clan Tumarian was the most Continental of the Archipelagan clans, and viewed as being the least dangerous.

Going into the undersea harbor to check that Demaratus's ship was, indeed, where and what he said it was, I managed to wheedle out a few details about Midian and his entourage. They had come in three mantas chartered from Tanethan Great Houses, and they had sealed off an area of the undersea harbor, leading to a considerable amount of chaos as Tumarian naval officers rushed around trying to free up berths.

Three mantas. That almost certainly meant that after Tumarian the tribunal would gradually split up, with only Midian and his immediate followers going on to Qalathar. At a guess I would have said there were two other groups, one heading for Mons Ferranis and the other for Selerian Alastre, to split up in their turn.

Leaving the undersea harbor, I went past rows of bars and ships' outfitters, walking along the shoreline to the small headland where the oceanographic station was located. To attract less attention I had been traveling as an oceanographer, wearing the Guild's light blue tunic, so there would be no reason to question my authenticity. Generally, sons of clan leaders—Continental ones, at least—didn't become oceanographers.

I was lucky, really; the dialect we spoke in north-west Oceanus was the same as in many of the islands, I was Archipelagan by birth and was traveling with two Archipelagans. Among the clansmen of Ral Tumar, I would only stand out as being strikingly Thetian. And Thetians, by and large, weren't heretics. Not that I felt any less nervous around the Sacri because of that.

Ral Tumar's oceanographic station was bigger than Lepidor's, and in a different style, but the feel of the building was the same. Although the entrance hall was smarter and bigger, there was still equipment stowed away around the edges, and that faint, indefinable smell of equipment which spent most of its time in the water.

There was nobody in the hall when I entered, but a couple of minutes later a bearded man in his thirties came down the stairs holding a piece of paper. He stopped when he saw me, and looked mildly surprised.

"Good afternoon? What can I do for you?"

"I'm passing through Ral Tumar, and I wondered if I could use your library. I have station bulletins from north-west Oceanus with me, if they're any use to you."

"By all means. Come, I'll see if I can find the Master's assistant. The Master himself is away at the moment, at a conference in Sianor. Which station?"

"Lepidor."

"That's good. Haven't had anything from Haeden Island for a while." That sounded slightly worrying to me as an oceanographer, given that both stations were on the same current cycle and needed to be in touch.

He led me down a corridor to the assistant's office, a larger one than the Master's cubbyhole in Lepidor. The Master. I didn't want to think about him. This man's door was open, and he looked up as we came in.

"Ah, Ocusso. Have you done the budget request yet? And who's this?" Some things didn't change, at least. The budget always came first.

"He's an oceanographer from Lepidor; he wants to use the library. If I can leave him to you, I'm just on my way to give the request to Amalthea."

The assistant nodded and my guide disappeared as quickly as he'd come.

"Welcome to Ral Tumar . . ."

"Cathan."

"I'm Rashal, first assistant to Master Victorinus, who's away." He might have been from anywhere in the Archipelago: his olive skin and long hair gave him an almost leonine look. He couldn't have been more than forty, I judged.

We made polite conversation for a while, about various oceanographic matters, and I handed over the station bulletin. It was essentially a summary of the major observations over a certain period of anything that would concern other stations. It was considered normal courtesy for a traveling oceanographer to carry copies for any stations he happened to go to. A station was supposed to send one to Guild Headquarters in Selerian Alastre every six months, but often they got lost or took a long time to arrive. Mine would probably reach Headquarters before the official one.

"What do you want to look at?" Rashal asked finally. "We've got quite a big library here, we should be able to help you."

I told him about the kraken's visit and explained that I was doing some work on deep-ocean conditions. Which was at least partially true. I'd always been more interested in currents and the behavior of the ocean as a whole than in, say, the inhabitants. Kraken were an exception. Everyone was fascinated by kraken.

Rashal's eyebrows shot up.

"That's a good field to be in at the moment. Have you heard about the *Missionary*?"

"*Missionary*?"

Rashal grinned, and pulled a couple of sheets of paper out of a drawer in his desk. "She's what all the deep-ocean people have been waiting for these last forty years, ever since the *Revelation* was lost. Essentially, she's a modernized *Revelation*. She's being converted from a war-manta in Mare Alastre, and they're planning to build a new one from the keel up, just for deep-ocean work."

That would have made my ears prick up, even if his first piece of news hadn't. Only once before had the Guild been able to afford to have a manta converted to work in the deep ocean, and even then the Empire and the Domain had contributed heavily. The *Revelation* had been the result, an exploration vessel that had provided answers to a lot of the mysteries surrounding the deep oceans and set the diving record—or so everyone thought. She'd been lost with all hands off the coast of Tehama nearly forty years ago, something nobody had ever explained.

"In cooperation with the Empire and the Domain again?"

Rashal nodded. "Read this," he said, giving me the paper. "That's everything I know at the moment."

It was a circular from the Guild's chief researcher in Selerian Alastre announcing that the Guild had secured the recently decommissioned war-manta *Despina* for conversion into a deep-ocean exploration vessel. The Emperor and the Domain had kindly agreed to sponsor the project in return for details of any discoveries made and the right to use the ship for a month each in the year. What did the Domain want to do with it? Then there were the technical details, the renaming of the ship, and a request for suggestions on what specialized equipment to mount. At the very end, three lines stated that the sponsors had also agreed to fund the construction of a specialized manta entirely for deep-ocean work, building to commence within a few months.

"Thank you," I said, handing it back. "We haven't heard anything about this yet."

"Good news, isn't it?" Rashal almost beamed.

"Especially since I wouldn't have thought anyone would have been interested now."

Rashal shook his head sadly. "The Emperor's too busy killing off his subordinates, and it's a miracle that the Domain's interested, what with all the troubles." He wasn't expressing any opinion at all, a prudent course in front of an almost complete stranger. Oceanographers were rarely fanatics, but it didn't do to be too sure. "Anyway, you won't want to be wasting time here. I'll take you down to the library and then leave you to get on, if that's all right with you?"

"Fine."

He took me down the corridor and through the door at the end into a large, low-floored room lined with books and files. There were a couple of weathered tables in the center and a few chairs, but nobody else was there.

"I'll tell anyone else I see that you're here, and just tell me when you're leaving. Deep-ocean works are over in the far corner."

There wasn't that much in the deep-ocean section, because there wasn't that much to write about. The *Revelation* had been the only ship ever to have gone below eight miles—as far as anyone was allowed to know—and there was an account of her explorations along with two thick volumes of detailed soundings and information collected. A slim book on kraken, by somebody who'd spent his life chasing them and seen four in the course of fifty years. Some theory about what might go on far below the surface, and finally a detailed survey of the caverns underneath the islands of Tumarian.

I was rather disappointed. There was more here than there was in Lepidor, but since Lepidor had the account of the *Revelation*'s voyages and nothing else, that was hardly surprising.

The book of theory was dry and technical, with occasional flashes of humor when the writer drifted off current mechanics on to another subject. The work's Thetian author seemed to have been a musician as well, and once digressed for ten whole pages about whale-song. No book I'd ever read by a Thetian had been without its digressions; they seemed to be a scatty people.

I read as much of that book as I could take, then skimmed through the cave soundings. All the islands had cave systems far below the surface. Some were little more than indentations in the rock, but some, like those beneath the island of Ilanmar in Thetia, stretched for hundreds of miles and included caverns big enough to hold a small fleet. That had happened once, I vaguely remembered. In the Thetian war with the Tuonetar, one side or another had hidden a squadron in those caves and ambushed their unwary enemies.

It was only of passing interest, though, because the *Aeon* was far too big to have been hidden in any known cave system. Although I had no idea what the ship herself looked like, she had apparently been built on a titanic scale, more like a mobile city than a ship. The picture I had gleaned from references and descriptions in the *History of the Tuonetar War*, written by a Thetian leader but since banned by the Domain, raised more questions than it answered.

I wasn't actually looking for the ship itself, but for what was on board. The *Aeon* had been the control center for a surveillance network of some kind, named the SkyEye system. Through some arcane means the SkyEyes had an outside view of the whole planet—and the storms. With them I might be able to understand the storms and, as the Master had accused me of doing, use them against the Domain.

But the *Aeon* had vanished during the Domain's violent rise to power, lost to view during the vicious infighting that followed the murder of an Emperor two hundred years ago. And since then—nothing. No trace of the ship, her crew, her commander, only a deafening silence.

I picked up the account of the *Revelation*'s voyages and stared at it. This was the only authorized account of the abyss far below the ocean's surface. An abyss that the *Aeon*, built hundreds of years before the war, had been more than capable of navigating. And if, as I believed, she had survived the brief civil war and then been hidden by her crew, the logical place to hide her was somewhere so deep that nobody would ever stumble on her by accident.

"Lost in thought?"

The soft voice cut through my reverie like a red-hot blade. I dropped the book and twisted around in the chair. My eyes widened when I recognized his face.

"Who are you?" I demanded.

"That's a question I could just as well ask you." With an uncanny grace, the visitor walked down the three steps from the doorway and across the floor to where I was sitting. He picked up the book and regarded it with a detached interest. "Voyages of the *Revelation*. That's a good field to be in at the moment, isn't it?"

I stood up, feeling at a disadvantage as long as I was sitting down. "Who are you?" I repeated. "You're not an oceanographer."

"I have no interest in oceanography at all, except where it directly concerns me." His naval tunic rustled slightly as he pulled a chair over and sat down facing me.

"Does Rashal know you're here?"

"If you mean the oceanographer, he will not trouble us. You're not going to get rid of me that easily."

"I can leave any time I want to—or have you put guards outside?" I said, thrown off balance by his emotionless detachment.

"Oh, I wouldn't do that if I were you. There are no guards, but you will stay here because I wish it. If you try to leave, I will have to keep you here, which will be rather humiliating for you." Unblinking violet eyes stared into mine as I glanced down to his waist, where a slightly curved sword hung from his belt. I might be unarmed, but . . . "And should you have . . . other talents, I can deal with those as well. So sit down, and we will have a civilized conversation." It wasn't a request.

"I prefer to know who I'm talking to," I said as I sat down sullenly. He could be bluffing, but there was something about him that made me reluctant to risk it. My heart was pounding in my chest.

"I believe I hold all of the advantages here, not least because you have something to hide and I do not."

"Then what's the loss in telling me your name?"

"Names can be power . . . Cathan. And in this room there's no one else you could possibly speak to, so you have no need to know my name."

"Then why did you say earlier that you could ask me who I was, if you already knew? Is this some Domain game?"

"Do you imagine the Domain are hunting for you as well? How self-centered you all are. Both of your friends seem to have the same failing—I wonder how you ever manage to get along." His angular features twitched with momentary amusement. "Do you quarrel frequently over which one of you is in the most danger?"

I said nothing, and after a moment he smiled.

"The Domain has no need of subtlety. If I were hunting you for them, I would know of your guilt and would have come to arrest you. If they weren't looking for you in particular, do you imagine they'd waste time like this? No, I can assure you I have nothing to do with them."

"Then why bother? Because you noticed us earlier, and don't feel satisfied unless you investigate everyone you see? I may have maligned Pa— my friend," I corrected myself, cursing inwardly at letting anything slip.

"Don't imagine I don't know Palatine's name. And I'll pose a question of my own: why were you so nervous about passing the Thetian embassy? That tends to indicate a guilty conscience of some kind. An embassy's hardly something to inspire fear."

"Don't you have anything better to do than check out possible guilty consciences? Heaven knows, there are enough people in this world who don't like Thetians. If you investigated every one that went past, you'd be here forever, and your Emperor none the wiser. Besides, you're not Thetian, are you?"

"How very observant of you. No, I'm not, but you obviously are."

"Are you just here to make clever comments and hint at things? I haven't got time for this." I stood up, determined at least to make a try. Better to take a risk than be cowed by smooth words.

As it turned out, he was capable of more than smooth words. With dazzling speed his sword was out and touching the skin of my throat before I'd taken more than a single step.

"This conversation is on my terms, Cathan," he said, his voice sounding bored rather than threatening. "You will stay here until I decide to let you go. Now sit down before I decide not to give you the choice."

I stared at him for a moment, almost livid with frustration and a sudden hatred. Who was this man, and why did he feel he could do this? But he was holding a sword to my throat, and there was nothing even magic could do about that. Shaking with rage, I stepped backward and sat down heavily.

"That's better." He resumed his seat and laid the sword across his lap. "Someone with more sense might have done that earlier. Someone with less pride might not have done it at all, but pride is something you have plenty of. Too much, really, for someone in your position. I, personally, have no objection to that, as long as it goes hand in hand with other qualities."

"Do you think we could get to the point? Or are you just massaging a large ego by lording it over me?"

"Why would I want to do that? And, in any case, you should already have guessed what, or rather who, I'm here about."

"You want me to tell you everything I know about Palatine so you don't have to ask her yourself." I might be at his mercy physically, but I wasn't going to let any other opportunities pass.

"I know a fair amount about Palatine Canteni, but I was under the impression that she was dead." There was a faint accent to his Archipelagan, hidden among the slightly formulaic speech. Like somebody who'd learned the language from scratch, but, I thought, not a native Thetian speaker. Thetians tended to miss out pronouns, not add them. Something to do with the peculiar way the High Thetian language worked.

"Do you think she is?" I challenged him. "Obviously not, otherwise you wouldn't have come here to ask me."

"I was also under the impression that she has only one living male relative. You and she look very alike, far too much for it to be coincidence." Which was entirely true. Despite her curvaceousness and much lighter hair color, everyone who saw us assumed we were relatives of some kind. Ravenna had thought at first that I was her brother. "That raises more than a few questions about *you*, which I believe you'd rather were not asked. I might, if you don't cooperate, be forced to draw some uncomfortable conclusions about who you might be."

Did that mean he knew something, I wondered, or was he just following a chain of thought? More likely the latter, because it didn't take a genius to make the connection. It was why Palatine was worried about going to Thetia. And, despite a mind clouded by anger, I was concentrating very hard. Almost certainly this man, whoever he was, was working for the Thetians. But which Thetians? The Emperor, the Navy, or one of the clans? There was no way to tell yet, but with any luck he'd say enough for me to place him.

"You're afraid of the Domain, for whatever reason. I'll find out soon enough. But Palatine Canteni used to move in high circles and provoked strong feelings in friends and enemies. A relative of hers with your features could be used by anybody. Thetia too has friends and enemies."

"You're losing your touch," I said with satisfaction. "Resorting to threats of violence, referring to mysterious factions. Usually a good indicator of someone without a leg to stand on."

"As I suspect is frequently the case where politics is concerned, you're quite wrong there," he said crushingly. "It seems my judgment about which of you was the most naive was quite correct. You can't go through life, especially not in the Archipelago, with a face like that and expect people to ignore you. Tell me, which continent are you from?"

"Oceanus," I said, a bitter taste in the back of my throat. I thought I'd been so clever, but he was running rings around me. There was no point in lying when I could get caught out so easily.

"And have you ever had the honor of seeing, or meeting, the Imperial Viceroy there?"

"I might have done."

"Not good enough."

"I've seen him," I grated, somehow unable to defy him.

"Viceroy Arcadius is a distant cousin of the Emperor, son of his grandfather's concubine. Thetian Emperors aren't supposed to have concubines, but never mind. At the moment, incidentally, he's heir to the throne. Anyway, he's pure Tar'Conantur: black hair, thin, finely carved face, sea-blue eyes. He's aged very well, don't you think?" He leaned forward and as he mentioned each feature he rested the point of his sword very lightly against the corresponding area of my face. I stayed completely still.

"I'm hardly unique," I said, as bitingly as I could, but I knew I didn't sound convincing. "Your royal dynasty's had a lot of children over the years, and apparently some things come through in every generation." Tar'Conantur was the clan name of the Thetian royals.

"Yes, but something is always lost. Tar'Conanturs always marry women of one particular race, which somehow reinforces the connection." That was something I'd read about but had never fully understood. Most royal dynasties interbred to reinforce their characteristics, eventually producing idiots. The Thetians seemed to have made it a rule that the Emperors nearly always married Exiles, a peculiar tribe who lived nomadic lives out in the ocean, rarely coming into contact with others. "I'm no expert at genealogy, but I do know Tar'Conanturs are hard to mistake."

"You think I'm a threat to your Emperor?"

"What I think is irrelevant," he said tersely. "I asked you a question about Palatine, and you chose not to answer it. I'm merely following the line of reasoning that anybody with half a brain would take. Whether you are a threat to the Emperor is immaterial, because, like beauty, the threat is in the eye of the beholder. So, I will say again, is this the real Palatine Canteni? Be careful; don't try to sidetrack me this time, unless you actually *want* me to teach you a lesson in humility."

"She is," I said, feeling trapped like an insect in pine sap, "as far as I know." I didn't want him to go any further, but part of me was shouting that I was giving up far too easily. Why was I so prepared to give in to mere threats? The sword was just to keep me in my place, nothing more. Or so I told myself.

"Has she told you what happened to her, how she escaped from Thetia?"

"She's not sure, but I know she was picked up by—" I began, then forced myself to stop. "I'm not betraying her. For all I know, you could be one of the people who tried to kill her. I'm not telling you any more."

"Fine," he said expressionlessly, standing up and sheathing his sword. "I'm sure that the new Inquisitor-General will be very interested to hear that a high-ranking Qalathari heretic girl is staying in a hostel on Bekal Square." He walked over to the short flight of stairs leading out of the room.

My heart felt like it had stopped for a second, and I stared at him in horror. Surely he wouldn't— But he was just about to open the door.

"No!" I shouted desperately, running across the room in an unthinking effort to stop him. I skidded to a halt without even touching him as the wicked-looking sword came out.

"I don't make idle threats, Cathan," he said, with a pitiless smile. "How much of your precious dignity are you prepared to sacrifice to save her?" He didn't move except to tap me on the shoulder with the point of his sword, and I stared at him uncomprehending for a minute.

"You bastard . . ." I said, finally realizing what he meant and choking on my words.

"I have been well trained," he said, waiting.

Filled with a blind, volcanic rage, I almost rushed at him, ignoring the sword and his superior strength. But he would only win, and then . . .

I kneeled very slowly on the floor below the wooden platform of the steps, my head level with the tip of his scabbard. Twice before I had been in a similar situation, but both times I'd been bound and vastly outnumbered by my captors. Although this time I didn't think I was in danger, it felt far worse to be forced into this kind of surrender to a single man who didn't even seem to be a mage.

"Well?"

"What do you want? For me to apologize, or plead?"

"Beg," he said. Just a single word. I was going to kill this man, whoever he was. It was the only thought that sustained me through the next sentence.

"I beg you . . . I beg you not to tell the Domain about Ravenna. Stay here and I'll tell you whatever you want to know."

For a long moment he stood there, while I stared up at him in consuming, impotent fury. Then, perhaps having watched me squirm enough, he let go of the door handle and went over to sit in his chair.

"Don't bother standing up, Cathan, just turn around and look at me."

When I reluctantly obeyed, he was sitting down as if on the Dolphin Throne rather than a nondescript wooden chair in a provincial library.

"Now you will tell me everything about Palatine that I ask for."

His interrogation of me was relatively short, considering all the fuss he'd made, but it seemed to go on forever. When he finished, my knees were aching from contact with the hard stone of the floor, but I was still angrier than I'd ever been before. He stood up again and went back up to the door. Not daring to stand, I resumed my previous position, craning my neck to look up at him.

"Palatine is of less consequence to me right now than you are, Cathan. It is you, even more so than her, in whom I am interested. I know who she is and what she is like, but you are another matter. I came to set my mind at rest, but that is far from what has happened."

His form seemed to blur for a second, as if I was looking at him from underwater. Then the foreign-looking agent from the Embassy was replaced by a slightly smaller but much more intimidating figure: slender, with black hair, a finely chiseled face, and sea-blue eyes that glittered with an unholy passion. He was slightly broader, taller and much more commanding than a mirror-image of me would have been.

For the first time, I was genuinely afraid.

"Do you perhaps recognize me now, Cathan? Do you know this face? It is the face of the one true crowned Emperor of Aquasilva. It is me to whom you have been talking, to whom you have kneeled, the first of the many people in the world of whom you should be afraid. You will see my agent again, as you will see me again.

"There will be times ahead when you will long to be back here, Cathan. If you live long enough, our paths will cross again. You are terrified of the Domain, but now you have something much more to fear. One day you will present yourself at my court and kneel to me in person, because if you do not and I have to bring you there, you will wish you had never been born.

"I give you a time of grace now. But remember I know that you exist and that I will be with you. Wherever you go, wherever you try to hide, somebody will find you. Perhaps me, perhaps an Inquisitor. Make sure you do not forget."

His form blurred back to the foreign agent, who went out of the door and closed it behind him without saying another word.

It wasn't possible.

But it had happened. That had been no illusion, however he had done it. It was small comfort to know that it hadn't been just anyone who'd been able to control me so effectively.

It had been the Emperor Orosius.

Chapter VII

I sat there in the library for a long time after Orosius had left, not moving except to stagger across to the chair I'd been sitting in before he'd arrived. After the sound of his retreating footsteps had died away there was no noise except a faint, tuneless whistle coming from somewhere else in the building. An apprentice at a boring task, completely unaware of who had just been in this room. Or rather, whose *presence* had been here.

It was supposed to be impossible, what the Emperor had just done. A lot of things were impossible, if the mages who'd taught me were to be believed. Including linking minds, and influencing the storms.

There were people out here, though—and probably in the rest of the world—who had never heard of those rules. And some for whom no rules, if the stories were true, meant anything. Foremost among them was the man I'd just been talking to—if "talking" was the right word.

The heretic council had, in their jealous, protective way, been right about one thing. It was far harder to remain anonymous than we'd had any idea of. At least for the three of us. Perhaps, with none of the Imperial complications, there wouldn't have been a problem. Certain things, though, were known to run in families, and magic was one of them.

I stared down at the books on the table, trying not to feel ill. I couldn't remember any time when as many things had gone wrong. Two days in Ral Tumar, and we'd already run into the Domain and the Emperor. Bad things were supposed to come in threes, and I didn't want to think who else we could meet here.

The copy of the *Revelation*'s voyages was lying where the Emperor's agent had put it down, open a little way on from where I'd been looking at it; the pages had fallen back into their natural position. I picked it up again and half-heartedly flicked back to where I'd been, trying to distract myself, but it didn't work. After a moment I found myself staring off into space again, thinking about what he'd said.

I couldn't think of any way he could fail to make the connection between the *Revelation* and the *Aeon*. He probably knew more about the *Aeon* than anyone else alive. Except for Tanais, who we might or might not be able to find in time. The Emperor wouldn't want anyone else to get hold of the *Aeon*. Too dangerous, for a man who claimed to command the seas. Thetian naval supremacy was a thing of the past, one of the Empire's many lost glories, but Orosius, I knew, had ambitions in that direction.

Then, belatedly, I realized something else. Something that confused and worried me in equal measure.

One day you will present yourself at my court and kneel to me in person.

Two things, in fact. One only implied, one glaringly obvious, something I'd been afraid of the whole time. He'd been able to dominate me effortlessly, and if the agent wasn't a mage, the Emperor certainly was. It would have been simple, easy, to take me back to the Embassy and have me shipped back to Selerian Alastre. Only a mind-mage could have used magic to do that, but there were other, more subtle ways.

One point stood out, though, however I interpreted it.

He had let me go. I was still here because he wanted me to be, because he didn't want to bring me back yet.

The second thing, more subtle, had taken me much longer to realize. For some reason my going there at all was important. Why? Why did he want me in Selerian Alastre? Whatever the reason, he'd decided that it could wait, but I already had a good idea what it was. Something that had been at the back of my mind since before I left Lepidor.

Our Thetian system of government is a source of confusion to the rest of the world, Hierarch Carausius had written more than two hundred years ago. *While other nations can be called republics or monarchies, we are neither, or somewhere in between. A Huasan delegate to the Assembly once likened it to a flailing octopus, a creature whose limbs are difficult to count and seemingly too numerous for what it needs to do. It is, I believe, the best analogy I've yet heard, although someone else once suggested I change it to a two-headed octopus. I don't know whether he was flattering or joking, but I will never have the chance to ask. The beauty of it, as far as I am concerned, is that anyone trying to seize power would be so confused by the time he'd dealt with each part that he'd just give up. I have wished I could do the same thing myself, once or twice.*

Even Palatine's impromptu briefing in Lepidor had left out a lot, only mentioning the Assembly and the Emperor. For all his power, Orosius's position was always precarious, something he obviously wanted to change. And the most striking peculiarity of the Thetian system, the biggest check on the Emperor's power, hadn't existed for more than two centuries. There had been no hierarch, no Imperial priesthood since the time of Carausius.

It was becoming more and more important for me to talk to Tanais, but I doubted that I'd find the Marshal if I went looking for him. I just hoped we were important enough for him to actively try and find us. Palatine seemed to have been his protégée, and he'd said, two months ago in Lepidor, that there was more he needed to tell us.

I had lost all patience for oceanography. There would be more opportunities to come back here and study what little there was, but it was early evening outside and my concentration was gone. I carefully replaced the books on the shelves, folded up the still-blank pieces of paper I'd brought in case there was anything worth recording, and left the library.

Rashal wasn't in his office, and the only oceanographer I could find—working late in the testing room—didn't know where he was. I asked her to pass my thanks on to Rashal, and let myself out of the Guild building into the limpid evening air of Ral Tumar. Even this late in the year, it was still pleasantly warm, and the soft aether globes that lit the streets were coming on. Ral Tumar had an entirely different feel from any city I'd been in before; I wasn't sure if it was Ral Tumar in particular, or because I was in the Archipelago now. Palatine and Ravenna, who'd both spent most of their lives here, would know what it was.

That was something else I had to decide. Was I going to tell them what had happened? I ought to, but then Palatine would probably declare Thetia wasn't safe either, and we'd end up doing nothing at all. Ranthas knew, there seemed to be enough places we had to avoid as it was, and there was no telling what Palatine would do once she knew the Emperor was involved. The invasion of Lepidor had changed her, and not for the better.

I wandered distractedly along the waterfront and up the main street, now empty of the elephants and heavy traffic that normally threatened to run me over. The clamor of the surface docks had died away, and most of the ships lay still in their berths, deserted except for a few watchmen regretting the fall of the dice that had left them there while their comrades ate ashore.

Lights still blazed in the undersea harbor, and I couldn't repress a shiver as I saw two hooded figures conferring in the doorway, black shapes against the yellowish glow. What were they doing down here so late? Making sure there were no unbelievers in the harbor, that no heretics were trying to make off with their ship? No one would try that at the best of times, let alone after this morning's display of power.

I quickened my pace as I turned up toward the center of town, eager to leave them behind. Not a wise thing to do, ever, but an instinctive reaction I found it impossible to suppress. There was no cry of "Heretic!" though, no sound of running feet. Why should there have been? Two priests talking about some trivial matter of administration, perhaps, as uninterested as any of their kind could ever be about passers-by.

All the way up the main street, tables and chairs had been set out and lanterns hung from foldaway wooden frames, creating the same kind of atmosphere in the street as in the squares, transforming a busy highway into a boulevard of coffee houses and tavernas. Many of them belonged to individual Houses and were places where members of the interconnected families who made up the House could sit out before the evening meal. But just as many were open to all. This was a major trading center, after all.

Open to all theoretically, but, as I gradually noticed, Continentals weren't to be found in all of them. In Ral Tumar, as everywhere, there were subtle differences in certain areas, places where outsiders weren't welcome. People accused Archipelagans of being excessively clannish and close-minded despite their courtesy, and the reputation didn't seem to be entirely unjustified. Not surprisingly, we hadn't had any problems, because there was nothing to link us with the Continents, but I'd seen obviously Continental people received somehow differently in shops and tavernas.

Even here in Ral Tumar, said to be the least Archipelagan of the island cities, there were undercurrents. What Qalathar was like, in that case, didn't bear thinking about.

I reached our lodgings eventually, having decided not to mention the incident at all. It wasn't fair to them, I knew, and it made me guilty of the same kind of mistrust I'd accused Ravenna of earlier. If it became important, I'd tell them, but, for whatever reason, it was me the Emperor was interested in.

No one answered when I knocked on Palatine and Ravenna's door, but I found a note slipped under the door of my room.

No sign of Palatine yet. Join me at that taverna you pointed out yesterday; I've left a note for her too.   R.

Earlier I might have wondered if it was taking discretion a little far not to put the taverna's name, but not now. I knew which one she was talking about, so I left my bag and the note on my bed and went to find her.

The Casa al-Malik was on a terrace overlooking the city's main park, its tables looking down on to an oasis of greenery. The disadvantage of its position, from the taverna's point of view, was that the road actually ran between the building and the tables, so anyone walking along the road had to avoid the waiters. A minor disadvantage to put up with, really, for such wonderful views, and the fact that it served dishes made from the meat of some of the wild birds found only at the very edge of the known Archipelago.

We'd passed it during a walk around the town the evening before, which was when I'd noticed the menu and the number of copper-skinned Southern Archipelagans eating there. Evidently it was good enough for them, as well as for the Mons Ferratan merchants who'd been eating there too. Mons Ferratans tended to be notorious gourmets, though not fond of fish because of some peculiarity in the water around Mons Ferranis that gave everything a certain tang. An acquired taste, I'd been told while at dinner with a Mons Ferratan more than a year ago.

It wasn't hard to spot Ravenna, waiting with a wine bottle and glasses ready at a table near the terrace's edge. She greeted me with a slight smile, her way of telling me that she'd forgotten any disagreements we'd had earlier.

"Any luck?" she asked, pouring me a small measure of the wine, Lionan red. Not meanness, she just knew that I had a weak head for drink.

"Not really," I said, silently begging pardon for the monstrous lie. Perhaps it was true, if she meant *good* luck, but that was a feeble excuse, and unworthy. "There's not much more here than at home. What I did find out is that they're building another *Revelation*." I told her what I knew about the *Missionary* project.

"Strange thing for them to do at a time like this, with the Prime needing all the funds he can get for his new schemes." She kept her voice down. Talking about Lachazzar at a time like this wasn't a good idea. Especially not in the Archipelago.

"Especially since they haven't shown the slightest interest in the deep ocean since the *Revelation* proved there isn't anything down there." There'd been a lot of muttering after the *Revelation*'s disappearance that the ship had broken some kind of divine law by going too deep. Only the Continentals had been uneasy, of course, because they saw the sea as a highway rather than the cradle of life.

"Maybe they're looking into a new kind of prototype warship, to achieve the element of surprise," Ravenna suggested, but didn't even seem to have convinced herself.

"They don't need surprise. But having a ship like the *Missionary* will give them an advantage over us. A way to reach . . ." I deliberately didn't say the name. Some things were too sensitive.

"I can't believe they've suddenly found an interest at the same time as us."

"It's possible it may have come to the Thetians' attention somehow," I said, choosing my words carefully. Almost certainly it had, but possibly not until today.

"Their timing can't be a coincidence, although I can't think why they'd suddenly be so interested in the deep ocean. It can't be anything to do with us, because a month simply isn't enough time to arrange something like that."

"Which raises more questions than it answers."

"Still, at least we know there's something going on," she said, sighing. "Another complication, another thing for us to be afraid of."

I didn't mention that Ravenna was the principal offender as far as that was concerned. Palatine might be wary about visiting Mare Alastre, but at least we were still going there. That was something I wasn't going to give way on. I wanted to see Thetia for myself, even if it wasn't safe to go to Selerian Alastre.

"They don't have all the advantages, though," I said, after a pause, as we both looked out across the garden and the domes of Ral Tumar. "If they're really searching for the same thing, I don't see how the agreement can last. If they find it, there's no way the Emperor will give it up, or the Domain let him control it."

"Either way we don't have it," Ravenna said, pointing out the biggest flaw in my argument. Perhaps the Thetians and the Domain would disagree, but not until they had the ship in their grasp.

None of us had, as yet, any idea about what to do with the *Aeon* if we were lucky enough to find it. Although all three of us had some slight experience with mantas, the titanic Imperial flagship would be another matter entirely. Carausius had stated quite clearly that the ship wasn't Thetian built; in fact, it was much older than the Empire that had used it. Who had originally built it was uncertain, and there were no mentions of it in pre-Imperial days. There was only the story of how it had been found, adrift in a dead, empty ocean beyond the Archipelago's known limits.

The fact remained that the three of us, without naval experience or even a ship of our own, would be hopelessly lost if we found the *Aeon*. To some extent, it didn't really matter if we couldn't move her, because it was the SkyEye system, not the ship itself, that I was interested in.

That wasn't something to discuss now, in a crowded Tumarian taverna on the day Midian had arrived with an Edict Universal from the Prime to root out heresy in the Archipelago.

We were joined, about quarter of an hour later, by a worried-looking Palatine, her expression grim.

"You've heard?" she said almost as soon as she'd sat down, taking the proffered—full—glass of wine with a gesture of relief.

"We were there."

"How—"

"An accident," Ravenna said quickly. "Just our bad luck to have been near the harbor when they arrived."

"The Harrowing, they call it." Palatine drank her wine far more quickly than etiquette dictated, but Ravenna poured her another without comment. "You can tell me exactly what they said when I can bear to hear it."

As we waited, I realized we had little to worry about in talking of the Domain. There was virtually no other topic of conversation in the taverna and the prevailing mood was more sober than it first appeared. It would probably attract more attention *not* to be talking about the Domain than otherwise.

"Where have you been?" I asked. Somewhere fairly stressful, to judge from her appearance.

"You remember Phocas, the boxer?"

That was the name we'd been trying to recall, the Citadel connection in Ral Tumar. Not a man who looked like a boxer, I thought, my memory jogged by the name. Tall and thin, fond of starting amusing rumors. Never malicious, just a joker. That was really all I knew of him.

"What about him?"

"I remembered the name finally and went to see him. He was friendly enough, considering he hardly knew me. Turns out his father's in charge of public works in the city this year, and got called in by the Viceroy to help deal with all the new arrivals. Would you believe Midian's worse than he was in Lepidor? He doesn't even pretend to be friendly now."

"How did you come to meet him?" Ravenna asked, a set expression on her face.

"I got Phocas to dress me up as a servant and take me with him when his father needed help."

She'd actually gone into the temple? When it was swarming with Inquisitors and Sacri?

"Before you say anything, it wasn't all that dangerous," Palatine said quickly. "The place was full of people—even the Emperor could be there and nobody would notice." She was right, of course, but not in the way she meant. "Most of them won't be here that long. Sarhaddon and Midian are staying long enough to officiate at a High Rite service in the Temple and receive the first batch of penitents, then they head on to Qalathar."

High Rite was a celebratory service only ever conducted by the most senior priests of the Domain. I'd been to one once, in Pharassa, when I'd been quite small. Mostly I remembered the incense, from braziers all around the ziggurat, its smell overpowering even in the raised pavilion reserved for Counts and their families. It would probably be even worse in the interior of the temple here. Not that it was a bad smell, just that there was always far too much of it.

"The other thing he's going to announce is a new *Index*, with a lot of books on it that weren't there before. They'll be organizing book-burnings all over the Archipelago soon."

"To tide them over until they can find some heretics," Ravenna said savagely.

That would be bad news for the oceanographers, because some of their books would inevitably suffer. I wondered what it would be this time, and hoped that the Guild Masters would be able to hide their copies in time. But works would be lost nonetheless, as they had been when Vararu was burned during the Crusade, just to satisfy the Domain's seemingly insatiable appetite for destruction.

"Has the Viceroy met Midian yet?" Ravenna asked. Her fingers were clenched around her wineglass, so tightly that I was worried she would crush it.

"He turned up while I was there. Very friendly to Midian, of course, said that the Emperor had ordered him to help them as much as he possibly could. He doesn't matter, actually—he's just a cipher. Admiral Charidemus is the real power in Ral Tumar, but I didn't see him at the temple. He's not the slightest bit concerned about religion, so he'll follow the Emperor's instructions as far as the Domain are concerned."

"Is that normal?"

"In the Navy it is. Most of the officers aren't very fond of Orosius, because they ran things under the old Emperor and now Orosius is reining them in. They're loyal to the throne and the Assembly at the moment. If Orosius were to win some campaigns, things would be different."

"Are we going to have any problem getting out?" I asked her.

"Difficult to say." Her expression became even grimmer, which I hadn't thought possible. "I know they have a list of people they're looking for, and they're keeping guards on the harbor already. They won't stop anyone else leaving—"

"It's not the way the priests do things," Ravenna interrupted. "They'll let people spread fear, start rumors, so that everything's tense when they finally arrive."

"Exactly. What I don't know is whether we're on the list or not. Perhaps not officially, but for Midian we're fair game, and he may have added Cathan at least. I'm afraid you're legitimate quarry here, Cathan. We have to assume that they'll try to capture us if they know we're here."

I glanced around worriedly, but everybody seemed to be engrossed in their own conversations. There was no way to tell, though.

Nobody got a chance to say anything more just then, because a waiter— obviously hired for his wild Southern looks more than anything else—came over to ask for our order. I didn't have much appetite after what Palatine had just said, but chose one of my favorite dishes from the Citadel all the same. I probably wouldn't find this kind of cooking again for a while.

We didn't talk much as we ate, and I was too anxious to enjoy the food, well prepared as it was. It was only after we'd paid and left that anyone dared to mention the Domain again. We were walking back along a tree-lined avenue, some of the light globes partially obscured by the branches and casting dappled shadows on the street.

"Do we have any idea how to get out of Ral Tumar, then?" Ravenna asked softly. The hills behind the city hid what sunset there was, and there were no stars or moon in a nearly black sky. The lights of the city sprawled around us like constellations in miniature, a sight that must have been even more impressive when seen from out at sea.

"We don't know that there'll be a problem," I protested, somewhat feebly. "We're not particularly conspicuous, and they don't have a description of us."

"You're too like the Emperor to be inconspicuous. We *might* be safe, I suppose, because nobody here knows us."

"Except perhaps that Thetian agent we saw this morning," Palatine said, and I felt a sharp twinge of anxiety. But she wasn't looking at me— she had no idea what had happened this afternoon—and I gave a small, silent sigh of relief. "But we can't be sure."

"How else can we get out?" I said. "If we go by sailing ship, it'll take months, and we risk getting caught in every port along the way. By the time we reach Ilthys or Qalathar there won't be any dissidents left to contact."

"He's right, Palatine," Ravenna said. "They don't know we're here. There's no way they could have heard since they left Taneth. Midian won't be looking for us here, but in Qalathar. That's the center, and that's where he'll expect us to go. He's not even sure we'll be in the Archipelago at all."

I wasn't so certain, and I could feel the gnawings of doubt. What if the Emperor—or his agent—had decided to tell the Domain, to have us brought in? I pushed the thought as far back in my mind as I could. It was too uncertain, when he could simply have made me follow him, and who knew what Midian would do if he got hold of me? If I'd understood him properly, the Emperor wanted my surrender, not my death. Or so I hoped.

"But he'll issue descriptions just in case," Palatine pointed out. "And none of us are nondescript. It might be an idea to get rid of that oceanographer's tunic."

"That'll attract its own attention," I objected. "I can't be a part-time oceanographer. I'm traveling as a journeyman oceanographer, not the Escount of Lepidor. Better if I stick to that."

"So what do we do, then? Go into the harbor in two days' time and hope we don't get arrested by the Sacri? There's no halfway if that happens."

"You're being paranoid again." I could understand her fears, but I was afraid we'd end up here in Ral Tumar forever. And, logically, if we moved fast enough, then anyone reporting to Midian would always be out of date.

"It's called being sensible, and it already saved my life once." In Thetia, I guessed, where assassination was rife. Most of it, as far as I could see, inspired in one way or another by the Emperor.

"Once on that ship we can be in Ilthys long before any Inquisitors get there, make contact with the dissidents while they can still show their faces . . ."

"And then what?" Ravenna interrupted, stopping us in our tracks and turning on me, her eyes flashing dangerously. "You're both acting as if this was some kind of real-life chess game. We can't stick to our old plans anymore, because things have changed. The Inquisitors are here to ruin the Archipelago, and in the process they're going to kill a lot of people. My people, although that may not matter to you. It'll take months to organize this arms trade, and what help will it be? There may not be enough heretics left by the time we get anything done."

"Sarhaddon is out for our blood, but he's also out for everybody else's. All the people we knew at the Citadel—Laeas, Persea, Phocas, and their families. All the people whose lives we tried to save a month ago, who don't have Continental cities to flee to when things go wrong.

"I don't want to be captured by the Domain any more than you do, but if the Inquisition succeeds, I might as well be. If we just make contact for Hamilcar, we'll have helped. If we can find the *Aeon*, we might be able to turn things around. It might need more than that, but it'll be a start. And a place of refuge."

We talked on, not knowing that the choice had already been taken out of our hands.

Chapter VIII

The next morning started peacefully enough, if without any obvious solution to our problems. At Ravenna's insistence, I went back to the oceanographic library to see if there was anything I could glean there. I didn't hold out much hope, but it was worth a try, especially now that other avenues were being closed off.

Surprisingly, Palatine hadn't objected to the change of plan after Ravenna's impassioned words last night. I felt sure she didn't agree but had held her tongue to avoid starting another argument that might attract attention. She was more of a realist than Ravenna, but I wasn't sure that was very helpful at the moment. Things weren't looking very promising.

She decided to try and get into the Temple again, which sounded a lunatic idea. She was as adamant as Ravenna had been, though, and wouldn't be dissuaded.

Ravenna insisted on coming with me to the Guild, even though I didn't want her to. Especially if the Emperor's agent chose to put in an appearance again. It might make the oceanographers suspicious, but that couldn't be helped, and Ravenna was insistent that she wasn't going to sit around all day.

Neither of us was very keen to go past the undersea harbor, so we plunged into the confused warren of the old part of the city, clustered around a small hillock that must have held the city's first palace and fortress. A fairly ordinary Tumarian House residence was perched on top of massive stone foundations rising from the street below. The foundations were built of large stone blocks, rather crudely fitted together; not Thetian construction at all. Had Tuonetar control extended this far south?

We found Rashal in his office at the oceanographers' station, going through the budget request with his bearded colleague Ocusso.

"Cathan," he said cheerfully. He didn't seem surprised to see me again. "Who's this?"

I introduced Ravenna. Thankfully, Rashal didn't see anything strange about her being there, or at least didn't show it if he did. He was preoccupied with wresting the last possible coron out of Guild Headquarters, and didn't talk for very long before telling us to go on to the library. He'd come in later, he said, to see if he could be of any help. Ocusso gave us a friendly if distracted nod. From his expression, he was rather less interested in the budget than Rashal. That kind of attitude would never get him a Mastership.

The library was empty again, but I knew we couldn't rely on not being disturbed for long. I explained to Ravenna as best I could what we were looking for, and gave her the account of the voyages of the *Revelation* and some paper. I found an intriguing papyrus on manta construction that had to be at least a hundred years old, if not more. What caught my attention was that it had been written at and issued by the Imperial shipyard at Salemor, in southern Thetia. The yard where the *Aeon* had been taken after Carausius had salvaged her from the Ocean.

"What exactly happened to the *Revelation*?" Ravenna asked, after what seemed like only a few minutes of silence.

"Didn't you ever hear the story?"

"My teachers always had more immediate things to drum into me, like the history of the Crusade."

"Your loss. The Domain and the Thetians converted her from a decommissioned war-manta, the same as they're doing now with the *Missionary*, to explore the deep oceans. No one knew if there were hidden civilizations down there, or remnants of the Tuonetar. The Emperor, Aetius V I think it was, poured huge sums into the project to make her the best-equipped research vessel ever built.

"She spent a couple of years making ever deeper and deeper dives. Her crew made maps of the abyss and took readings all over the Archipelago. Very valuable for the Guild, and the Thetians and the Domain were delighted to discover that nothing could survive at that depth, so they didn't have to worry about being attacked by submarine Tuonetar survivors. The Domain gradually lost interest, but it was the Emperor's pet project and he kept the funding up.

"About three years after the *Revelation* was launched, someone decided to test her diving limits, to see just how deep she could go. They sent her with a naval squadron to somewhere off Qalathar—Tehama, I think— prepared her as much as they could, and then ordered the dive. She reached nine miles before they lost track of her completely. There was no emergency message, no sign of the ship actually being destroyed—they just lost her."

"Couldn't they use magic to track her?"

"The Domain tried. They still had a mage on board, but they couldn't locate him or even tell if he was alive or dead, although you're supposed to be able to. There was something strange in their last transmission, I can't remember what."

Ravenna was flicking through the book, scanning pages near the end.

"Their last message was: *'Report fifteen. Nine miles and counting, angle of descent one over eight, all conditions stable. The temperature is unbelievable: I have allowed the crew to change out of uniform because of the heat. We have encountered a strong cross-current of several knots, direction south-south-east, which appears to be very localized. Revelation out.'* "

"*That* was what was unusual, the localized current," I said. It would only seem mysterious to an oceanographer, because he would know that at that depth currents were hundreds or thousands of miles wide, not *localized* as the *Revelation*'s captain had reported. An eddy current or cross-current such as they'd reported would be feasible near the surface, because the Tehama coast of Qalathar was a peculiar one, with a current system all its own. There were coastal features, promontories and caves, that could cause such a phenomenon. But not nine miles down, and nowhere near Tehama. "There are treacherous waters nearer the coast where it's shallower, but nobody ever explained that cross-current."

"Why were they so close to the island?" Ravenna asked. "I know the coast you're talking about. We call it Perdition's Shore because so many ships have been lost there."

"They weren't that close. For some reason, the powers that be chose Tehama, and they had to dive close enough to be able to reach one of the nearby islands if a storm blew up. I can't think why they chose the most dangerous coast on the island."

"It's a strange place, Tehama," she said, musingly. "You know, there's a lake up there, four or five miles above sea level, and on the west coast the water falls all the way down to the sea. I've only ever seen it from the top, but it must be so beautiful from below, on a clear day. It was our only way out in the old days, before Valdur blew up the road and sealed the plateau off. Or so he thought."

The rest of Qalathar was mostly forest, like every other Archipelagan island, only on a larger scale. The interior had been charted and explored long ago, and had been found to be nothing more than endless narrow valleys full of trees. The area known as Tehama, rising from Qalathar's western end, was different. Its mountains were shrouded in clouds, and the interior remained a mystery. Except to those like Ravenna, who'd lived there.

"You've never told me what Qalathar itself is like. That's the place you seem to call home, not Tehama."

"Haven't I?" She seemed genuinely surprised. "I thought you knew."

"I know about the forest and the sea, but that's not what I mean."

Ravenna laid the book down in front of her and stared off into space. "I don't know how to say it, really. It's always warm, never hot like Thetia's supposed to be, and not as wet either, except during the winter when everything's soaked all the time." She paused. "I'm making it sound terrible, aren't I? Green wherever you look, forests inland and along the coast, but never depressing. Tehama's very clear and cold, but Qalathar's not like that. It's beautiful, that's all," she finished lamely, and gave me one of her half-smiles. "You picked the wrong time to ask me."

"You never talk about it, that's all."

"I don't like to think about it. When we go there I'll take you to see the ruins of Poseidonis, and you'll see why. That's if they're still there, and the Inquisition hasn't built a ziggurat on top of them."

Neither I nor Palatine had any right to challenge her decisions where Qalathar was concerned, I'd begun to realize. It was her country that was being systematically destroyed by the Domain in the name of religious orthodoxy, and her people who were dying.

Ravenna returned to the voyages of the *Revelation*, and I started reading the comprehensible bit of the manta papyrus, about the history of the Salemor yard. Most of the rest was devoted to various aspects of manta construction, complete with examples, specifications and technical details. There might be gems to be found in there, but it would take time and would have to be set aside for now.

The Salemor yard was much older than any others I knew of, dating back to early Imperial days with a charter issued by Aetius II, grandson of the Founder. No wonder they'd sent the *Aeon* there to be fitted out. I more or less skimmed through the early years, the building of the great fortress above the shipyard, and how the shipyard gradually expanded to meet the demands of successive Emperors in their war against the Tuonetar.

Then I reached the year of Aetius IV's accession, and found that, without warning, the chronicle skipped the following twenty-one years. In one paragraph it was talking about an improved weapons system that wouldn't freeze up in icy northern waters. And in the next, Valdur I was attending the launching ceremony for the first of a new class of ships to replace war losses—Valdur, who'd betrayed and murdered Aetius IV's son Tiberius a year after the end of the War. The man who'd established Domain supremacy and been a friend of the first Prime.

"Damn!" I said, resisting the urge to throw the offending document across the room. It didn't *seem* to have been censored, just written as if the years of the Tuonetar War had never happened. So much for history.

"What now?"

I pushed the papyrus across the table to her, pointing to the break in the text.

"The Domain again," she said with an expression of disgust. "The penalty for writing about those years is burning at the stake. Are you surprised nobody dares to?"

The Domain couldn't afford any mention of the final years of the War. If the real history were general knowledge, the Domain might lose more than a little support, because the story of their rise to power was far from edifying. Especially the persecutions in Thetia, carried out by the Domain in the Emperor's name, hunting down every last mage and priest of Elements other than Fire.

Someone, somewhere, must still have books recounting the events of those years. We'd had three at the Citadel, but surely there must have been more, accounts written in the brief, halcyon period after the Tuonetar's final defeat. When Carausius and his family had hoped there might be a chance for a new beginning, a chance to rebuild homes and lives after the devastation of the War.

I returned to the shipbuilding scroll, now thoroughly fed up. The chances of finding anything in any library seemed remote if the censorship was this effective. Taneth's Great Library was only as old as the city itself, and thus more recent than the War; I was unlikely to find anything old enough there. And Selerian Alastre, with the largest library on Aquasilva, was also where the Emperor was.

I wasn't concentrating that closely as I read on, not really taking in very much. No one came into the library, but I heard running footsteps and a door being thrown open somewhere down the corridor.

I was just about to roll another section on when something caught my eye.

It was also in that year that work finally began on repairing the damage done several years previously when a reactor-core overload had melted the conduit network and destroyed the deep-water construction gantries. Superheated aether had twisted the gantries beyond recognition, and continued to cause trouble for traffic within the shipyard. Nicephorus Decaris, who ordered the work, was to go on to preside over Salemor's longest period of prosperity, and was determined to make his mark from

the outset. He personally devised the technique that removed the accumulated power
residue from the remnants and made them safe for reclamation teams, a technique
that is still used, in a modified form, to this day.

Even I knew enough about manta construction to recognize some
glaring inconsistencies in that. Aether charge wouldn't have remained in
the gantry for more than a split second, nor, in any circumstances, was it
capable of inflicting the damage described there. And there had been no
mention of such an accident. Perhaps—

A loud crash cut off my train of thought. A dark-haired apprentice
with a worried look on his face was standing beside me.

"Rashal says to put the books away and come to the hallway. There
are Inquisitors coming."

Our gazes met for a split second, and then we closed the books and
bundled them away as fast as possible. The apprentice didn't wait, but
dashed off down the corridor again. A moment later I heard his voice
calling upstairs, someone answering and more running footsteps.

"Have you taken any notes?" I asked Ravenna as we left the library.

"Yes, but not many."

"Give them to me. I'm the oceanographer, and if—"

"We can't stay here," she said. "Rashal knows who you are, we can't
risk it."

Most of the station staff were standing in the main hallway or on the
stairs, and every face bore a look of grave concern—or worse. Rashal was
standing on the bottom step, looking around to see who was there. A
moment after we arrived, the apprentice and Ocusso appeared on the
second flight of stairs.

"You'll all have heard by now," Rashal said. "Ocusso's son ran down
from the temple with the news. Apparently a group of zealots has
denounced us for practicing forbidden arts, and some Inquisitors and
Sacri are on their way."

Forbidden arts? What was *that* about? A moment later my silent
question was answered, at least in part.

"Since when has using dolphins been a forbidden art?" a sultry-
looking woman demanded angrily. "Try telling that to the fishermen."

"We've been doing more than that, Amalthea, but that's irrelevant."
Rashal swallowed nervously, and I realized he wasn't as confident as he
appeared. He'd probably never expected to have to deal with a crisis like
this, and was wondering what the absent Master would have done had he
been here. "It's not enough to warrant this."

"Surely they won't arrest us just on the word of a few zealots?" Ocusso said, but he didn't sound very sure of himself.

"We're oceanographers," someone else exclaimed. "They need us."

"I wish I could share your confidence. But if the Inquisitors think we've been using the dolphins in connection with magic, they won't be inclined to forgive us. Amalthea, you're the expert on the dolphins. The Inquisitors will be here any minute now. Can you gather up as many of your notes as you can and get to the sea-ray bays?"

"You're suggesting I run away?" Amalthea said, disbelievingly. "Flee the Domain? I'll be denounced as a heretic."

"You've got to get to Headquarters, give them the data, and tell them there's going to be a purge. Get everything you can and go down the back stairs. If nobody's there to help, just set off. Now!"

After a moment's hesitation, Amalthea pushed past him and ran up the stairs, her face white. Ocusso looked as if he was about to be sick.

"She won't make it," said a voice I knew too well. I spun around, feeling a sudden stab of panic, to see the Imperial agent from yesterday coming out of the library corridor. Orosius in person, or just his mouthpiece? I couldn't tell. "There are Sacri watching the harbor."

"Who are you?" Rashal demanded, his expression full of fear. There was stark terror on some of the others' faces, and I could well sympathize.

"I am not a priest. That is all you need to know for now. However, your guests are personal enemies of the Inquisitor-General, and will be executed if they are caught."

Rashal looked at me as if I'd just stabbed him in the back, and I felt like crawling away into a corner. "Is this true?" he asked, his voice barely more than a whisper.

I nodded miserably.

"There's still a chance, however. If Cathan and his girl will help me, I'll get them and Amalthea out of here, and you'll have a lot less to worry about."

"What do you get out of it?" the dark-haired apprentice demanded.

"Them."

"For Ranthas's sake, help him," Rashal said, a note of pleading in his voice. I fought down an urge to lash out at the agent, who yet again was treating me like a commodity. I turned to him, keeping my voice as neutral as I could.

"What do you want?"

Thankfully the strange, angular face showed no satisfaction. Ravenna was looking daggers at him—and at me, which only made me feel even more wretched. Why hadn't I told her last night? Why hadn't I trusted her?

"Somebody show us to the bottom of those back stairs, where we can meet Amalthea," he instructed. "Assistant Rashal, I suggest you hide well any banned books you may have in your library, and prepare your defense. You are unwise to have undertaken such a project without the sanction of the Guild, but I believe you will escape. Do not mention me—although you are welcome to mention your guests."

"Ocusso will show you the way," Rashal said. "Myroes, you heard his instructions. Use the secure place. The rest of you, we have some thinking to do."

"Me?" Ocusso asked fearfully.

"Yes, you. Be quick."

Suddenly galvanized into motion, Ocusso raced down the stairs and along a small side corridor, not waiting for us to follow.

"After you," the Imperial agent said, gesturing toward the corridor. Through the windows I could see a column of Inquisitors and the dull crimson of Sacri helmets farther along the shoreline, unmistakably headed toward us. This once, I wouldn't protest. Pushing Ravenna along, I ran after Ocusso.

He led us a short way down the corridor, then into a high-roofed warehouse-type room with a rough stone floor. It was piled high with oceanographic equipment of various kinds, from testing stations to a collection of nets that wouldn't have been out of place in a fishing boat. Over on the right-hand side, a set of rickety wooden stairs led to a door on the upper level, while opposite was what I guessed to be the way down to the sea-ray berths. Oceanographic sea-rays, like escape subs, were sometimes kept in bays rather than anchored to gantries; obviously Ral Tumar's station could afford the expense. After seeing the way Rashal dealt with the budget, I found that very plausible.

Ocusso paced nervously up and down the small area of uncluttered floor, looking up at the staircase with almost every heartbeat. Amalthea seemed to take forever, but at last the door opened and she clattered down the steps.

"Rashal says these people will help you," Ocusso muttered. "Something about Sacri watching the harbor." He turned and fled without waiting for a reply. The impending arrival of Inquisitors had turned the mild oceanographer into a frightened rabbit, and from the looks I'd seen in the hallway, he wasn't the only one so affected. For Thetis's sake, why pick on the Guild? What had this bunch of amicable, squabbling scientists done to deserve Midian's attention?

"Can I trust him?" Amalthea asked me, indicating the agent.

"He's a vicious, unpleasant Imperial spy," I said savagely, glad of a chance at revenge. "But otherwise we're trapped." That, unfortunately, was also true . . . or was it?

"If I didn't have to keep you alive, I'd willingly hand you over . . ." the agent said. Then he paused and shook his head slightly. "There's no time to argue."

"Are there really people watching the harbor?"

"There are," the agent replied. "If any of you want to live, you'd better do exactly as I say. Amalthea, please exchange tunics with Ravenna here."

Both of them began to protest, but at that moment we heard, quite clearly, the sound of a staff rapping on the main doors. The agent moved across to shut the door of the room we were in, and Ravenna and Amalthea turned their backs. I looked away as they exchanged tunics; Ravenna's would be a tight fit on Amalthea, but thankfully the oceanographer wasn't as buxom as some of her fellow Tumarians.

"Amalthea, take us out of the yard," the agent instructed. She didn't question us this time, but opened one of the large double doors at the end of the storage room, allowing gray daylight in. The cluttered yard was deserted, but I felt a tingling between my shoulder blades, expecting every second an Inquisitor's shout behind us.

It didn't come, and we reached the small wooden door on the other side of the yard unimpeded. Amalthea slid the bolt back and we slipped out into a back street between the oceanographers' station and some small warehouses. It felt uncomfortably similar to my experiences of a few weeks before, eluding Sacri patrols in the harbor quarter of Lepidor.

Two sailors were the only people in the street, and after staring at us for a moment, they moved on again as if we didn't exist. The agent led us a little way along, into a narrow side-alley and around a sharp corner to a tiny square between several warehouses, a forlorn fig tree standing desolately in the center.

"This is where we go our separate ways," the agent said, reaching into a cleverly concealed pocket of his tunic and pulling out a thin square of copper. He then fished out a medallion that hung around his neck, under his tunic, and pressed it hard into the copper. Once he'd hidden the medallion again, he handed the copper square to Amalthea.

"This is an Imperial safe-conduct. Use it to get to Selerian Alastre, and hand it over to your superiors. The warship *Meridian* is leaving from the forty-fifth gantry in a couple of hours' time: make your way by the backstreets to the harbor and get on it immediately." With some reluctance, he also gave Amalthea a small purse of coins. "This will help you get there. Don't go home, whatever you do. And if you're questioned, you were given this by Imperial Intelligence, for whom you are carrying messages to the Guild. Do you understand?"

Even Amalthea, who so far had been the calmest of the oceanographers, wilted a little now. But then she nodded and set off. Almost as an afterthought, she turned around and said, "Good luck." She wasn't talking to the Imperial agent.

The sound of her footsteps had barely died away when Ravenna turned around, eyes flashing, and gave me a violent slap that almost sent me reeling.

"That's for not telling me," she said, before inflicting the same injury on the Imperial agent, a blow that he could almost certainly have avoided if he'd wanted to. "I am nobody's girl, mercenary, and nobody's to bargain with."

Still smarting from the slap she'd given me—which I'd deserved, however much my anger threatened to obscure the realization—it was more than a little satisfying to watch her deal out the same punishment to the arrogant Imperial agent. This time it wasn't Orosius himself, I was fairly certain of that. There were subtle differences in the way he carried himself and spoke today, and I couldn't imagine Orosius taking that blow.

"You are, however, in a hostile city and at my mercy," he said after a moment's silence. "Not to mention wearing colors that are virtually an arrest warrant."

"In which case we'll go back and change," Ravenna said. "Coming, Cathan?"

What happened next was very hard to describe, but as I began to move, I felt a fog falling over my mind and my muscles refused to obey me. Ravenna seemed to be wading in treacle for a second. Then we both stopped.

"I've just frozen you to prevent you doing something extremely unwise," the agent stated calmly. "There are Sacri all over the city, conducting searches of various kinds, and they all have orders to arrest any escaping oceanographers. I doubt you'll get as far as your lodgings."

Once again I'd been completely outmatched, although this time it was worse, because now Ravenna was standing a few feet away, fury and astonishment written across her features. What was even more galling, and the reason I'd deserved the slap, was that the Emperor obviously wasn't willing to wait. I'd been wrong, and who knew what my wounded pride was going to cost us now?

"So how do we escape this trap you've so kindly set for us?" Ravenna demanded. "Or aren't we supposed to?"

For answer, the agent walked over to one of the small warehouses and knocked twice on its square wooden door. It swung open, and I suddenly felt an irresistible urge to walk inside. An urge that, thirty seconds later when he closed the door behind us, I was finally able to explain.

"I thought all mind-mages were supposed to become priests."

"There are no rules where the Emperor is concerned," he said, smiling grimly.

The warehouse was much like the one we'd just been in, apart from being slightly larger and gloomier. It was lit only by two small skylights. And a torch, held by a squat man wearing a scarlet tunic bearing silver insignia.

It wasn't the torchbearer who demanded attention, though. There were three other people standing amid piled boxes and crates. One was a maidservant, I guessed from her rough tunic, though she was not the timid, self-effacing kind.

The other two were most definitely not servants.

"Oh my," said Mauriz Scartaris, a commanding presence in the flickering torchlight. He had a singer's voice, one that would have been a credit to any opera house on Aquasilva. "You were right. The resemblance is unmistakable."

His words failed to mask a sharp intake of breath by his companion, who *was* unfamiliar, a Thetian woman dressed entirely in black and with gold flashes on her collar. Not that that meant anything to me—I was completely out of my depth here.

"If that resemblance is true," she said slowly, "it casts doubt on a lot of things we've all believed for a very long time. It also takes us into very deep waters, Mauriz."

"The deepest waters contain the highest mountains," he said, which might have been a quote. He smiled the smile of one who had just discovered a treasure and knew it, his saturnine, patrician face very pleased all of a sudden. "And torches glow brightest in the dark. I have seen very few dreams come true, Telesta, but here and now I am living one that we have been dreaming for generations."

"Dreams . . . or nightmares?" the woman he'd addressed as Telesta said softly.

"You never see the bright side of things, do you? Like a bird of ill omen, crying into the wind."

She didn't seem insulted. "Not all omens are good, Mauriz. Remember that."

Chapter IX

"Might I suggest that we hurry?" the agent said, breaking the silence that followed Telesta's last words. "If the Inquisitors discover that people have got away, they might begin searching this district."

Mauriz nodded, and spoke to the servant without turning around.

"Open the trapdoor again, Matifa."

Matifa ducked behind a pile of crates, and a moment later one of them slid aside with a slight creaking sound.

"Tekla, you bring up the rear," Mauriz said, then gestured to the torchbearer to lead the way. So *that* was the Imperial agent's name, which he'd so assiduously kept from me—or at least it was the name he was known by. It wasn't a Thetian name, or one I'd ever heard before. "Cathan, I hope I can trust you and your friend to follow without any further compulsion."

I nodded and felt the mind-mage's fog lift from my mind. It was like stepping out of a pool of honey, but I barely had time to regain my bearings before Tekla pushed me toward the opening.

A flight of stairs led downward into a passageway that was fitfully illuminated by the torch. My arm brushed against a damp stone wall, with what I hoped was only moss growing out of the cracks. A little way along, Mauriz stopped until we heard a creak from behind, and Matifa's voice rang out saying that the trapdoor was shut again.

The air in the tunnel was close and oppressive, and the ceiling was so low that the torch couldn't be held any higher than its bearer's face. Thankfully the passageway was quite wide, but, hemmed in by Telesta and Ravenna in the semi-darkness, I felt a twinge of claustrophobia. All my other fears rose to the surface again as I walked along an underground track, more or less taken prisoner by an Imperial agent I hated. Not to mention Mauriz and that black-garbed woman he'd compared to a bird of ill omen. We couldn't have gone far before the tunnel widened into a cave that seemed to be slightly drier and had a higher ceiling than the tunnel. Our little procession didn't stop, though, but kept on toward one of two openings on the far side.

"Where are we?" I asked.

"It's a warehouse," Tekla said. "Of a kind."

"Smugglers' lair, he means," whispered Ravenna. "So that Clan Scartaris don't have to pay customs duties."

We passed several wooden doors, locked and barred, set into clefts in the rock. Somehow I couldn't imagine Thetian clans involved in small-time smuggling, but I quickly realized how naive I was. This was smuggling on a huge, Thetian scale, with a large complex of warehouses cut out of caves. Perhaps the clans hadn't originally constructed the system, but they were certainly making use of it now.

We walked on through a seemingly unending network of caves. The only sounds were those of our footsteps on the worn stone floor, cut level so that generations of clan smugglers could transport their cargo more easily. Mauriz, powerfully built for a Thetian, set a quick pace and kept to it, never stopping.

We crossed a stout wooden bridge over a hidden stream and then walked alongside an underground lake through a long, twisting gallery from whose upper reaches hung a mass of stalactites. The sound of dripping water echoed eerily off the high ceiling, and in the distance I could hear the faint, unmistakable sound of surf.

Then, at the end of a shallow incline, we arrived at a small cavern. I looked around and saw that it was mostly flooded and that there was a large sea-ray moored to a short quay. The cavern's walls disappeared into blackness above our heads. I stared at the sea-ray's horns for a moment, squinting in the light from flickering torches set in metal brackets along the quay's edge. *Scartaris red and silver*, I thought.

"Have we had any more visitors?" Mauriz asked the wiry marine sitting on the sea-ray's dull blue roof. The man shook his head, and Mauriz turned to me. "Cathan and . . ." He looked at Ravenna, who stared sullenly back at him, eyes like chips of ice. "Ravenna," she said mutinously.

"Ravenna. For your own sakes, do exactly as I say. We have to be in Ral Tumar for another day or two, and since the Inquisitors have your descriptions we're going to disguise you. Matifa will deal with that." He motioned to Telesta and Tekla and walked out of the cavern with them, a little way up the passage, until their voices were nothing more than murmurings obscured by the not-too-distant surf. Mauriz had the unmistakable air of one used to giving orders, orders that he assumed would never be questioned.

"Both of you go and get yourselves wet," Matifa said curtly, before disappearing inside the sea-ray.

Ravenna and I looked at each other for a second. Then she shrugged, took the paper and purse from her pocket, and removed her shoes. "We'll find out soon enough."

We jumped into the water from the wooden quay, whose upper surface was a couple of cubits above the lake, and instantly regretted it. The water was shockingly cold and deep enough that I couldn't feel the bottom. We both climbed out as fast as we could and stood shivering on the planking.

"Cold?" Matifa inquired, smiling humorlessly. "We got you out of hot water, so it seems only fair you have to jump in there. Kneel down, I can't do this standing up."

She came over to us, carrying a small pair of scissors and two glass vials full of a dark brown liquid. Even so, Ravenna realized what Matifa was up to before I did and pulled her sodden hair back, away from her face, before kneeling down. For all her outward cooperation, I could tell she was still seething—even more so after Matifa had cut a couple of inches off her hair. And I knew who would be the target when she finally got a chance to air her grievances.

I reluctantly followed her example, then watched as Matifa uncorked a vial and poured a fair measure of its contents over Ravenna's hair. Even Ravenna seemed surprised at that, and I wondered if dyeing was normally done some other way.

My knees still hadn't recovered from their unfair treatment of the day before and I was silently urging Matifa to get a move on, while hoping my own hair wouldn't look too obviously dyed. From the way she worked the dye into Ravenna's hair with stained, worn hands, occasionally pausing to pour on some more, Matifa was probably an expert. Mauriz didn't look the type to employ amateurs.

By the time Matifa moved on to me, Ravenna's still-wet hair was noticeably lighter, glistening in places from the dye. Her borrowed tunic had streaks of brown running down it, but with any luck Mauriz and his companions would be giving us new clothes. I was still cold, and having warm dye poured on my head—from the second vial—came as something of a relief.

Thankfully, I didn't have anywhere near as much hair as Ravenna had so it wasn't that long before Matifa stoppered the bottles and stepped away. "You can get up now," she said, almost as an afterthought. "But there's more to come."

"More to come," I discovered, involved rubbing sickly sweet oil into our faces and forearms—to lighten the skin, was Matifa's answer to my question—another concoction on our hands and feet to toughen them and, finally, changing my eye color.

Thetian alchemists were the envy of the world, but where their Continental counterparts still pursued arcane studies and the transmutation of metals, they had long moved on to more practical applications of their art. Palatine had once said that her country's alchemists and beauticians could change a vulture into a bird of paradise. These talents had other, more sinister, uses in the game of Thetian politics. The Thetians produced everything from poisons to aphrodisiacs—including, I soon found, a potion capable of changing the color of one's eyes.

It was only then that I appreciated what Ravenna had been going through all her life, subtly changing her appearance, straightening her hair and, most of all, changing the appearance of her eyes. And she'd mostly had to do it on her own.

"Keep your eyes open, or it'll be a lot worse," Matifa warned as I lay down, with some trepidation, on the uneven rock. Ravenna and Matifa had brushed aside my protests, pointing out that the number of people in the world with brilliant sea-blue eyes was few enough for me to attract notice. I would have been fine as an Exile, she said, but they all had red hair, which was even more noticeable. Ravenna was holding my head very firmly, which didn't inspire confidence in what was about to happen.

"You're a man, so of course this is a terrible experience," Matifa said, leaning over me with a delicate glass dropper poised.

I didn't have time to reply before a stream of liquid poured into my left eye, then, a second later, into my right. For a moment I wondered what she meant, then my eyes began to sting excruciatingly. Instinctively I cried out and shut my eyes, only to force them open a moment later when I discovered that closing them didn't help at all. Everything faded to a fuzzy blur until Matifa blindfolded me with a strip of linen.

"Make sure he doesn't take it off for at least five minutes," she said, getting up. "You know the routine. We're almost finished now."

With a ruthlessness that was entirely in character, Ravenna kept me lying there for ten minutes before she took the blindfold off and let me sit up. I could see her through a slight haze, peering into my eyes.

"Were they supposed to be this dark?" she asked Matifa, who'd come back by now.

"That's fine," the other woman answered. "Just a normal blue now, nothing unusual in that. Now, there are clothes in Scartaris colors inside the sea-ray. Go in there and change completely, throw what you're wearing now into the bag. Be quick, please, we have an appointment to keep."

The blurriness had more or less disappeared when we got inside the sea-ray's passenger cabin, although my eyes still stung. It was an escape pod from a Scartaris manta, I guessed, used for errands and for saving the crew's lives if their ship was mortally damaged. The aether lighting was painfully bright after the gentler glow of the torches, but only for a few moments.

"Here's the sack," Ravenna said, standing by one of the padded chairs. She pulled out two complete sets of servants' clothes, tunics in the Scartaris colors. No trousers, which wasn't surprising; the only materials light enough, even in winter, for the Archipelagan climate were too expensive for mere servants.

There was no privacy in the cabin, so we changed as quickly as we could, retrieved everything from the pockets of our own clothes and stuffed the discarded garments into the bag. The tunics were a little on the baggy side, but would probably pass muster for whatever Mauriz had in mind. Then we looked at each other in our new garb for the first time. I saw a grin spread slowly across Ravenna's face and, a moment later, she burst out laughing. Then I saw my reflection in the window, and despite the incongruity of the situation, I joined in.

Matifa had transformed us from undeniably Central Archipelagan, dark-haired oceanographers—as it would have seemed—into brown-haired outlander servants. Not especially similar to each other, by any means: our faces were too different for that, and there were subtle differences in the things Matifa had done to each of us.

I found it rather humbling that the change had occurred in less than an hour. Not to mention disturbing, seeing a stranger in my own reflection. But, somehow, there *was* a funny side, and the urge to laugh was strong.

Even when Matifa interrupted sharply, summoning us outside again, some of the tension had been relieved. Not all of it, but some.

Mauriz and his companions were waiting opposite the door, while Matifa and the torchbearer watched from the sidelines. We stopped at the edge of the quay on a gesture from Telesta, and stood there self-consciously while the three of them looked us up and down.

"Well done, Matifa," Mauriz said after a while. "It should be more than enough to mislead any of those fools watching the harbor."

"There are still things I should do," Matifa said, not acknowledging the praise. "How long did you say this has to last?"

"It depends. I'll tell you when I know for certain." Like Tekla, he deliberately wasn't giving anything away.

"In that case, there's a bit more to be done. This will be fine for a few days, but not if you want to keep the deception up for much longer."

"You can do that when we're at sea. For now, they'll easily pass for servants. Cathan, Tekla's now going to find Palatine and bring her to the Embassy. It would make things much easier if you'd use some of that paper to write a message for her. Don't refer to Clan Scartaris."

I hadn't mentioned Palatine in the hope that they might forget about her, but I should have realized they were too well organized for that.

We wrote the message, using the surface of the sea-ray to support the paper, while everyone except Tekla and Mauriz boarded the craft. Mauriz dismissed our first attempt, pointing out that it was too ambiguous, but the second met with his approval and he gave the piece of paper to Tekla. I'd put the closest thing to a warning there that I could, but there was little hope that Palatine would get away—and even less point. Where would she go—back to Lepidor, to tell my father that I'd disappeared? On to the unfamiliar land of Qalathar? No, she was caught in the Thetians' net as surely as we were.

I was still wondering, as we boarded the sea-ray, whether I had just betrayed her. Someone had tried to assassinate her in Thetia, a plot only foiled by the intervention of an unknown mage. She'd always maintained that it had been the Emperor, acting to remove the republican party's sole remaining figurehead. Even I, with my scanty grasp of Thetian affairs, knew that Clan Canteni and Clan Scartaris didn't see eye to eye. Was I delivering her into Mauriz's hands? But, I reminded myself, if Mauriz wanted my cooperation, he wouldn't start that way. He seemed absolutely lacking in tact and sensibility, but he was probably dangerously clever. And if the oceanographers talked, Palatine would still be in danger.

Sitting in one of the comfortable padded chairs, I watched Tekla extinguish the torches and disappear up the tunnel, a small pool of light fading to leave the sea-ray in darkness.

"Take her out," Mauriz said to the pilot, before coming to sit down in the seat opposite mine, next to Telesta.

"So when do we find out what this is all about?" Ravenna asked Mauriz, as the sea-ray backed slowly away from the quay. The Thetian's casual arrogance was nettling her, I could tell. I could understand it, because I felt exactly the same way.

"You're not our prisoners," Mauriz said, with a shrug. "Under Thetian law you're something called *Terai*, a sort of indentured servant. That's only a technicality as far as you're concerned, but it'll come in handy if the Domain interferes."

Ravenna's temper was almost boiling over by now, and I could see from the tightness of her expression that he was pushing her too far.

Who exactly was Mauriz working for? He had nothing to do with the Domain but here he was, working alongside an Imperial agent of some importance. Tekla wasn't a mere underling, not if he was a mind-mage with some kind of link to the Emperor. But if we were being taken before the Emperor, as seemed likely, why bother with the disguise? Mauriz or Tekla could simply brandish an Imperial warrant at any Inquisitors and say I was already under arrest.

"If the Domain interferes with what?" Ravenna demanded. "You were talking about Cathan as if he was some sort of messiah, and you've gone to some trouble to help us escape. Is this another of your pointless little Thetian plots?"

The sea-ray dived and circled around, water gradually rising up the windows until we were submerged in the dark water. There had to be a submarine passage leading out to the sea, I realized; how else could they have got in?

"This is more than a plot," Mauriz said. "Much more. You could say it's about redemption."

Half an hour later and none the wiser, we stood in the well of the Scartaris Clan Ship *Lodestar*, waiting for Mauriz to finish talking to the captain. From the way he gave orders, I'd guessed he was somewhere very close to the top in the Scartaris hierarchy. The captain had been waiting outside the sea-ray bay, and Mauriz had led him off to issue orders, leaving us standing in the manta's central well under Matifa's watchful eye. It was strange to see the way everyone else faded into the background when Mauriz was around, as if he attracted all the light himself.

Ravenna and I were servants of Clan Scartaris now, two Worldsend Islanders who'd managed to escape the desolation of Worldsend by taking service with the clan. None of that was unusual, and people didn't look at servants anyway. Since anybody who *did* look could tell that we weren't used to it, we were supposed to be new to the clan, having just arrived on the *Lodestar* and been appropriated by Mauriz.

The door to the chart room opened, and Mauriz swept out and past us, a curt gesture of his hand indicating that we were to follow. None of the sailors paid us more than the slightest attention as we followed him out of the main hatch and down the long, glass-roofed gantry into Ral Tumar's undersea harbor, a column of lights in the blue-gray murk.

The harbor was as busy as ever, bustling with people and sailors shifting cargo. Below us, on the cargo level, I heard Thetian voices raised in argument, and someone swearing, but as my attention wandered, a sharp jab in the ribs from Matifa concentrated my attention. I glared at her, and half-ran into the flamewood lift, where Mauriz was waiting, an impatient expression on his face. He said nothing, though, as the gaunt naval rating manning the lift activated the aether controls and it began to move upward. I felt my heart pounding as we rose: somewhere up there were Inquisitors who had my description and orders to arrest me for heresy. *Please, Thetis, let the disguise work,* I prayed silently, watching levels move past, people getting on and off the lift.

Time always moved too slowly or too fast, and it felt like only a moment later that we reached the surface, emerging into the bowl-shaped hall at the top of the undersea harbor. Ahead of us were the doors and steps where, only yesterday morning, Sarhaddon and Midian had stood to read their message of death. And on either side, faces hidden behind crimson veils, Sacri stood guard.

"Don't look at them like that," Ravenna whispered.

Mauriz moved swiftly out of the lift then stopped, a little way on, still looking impatient. "You two will have to learn to follow me," he said. "Matifa, make sure they keep up." Then he looked around, and I saw Telesta coming down to join him. She'd disembarked earlier, Mauriz had mentioned, to check something with the port authority.

"That'll be fine," she said, falling into step beside Mauriz. "The Jontians aren't leaving until the day after tomorrow."

Who on earth were the Jontians? Another clan?

"As long as they keep to that schedule, there won't be any problems."

As we went up the ramp toward the door I was sure the Sacri were looking at me and that any moment one of them would shout "*Halt!*" and step forward to block my way. But they didn't move, or even give any indication that they knew we were there. And then we were outside the harbor and walking down the steps.

I gave what must have been an audible sigh of relief, because Ravenna looked over at me and nodded in sympathy. We still had a long way to go, a night and a day in Ral Tumar before—before what? Wherever Mauriz took us that was safe, it would be where he wanted to go. Not our choice, and no help as far as the *Aeon* was concerned.

As it happened, we came out of the harbor just in time to see the oceanographers marched past under Sacri guard. A sight that fouled the humid afternoon air with the ghosts of pyres, smoke, and burning books. Sacks and sacks of books, being carried by more Sacri walking behind the captives. The accumulated knowledge of centuries of research, destined to be flung into the flames and reduced to ash.

Reluctantly I looked to the left, along the quay. To where a banner with the Flame of Ranthas had been hoisted above the oceanographic station, hanging balefully over the blue and white building. There were no oceanographers in Ral Tumar now. No one to warn sailors of undersea storms, to detect minute changes that signaled massive tempests elsewhere in the world-ocean. All to satisfy a Halettite's lust for a cleansing, his precious scourging of the god.

There was more to Midian than just his fanaticism, actually, as the frightened oceanographers being marched up for questioning in the temple would soon discover. The man who hunted us was a politician as well as a fanatic, as the Primes from Temezzar to Lachazzar had been. A Halettite for whom all the other peoples of the world were inferior by not being born in the Equatorian heartland.

And a man with a burning desire to dominate who had been defeated and humiliated by the people he despised. Specifically, by an oceanographer, an Archipelagan and a Thetian, two of whom were women. Hamilcar, whose intervention had been crucial, was less important. Because of what the three of us had done to save our own lives, Midian would devastate the Archipelago with fire and chains, in the name of Ranthas.

It had gone far beyond Lepidor now, I thought sadly as we followed Mauriz and Telesta, now accompanied by two Scartaris marines in scarlet scale armor, up the main street. Midian's anger must have festered since the liberation of Lepidor, becoming a canker eating at his soul. Something we had never thought of, but should have, was that if he survived Lachazzar's anger—as he had done—his desire for revenge would make him the perfect instrument to lead an inquisition. One of us should have known better, but we'd all been busy celebrating—and recovering. I doubted that even our capture and execution would assuage his wrath. It had become a matter of pride for him.

I thought Mauriz had chosen not to travel by elephant in order to attract as little attention as possible, but I was wrong. Little more than halfway up the main street we turned off into a narrow side-road that would have been too small and crowded for any elephant. Past the day-to-day entrances of the street-front Houses, then along another alley, emerging into a small square with orange trees growing outside the Scartaris consulate.

There were nine Thetian consulates in Ral Tumar, Palatine had said, as there were in every other major city; the reason was lost somewhere in the bewildering intricacies of Thetian politics. What mattered was that this was Thetian—or, more specifically, Scartaris—territory, where we were under the protection, or guard, of Thetia's second most powerful clan. A clan that once had wielded more power than entire continents, in the old days of the Empire, but had now sunk into decline, along with the Empire itself. Somehow I didn't think Mauriz's highest ambitions centered on prominence in the social circuit of Selerian Alastre as did those of so many of his compatriots.

The door was opened even before we reached it, and Mauriz was ushered into a marble-floored entrance hall that managed to be light and airy despite its ochre-red walls. I could hear the sound of running water coming from a courtyard farther inside, a rather soothing sound. There was a faint trace of perfume in the air.

"Anything new?" Mauriz demanded of the man who'd opened the door; the consulate steward, I thought, a fairly young man who looked as if he had more rungs to climb and was determined to make the climb as easy as possible.

"The Consul is meeting with an Eirillian representative, High Commissioner. Lunch has been prepared."

"Telesta and I will eat now—we have business to conclude. These two—" he pointed a commanding hand at me and Ravenna "—are assets to the clan who will be treated as new servants from Worldsend. Matifa is in charge of them, and I'll be taking them with me when I go. Make sure they have somewhere to sleep tonight."

The steward's gaze flickered over us briefly and then returned to Mauriz before he led the High Commissioner and Telesta off into the courtyard, a reminder of Ravenna's and my importance in the general scheme of things. He'd called a name, though, and a moment later an older woman appeared from a door to the left. She wasn't a Thetian, unlike the steward.

"Besca," Matifa said, in a tone that indicated she considered the other woman an inferior. She more or less repeated what Mauriz had said about us, adding that we'd need some more kit. Our bags would be collected from the hostelry, she'd assured us earlier, but we wouldn't need them now. Presumably they'd be searched thoroughly, but I didn't think there was anything dangerous in them. I still had the credit note from House Canadrath hidden in a pocket, and they already knew I was a heretic.

"We're short of space at the moment, with all these marines," Besca said. "I'll have to put them in a storeroom, if I can find room in one." Why were there so many people here? Was it a routine movement of troops, or part of Mauriz's plans?

"You aren't sleeping together, are you?" Matifa asked bluntly.

"No." We said it at the same time. Ravenna's voice was angry, I was just irritated. It was the assumption that annoyed her, I thought, but I'd never been sure why.

"Could have told you that for nothing," Besca said to Matifa. "We'll find somewhere. Does His Lordship want anything with them today?"

"He may this evening, but not before. They're not to go out. You can put them to work, if you want." Matifa smiled sourly. "Teach them how to act like servants."

It was almost like being a child again, hearing the women talking about me as if I wasn't there, but I found it hard to place all the blame on Mauriz, abrasive as he was. If I blamed anyone, apart from myself, it would be Midian and Lachazzar, perhaps, or those nameless zealots who'd denounced the oceanographers. Just what *had* they been working on with those dolphins? I longed to know, even though it was a part of oceanography I didn't know much about.

Despite the prevailing hatred for the Domain, I thought as Matifa stalked off and Besca led us back through the door she'd emerged from, there would be other such zealots across the Archipelago. Fanatical bigots with a thirst for revenge on ungodly fellow citizens—puritans of the worst kind.

It wasn't until several hours later, sluicing down the floor of the colonnade and silently wishing a thousand tortures on Besca, that I saw Palatine arrive. The steward obviously had an office looking out over the square, because, once again, he was there opening the door before anyone knocked. A moment later, Tekla, two bags slung over his shoulders, ushered Palatine into the hallway.

"Commissioner Mauriz! Your guest," the steward called. Palatine saw me, ignored me completely, and then, a moment later, looked back again incredulously. She didn't have time to say anything, because Mauriz, who must have been nearby, came out into the hall and stood almost blocking my view of Palatine.

"Palatine! You're alive! It's a pleasure to see you again." He invited Palatine out into the colonnade with a flamboyant sweep of his hand. Away from all sets of ears except one, and I was sure that was intentional.

"You were dancing on my grave, Mauriz. I can't imagine anything that would have ruined your day more."

"You were just an irritating Canteni back then, Palatine. Things have moved on, the situation is different now. We've got a chance at last, a chance to do what your father was killed for."

"And what is that?" I was sure that Palatine already knew what Mauriz was talking about. And a second later, crouching on the wet flagstones by the sluice gate, my guess was confirmed when I heard him say, "Found a republic, of course."

Chapter X

Four exhausting hours later, when Mauriz finally summoned Ravenna and me, I wasn't quite as ready to forgive him as I might have been earlier.

They were short-handed, Besca had informed us gleefully when she'd first taken us off, on account of all the marines staying there. Not just marines, but *elite* marines, Scartaris Presidential Guards and a number of staff officers accustomed to the easy life in Selerian Alastre. Thankfully, they were leaving tomorrow on the *Lodestar*, she said, but for now we'd be very useful in freeing up more experienced servants to deal with the marines.

Besca had given Ravenna and me enough lunch to keep us going and had then set us to the pressing task of sluicing the courtyard. It was their turn to use the water flue running beneath the block only once every few days and today was the day, when they had fewest people to spare. We had to work the flue gates so that the water was dammed and came up to irrigate the courtyard, more or less flooding it, and then open all the outlets to drain it again. This was good experience, according to Besca, because every House throughout the Archipelago did this, and it couldn't hurt to know how.

Novices that we were, it took us far longer than it was supposed to and got us very wet in the process. Which wasn't a pleasant experience in the damp, mild air of Ral Tumar, where nothing dried. After that, because Ravenna and I were both quite short and fairly agile, we were landed with the equally unpleasant job of scouring the guttering of wind-blown leaves. By the time we'd finished we had blisters on our hands, aching muscles, more than a few bruises and, in my case at least, an itch to throw Matifa off a cliff, with Besca to keep her company on the way down if possible.

Besca gave us new tunics to wear that evening, when we were to wait on Mauriz, Telesta, Palatine and the Consul. We'd both done it before at one time or another, though never in quite the same circumstances.

Palatine made a point of treating us as friends and talking to us whenever possible, because it annoyed Mauriz, I suspected. The Consul, stooped, gray-haired and looking ill, ate very little and watched the byplay with an other-worldly detachment. He was, Ravenna said in a spare moment, almost certainly dying. Tekla wasn't present.

Only after they'd finished and the Consul had retired to bed did Mauriz finally deign to notice us as anything more than servants, telling us to come to the reception room after we'd cleared up.

"Let him wait, the arrogant bastard," Ravenna said after they'd gone, stacking the dishes from the dessert course. Three-course meals weren't customary, apparently, but Mauriz and Telesta were treated as honored guests. Thetians, among their many other traits, were fond of good food. A sin, some of the ascetics called it, to devote so much time to enjoyment and so little to Ranthas. They were ignored in Thetia, as they always had been. For once, I almost agreed, though not for the same reasons. That was all Thetia seemed to be about under Orosius: a façade of culture with no substance.

"By all means. Slow down, then."

We cleared the table as slowly as we could, and I ambled across to the laundry with the linen, unconcerned whether or not Besca noticed me. But although some of the other servants passed through the room, giving me wary or hostile glances, knowing as well as I did that I wasn't really one of them, she didn't appear.

Ravenna was sweeping the mosaic floor when I got back, and taking her time about it. It was a childish thing to do, but both of us were feeling angry and humiliated. I was grateful to Mauriz for arranging our escape from the oceanographic station and probably saving our lives. Since then, though, he'd been playing with me for some purpose of his own, something I wasn't going to accept. Either that or he simply didn't care what happened to me when I wasn't needed. If he wanted to use me to help him found a Thetian republic, he wasn't going the right way about it.

Although we dragged our tasks out for as long as we could, eventually there was nothing more to be done except walk across the courtyard to the reception room where Mauriz, Telesta and Palatine were sitting on low cushion-covered divans, as was the Thetian custom. All three had glasses of blue wine, and this time they noticed us, the conversation breaking off as we approached.

"Do have some wine," Palatine said. "Mauriz, why don't you offer them some of your splendid vintage? We wouldn't want it to go to waste."

"As my friend suggested, Cathan," Mauriz said smoothly, immediately. "Don't stand on ceremony." There were no servants—real servants—to be seen, and a bottle with three more glasses stood on a low side table. I crossed over and poured wine into two of the glasses, cut-crystal goblets that were intended for special guests. "And take a divan."

I offered one of the glasses to Ravenna and looked at the divans. There were always three in such a room, I knew, each with room for three people to recline or sit cross-legged. But how to conduct myself on one was something I didn't know.

I waited to see how Ravenna dealt with the problem, and watched her arrange herself on the one empty divan. She invited me to join her, tilting her head.

The divan was harder than I'd expected, covered though it was with cushions and a richly woven throw rug, and it was difficult to recline on graciously unless you knew how. It was all too apparent that I didn't, even without a glass of wine in my hand, and I cursed myself for appearing like a country bumpkin in front of the three Thetians. They didn't expect me to know, of course, but that only made matters worse.

"Thank you for joining us," Mauriz said, after a moment. They were empty words; his voice didn't hold a hint of gratitude. The room was lit by tinted aether torches positioned around the edges and by a lamp hanging high above the cedar table in the center of the three divans. There was a complex scent in the air—incense mixed with something unfamiliar—that was slightly bitter but not unpleasant.

"I wouldn't want to miss this after the wonderful reception you've given us so far," said Ravenna, her voice brittle.

Mauriz fixed his gaze on her and said, "Speak not to me of the gratitude of kings."

"Never eat at a Tanethan feast, for they expect you to pay," Ravenna replied, but I'd heard her slight intake of breath at Mauriz's words. He *couldn't* know who she was. Not unless Palatine had told him.

"Only those who have been slaves should ever keep them," Mauriz replied. "Third verse of the Code. Written at a time when slavery was still common in Thetia, before the Lawgiver, Valentine II, declared it an unjust and evil practice. Henceforth those who would have been enslaved were to become *Terai*, sworn to serve for three years only."

"A practice forgotten outside Thetia," she replied.

"You appear to have missed my point. Aetius IV put it much more clearly."

"No one commands in my army who's never been at the bottom of the heap," Palatine said, and shrugged apologetically. "It loses something in the translation." Her Archipelagan seemed rough and clumsy beside Mauriz's perfect, unaccented phrases.

"So why are we speaking of armies and commanding? What does that have to do with a republic?" Ravenna shifted position slightly, as unaccustomed as I was to this position. This close to her, I could smell the residue of the dye in her hair. "I'm sure all of you have gone through the same experience, in any case."

"It's a mark of honor in Thetia." He didn't look like he'd ever served anyone.

"And how far does it extend? It's a powerful principle, one that can be taken to extremes. I'm sure the philosophers argue it in the market places. Can you only condemn if you've been in the dock? Can you only kill if you've been killed?"

"That's not a remark worthy of you," Mauriz said, at the same time as Telesta spoke for the first time.

"We are getting nowhere with this, Mauriz," she said. It was the first time I'd had a chance to see her properly, overshadowed as she was by Mauriz. Why was she dressed all in black, with just that gold on the high collar of her tunic? And her hair was tied back tightly, unadorned—it was a severe style, more like that of a priestess than anything else. Black and gold were mind-mage colors, but surely she wasn't one? The Domain had a monopoly on mind-magic, as on all other magic except for healing. Or they were supposed to have. Tekla must be a maverick, protected by his service to the Emperor.

"On the contrary, this is something of great importance. My guests implicitly accuse me of humiliating them, a charge that isn't often thrown around. I will reply to it first." It was, I thought, only a new experience because no Scartaran clansman would cross this man. Anyone else would have ample grounds for complaint.

"So how do you plead?" Palatine said immediately.

"Guilty. But since in this court I preside—which makes it rather like an Imperial one, don't you think?—I grant myself an explanation." His gaze shifted from Ravenna to me before he said, offhandedly, "A test."

"So a deliberate act, not an oversight?"

"Would I miss that? A test, though there wasn't much time." He made it sound as if that was someone's fault, that he'd wanted a longer period of trial. "A test of observation, of reaction. And of whether I've saved a tyrant or a liberator."

"You speak as if your plan were a certainty, Mauriz," Telesta interrupted. "A liberator . . . perhaps. Equally, a tyrant . . . possibly. But you say nothing of the man. Things are seldom so simple."

"You can't distinguish so easily," Palatine said. "There are subtleties, reflexes of years of conditioning. If he'd grown up as, say, a tailor's son, the test would have meant nothing at all."

"He *didn't* grow up as a tailor's son, though. And neither did Ravenna. Of course they resent it. If either of them didn't, they'd be marked for a monastery, spending their lives with gutless monks. The fact remains that neither of them made trouble."

"You're making too much of this," Palatine said, shaking her head. "Maybe it means something, but not as much as you say."

"Would you have done the same thing? Not a fair question, because you would. If you thought it would gain you information. But of those you meet outside Thetia—how many, do you think?"

"Few. But you want to compare him with the Emperor, don't you? What's to say that if Orosius had been brought up like Cathan, he wouldn't have put up with the experience in the same way?"

"Someone who's born cruel and arrogant will grow up that way wherever they live. Like petty officials, kings of their own little worlds, and as stiff-necked as any Emperor in a palace." *Mauriz* was saying this?

Palatine shook her head as Telesta shifted impatiently. She was sitting on the first divan, next to Mauriz. I shivered slightly as a cool breeze gusted through the room from one of the unshuttered windows. I wondered about them, but then realized there would be a guard outside. Mauriz's marines, or perhaps someone more trustworthy. Like Tekla.

"You disagree, then? Orosius isn't naturally arrogant?" Telesta said, with some reluctance. If she wanted to get on to the real topic of conversation, why prolong the discussion?

"The Emperor is different," Palatine said. "Uncontrollable—no one has given him an order for ten years or more. With his power, none dare. There is no way under the stars that Orosius would ever have played a servant's part."

"You've misunderstood me again." Mauriz sounded as if he was talking to a child. "We all know that Orosius would never have accepted a menial role as Cathan did, even for a moment. But it wasn't Orosius we were testing. I don't know any more about Cathan than I've been told, so I have to judge for myself. It will be . . . crucial."

I took a deep breath, aware that there were nuances in the conversation that I must have missed. "It seems," I said, very deliberately, speaking for the first time, "that you see me as a tool, Mauriz. Someone you are employing to do a job. I'll assume that it requires my consent."

"You want me to treat you as an equal," he said, pre-empting my next words.

"Yes. You saved my life today so that I could help you. That puts me in your debt. And I will, if it is necessary, stay in this disguise until we have agreed on a repayment. Does it take so much effort to treat me as more than an instrument? You wouldn't treat a real servant so abruptly, would you? After all, today's servant is tomorrow's President. Isn't that the case?"

I saw a momentary tightening of Mauriz's expression and knew the barb had struck home. Most servants in Thetian households were either young and starting a career or old and earning money in semi-retirement. There had been a time when things weren't so fluid, two hundred years ago, when a Scartaris servant had schemed his way to the clan presidency by masquerading as a clan-born.

"Tonight, you are disguised as a servant," Mauriz said, with a shrug. "You aren't safe in this city, and there are plenty of spies about. Would you rather I had proclaimed you an honored guest this afternoon?"

"I think," Ravenna said, very carefully, a moment later, "that you wanted the satisfaction of seeing a Tar'Conantur in a servant's tunic and washing your floors. That this, in fact, has everything to do with the Emperor and nothing at all to do with Cathan." And with those words, the tenor in the room subtly changed—it moved on to an entirely different level.

I saw Telesta look at Mauriz, her green eyes watchful. She was waiting for his reaction. This time the silence lasted longer, long enough to hear a nightbird—I didn't know what sort—call softly outside.

"What makes you think that?" Mauriz said finally. It wasn't enough of an answer, not by a long way.

"Tell us what it is you want to do," Palatine said. "We'll keep your silence."

It wasn't Mauriz who answered, though, but Telesta, alert now.

"Twenty-five years ago next month, Prime Kavadh proclaimed a holy war against the Archipelago. He offered, in the name of Ranthas, a place in Paradise for all those who fought. It was a Crusade, a glorious enterprise of the Faith.

"You all know what happened. The fires, the destruction, the massacres. Flames, flames everywhere. More than a hundred and fifty thousand dead in the heartlands alone. So much that was beautiful, irreplaceable, was lost in that devastation. They destroyed nineteen cities, until the Archipelago surrendered at Poseidonis, to save the island of Qalathar itself from destruction. They had no leaders, no fleets, no armies. They called for help, and it never came."

She was recounting it as a historian might, in a way. Not a dry academic, closeted in the halls of the Great Libraries, but one who knew what life was like. Someone who knew what a tool emotion could be, but used it essentially *as* a tool, nothing more. Her voice was calm after Mauriz's astonishing expressiveness, which made his voice hard to ignore even with the man's arrogance. But I listened nonetheless.

"The one nation in the world that could have helped, whose people are cousins of the Archipelagans, did nothing. Emperor Perseus sent no reply to their appeals, nothing more than a message: he could not intervene.

"The Domain imposed religious rule on Qalathar, set up zealots as city governors, with foreign Avarchs pulling their strings. The Exarch of the Archipelago holds the power of life and death over the Archipelago, even in those islands outside his immediate control. There have been several purges in the years between then and now, a repression that has gone on and on.

"I have lived in the Archipelago for some time now, chronicling what remains of their history before the darkness descends again. They've always known that this Inquisition would come, that they were still too independent for the Domain's liking. The Inquisition is here to crush Archipelagan resistance, to burn every last heretic, and make the worship of Ranthas supreme again. And they're less well suited to resist than they were last time, now there's no leader at all. No one but a tyrannical Emperor—a man who should have been drowned at birth." Her last words came from the heart, perhaps, but I couldn't tell. I didn't know what to make of her.

But I was, uneasily, beginning to see where she was leading, though one question still remained to be answered. It was, I hoped, an answer that none of them yet knew, but almost certainly that hope would prove forlorn. Mauriz's next words, though, concerned something quite different, and were to prove fatal. Time and time again I would wonder if there was something I could, or should, have said, an interruption of any kind that would somehow, miraculously, have prevented him from going on. From setting forward a case, a proposal, that would have been merely heretical and seditious had there not been five people in that room.

"There is the Pharaoh, naturally, and many people revere her, whoever she is. But her value is mostly symbolic, and they've made a mistake by keeping her hidden. She'd have a hard time proving she was genuine if she *did* appear, and almost certainly she'd end up as a Domain puppet."

I felt as well as saw Ravenna tense in a fury, a gesture Telesta noted and must have misinterpreted. They didn't know who she was, and I wished they did.

"You're Qalathari, aren't you?" Telesta said to Ravenna, daring to interrupt Mauriz's speech.

"You," Ravenna said to Mauriz, throwing protocol to the winds, "aren't."

"The Pharaoh has great value as a symbol," he repeated. "Not as a leader. She's untried, no experience of war or of what it would take to save Qalathar. A symbol isn't going to be enough, I'm afraid."

"Who would be better, then?" Palatine interrupted. She'd kept her composure, but she must have been as worried as I was. How could he have said that, with Ravenna in the room? There was no way he could have known, of course, but he understood, at least, that she was a supporter and perhaps a confidante of the Pharaoh.

Palatine's question, as an attempt to pour oil on troubled waters, was a mistake. I should have realized that before Mauriz went on, but I was too worried about Ravenna to take in the obvious implications of what Telesta said next.

"I'm sure all of you know about the old Thetian tradition of twins in the Imperial House. It happens every generation—there's only been one interruption in four hundred years."

That was true, and nobody had ever explained either the tradition or the interruption. It was believed that the line of twins had ended with the murder of Tiberius two centuries ago. The interruption when Tiberius's cousin Valdur, Carausius's son, had usurped the throne. And founded the Domain.

There had been twins in the intervening generations, though, as it turned out, and as he explained I finally understood the last, terrible secret of my own life.

"Before the Domain and the usurpation, there were eight religions, more or less, in the Archipelago and the world." With the usurpation and the purges that followed it, the Domain version of history rejoined reality.

"More or less" was an entirely apt term. Eight elemental religions, but not all with followers, or even the potential for followers. Water, Earth, Fire, Wind, Light, Shadow, Spirit and Time. All except Time had had their mysteries and their mages, their followers and their schisms.

As Mauriz then went on to remind us, there had been plenty of confessional disputes, wars fought between followers of one elemental order or another. These had never been carried on in the name of religion, though, always for political reasons. Religious war had been the Domain's invention, something Mauriz was careful to stress even though we all knew it.

"It was set down by Aetius II that the twins of each generation would inherit the throne." In his somewhat patronizing way, Mauriz was coming to the heart of his proposal at last, and I couldn't think of a way to stave off the inevitable conclusion. I felt my stomach clench in painful anticipation. "The elder became Emperor, while the younger, even on the rare occasions when he had no magical talent, was made Hierarch, high priest of high priests. He commanded the Empire's mages, most of whom were followers of Water, and was the supreme religious authority."

I suppose I ought to have been happy at his next words, as he made clear that he wanted me to take the Hierarch's diadem, to rise to a power most people could only dream of. In an ideal world, perhaps I might have done, but in an ideal world such things would not have been needed.

Aquasilva was not an ideal world. There was the Domain, which couldn't in a thousand years accept a return of the Hierarchate, and there was the Emperor, whose need to have me in his power now became terribly clear. Under the system he followed, the system legitimized by Valdur's seizure of the throne, as Orosius's twin brother I was heir apparent to the throne of the Empire. The Hierarchate hadn't existed for two hundred years; only the throne mattered, and my very existence was a threat to Orosius's power.

"The Hierarch is the only figure who'd be accepted by the whole of the Archipelago and Thetia. He's not linked to any particular order or heresy, and he's someone the Thetians, and the fleet, would follow."

"Someone who would draw support away from the Emperor and found a Thetian republic," Palatine said. "That's what it's about, for you at least."

"There are more who feel this way," Mauriz said evenly. "Archipelagans and Thetians. We just happened to be in the right place at the right time."

Three of them were looking at me now, waiting for me to state the obvious, that I understood and would be prepared to accept. Accept a title that no longer existed, go against every secular and religious authority on Aquasilva. Who, I had to admit, were already hunting me for one reason or another.

It might, conceivably, be a way to end the terror of the Inquisition, and defeat the Crusade that would inevitably come once that happened. Thetia's fleet would have tipped the balance in the last Crusade, and could just as well do so this time if it was ordered to intervene.

Finally, as, with growing distress, I acknowledged that Telesta might well be right, I could see that there were two problems.

First, I didn't want to become Hierarch. I had found out the hard way in Lepidor what having power meant, and my decisions had nearly lost the city and killed all of us. I never wanted to be in that position again.

Second, agreeing with Mauriz, even in principle, would lose me Ravenna. Whatever there was, or might be, between us would die in an instant. Much as she hated the inheritance, her pride wouldn't allow her to agree with Mauriz, or to sit by while a foreigner—no matter how much of a friend he might be—became the Archipelago's savior. She was the Pharaoh, and in her eyes the only ruler whom the Archipelago acknowledged. If I played my part in Mauriz's plan, there would be no need for a Pharaoh.

"How do you propose to do this?" Palatine said, seeing the stricken look on my face. "In the middle of a purge, with the Emperor's agents everywhere?"

"You do know that Tekla works directly for the Emperor?" I said, stepping in blindly, trying to divert them any way I could. "That he's been the Emperor's mouthpiece?"

"Tekla reports to the Imperial spymaster, who has been taken care of. In any case, that isn't the biggest problem. If we can't secure the support, or at least the neutrality, of Marshal Tanais, it will be more difficult to succeed."

"You think Tanais will allow you to depose the Emperor just because you've got Cathan?" Palatine demanded. "Even more foolish than I thought."

"His concern is for the Imperial line, the family. Not for individual members."

"And for Thetia. What price that family, if they don't have a throne?"

"Tanais was your tutor," Mauriz said quietly. "You were a republican. I want to know if you still are."

"Whether I am with you or against you on this?"

Mauriz nodded, and this time it was Palatine who became the focus of attention. She paused, as if unsure what to say. I shifted my weight from one shoulder to the other as I tried to ease my soreness. After a day spent in unaccustomed hard labor, lying on a Thetian divan for an extended period of time was beginning to hurt. My shoulders ached now, as well as my arms and back. The growing physical discomfort was, however, the least of my worries.

"You still haven't told me your plans."

Mauriz shook his head. "And I won't, not until I know Cathan's answer."

"And if I refuse? If Cathan refuses, as he might well?"

"The Inquisition have free rein, Orosius remains in power, you stay exiled from Thetia."

"By choice, Mauriz, a choice that you've only justified so far. Isn't it arrogant to say that yours is the only way forward?"

"Then tell me," Mauriz said, "another."

"She will tell you as much about our plans as you have told us about yours," Ravenna cut in, the fury in her voice barely suppressed. "One that does not involve supplanting the Pharaoh."

"Your loyalty is commendable, if misplaced."

"I think you'll find this loyalty more widespread than you think."

I remembered the Archipelagans who'd been shipwrecked in Lepidor, their almost fanatical defense of the Pharaoh's name. None of them had known who she was, none except their leader. And Mauriz's loyalties, divided as they already were, couldn't be guessed.

"You know what's coming as well as the rest of us. What the Inquisition will do across the Archipelago." Mauriz was replying to Ravenna, but she wasn't looking at him, rather at the rest of us, her stare fastening on each in turn.

"I don't need to describe it again," Mauriz went on. "Tell me, if a leader appeared, someone who stood for the Archipelago against the Domain, the Emperor, the Halettites, do you think people would care whether it was the Pharaoh or the Hierarch? If this person had support, enough to make them a serious challenger, who would follow? The Archipelagans want an end to persecution. The Thetians want an end to Tanethan supremacy, and a saner ruler."

"The only difference," Telesta finished, "is that the Hierarch would have wide enough support to bring down Orosius. And once Orosius is gone, the Domain can't control Thetia."

"There is a word you use for such a person," Palatine said. "*Messiah.*"

It was true, all of it. Properly organized, Mauriz's plan had a chance. He wouldn't tell us exactly how it would work, but he was right, as long as the Thetians kept their promises once Orosius was gone.

It was crucial that they did. This was the question I asked Mauriz a moment later, a question that he had to answer. Thetians were as capable of duplicity as anyone. But if Telesta and other senior people were involved, I couldn't see how they could renege, if things came to that point. I still knew very little about Telesta. She couldn't be a minor player, though, in whatever circles she moved, because Mauriz treated her as an equal, in his way.

She was the one who stated the fact we'd skirted around all evening, and finally brought the fateful discussion to a close.

"Cathan, you are the Hierarch, Orosius's twin. Whatever you may feel about it, you may be the key to driving out the Domain, something the Archipelago has been awaiting for a quarter of a century. That's why we rescued you."

I could see the tautness behind her and Mauriz's expressions, and knew that I couldn't evade anymore. I felt sick. There was nowhere I wanted less to be than in this room, on this divan, being asked this terrible, impossible question. Would I lead a holy war for political gain? To try, at least, to free the Archipelago from the Domain?

To agree would be to burden myself with a nightmarish responsibility, far worse than any I could ever have met as Count of Lepidor. I would make a bitter enemy of the woman I loved, who I would be, in effect, sidelining. And I would have to face Orosius, my hated, twisted twin brother.

I wasn't strong enough. In a sense, I realized, it was over before it had even begun, because I couldn't decide. More political ambition, a genuine relationship with Ravenna, might have tipped the balance either way. As it was, I did the worst thing I could possibly have done, because they saw me as I was. And in not deciding I put myself into their hands. Because I couldn't decide, they knew that they would be able to control me, that there was no problem with my assent because I wasn't strong enough to stand up to them.

Shaking my head in agonized silence, I threw away the chance they'd given me, and the respect of the person who mattered most to me. I had been given an opportunity as few people ever were, recognized it as few people ever did—and then lost it. The most fatal trait of all in any leader. It didn't help to know that I had inherited it from my real father Emperor Perseus. Nor that there would be no chance at redemption, for me or for the people who would suffer because of that unmade choice.

No one said another word as we got up from the divans and left. I went back to lie on the floor in a dark storeroom, there to spend a night of silent, lonely misery and pain.

Part Two
Illusions of Glory

Chapter XI

My first arrival in Qalathar was not a happy one, but I was never to forget it. Qalathar was not a sight one *could* forget.

Normally only those who couldn't afford a manta passage traveled by sailing ship. The conditions were chancier, the risks greater, and it was far less comfortable. In winter, with violent weather almost guaranteed for anything longer than the shortest voyage, only the truly desperate would make such a journey. But in braving the elements to travel to Qalathar, those who made the crossing had the compensation of seeing it for the first time with their own eyes.

Huddled in a voluminous cloak that wasn't doing its duty—keeping out the spray—I wedged myself into a narrow space on the foredeck to watch the green cliffs of Qalathar gradually rise up from the sea ahead of us.

How much more impressive it would have been to arrive on a summer's day, gliding through a calm blue sea, with the mountains revealed in their full glory. I might also have escaped being chilled to the marrow by a biting wind and drenched with spray every time the bow dipped down into a trough.

As it was, though, my first sight of Qalathar, under heavy, dark skies, the mountains shrouded by clouds, imprinted itself indelibly on my mind. Dark green forest met gray sea in a wall stretching away in both directions, the two separated only by a line of white where the surf, audible from miles out, pounded the rocks. Only the faintest dip in the shoreline, its upper reaches hidden behind the veil, betrayed the presence of the Jayan Strait. Beyond that was Qalathar's Inland Sea, and, somewhere, the person who had promised to show it to me.

Hard as I looked, nowhere along the coastline could I see any signs of life or habitation. Almost no one lived on this shore, battered as it was by constant storms, where waves birthed far out in the reaches of the Ocean crashed endlessly and with terrible force on to the dark gray cliffs and coves.

The Island in the Clouds, it had been called since time immemorial, a place of mists and valleys during winter, sun-dappled forests and beaches in summer, its cities clustered around the Inland Sea. There were peaks here that towered higher than any I knew: it was almost the only place in the Archipelago to have mountain ranges. The shoreline, for all its greenness, was dark and ominous, as if shadowed still by the hidden crags.

It was wild, and beautiful, I thought, watching the contours gradually resolve themselves as we crept nearer, the outlines of the Jayan Gap becoming visible. I shivered and pulled the cloak tighter as moisture trickled down my neck. The air was filled with flying foam and salt water, the creaking of the masts and timbers an accompaniment to seagulls' mournful cries.

It should have been something to celebrate, arriving here— somewhere I'd for so long wanted to come—after three weeks at sea. Three weeks of being almost continually wet and permanently miserable, avoiding Mauriz and the one other passenger not suffering from seasickness. We had barely survived one of the storms, and two others had been bad enough to make even me ill. I hadn't been seasick since I was four. My one consolation, as I'd lain in a perpetually moving, drug-induced nightmare, had been that Mauriz was ill too.

Now, though, as the chartered Ilthysian galleon plowed its way through wave after wave toward that strange, primeval shore, I would have given anything to be somewhere else.

I very nearly had been, as a matter of fact. And more than once, during the galleon's awful voyage, I'd seriously wished I was.

I'd almost ended up as a floating corpse, one tiny part of the flotsam on the Ocean's vast surface, my soul in a happier place. Thetis looked with favor on those who had been drowned at sea or committed to the deep: they became true sea elementals, formless currents on a higher plane of life.

That I hadn't been received into Thetis's blessed peace could have been an indication of either divine displeasure or favor. It didn't really matter, though, because I was still alive despite everything that had happened. And, a month and a half after leaving Ral Tumar, we had finally reached our destination.

"We" was perhaps the wrong word to use. Only a few of those who had left Ral Tumar with Mauriz would see Qalathar, for the time being, at least. Some never would, unless their elemental spirits chose to visit it.

Some would need weeks, months of convalescence before they could even contemplate it. One was already there.

For that last and most painful absence from our group, I could blame Mauriz, but only for that one. For all the rest, everything else we had gone through since leaving Ral Tumar, the Domain were at fault. They seemed to have jinxed our luck right from the outset, with that frustrating, time-consuming and utterly futile search of the *Lodestar*. There were known heretics in Ral Tumar, the leading Inquisitor had said, his eyes alight with fanaticism. They must not be allowed to escape.

Even Mauriz's rank and connections had been ignored, and the Sacri had systematically combed the *Lodestar*, while the Inquisitor subjected a fuming Mauriz and his suite to a harangue on the dangers of heresy. I didn't remember having breathed once as he'd looked across us all. But he was looking for the Escount of Lepidor and his entourage, not two sullen, dispirited Worldsend servants and a Thetian aide. Mauriz's pleasure at introducing Palatine as a member of Clan Scartaris must have been considerable.

Eventually the thwarted Sacri disembarked, and their leader came up to the Inquisitor to tell him there were no stowaways, and no sign of the renegade oceanographer. The Inquisitor had looked slightly disappointed, I remembered, but no less eager.

"There can be no hiding from the Inquisition," he declared. "The eye of Ranthas sees all, and in His infinite mercy He will show us what we seek."

There was no apology for the delay, only an injunction to walk in the light of Ranthas, as the Inquisitor swept off again. At one point his robe had brushed against my leg, and I wondered how anyone could wear fabric that rough. He was an ascetic, of course, as many of the Inquisitors were. There were those who liked their food and drink, their soft beds and concubines, and there were those who scourged themselves and wore hair shirts. I suspected that the latter were in a minority.

The disguise arranged by Mauriz had saved us from arrest, there was no doubt of that. The Sacri were terrifying in their efficiency, faces hidden behind crimson veils, moving with the deadly grace of trained killers. Had it been the novice Sarhaddon who'd said there were no soldiers in the world to equal them except the elite Thetian Ninth Legion? The cynical, good-natured companion of my first long journey had taught me a lot, and I still wondered what had turned him into the pitiless fundamentalist he seemed to have become.

Even when we finally boarded the *Lodestar* and were given permission to leave by the port authorities, the atmosphere was uneasy. The crew's attitude wavered between resentment and fear; three times that afternoon I heard the even-natured captain turn on one of his subordinates. Even Mauriz's forced calm began to fray at the edges.

Palatine and Ravenna did their best to pretend the previous night's conversation had never taken place, but I saw a new, pitying look in their eyes. I silently cursed Mauriz, Telesta, the Emperor, but I couldn't deny even to myself that I'd done the wrong thing. Worse than the wrong thing.

Only when the *Lodestar* had left Ral Tumar and was heading out to sea, the outer islands of the Tumarian archipelago slipping past, did Mauriz tell us that we were going to Qalathar.

"Why?" Ravenna demanded. "Why go where the Domain's attention is focused? How are you going to hide Cathan there?"

"That's where the resistance is," Mauriz replied, shrugging. "We have to start a rebellion, it has to be in Qalathar, at the center of things. There's no point in beginning out on the rim somewhere that can easily be cut off, even if it's less dangerous."

"That's not an ideal plan either," Palatine said. "The Domain have informants, stooges, people who will tell them at the first sign of trouble."

"They expect discontent in Qalathar. If, say, Ilthys suddenly became a hotbed of rebellion, they'd crush it instantly. They know Qalathar will be difficult."

"And if we can win Qalathar, that's the Exarch's headquarters destroyed," Telesta said, a note of finality in her voice. Perhaps it was her plan, or something she strongly supported, but she was much firmer about it than Mauriz. "Once we've done that, they have nowhere very safe in the Archipelago, and they'll have to summon reinforcements from the Holy City. That should give us enough time to deal with Thetia."

But still, despite the confident assertions, there were no concrete plans, no signs that they had a considered plan of action. It was entirely probable that they didn't have anything more than a vague outline. Perhaps the guiding force of the movement was currently in Qalathar, or perhaps Mauriz hoped to upstage the scheme's leader by starting without him— or her. Her, quite possibly, if it was a Thetian scheme, originally conceived by the republicans.

There was, in any case, no more argument. Ravenna became even more withdrawn and hardly spoke to me or anyone. Mauriz more or less ignored her, a mistake which was entirely pardonable, given that as far as he knew Ravenna was just a Qalathari heretic, if of fairly noble birth.

Perhaps she intended to tell us her plans at the end of the two-week journey to Qalathar, but five days after leaving Ral Tumar, bad luck caught up with us.

I was more or less killing time, skimming through some bad Thetian poetry in the mess hall—there wasn't much of a selection of reading matter—when I felt the ship's motion slowing, the deep thrumming of the flamewood reactor changing tone. None of the marines sitting around the tables, gambling and telling each other ridiculous stories of their exploits with women, seemed to have noticed.

I put my hand against an exposed bulkhead to feel the motion—we were definitely slowing. After a few days at sea, the reactor's pitch had become familiar enough that I noticed the change. But why? We were passing through the edge of the Sianor island group, but not close enough to any islands to warrant a reduction of cruise speed.

I returned the book to its case in the small library corner of the mess hall and threaded my way between the tables to the door. Almost as soon as I'd got into the passageway, though, the captain's disembodied voice sounded over the message system.

"All crew to duty stations to prepare for salvage operation. Marines to arm and assemble in the well."

There was an immediate commotion behind me, the sound of chairs being pushed back. Salvage meant something to do, a relief from the boredom of a long voyage. More importantly, it meant money for all those on the salvaging ship.

When I reached the well, as yet empty of marines, I met Palatine coming down the stairs from the upper deck.

"There you are," she said, impatiently. "Come up to the observation room, you can see it from up there."

"What is it?"

"Drifting manta. Being Scartaris, they're ready to drop everything for a chance at profit. Mauriz wants to salvage it."

"Typical Canteni," remarked the second officer from the chartroom. "Why make some money when you can do target practice instead?"

"And where does that get us?" Palatine shot back as we climbed the stairs again. "Who wins all the battles?"

"Who's richer? That's what matters," was the second officer's reply, but after that we were out of earshot. It was friendly bickering at a time like this, but I knew that the two clans had fought wars in the past, and doubtless would again. From Palatine's accounts, they hadn't been very bloody, but some clans still held blood feuds against each other from past occasions when the fighting had got out of hand.

Ravenna was already in the observation room when we got there, looking out of the starboard windows, but she was alone. Everybody else had taken up their duty stations, while Telesta and Mauriz were on the bridge, no doubt. I had no idea where Matifa was, and I didn't want to know.

It was mid-morning by the ship's clocks, and we were in water shallow enough for the ocean to be murky gray-blue outside. I couldn't see the other manta at first, but then Ravenna pointed to a darker spot in the gloom just ahead. The *Lodestar* was only moving very slowly relative to it now, circling to come in alongside the other vessel. Linking mantas to board was a very precise maneuver, one only skilled helmsmen could do.

"Any word on whose it is?" Ravenna asked.

Palatine shook her head as we stood there and watched the dark shape slowly growing in size. It was more or less tail-on to us, the horns with their identifying markers hidden from sight.

Even at this distance, though, surely those were faint points of light here and there along its sides, and stray bubbles drifting from the engine vents? That would mean the reactor was still on, possibly even that the ship had only just stopped moving.

"Very suspicious," Palatine said when I told her, taking advantage of my mage's shadowsight to see better in the gloom. "We use this to ambush people. Scartaris, Jonti, Polinskarn, they all fall for it. They see a ship floating, they have to try and salvage it."

"And you never get tricked yourselves?" Ravenna said innocently.

"Of course not. We invented that trick in the War." Palatine glanced over her shoulder to check that nobody else had come in. "A Canteni captain did it to a Tuonetar arkship—pretended to be dead, then swarmed them when they boarded."

Like the Domain, the Tuonetar had hated the sea, always preferring to board and fight hand-to-hand. It was something that more or less guaranteed them victory when they managed to do it, because their ships were always huge and equipped for invasion, with more soldiers on a single one of their arkships than an entire Thetian fleet could muster.

That was one of the reasons the *Aeon* had been so useful during the war, because it reclaimed the advantage of size for the Thetians. Although virtually unarmed, it had space to fit the Thetian armies inside ten times over—something Aetius IV had used to good advantage in his last assault on the Tuonetar capital.

The characteristic faint blue glow of the aether shields showed around the edges of the other vessel's windows. The *Lodestar*'s captain wasn't taking any chances but it struck me that there must have been more subtle ways to lay an ambush than this; the lights and engine activity would only make the captain warier.

It seemed to take forever for the *Lodestar* to coast in, the helmsman laying a course exactly parallel to and slightly above the other manta. Aside from the obvious difficulty of matching speeds and courses, the other problem of linking two mantas was the shape. Because of the wings, they couldn't come alongside each other and link forward hatch to forward hatch. That was why there were two passenger hatches at the rear, on the cargo deck, where the mantas' shapes allowed them to more or less touch bow to stern.

There was a lot of noise from down below now, abruptly silenced by a shout of command, then the sound of many people moving at once; presumably from the well to the aft cargo stairs. It was always safer to board from a confined space into a broader one rather than the other way around.

The other manta was very close now, its dull, almost smooth blue hull curving away on either side of the wings, which blocked our view directly downward. The *Lodestar* was hardly moving, its motion only perceptible when we looked at the other ship. We were very close to the surface now, perhaps thirty feet down, the wings reflecting a dreary gray light. The sun wasn't shining above the waves.

A moment or two later a shudder ran through the *Lodestar*'s hull, followed by a sharper, more definite sound as the mantas touched. It was frustrating, standing up here doing nothing, only awaiting the outcome, but all of us knew we'd only get in the marines' way if there was a fight.

Another thump—the hatch-cover connecting, giving the marines dry access. Then nothing. There was very little to see from up here now— the other manta was almost entirely hidden by the *Lodestar*'s wings—so we went back down to the well. It was deserted, and the door to the bridge was closed, but a moment later a marine came running along the corridors and on into the bridge. He looked rather disappointed, I thought.

"Qalathari?" Mauriz's voice said, very clearly, from inside the bridge. "Are you sure?"

I didn't hear the marine's reply, but a moment later the captain's voice rang out over the comm again.

"Healer to the other ship immediately."

The marine emerged, Mauriz and Telesta behind him, and headed off down the corridor, but not before Mauriz had ordered the three of us to follow them.

"What is it?" Palatine asked.

"Qalathari manta, heavily damaged off Sianor. They made it this far but their reactor's given out."

That would explain the disappointment. The Scartarans might be able to extract something in return for their help—which they were obliged to give, under Thetian law. But if there were still people alive and in control on the other ship, there would be no chance of salvage.

In the other ship's damaged, half-lit well we were met by a haggard-looking old man in a red tunic, which looked like part of a uniform. The ship belonged to the nominal civilian government of Qalathar, Ravenna whispered, although they had virtually no power, caught between the Domain and the Viceroy.

"High Commissioner, my thanks for your assistance," he said gravely. "I don't want to keep you here, but we have wounded and our reactor is damaged."

"Where is your captain?" Mauriz asked.

Whoever the attackers had been, they'd certainly hit hard. Only one aether light survived in the well amid a mess of bent metal; the walls had buckled or collapsed completely, and the stairways were gone.

"The captain's injured, and the lieutenants both gone, so I'm in charge now. I'm Master Vasudh."

"Who was it?"

Vasudh paused for a minute, then looked him in the eye and said, "Domain."

"Domain? Why?" Telesta demanded. The two or three marines in the well glanced uneasily around.

"They tried to take over the ship at Sianor, said they had orders from the Inquisitor-General that all Qalathari ships were to be put at the Domain's disposal. The captain wouldn't let them, so they tried to impound us. We broke out, but they chased us and used pressure charges—so much for them being evil and heretical weapons. That was three days ago, we've been trying to escape ever since. None of our communications survived, which is why we couldn't warn you."

"How far behind are they?"

"I've no idea. I thought we lost them, but the captain says they can track us much farther. He wanted to make for Beraetha, scuttle her and hide on the island."

"You put us in a difficult situation," Mauriz said, looking worried now. "If they catch up and find us helping you . . ."

"It is demanded by the Law of the Sea," the old man said fiercely. "A law far older than these Continental upstarts with their phobias about heresy."

"I won't leave them behind," the Scartaris captain said, emerging from behind us. "I won't have it, the crew won't have it. Master . . . Vasudh, if we repair your reactor and give your injured what treatment we can, will that be enough?"

"Thank you, Captain," Vasudh said, with a stiff bow. "That's all we ask."

"I'll send some of our engineers over right now," the captain said to Vasudh. "Can your men help?"

Mauriz looked reluctant, but stood by as the *Lodestar*'s captain coordinated the repairs. Engineers were brought over, the ship's healer attended to the wounded, and the marines helped shore up some of the worst damage. There were no repairs to weapons systems or shields, but Vasudh hadn't requested them.

Mauriz and Telesta became more and more impatient as the hours dragged on. Of very little use to anyone except as light labor, the three of us ended up in the *Lodestar*'s empty mess hall.

"So much for profit," Palatine said with satisfaction, watching the Scartaris marines take off their armor before they went back to prop up bulkheads in the other ship—it was called the *Avanhatai* after an ancient Qalathari ruler. "They have to spend the afternoon working and don't get a penny for it."

"Yes, and if the Domain catches up with us, will it be so funny then?" Ravenna snapped, ill-tempered as she so frequently was these days. It was different from her usual rages, more intense, more sullen, and more long-lasting. If I hadn't been so weak and vacillating in Ral Tumar . . . but in that case, I might have agreed to Mauriz's proposal and alienated Ravenna entirely. It was small comfort that her anger was directed at everyone, not just at me.

It was three hours later, with the repair work almost finished, that the shrill of the battle alarm shattered the near-silence in the *Lodestar*'s mess hall. We looked at each other for a second, then jumped up and ran along to the well again. We met the second officer coming out of the bridge.

"Tell everyone to get off the *Avanhatai*," he said. "Now! Run! The Domain's here. Ten miles away."

The panic in his voice would have been enough, even without the mention of the Domain. As we ran back along the corridor, we met

Mauriz and Telesta coming up the stairs and passed the news along. It wasn't welcomed, but I ignored their expressions of dismay and ran down the steps, past the marines, to the *Lodestar*'s captain, who was talking to Vasudh.

"We have to leave now, I'm afraid," the captain said to Vasudh, once I'd told him. "Your reactor can be started up, but you'll have to repair it again in a few days."

"We only need a few days," Vasudh said, then cupped his hands and bellowed, "Everyone off!"

His voice was deafening, reminding me vividly of a training officer's bellow. Vasudh was just the sort of man who'd retire to a sailing instructor's post.

The Scartaris crew and marines were nothing if not disciplined. In less than a minute they were pouring through the *Avanhatai*'s well and back on to the *Lodestar*, engineers carrying their tool kits. The Qalathari manta's grim-faced, blackened crew hurried to their battle stations at the same time, their faces set with a kind of defiant resignation—I only hoped they got away.

It was a very quick, well-practiced and efficient evacuation. We were hustled back on to the *Lodestar* by Vasudh, wished him good luck, and just over five minutes after the second officer's warning the hatch was sealed and the *Lodestar* was ready to break away. Against any secular attack, it would have been enough.

As the crew went to their battle stations, marines retrieving their armor and moving to their stations, we were banished to the observation room again, the traditional place for passengers during battle. The edge of the room was clear, but there were chairs around the aether table in the center with straps to stop their occupants falling out if the helmsman got imaginative.

The aether table showed the same image as its companions on the bridge, the *Lodestar* and everything within its sensor range, about twelve miles. With our view out of the windows, we thus had a good view of the battle.

As it turned out, there was no battle. The Domain ship was still five miles away, well out of weapons range, when we broke from the *Avanhatai*, lifting slightly to get clear. The engine had just cut in again, pushing the *Lodestar* about a hundred yards away from the other manta's hull, when I felt a vast surge of magic.

It hit me like a whip, an agonizing pain lancing through my skull. I screamed, caught completely unawares, and heard Ravenna's tortured shriek.

"Are you . . . Sweet Thetis!" Palatine said.

Both hands holding my head, I looked up at the aether table. An incandescent spark flared under the *Avanhatai*, so bright that it sent a fresh wave of pain through my skull. Seconds later the spark extended lengthways, like a brilliant white rip in the water, then expanded.

The water outside the windows turned to bubbles, a frothing nightmare of air and steam, and I felt the *Lodestar* thrown bodily up as if it was no lighter than a feather. My chair tilted sideways with appalling speed, leaving me almost hanging by a thin strap, desperately praying that it wouldn't break and drop me into the far well a dozen feet below. My right leg was driven against the chair arm so hard that I thought for a moment it had been broken, the impact triggering fresh waves of pain.

Something heavy clanged against something else, and there was a high keening like souls in torment, a chaos of sound and motion.

A second later, an even brighter white light flooded the room, and in the second before I screwed my eyes shut, I saw the *Avanhatai*'s image consumed.

Another shock wave slammed into the *Lodestar*, throwing it end over end, the world twisting around in a whirl of noise, heat and pain. I didn't black out, although I wanted to; somehow I managed to retain my senses as the manta rocked wildly. A concussion shook the hull, but I couldn't tell where it came from.

With the ship still out of control, I felt more violent impacts, things crashing against the hull, a force from somewhere pushing me into my seat at an awkward, painful angle, the chair digging into my painfully bruised leg and thigh. The water outside the windows seemed to be white, for some reason, with everything else just dark outlines. The *Lodestar* reared up again, and for a terrible moment I thought it would fall upside down. Then it slipped back, and I slumped forward in my chair, almost deafened by the unearthly groaning of the dying manta.

Chapter XII

It was several moments before my head stopped spinning enough for me to risk opening my eyes. For a moment all I could see was whiteness, and I was gripped by panic. Had I gone blind?

It only lasted a second or two, because I gradually made out shapes, the outlines of the room—all in shades of gray. Here and there I saw a flash of color at the corner of my eyes, but I couldn't focus on it. I closed my eyes and opened them again, hoping the color would come back, but it didn't.

I unfastened the strap that had held me in the seat and stood up as slowly as I could. I almost collapsed, and only stayed upright by grabbing hold of the broken aether table. My right side seemed to be a mass of bruises, but as I gingerly ran my hand down it there didn't seem to be any blood.

That awful shrieking was still there, as if the manta was being crushed in a giant vice. A manta's outer skin was more or less impossible to break, but that didn't mean it couldn't collapse in on itself.

"I think it might be a good idea to go down to the main deck," Palatine said unsteadily, standing up next to me. "You both look awful. What happened just before they blew up?"

"Magic," Ravenna said. "Far too much of it." She was still sitting down, and when she tried to stand up she staggered and fell back into the chair.

"I think at least one of the Gods has a sense of humor," said Palatine, smiling faintly. "Cathan, she can lean on you, if you're up to it."

I remembered Ravenna's scathing words eighteen months ago, when I'd been too weak to stand up after being knocked out. Small justice, really.

It was very dark in the manta's interior; once we were out of the observation room, without the gray light from the surface, we were more or less feeling our way. Palatine led, moving cautiously down the stairs to the main deck; the *Lodestar* was big enough for the observation room to be on the third, top deck. I heard cries of pain from the darkness below, but I had to ignore them: I was too preoccupied with trying to support myself and Ravenna without falling down the stairs.

"This ship doesn't have long," Palatine said as we reached the gallery on the upper deck. "Ravenna, can you get down these next stairs on your own? They seem to be twisted."

"I'll try," Ravenna said, but didn't shift her weight yet. "After you."

That was so unlike Ravenna I couldn't believe it. *I'll try?* There had been times when I'd have been savaged for suggesting she couldn't do something.

"Wait here until I'm at the bottom," Palatine said.

"Who's that?" a voice called from below.

"Palatine Canteni," she called back. "Where's the captain?"

"I don't know. All injured. Must get off, the ship's going to explode." The speaker sounded dazed; I thought it might be one of the engineers.

"We've got to get everybody into the escape subs. Cathan, I'm at the bottom, the fifth step from the top is gone." I heard Palatine's footsteps, and she said something else to the engineer that was drowned out by the screeching of armor on metal; one of the marines getting up, I thought.

"Are you all right?" I asked Ravenna. "Can I go?"

"Yes. I'll join you."

I gently removed the arm that was supporting her and made my way backward down the stairs, my head still reeling slightly. There was a faint light again now; someone had opened the door to the bridge, and light was creeping in from the windows at the front.

"Where's the captain?" someone else asked. I stepped away from the ladder to leave room for Ravenna and almost tripped over a marine, who gave a muffled groan.

"Out cold," someone said from inside the bridge. "And the aether table's . . ." I heard a faint curse, then another voice. There was a crash from somewhere aft, and a shout for help.

"That's the engine room," said the voice I thought was the engineer's. He was standing next to Palatine, whose face I could just about see in the light from the bridge.

Ravenna reached the bottom of the ladder and came, rather unsteadily, on to the bridge with me. Most of the bridge crew were unconscious. Some were still in their seats, but a few lay on the floor.

"We've lost the reactor," said the second officer, who was sitting in the chair to the captain's right, holding one hand to the side of his head. "She may collapse, she may not."

"Give the order to abandon ship, then," said the first person I'd heard from inside the bridge, perhaps the junior lieutenant. "No point staying here."

"Do you want to drag everybody to the rescue subs yourself? They're not going to make it on their own."

"Would you rather explain this to the Domain?" the other snapped. "I don't know if the captain will regain consciousness, so you're in charge." He turned to look at the two of us. "Who are . . . Oh. If you two can help me take the High Commissioner and his friend to an escape sub . . ."

He was interrupted by the second officer. "And what then? The Domain ship will be here in minutes, and they'll do just the same to your escape sub as to the ship."

"I don't think they've got the power left," Ravenna said hesitantly. "Whatever they did, it must have exhausted them."

"Magic," the lieutenant said bitterly. "They boiled the water underneath the other ship, created a shock wave that hit us as well. That's why we were shaken up, and they weren't even aiming for us."

"They'll have more where that came from," the second officer said. "Are you planning to abandon ship without orders and get yourself court-martialed?"

"I'm making sure the High Commissioner doesn't get captured."

"I see. Currying favor is more important than the ship. Very well, go if you must." His tone was contemptuous, and I saw the other officer bridle, but he just turned on his heel and ignored his superior. The second officer didn't get a chance to issue any more orders, though, because at that moment there was the heavy, familiar bump of another ship coming alongside.

"Too late," the junior lieutenant remarked. "Well, it looks like you'll have to explain why we were helping those heretics."

Ravenna and I left the bridge. I glanced uneasily up at the ceiling, as if I could see the Domain ship through it. They were about to board, and unless I used magic there was nothing I could do about it. If I tried, and failed, our disguise would be ruined.

Ravenna shook her head.

"Not worth it," she whispered, somehow reading my intentions. "We've played servants as best we can—we'll try keeping on with it."

"Good idea," said Palatine from behind her, making me start. "It's not Sarhaddon or Midian, because they can't be in two places at once, so we've got more than a chance. Mauriz is the one who'll have to answer their questions for us."

"And the captain."

"The law will support him. Now find a corner and look like terrified servants."

It was nerve-racking, waiting for the Domain ship to complete the docking. As Palatine conferred with the second officer and tried to revive Mauriz, a succession of noises echoed through the well.

Then, finally, the hatch swung open and Sacri came marching on to the *Lodestar*.

They must have done this before, I thought a minute or two later, as one of the Sacri reported to his commander that the ship was secure. They'd been utterly confident that there would be no resistance, and they'd been right. No one had been in any condition to lift a finger.

I was feeling sick with fear, still certain that at any moment one of the Sacri would point to us, but they didn't. Ravenna and I were sitting almost under the ruined stairs, knees drawn up to our chins, looking—we hoped—for all the world like what we supposedly were. A Sacri soldier stood nearby nonetheless, even more menacing in the light of flamewood torches. We'd been scrutinized by the commander and told to stay put while he went to find someone in charge.

Palatine and the two officers, one reluctantly propping up the other, had been brought into the well and were waiting for the Inquisitor to come across from the Domain ship.

He didn't take long to arrive, preceded by two less-senior Inquisitors and another priest in brown and red robes. Palatine and the others tactfully made the customary bow to a senior official. There was no point in putting him in a bad mood.

"Who commands here?" he demanded. This was a different type of Inquisitor from the ascetic who'd searched the ship in harbor. He was a heavy-set, gray-bearded Halettite who, though not running to fat, looked as though he enjoyed his food. He wasn't any less intimidating for that, and was possibly even more dangerous for being more of a man of the world.

"I am Second Officer Vatatzes Scartaris," said the senior of the *Lodestar*'s conscious officers. There was blood on his hand and the side of his head, and he seemed to be white-faced even in the torchlight. "My captain is unconscious."

The junior officer looked as if he was about to say something, but sensibly kept his mouth shut.

"You were aiding and assisting heretics and renegades, which under the Edict Universal of Lachazzar is heresy in itself."

"The Imperial Law of the Sea requires all vessels in the vicinity to help a vessel in distress, unless they are enemies," the second officer said, his words very carefully enunciated, as if he was afraid he couldn't say them.

"The law of Ranthas is higher than any earthly code," the Inquisitor said harshly. "He requires that heretics be hunted down, not aided."

"I will not abandon . . . men in distress," the second officer said through gritted teeth, then swayed, his legs buckling. His junior caught him, but a moment later eased him to the floor.

"He's badly injured—he needs medical attention," the other officer said challengingly. "He's not a heretic, he's a wounded officer of a Thetian clan who obeyed his captain's orders."

The Inquisitor looked murderous, but the priest in red and brown said something in a low voice.

"This man is a monk of the Jelath Order. He will attend to your wounded," the Inquisitor said a moment later, and the monk detailed two Sacri to carry the second officer away. I silently prayed to Thetis that he'd recover; the Jelathi monks were a healing order.

The Inquisitor turned to Palatine now, ignoring the junior officer.

"Who are you? Do you have any authority?"

"I am Palatine Canteni, Your Grace, a passenger and guest of the High Commissioner Mauriz, who is injured."

"A Canteni traveling with a Scartaris?"

I sharply revised my opinion of the man. Any Halettite Inquisitor who knew more about Thetia than merely the Emperor's name was very dangerous indeed. Usually they ignored the place and its internal affairs, in which they were forbidden to intervene by the original agreement between Valdur and the first Prime.

"We aren't at war at the moment."

The Inquisitor seemed suddenly to lose interest in her, and summoned another Jelathi monk to rouse Mauriz. The monk reported a moment later that Mauriz too would need medical attention.

"We have no more time to waste here," the Inquisitor said finally. "This ship is now under Domain control. Preceptor Asurnas, bring some of your men and some sailors over to take control of this vessel. We'll head for Ilthys."

"What about the crew?" the man I guessed was Asurnas asked. He had a gold border around the flame on his surcoat, which made him an officer of some kind.

"All the officers and passengers will be moved over to our manta. Put them in the cells for heretics, since they're empty at the moment."

The junior officer tried to protest but was silenced by a blow to the head that sent him reeling.

"Who are you?" the Inquisitor said, his gaze falling on Ravenna and me for the first time. I felt his dark stare boring into me.

"The High Commissioner's servants, Your Grace," I managed to stammer.

My fear was genuine enough, so I hoped I looked as terrified as a servant from the remote Archipelago would, if he was caught up in this.

"We are rather short of servants. You will serve my brothers and myself for now. The novices may have a day off from that privilege to celebrate our destruction of the renegade ship."

So the *Avanhatai* had been destroyed, as I'd feared, and the explosion had caused the second shock wave which had hit the *Lodestar*. The captain's help had been for nothing; we'd ended up prisoners of the Domain, and Master Vasudh would never reach Beraetha. As we were herded over to the Domain manta, I was wondering whether the Inquisitor knew enough about Thetia to have heard of Palatine Canteni.

After a day and a night in the close atmosphere of the Domain manta, I was only too glad to emerge into the warm, humid air of Ilthys. There were one or two breaks in the clouds, and the water offshore was tinted green by sunlight, the first I'd seen since leaving Lepidor. There was something beguiling about the Archipelago's constant warmth, even the wetness that pervaded everything. Except for the presence of the Domain, I felt it was a far better place to be in winter than my own home.

Especially when the manta had been full to bursting with priests, Inquisitors and Sacri, to the extent that its inside had been converted to allow room for monastic cells and a refectory. It was one of the few vessels owned entirely by the Domain; most of the others they were using in this purge, I gathered, had been hired from Tanethan Great Houses. There had even been a row of cells for captured heretics to be confined in, though why there was a need to transport them, I didn't know. The Domain wanted examples, interrogations and burnings to subdue the local people, so what was the point in moving heretics around?

Those of the *Lodestar*'s passengers and crew who were in a condition to walk were being escorted ashore by Sacri, who seemed to have assumed already that we were all heretics. Mauriz, hit hard on the side of his head, hadn't been in any condition to talk until an hour or two ago, so the Inquisitor had decided to question him in the Ilthys Temple.

Ilthys was similar to Ral Tumar in many ways: the same architecture, the same mix of domes and gardens and arches. Unlike Ral Tumar, though, most of the city was perched on top of the cliffs, its sheer walls running around the edges. It was an impressive sight. I wondered why it had been built like that since, as far as I could remember, Ilthys had never been attacked.

The Domain were already on the island, I realized as we started to climb the steep, curving road up the side of the cliff from the lower town, and in force. The Inquisitor had been welcomed at the undersea harbor by the Avarch and a fellow Inquisitor who looked like a dyed-in-the-wool ascetic.

Although he was going on to Qalathar, our captor obviously had plans to stay overnight in the Temple, because Ravenna and I were both carrying heavy bags. It was better than being marched up as prisoners, I supposed, but less comfortable.

"Did you leave brethren behind in Sianor, to carry out our work there?" the ascetic asked our captor, who almost blotted him out by bulk and force of presence.

"As many as I had time for. I'll leave some brothers with you before we go on to Qalathar, to return to Sianor by another ship."

"A pity, perhaps, that the renegade ship was destroyed," the ascetic remarked. "It might have been useful."

"It resisted too long."

"It occurs to me that the technique is a little heavy-handed. These heretics must be made an example of, not killed outright. There is nobody to watch in the deep ocean."

"If you wish to suggest some modifications to the mages, I am sure they will listen."

"I will, and I shall send a message on to Midian in Qalathar. It is our most potent weapon and should be used accordingly, not to kill, but to bring to justice. Ranthas judges all, but He should not have to deal with the souls of heretics."

My shoulders aching beneath the load, I listened in horrified fascination as the two calmly discussed their butchers' trade. Twelve men whose lives, even as potential heretics, were of no account had died on the *Lodestar*. As for the *Avanhatai*, they weren't content with its utter obliteration, but regretted that its end had brought no terror.

Even more interesting was the tension between the two men. Overshadowed as he was by his more dynamic colleague, the ascetic had delivered a stinging reprimand of the other's heavy-handed tactics, and that hadn't gone down well. Was it a professional rivalry, I wondered, or a personal animosity? They didn't seem to know each other that well, and their greeting had been rather cold and formal.

As for the casual assumption that the Domain was better suited to judge souls than the god they worshiped . . .

"I am eager to hear of your successes, Brother," the Halettite said, a not very subtle approach. "Leaving Sianor as quickly as I did to catch those heretics, I haven't yet had a chance to see how effective our arrival has been." In other words, *I've caught a load of heretics and killed some more; what have you done?* It seemed strange, considering his political knowledge, that he was so tactless in dealing with this unworldly ascetic.

"The three days of grace finish tomorrow. I've already seized a known heretic wanted by the Inquisitor-General—she will be tried and burned on market day. It is a slower process within the confines of the Rule. If you should find your prisoners guilty, we could arrange a larger ceremony."

The Halettite's face darkened at that, but he'd left the tribunal in Sianor staffed with only four Sacri and two Inquisitors, in order to catch the *Avanhatai.* A few minutes to disembark some more to ensure that everything went smoothly probably wouldn't have made a difference to their pursuit of the Qalathari ship.

"I expect the Inquisitor-General himself may take an interest in this case."

"I'm sure he'll commend you for your good work."

They fell silent again, and my attention wandered. I looked out through the arches of the wall over the sea, now quite a way below us. Like the upper town, the road was walled on its outer edge, only it was an open wall allowing a view of the sea beyond. It would be a lovely scene on a summer's day, when the ocean was blue rather than gray and green.

We hadn't quite reached the top when I heard the sound of hooves ahead and, peering between a Sacrus's head and the ascetic's horse, saw three riders emerge from the gate to the upper town and stop, deliberately blocking the Inquisitor's way.

The Halettite reined in with the skill of a born horseman, while a Sacrus caught hold of the ascetic's bridle and more or less pulled the horse to a stop. The Sacri stopped with their masters, and behind us the column came to an abrupt halt.

"Who dares to obstruct agents of the Domain?" the Halettite demanded.

The leading rider, on a splendid gold-maned stallion a good two hands higher than either of the Inquisitors' mounts, stared at him for a moment.

"I believe you have illegally attacked a Scartaris manta and taken its crew prisoner. Is this true?"

He was quite a young man, I judged, quintessentially Thetian with that dark brown hair and olive skin, a very dramatic face with flashing eyes. Silk clothes, a gold brooch on his tunic—he had to be someone fairly senior. And he was the first person I'd met in the Archipelago who seemed willing to stare down an Inquisitor. His companions, equally gaudily dressed, both had the air of people expecting to be obeyed. One was a woman, her hair golden, which couldn't be natural, not with that skin color. The Scartaris consul, maybe—she was certainly wearing their colors.

"Who are you, presuming to interrupt the work of Ranthas?" the ascetic snapped.

"Ithien Eirillia, Governor of Ilthys in the name of the Assembly. I'm responsible for the welfare of my countrymen in Ilthys, which includes these people."

I looked around, hesitantly and still acting my part, at Mauriz, who was smiling slightly. The scowl he'd had earlier had disappeared now.

"They have been arrested on suspicion of heresy."

"On what charge?"

"I do not have to answer your questions. Now move out of the way before I arrest *you* for abetting heresy."

The Halettite leaned over and whispered something in the ascetic's ear.

"I am an officer of the Thetian Empire," Ithien said, not moving. "Your Edict gives you permission to root out heresy across the Archipelago. These are Thetian citizens, and they are not covered by your Edict."

"The Edict demands that all secular powers cooperate with us on pain of excommunication." Whatever the Halettite had said, it hadn't moderated the other's tone. Although the ascetic wasn't Halettite or Tanethan, it was hard to tell where he was from. I guessed it was somewhere a long way from Thetia.

"That's as may be," said Ithien. "You will explain the circumstances, and should it be deemed a genuine charge there will be a secular trial."

"Out of the way!" the Halettite commanded. "We are men of the cloth, representatives of Ranthas on Aquasilva. He who obstructs us obstructs the work of Ranthas. Your Emperor has given his full support to this, so let us pass."

"The Emperor does not have as much power as he thinks he has," Ithien said. "I shall be back."

"Bring a Canteni with you, Ithien," Mauriz called from behind me. "They're in for a shock."

"A Canteni? I'll bring one, and more besides. Trust me, Mauriz."

Ithien and his companions turned their horses and trotted away, for all the world as if the Domain wasn't there. It seemed that Thetia, and its people, were more complicated than I'd ever imagined. It was breathtaking, the arrogance Ithien had just displayed toward people feared by the rest of the world. He was, as I was shortly to discover, unusually self-confident as an individual. But not for a Thetian representative. And his authority was even higher than Mauriz's.

As the Inquisitors started moving again, I still couldn't imagine how Ithien could secure our release. There would be Scartaris troops in this city, but they would be in no way a match for the Sacri, and it was unthinkable that the imperial garrison would intervene. To take up arms against the Domain would be a condemnation, no matter how powerful the clan. And he couldn't know the circumstances, so why was he that confident?

People moved out of the little procession's way as it passed through the streets, unguarded faces showing fear and unease, some even bitterness. Which, I realized as they looked pointedly past me to fix on the Sacri, was directed at the captors, not the prisoners.

Thankfully, the upper town was more or less on a level, only rising slightly toward a fortress-palace at the far end of town, visible here and there through the rooftops. It had a different feel from Ral Tumar somehow, something I couldn't put my finger on. It was smaller, too, and I didn't see as many foreigners.

The temple was, as usual, on the main street near the market square, an unwelcome interruption in the colonnades that ran along both sides of the road. Ilthys was rather like Taneth in that latter respect, although the architecture was different. Even the temple, three stories high with a huge blind arch—too big for any door—dominating the façade, was in an Archipelagan style. Was it older than the Domain, perhaps, a temple of Thetis that they'd taken over and converted?

It was actually quite a pleasant temple, for all that the Domain had tried to alter it. They led us inside, through a beamed entrance hall with stars painted on the ceiling, around the sanctuary to the complex behind it. One of the ascetics escorting Sacri told Ravenna and me where to put the Halettite's luggage, which we dutifully did before returning, as instructed, to the hall. The temple was already crowded with the ascetic's tribunal, so I wondered where the other Inquisitors would lodge.

The two leading Inquisitors had disappeared, while their junior brethren were keeping a watchful eye on the people assembled in the hall. Novices moved the long table aside, setting up chairs for the Inquisitors on the dais. They were trying to hurry the proceedings, I thought, perhaps to secure a conviction before the Thetians arrived and complicated matters.

There was no way they could finish in time, however much they hurried. Trials took a couple of hours at least, Ravenna whispered, standing next to me at one side of the refectory, separate from the others. We seemed to have been dealt with already, as far as I could tell. Or were we to be put in with the Scartarans once the Inquisitors returned? I was still afraid, but not the way I had been before. Though it sounded selfish, it was because I knew I wasn't the focus of events. And Mauriz, who was, seemed to have more than his fair share of support.

The Inquisitors didn't reappear until everything was in place; then they made a ceremonial entrance through a side door. They appeared more daunting than before, gliding up to the chairs on the dais with that effortless walk that was one of their more unnerving characteristics.

Once they'd sat down and the two leaders had been joined by a third, the Halettite made a slight gesture to one of the Sacri, who pushed Ravenna and me to join the group in the center. I was an idiot to have imagined it would be otherwise.

There was a prayer before they began, intoned by another Inquisitor standing to one side, asking for Ranthas's blessing on their actions.

"You rendered aid to heretics and renegades in contravention of the Edict Universal of Lachazzar," the ascetic began, the formalities over. He was talking to Mauriz now, standing by the first and third officers of the *Lodestar* in front of the group. "This is a law made by Ranthas, superior to all earthly laws, which you have broken."

"We gave aid to a ship in distress," Mauriz said matter-of-factly, making no attempt to shift blame on to the captain, who had died the night before. "Until we docked, there was no way to tell it was, as you claim, crewed by renegades. We gave them enough help to make them seaworthy."

"This does not prove your innocence."

"I do not need to prove my innocence, Inquisitor. Under Imperial law I have committed no offense, nor have any of the crew of the *Lodestar*. We are Thetian citizens and we do not come under your jurisdiction." His tone was flat, contemptuous. He had been less sure of himself on the ship; this confidence had to be something to do with Ithien.

"This is a court of Ranthas, not a court of man. We do not answer to any law of your Empire, even without the Edict Universal. You have heard it, or read it, you know the letter of divine law. You are charged with aiding heretics, which is punishable as heresy under the Edict. Can you prove your innocence?"

It was a Domain court, working under Halettite law, where guilt was assumed. The exact opposite of the Archipelagan system, something the Domain had long ignored. Except perhaps in Thetia. In any case, Mauriz was saved from answering by the sudden and unbelievably prompt arrival of nine Thetian consuls and the Governor.

Chapter XIII

Emerging from the door that led to the sanctuary, the consuls strode out into the refectory between us and the Inquisitors. Some were wearing clan badges—Canteni burgundy and Scartaris red and silver I knew, but I didn't recognize the others. One was dressed entirely in black and gold, and I wondered if those were Polinskarn clan colors, nothing to do with mind-mages.

Ithien was there too, but to my surprise he stood aside, and it was one of the consuls who began to speak, an older man with iron-gray hair. His colors were sky-blue and white, another unfamiliar clan.

"Ithien warned me you'd be conducting a show trial." He showed no deference whatsoever, a sight that warmed my heart. "This is not permitted under Thetian law."

"You are interrupting the work of Ranthas," the Halettite said, but he didn't sound as sure of himself as he had a moment ago. I could understand his surprise—I'd never imagined that all nine consuls and the Governor would appear to rescue a Scartaris crew. Which faction did Ithien's clan, Eirillia, belong to? I wasn't sure—not Mauriz's or Telesta's, I thought.

"What is the charge?" the spokesman demanded.

"Aiding heresy."

Ithien made a disgusted sound and walked across to Mauriz to ask him what the Inquisitor meant. Three or four of the other consuls turned their backs on the Inquisitors and came over to listen. After a moment a fat man in green and white buried his head in his hands in an exaggerated gesture of despair, then looked up and shrugged sadly. Green and white: Clan Salassa, if I remembered rightly. There was such a bewildering array of finery in the hall that it was easy to get confused.

"What can we do?" the Salassan said, incredulity showing in his voice. "I cannot believe it this time, what they try." His accent was very thick, and it sounded as if he was still learning Archipelagan. He started talking to the woman I thought was the Polinskarn consul in rapid-fire Thetian, completely ignoring the Sacri, the Inquisitors and everyone else. After a moment the Polinskarn consul gestured to the Inquisitors, talking with her hands the way Thetians did. It was amazing how much smaller the room was with the ten Thetians in it, their incomprehensible conversations ringing off the vaulted roof. The hall had wonderful acoustics.

"This is a properly convened Inquisitorial tribunal," the Inquisitor shouted, as one of the Sacri thumped the table with the hilt of his sword to call for silence. "I will not have these proceedings interrupted."

"I wouldn't bother if I were you," Ithien said, his lip curling. He was speaking to the Inquisitor over his shoulder, not even deigning to turn around. "Save yourself the trouble and let them go."

"Be careful, Ithien," Mauriz said, a note of caution in his voice. "Don't go too far."

"They act as if they own everything," the Governor said dismissively. "Let them have a taste of their own medicine for once. Is that really all they're accusing you of?"

Mauriz nodded. "I don't think a Justiciar would even hear this case."

"Justiciars know the meaning of the word *law*," Ithien said, turning with a theatrical flourish to go and talk to the spokesman—in Thetian again, presumably to irritate the Inquisitors. His exaggerated gestures had the smoothness of long practice, but this wasn't a man I'd accuse of being a mere show-off.

I looked up toward the dais, where the Inquisitors were glaring down. The ascetic's face was pinched and tight. How could this be happening? It was unbelievable that the Thetians could defy the Domain's power like this with no regard for the consequences. Surely the clans were more diplomatic than this? I thought clan politics was about subtlety and treachery, not this casual assumption that they had the power to do whatever they wanted. The Assembly, from what I'd heard, was a collection of spineless sybarites who caved in at the first sign of pressure. That didn't fit with the reality I was seeing now.

Up on the dais, the Halettite shook his head in reply to something the ascetic had said. They seemed to be disagreeing again, which was all for the good. The Sacri stood immobile, as they always did, and my eyes kept drifting back to them. Surely the Inquisitors could order them to seize the consuls as well? It wouldn't be a very clever move, but the Thetians were cut off from support in here.

"As Imperial Governor of Ilthys," said Ithien, breaking off his conversation with the consular spokesman, "I am putting a stop to this trial as a violation of Imperial and clan law." That sounded a shade more diplomatic, but now he was backing them into a corner, giving them no easy way out.

"I think you fail to understand, all of you," the Halettite said slowly, as if speaking to a child, "that your cherished law does not apply here. We are acting under an Edict Universal which overrides all other jurisdiction."

"Something puzzles me, Mauriz," Ithien said, his attention diverted, ignoring the Inquisitor and going back to the Scartaran. "How did they damage the *Lodestar*?"

Mauriz's reply was in Thetian, but I more or less knew what he was saying. Ithien's expression was outraged, and the round-faced, expressive Salassan looked horrified. He said something else, and I cursed silently at not being able to understand the Thetian they were all talking in. Two more of the consuls came over, and I saw worried looks on their faces as they conferred.

"He's saying this is why the Inquisitors are so confident," Palatine whispered. The Canteni emissary didn't seem to have noticed her—he was talking to a sharp-featured woman in colors I'd seen before but didn't recognize.

"There is only one law that matters here," the ascetic Inquisitor said, looking more confident now, secure in the knowledge that his mages had the ultimate answer to the Thetians' arrogance. "That is the law of Ranthas, which—as the defendants have found—is above all other laws. His justice will strike down those who sin against Him."

"Ithien's saying there's nothing to worry about," Palatine said, keeping up her commentary. "He says it gives them advantages for now, but there'll be a solution found soon, it's nothing to worry about . . . the others don't agree."

The orderly trial of just a few minutes before was descending into chaos. The Thetian consuls dominated the room, talking excitedly in twos and threes, while Ithien and the spokesman had begun arguing points of law with the Inquisitors. The hall sounded more like a crowded meeting place than a court, especially with the fast, musical chatter of the Thetians dominating it.

"How can they get away with this?" a bewildered Ravenna asked Palatine, her sullenness gone for the time being. "I've never seen it happen before."

"Thetia may not be as powerful as it was, and the Emperor may have more control, but these are still the great clans. Ithien knows he'll be supported on this." Palatine seemed on edge, but more with anticipation than unease. She'd never given any sign that she missed Thetia, but now I was beginning to wonder whether that had only been a pretense. Among her countrymen, she moved and spoke with a new vitality, something that pleased and concerned me at the same time. Would she forget the reason she'd come here, and be drawn back into the world she'd inhabited before I met her?

"But why are they so confident?" I asked her, masking my concern.

"The Thetians still rule the seas here. And we will never be persecuted, not in a thousand years. Only the Emperor can do that, but not even Orosius will allow burnings or Inquisitors in Thetia. They aren't under his control, so if he allows them it diminishes his power. They wouldn't answer to him, and he can't stand the thought of that." She broke off as the Halettite Inquisitor thumped a book down on the table and spoke into the momentary silence that followed.

"Our rights in the Archipelago are absolute," he said, clearly expecting this to end the discussion. "The accused may be Thetian citizens, but they committed the crime of aiding heretics in the Archipelago."

"We don't have time for this," Ithien said testily, from his expression already fed up with the Inquisitors' obstinacy. The spokesman laid a placatory hand on his arm and whispered something. Ithien nodded, and the spokesman replied.

"According to the Compact of Ral Tumar signed by the first Prime, Temezzar, and Emperor Valdur I, Thetia and Thetian citizens are exempt from religious law. Those who are charged with religious crimes outside Thetia's borders must be tried in Thetian secular courts. Under secular law no crime has been committed, so this trial is illegal."

As he finished speaking Ithien went over to the door and clapped his hands. Looking suddenly alarmed, the spokesman followed him. Ithien said something fiercely, imperiously, gesturing at us; the spokesman, less excitable, pointed at the Sacri.

"You would do well to remember whose authority you go against," the ascetic said. "Even by your standards, the contempt you have shown for His representatives on earth is counted as heresy."

I heard more footsteps in the sanctuary, and a man in fish-scale armor and a scallop helmet appeared next to Ithien; a marine commander, I thought, judging by the waving blue plume on his helmet and the silver trim on his dark blue cloak. Perhaps the commander of Ithien's guard? I found the sight of the marine and the Sacri in the same room rather incongruous; the glittering, almost alien armor of the Thetian looked out of place next to the fanatics' quiet menace.

"Very operatic," said Palatine musingly. "Although in a real opera, the bigwig would appear now and sort everything out. The Inquisitors get their just deserts, the lovers go off together, the President gets his clan back and so on."

I found it more like a scene from a twisted, incredible dream: the dread Inquisition humbled by a motley crowd of Thetians. I just wished it could have taken away some of my terror of the Inquisition, but even now, with their authority gone, the two men on the dais were still figures to be feared. I knew that the Thetians weren't rescuing us, but rather Mauriz and his crew. Ithien was here to protect his fellow Thetians, because there were some loyalties that cut across clan boundaries.

By birth, I was as Thetian as any of them, and it was strange watching my countrymen argue among themselves in a language I didn't know. I didn't feel like I was one of them; they lived in a world I had no experience of. I wasn't entirely sure I wanted to get to know it, but then, nor did I want to cut myself off from it.

"Outside, everybody," Ithien ordered. "Be quick. We'll deal with people's belongings later."

"The Inquisitor-General shall hear of this," the Halettite snapped, rising to his feet and angrily waving away the Sacri who moved to block the exit. "He and the Emperor will hear of what you have done, and we will see if you can defy them."

"I shall have your luggage inspected for heretical texts," was the ascetic's parting shot.

"Do that," Ithien said, as we followed Mauriz and the rest of the *Lodestar*'s crew toward the door. Palatine tapped Mauriz on the shoulder and said something in Thetian, to which he mouthed a reply, and she looked relieved.

We'd been freed without a blow being struck, but as we left the hall, crossing around the edge of the sanctuary past the temple's eternal flame, I remembered the look in the Inquisitors' eyes, and didn't feel quite as relieved. Things would go hard for any of us who fell into their hands again, and Midian would hear of this as soon as the Inquisitor could get a message to him. Midian already hated Archipelagans, and this episode wouldn't endear Thetia to him.

The smell of incense from the sanctuary followed us as we came out into the afternoon air of Ilthys, surrounded by grinning Thetian marines who seemed only too glad not to have been called on to intervene. Ithien's guards weren't the only marines there; each of the consuls had brought a detachment, although only the Governor's were armored. I wondered if Ithien's men knew how to fight, or whether their armor and helmets were fit only for the parade ground.

There wasn't a throng of bystanders as I'd expected, but passers-by, probably amazed at the sight of all nine factions cooperating, were staring curiously at the large group of Thetians.

"Thetians have their uses, wouldn't you agree, cousin?" Palatine said, smiling. It was the first time she'd called me that, and it seemed somehow out of place. Then again, perhaps not. I nodded happily, glad to be out of the Domain's hands, but before I could say anything, there was an amazed cry from one of the less observant Thetians, and suddenly a crowd of people was gathering around her.

"Palatine!" The Canteni representative seemed dazed, as if he'd just seen a ghost. As far as he was concerned, he had. "You're alive! I thought I recognized you in there, but I didn't want to say anything in case you're in other trouble with those carrion crows."

"I'm very much alive," she said in Archipelagan. Then the conversation moved into Thetian. The others' actions spoke for themselves, though, because a moment later the Canteni consul, a tall man several years her senior, stepped forward and embraced her. It was the signal for a torrent of excited speech, the disbelieving consuls firing questions at her.

Ravenna and I stood back and watched. It was hard to feel left out at such an obviously joyful time. All of them seemed pleased to see her, but whereas for some—the fat Salassan, the spokesman, the harsh-faced woman and the two other older consuls—it was merely a pleasure to find that a colleague they'd thought dead was alive, for others it was different.

To the Canteni and the three younger consuls, Palatine seemed to be more than just a fellow Thetian aristocrat returned from the dead. The sober-faced, serious Polinskarn consul gave her an ecstatic hug, and a tall man in sea-green treated her like a long-lost sister.

Even more astounding, the arrogant, domineering Ithien treated her with more courtesy than he'd shown to anyone. She returned it, which surprised me; I remembered the way she'd treated Mikas Rufele, who wasn't unlike Ithien, in the Citadel; it was an amazing contrast. As I watched them greet each other, though, I realized that they were more than just acquaintances, that Ithien must have been one of her friends in Thetia. I saw him ask her something and noticed her expression of pretended outrage. Then I witnessed something I'd never seen before. She let him kiss her.

He did it very formally, but it was the first time I'd seen her allow anyone that close. This was a homecoming for her, in a way, and perhaps that had something to do with it. But, for Palatine, who was the most reserved person I'd ever met, it was unprecedented.

It was a brief, touching moment, and then the marines started moving, and we were more or less swept along with the tide. I didn't know where we were heading, and didn't like to ask. We'd be there soon enough.

"Palatine told me what's in your luggage," Mauriz said suddenly, appearing by my side. "It'll be taken care of."

"Why are they behaving like that with Palatine?" Ravenna asked. She didn't like speaking to Mauriz, but there was no one else available.

He looked at her keenly for a second. "With her supposed death, she became almost a martyr to the republicans. She was something of an icon before that, because of who her father was, but I think she means more to us than Reinhardt ever did. I think this time the Emperor will have to think twice before attacking her."

Then Mauriz was gone again, and in a minute or two I saw him talking to a dissolute-looking older consul; I didn't know the clan, or which of the many colors he was wearing were the official ones. They all had the looks of bon viveurs, the older ones, except for the harsh-faced woman. More like my image of a Thetian than Ithien or Mauriz were.

As we trailed along behind the Thetians, I felt left out for the first time. These consuls belonged almost to a different world, one that Palatine knew well and neither I nor Ravenna had ever been part of.

We crossed the market square, following Mauriz as the most visible of the people we knew, and the fragrance of roast meats drifting out from a shop made me feel hungry. The Inquisitors had eaten well enough on the ship, but as for the acolytes' food that they'd given us—no wonder junior Inquisitors were so eager to demonstrate their zeal and climb the ladder to status and power. Did they give acolytes such awful food deliberately to make them more bad-tempered? Mauriz had better include us with everyone else when we ate at the consulate, I thought grimly—I was fed up with being a servant.

However, we weren't going to the consulate now. Just ahead, behind an open space with a fountain, like a cross between a square and a bulge in the road, was the Governor's Palace. It was smaller than the one in Ral Tumar, and it lacked the huge gates and the fortifications. This was more like a large consulate.

Ahead of us, Ithien and some of the other consuls had stopped and were talking by the fountain. There didn't seem to be as many as there had been outside the temple, and they were accompanied by some of the marine contingents. The harsh-faced woman wasn't there, and I thought one or two of the others had gone as well. Palatine was deep in conversation with Ithien, slipping back into her old world as if she'd been here with him all the time.

As we stopped, the untidy procession fell apart, the consuls bidding farewell to Ithien and heading off with their escorts until only Palatine, Ithien, Mauriz and Telesta were left. Ithien's marine detachment stood at ease a few yards away, outside the door of the Governor's Palace.

Palatine looked around, saw us and waved us over to the fountain, looking contrite. "I'm sorry, I shouldn't have left you, but I got carried away. Come and join us. Ithien, this is Ravenna Ulfhada, who's actually a Qalathari, and Cathan Tauro of Oceanus, who's actually a Thetian."

"I'm pleased to meet you." Ithien's gaze swept over both of us, quite politely. Despite his arrogance, he wasn't lacking in manners. "So why are you disguised?" he asked, an inquiring smile on his face.

He'd seen through it straightaway—was some of the dye wearing off, or was he just very perceptive?

"We had a slight disagreement with some Inquisitors," I said, truthfully. "This was Mauriz's idea."

"Anyone who disagrees with those parasites is a friend of mine," he said. "Do come inside."

We followed this strange, recklessly confident man into the Governor's Palace, which was rather similar inside to the Scartaris consulate in Ral Tumar. More spacious, I thought, looking around, and the arches of the colonnade were more elaborately decorated. The scent of greenery and the sound of running water drifted in from the garden in the courtyard, where a fountain carved with stylized leaves spouted three thin jets of water into the air, the drops catching what light there was as they fell.

As the door was closed behind us and the noises of the street were cut off, I felt again that strange sense of being in another world that I'd experienced in the Scartaris consulate. Traditional Thetian frescoes covered the walls, and shears sounded faintly from somewhere in the courtyard: a gardener clipping one of the bushes. It was a place apart, on a different, more relaxed plane of existence from the outside world.

"It's quite sleepy, really, Ilthys," Ithien said apologetically. "Busy enough for the Archipelago, but not if you compare it with Ral Tumar, or even a smaller Thetian city like Sommur. Or Mons Ferranis; now there's a strange place."

"In what way?" Ravenna asked.

"It has a different atmosphere from any other Archipelagan city," he went on. "People say it's like Taneth, only more civilized." From a Thetian point of view, at any rate. It wasn't really surprising, given that the Mons Ferratans weren't related to the Archipelagans or the Cambressians.

Ithien didn't linger on the topic of Mons Ferranis, though. "Cathan, Ravenna, there's no need to wear those servants' rags while you're here. I'll have my housekeeper find something silk for you both; not too ostentatious, because you don't need to draw the Inquisitors' attention, but better than what you're wearing. Mauriz, you won't mind my clothing them properly? Governor's prerogative." He seemed to regard us as within his sphere, even though we were technically Mauriz's responsibility.

A little while later, feeling considerably more comfortable, we were led through the back rooms of the palace and out into a walled garden. Water flowed down a series of terraces cut into a sculpted mound, splashing gently through a series of little pools. A tall semicircular hedge by the lowest pool partially concealed some stone benches where the four Thetians were sitting. A servant had brought a tray of drinks out, blue wine in tall, slim glasses, and Ithien proposed a toast to Palatine. Then I leaned back against the hedge, sinking a little into the slightly scratchy branches, feeling relaxed for the first time since that morning, more than a week ago, when the Inquisitors had landed in Ral Tumar.

"Mauriz," Ithien said peremptorily, "I think you could explain why you've caused all this trouble, and why in Ranthas's name you were going to Qalathar."

Mauriz told him, and when he'd finished Ithien looked over at me thoughtfully.

"Yes, there is a resemblance, even more so if his hair was the right color. So all those stories we've heard about the night of the Emperor's birth must be true. It puts the Chancellor's supposed plot in a whole new light, if he did steal a baby."

"Do you mean Chancellor Baethelen?" I asked, uncertainly.

"You know about that?" Ithien's expressive eyebrows flew up. "You know what happened to you?"

"My Oceanian father took me from him when Baethelen died in Ral Tumar."

"There were rumors for years that the Chancellor of the time, Baethelen Salassa, had been plotting something with the Empress," Mauriz explained to Ravenna. "He was supposedly murdered the night after Cathan was born, but not everyone believed that story. The

Dolphin Crown went missing at the same time, and people thought he'd stolen it for some reason, even after it turned up again. We always thought it was one of those stories that go the rounds with no basis in fact, but obviously it wasn't."

"There's a lot more to be told," Ithien said. "Baethelen couldn't have done that on his own. He had to have had help, so at least one other senior official was involved. And why did they do it?" He paused. "You're his twin, aren't you, Cathan?"

I nodded.

"And we all thought the whole thing of the twins finished when Valdur seized power." He looked at the others. "What happened to all the other twins? All the Emperors since Valdur must have had brothers, but they all vanished without trace."

"More to the point," Telesta said, "did Cathan have another uncle? Think about it: Aetius V, Cathan's grandfather, had three children we know about. Valentine, Perseus and Neptunia. Valentine should have been the heir but he was killed in an accident, so Perseus succeeded. Neptunia, of course, is Palatine's mother. By rights Valentine should have had a twin brother."

"Past history now, Telesta," Mauriz said dismissively.

"No, it's not," she insisted. "If Valentine had lived, he'd be in his mid-fifties now. If there was a brother, he could still be alive."

"Then we investigate," Palatine said. "But if he exists, he's been kept out of sight his entire life, and he's no concern to us. What matters is that we've got a chance now, a chance to remove Orosius. There'll never be another opportunity like this." She was more alive now than I'd ever seen her before.

"What we're doing isn't just for Thetia," Telesta reminded them. "It's to help the Archipelago as well." Even though she'd brought it up, there was an underlying assumption that it was secondary and that Thetia was most important.

"Of course, of course," Ithien said. "That's where it all begins, in the Archipelago. This is an evil time, with the Inquisition loose, meting out their parody of justice. There's discontent already, and think what'll happen when they reach Qalathar."

"There'll be more than discontent," Ravenna cut in. "Trials, burnings, informants . . . Do you have any idea what that's like?"

Ithien looked slightly put out at being interrupted, but gave a nod to tactfulness. "It needs to be stopped, yes. They're killing the Archipelago." His regret was probably more to do with lost profits and lost opportunities, the damage done to clan balance sheets, than to the lives that would be lost.

"We can't be too open, though," said Telesta. "We must be sure of support before we move openly. There have to be enough people we can rely on in Qalathar."

"Use rumor." Mauriz, this time. "Rumor's always powerful. Spread it around that a leader is coming—it'll soon be all over Qalathar, and people will believe it."

I shifted position on the stone bench; the marble was still very cold, and the hedge's branches were now digging uncomfortably into my back.

"The trouble is linking up the independence movements in Qalathar and Thetia," Palatine said, looking doubtful. "Aren't you just using Qalathar as a platform to start a Thetian revolution? The Archipelago deserves more than that."

"We need the fleet," Ithien said, nodding in agreement. "If we can sway the admirals, we'll remove the Emperor's support and be able to protect Qalathar at the same time. And for the fleet we require the Marshal," he added, looking meaningfully at Palatine.

I glanced around the garden, wondering whether someone was hiding behind the hedges or the fig trees. This was high treason they were discussing, and Ithien's safeguards against eavesdropping seemed to be non-existent. Did he even care? In the two or so hours since I'd met him he'd publicly insulted the Inquisition, the Domain as a whole and the Emperor.

"The Marshal?" she said, doubt sounding in her voice. "We're talking about removing the Emperor, for Ranthas's sake. You don't want to bring the Marshal into this. He's served that family for more than two centuries—do you think he'll turn on them now? Even on Orosius?"

"He despises Orosius, doesn't he?" I said, remembering a conversation in the garden of my father's palace in Lepidor, a couple of months ago. If I could nudge them into bringing Tanais into this, it might give me more leverage one way or another. I might be in their hands, but that didn't stop me from having my own plans, small though they were compared to what the Thetians were talking about. "He said Orosius wasn't a credit to the Tar'Conanturs, and he wouldn't tell me who I was. Maybe that means he was up to something as well."

Palatine gave me a wary glance as Mauriz said, "The Marshal's away so often we might be able to do this without him. If we can sway Admiral Charidemus and a few others even to stay neutral, it should be enough. All that really matters is that the Navy doesn't support the Emperor."

"This needs a lot more planning," Palatine said firmly. "We don't have Cathan's consent yet, which we need, and we must plan properly. Call in our allies, make sure we act together and at the right time. Nothing hot-headed, and nothing on our own. Agreed?"

The Thetians looked at each other, and Ithien nodded reluctantly, not used to having the law laid down to him.

"Plan, by all means, but don't delay too long," Mauriz said authoritatively. "We have the opportunity; Thetia mustn't suffer under the tyrant's heel any longer."

As the conversation veered away toward other, less explosive, matters, and Ithien and Mauriz briefed Palatine on the events of the last two years in Thetia, Mauriz's last words lingered on my mind.

It was painfully clear to me now that religion wasn't the only way to produce fanatics. I'd seen religious fanaticism too closely for comfort, but politics had always been a deadly game, replete with intrigue and scheming. Power and ambition were constants in politics the world over, but the Thetian republicans were motivated by much more than that. They followed an ideology, which put them in the same league, in a way, as the Domain.

It was like having cold water thrown over me, the shock of seeing Mauriz's cultivated, elegant façade crack to reveal the fanatic underneath. A republican fanatic, perhaps, less bloodthirsty than the Inquisition, but it was only a matter of degree. Ithien with his superior attitude and his tactlessness was no better. His fanaticism was of a different kind, masked by arrogance and that astounding self-assurance, but it was still there.

And Palatine, who'd been my closest friend for two years, who I thought had left Thetia far behind, was at the center of it all. They looked up to her—she was as much an icon for them as Lachazzar was for the hard-line fundamentalists. She'd always been a leader, a strategist, but at the Citadel and in Lepidor that hadn't stood for much. Here in the heart of the Archipelago, only a few thousand miles from Thetia itself, the stakes were much higher.

I looked at Ravenna as we were left behind in the Thetians' conversation, and saw the expression on her face for a moment before she noticed me and gave a faint smile. It worried me, because there'd been a determination in that look, a certainty that I hadn't seen for a long time. She'd come to a decision about something, and she didn't want me to have anything to do with it. Had I been more observant, I'd have realized what it meant. But I didn't—until it was too late.

Chapter XIV

Two days later, I was lying on my bed in the Scartaris consulate, listening to the rain beating against the shutters, when Ravenna knocked on my door.

A winter storm had descended on Ilthys in the afternoon, driving everyone under cover. It wasn't by any means as bad as it would have been in Lepidor; with no mountains to cause turbulence, the storm just swept over the low hills of the island. It was strange not to look up and see the faint, almost invisible glow of an aether shield protecting the city, and I felt exposed without it.

There was really no need, though. All a storm meant in Ilthys was that the windows were closed and nobody went out. The consulate was on the seaward side of the upper town, and I could dimly hear the sound of waves at the bottom of the cliffs, but that and the rain were the only indicators the storm was there.

Ithien had introduced us to a Thetian game that evening, to pass the time. It was played with a peculiar deck that had substantially more than the usual number of cards in it, and involved, inevitably, an awful lot of trading. They called it *cambarri* and, in one form or another, it was apparently the most popular game in Thetia, capable of becoming bewilderingly complex when played by experts.

And Ithien and Mauriz were experts, all right. Palatine knew how to play but was very rusty; Telesta didn't seem to have played that much, while Ravenna and I were novices, and ended up being robbed of our counters very quickly. Fortunately we weren't playing for money, drinks or any of the other stakes that were mentioned during the game. Someone's hoard of low-value coins had been brought out and used instead.

Cambarri was a very open-ended game, and when I managed to hold my own against Palatine for about two minutes, I saw how it could become addictive. We stopped quite early by Thetian standards, because even when Mauriz and Ithien gave us all massive handicaps, they still won easily. It was hard to tell how many of Ithien's stories of past games were true, but I was glad we hadn't been guests of the President of Decaris, the Thetian clan leader with the worst reputation for decadence, whose parties were infamous.

The others seemed to take those accounts seriously. Eirillia—Ithien's clan—was part of the Decaris faction, I discovered, and had a lot of assets in Ilthys, enough that the Decaris faction representative there was an Eirillian, the consul clad in sky blue and white who'd been senior spokesman. Despite this connection, none of them had a shred of respect for the Decaris President.

It was nearly midnight when we finished, so I went back to my room, getting rather wet on the way. Palatine, Ravenna and I had been lodged in a separate building in the garden, connected to the consulate by a covered walkway that hardly provided any protection from the driving rain.

I was restless, unable to concentrate on the Archipelagan novel I'd borrowed and not at all sleepy, so it was a relief when I heard Ravenna's knock on the door.

She was carrying two steaming cups of Thetian coffee. I accepted one gratefully and offered her the room's only chair while I sat down on the bed. It wasn't a very large or impressive room, obviously designed for putting up junior members of any visiting delegation, but it was much more comfortable than a penitent's cell on board the Domain manta.

"Can't you sleep either?" I asked, not sure that I'd believe the answer. It was a kind gesture of hers to bring me coffee, but, I thought, probably not without an ulterior motive. Not the way things were at the moment.

She nodded. "I'm not used to the storms here, I suppose. Or perhaps it's the after-effects of that game. Hamilcar might have enjoyed it because of the trading, and Palatine already knows how to play, but I was terrible."

"No worse than me." I took a sip of the coffee, which thankfully wasn't too hot. They drank it almost scalding in other parts of the Archipelago, but it was probably too warm for that in Thetia. "Or Telesta. Some Thetian she is—she was almost as bad as the two of us."

"Ithien's stories worry me terribly. How can they hope to accomplish anything when they have people like that in charge?"

"I'm not sure." The difference between the Thetians Palatine had described and the ones I'd met was still puzzling me. Ithien and his companions obviously lived well and sometimes loosely, but their energy and commitment didn't fit with her savage castigation of the clans for their decadence. "They seem far too confident."

"You don't think their plans will work?"

"They've got a long way to go. But now Palatine's taken over, things may change. Without her I wouldn't trust them at all."

I'd hardly seen Palatine in the past couple of days; she'd spent a lot of time talking in private with Ithien, Mauriz and another clan consul. She'd warned us in advance and said she was going to try and unravel what their plan was, but she hadn't finished yet.

"I don't agree with them, as you've probably guessed. They want you for Thetia, and Thetia alone. Ithien and Mauriz certainly don't care what happens to the Archipelago; I don't know how far Telesta agrees with them." I was taken aback by her sudden openness, the fact that she was willing to talk about it directly. It was unlike her—but then, she didn't seem to be herself anymore. She'd changed.

"I don't think Palatine will forget the heresy," I said. "Even if all the other republicans see it as a battleground, I think the Archipelago means more to her. I hope so, at any rate. She might even be able to do more for the Archipelago in Thetia, if she can bring down the Emperor."

Ravenna drew away from me slightly, and I knew instantly I'd said something wrong. "Do you think so?" she said neutrally.

I wasn't sure that I did, to be truthful, but this wasn't the time to antagonize her. Even though Mauriz's plan struck me as being far more realistic than anything else I'd heard, her presence was one of its fatal flaws. As for the other flaw, my inability to do what they required of me, Ravenna and the Archipelagans were a way out of that. I didn't want to do anything that would hurt her, or drive her anger at Mauriz's casual presumption to something deeper and more long-lasting. I suppose it was an entirely selfish motive, needing her to give myself an escape route from Mauriz's scheme. But what motive, in the end, wasn't?

"It's just a thought," I said, anxious to placate her. "Orosius is too dangerous. If he helps anyone, it'll be the Domain."

"He's your brother. Doesn't that mean anything to you?"

It was the first time anyone had said that out loud: a bizarre, almost hideous concept. It was Jerian who was my brother—a small, wild bundle of mischief who was constantly getting into trouble like any seven-year-old. That distant, malicious figure in the Imperial Palace in Selerian Alastre was no brother of mine—only he was.

"What should it mean?" I asked Ravenna, using one of the pillows as a cushion so I could lean back against the wall.

"You can't just see him as another enemy, no matter how terrible he is. Mauriz wants to use you to overthrow him and set up a Thetian republic. How long do you think Orosius will survive after that? An

Emperor without a throne, one who wasn't loved even when he still had power?" Her eyes held mine.

"How do you think he'd treat me if he captured me?"

"That's not the question. You don't have to behave in the same way as he does. The fact is, for Mauriz and his friends the Emperor is an enemy, the greatest threat to their plans. They have no link to him at all."

Rain was drumming on the shutters, a steady accompaniment to our conversation, but it was pleasantly warm inside, and the coffee had been made by someone who knew what they were doing. Ravenna herself or one of the cooks, I wondered?

"What are you saying? That I shouldn't oppose him because he's my brother? Of course I don't see him the same way as Midian or Lachazzar do but, Ravenna, he's still an enemy. I haven't grown up with him, I've never met him, and he stands for all the things I'm opposing. How much farther apart can we be? All that links us is having the same parents." I was keeping my voice as quiet as I could in case anyone was listening, but few of the palace staff who could conceivably be spies had more than a little Archipelagan.

"Remember, if you go against him, one of you has to lose. And the loser will die."

For Ravenna, who had no family, whose brother had been killed by the Sacri, I could see why it was important. *Brother* for her was an empty space where someone should be.

"Do you really think I want to?" I said, very softly indeed. Mauriz just had no conception that I wouldn't want to take what he was offering me.

"I don't know," she said after a pause, her voice slipping back into its old flat, emotionless tone. "Why not?"

"What would I gain from being Hierarch?"

"Power? Prestige? Wealth? Why else do people spend their lives trying?"

We were skirting around each other, neither willing to answer. Neither of us was sure what to say, in fact. How could I put into words the reasons why Mauriz's plan horrified me? There would be war whatever happened, and death, and burnings. There were ways out; there had to be, but they didn't all have to involve me like this.

"A life of ceremonies, attendants, where you have to live your life as others have to see it. Petitions, disputes, courtiers . . . it goes on and on." I sipped at my coffee, which was just reaching a comfortable temperature, and looked at her. "Do you know me so little, that you really think I'd enjoy it? That I'd want it, after Lepidor?"

"As I said, I really don't know," she replied, brushing the appeal aside.

"I wouldn't have thought so, but—you've read the accounts of the Tuonetar War. Would you have said Valdur always wanted to be Emperor? He tried to refuse the Hierarchate, then a few months later he murdered his cousin and took the throne."

I looked away again, a cold, empty feeling in my stomach. Did she really see me that way now? Had Mauriz changed her view of me that much? Valdur had been a monster.

"I shouldn't have said that, Cathan. You're not like Valdur at all—he was just the only Thetian example I could think of."

"Why Thetian? I was brought up in Oceanus. And I make a bad leader, please remember. Not like any of the examples you could bring up."

My voice was bitter. Twice my clanspeople had acclaimed me as a hero, both times after my own incompetence and indecisiveness had brought disaster. The bravery they'd praised me for hadn't been enough. It never would be.

"You're the only one who thinks that," Ravenna said fiercely. Then, almost as if that had been a slip of the tongue, "That doesn't really have anything to do with it. Ambition and greed can get you to the top, and leadership doesn't have to matter until you're there. Even then, look how many of the Emperors have managed without it. And if you managed to topple the Emperor, you'll have served your purpose as far as the republicans are concerned."

"So then I'm free to go my own way? Where does the Archipelago come into this, anyway?"

"That's part of the point. The Archipelago doesn't benefit from this. Sorry, Cathan, but you're not the answer—not your name, at least."

"Everyone's trying to persuade me," I said, her words confirming my suspicions. The whole purpose of that conversation had just been to make the republicans' offer seem even less attractive. "Mauriz says that I can help the Archipelago, you say I'll only cause trouble."

"You can never be anonymous, I'm afraid. Not now. But that doesn't stop you going your own way. The longer you stay here, the more power they have over you, because since Ral Tumar they think they can control you."

"You want me to leave?"

Ravenna shook her head. "You're the only one who can decide that."

"In that case, where is there to go? I'd have the clans after me as well as the Domain and the Emperor. I don't know the Archipelago at all, I don't have enough contacts."

She looked troubled, almost remorseful for a second, but then shrugged. "You know people from the Citadel. Laeas, Mikas, Persea—

her family live on the next island over from here. Admiral Karao's not always reliable, but he doesn't like Thetians or the Domain."

"I have to find the *Aeon*. Even if Palatine's involved with the Thetians, I can rely on you, I hope." I'd drunk most of the coffee by now, and, strangely enough, it was relaxing rather than stimulating. "We've still got a lot of searching to do before we find the *Aeon*. But we mustn't let her fall into their hands, or the Emperor's or anyone's."

"Who is there to trust with something that big?" she said. "It'll need more than two or three people just to use the SkyEyes, I'd think. It sounds like a very complicated system."

At least I had an idea of my own here. "That's where the Citadel should help. I know the heretic leaders are all cautious old men, but we should find novices who are willing to help. Maybe at the oceanographic academies, too."

"Only the Archipelagan heretics, though. I wouldn't trust Cambressians not to tell their government. And there aren't any oceanographic academies in the Archipelago. Not anymore. It's hard to trust anyone, I'm afraid," she said, with a strangely expectant expression. I was about to ask what she meant when I suddenly began to feel dizzy and very tired. Ravenna reached forward to remove the coffee cup as I slumped back on the bed, struggling to keep my eyes open. *Almost as if she's been waiting for it,* I thought dimly. Then I saw her face again, and finally understood—too late.

My limbs felt like lead, too heavy to lift, and it was with a kind of detached exhaustion that I watched Ravenna drink the last of her coffee. Then she lifted my legs up on to the bed, turned toward the door, and stopped. I wanted to cry out, warn somebody, but I couldn't. My throat wouldn't open.

She put the two empty coffee cups down by the door, came back and knelt by the bed. She paused, biting her lip.

"I'm sorry I had to do this, Cathan, but I can't trust anyone anymore. I can't let them proclaim you Hierarch for their own purposes, so I have to get there first." I looked up at her helplessly, trying to resist the urge to unconsciousness that was falling on me so quickly. I felt like a puppet, thrown down with its strings cut. By Ravenna.

"Sometime, if you can escape that name of yours, we'll meet again. Not before. Never before." Her words were coming in a rush now, perhaps because I was blinking, feeling my eyes closing . . . "People are waiting for me. Goodbye, Cathan. Always remember I love you."

Her last words seemed to come from a great distance away, and after that I didn't remember any more.

Chapter XV

"A manta left during the night," Mauriz said, after the aide had delivered his message. "It was scheduled, a Polinskarn manta. Ravenna booked passage with their factor the day before yesterday."

There were expressions of bewilderment on the faces of the five other people standing in the atrium of the consulate. On all except Palatine's, that was. The other Thetians didn't know why Ravenna had fled, and they were very worried indeed that she'd been a spy for someone. Not even Palatine's previous account of what had happened in Lepidor had quelled their fears.

"But why?" Telesta demanded. "If not to give us away, then why bother fleeing?"

"She was going to give us away anyway," I said wretchedly, my head still pounding. I'd barely had time to recover from the Domain's savage attack on the *Lodestar* before Ravenna's sleeping drug had hit me. She'd had to put in far more than was necessary to counter the effect of the coffee, the apothecary had informed me. Where there were Thetians, there were apothecaries who didn't ask questions, and the gaunt man who'd been called in to identify it was the same one who'd sold her the concoction.

"And you didn't bother telling us?" Mauriz demanded. He was angry, the first real emotion I'd seen him display, and in the dull, wet morning light of Ilthys I couldn't blame him.

"Palatine warned you in Ral Tumar," I said, but even now held back the whole truth. "Ravenna's very close to the Pharaoh. I think she's gone to tell her your plans, so that they can organize something of their own."

"She's betraying us, you mean."

"Yes, but not to the Emperor or the Domain," Palatine said. "She hates both of them. She's just a patriot who doesn't want a Thetian to lead Qalathar. Cathan had no idea she was going to do that. Neither of us guessed."

"The fact remains that the secret's out," Telesta said, calmer than Mauriz but still grim-faced. "So much for rumor. She'll inflame the Qalatharis against us. Mauriz, I think you should issue a general order to your people there. She's to be brought in and interrogated—eliminated, if that's impossible."

"No," Palatine snapped. "Absolutely not."

"She may be your friend, Palatine, but she could have wrecked our best chance. She's been a traitor in our councils: she doesn't deserve your mercy."

"She's also been more loyal to her leader than any of us have ever been. She fled because she was putting the Pharaoh before her friends. You may think that's misguided, but she is *not* a traitor."

"If we don't find her, your republic may be stillborn. And this is a clan matter."

"Find her, by all means, if you can. But if she dies at anyone's hands, I will hold you responsible. You should also remember that Cathan's feelings for her were somewhat stronger than anyone else's. If anything happens to her, I guarantee you'll have no chance at all of him helping you." Palatine said it better, and with more authority, than I could have. Like the others, she was angry, but all I felt was despondency.

"You won't be in time," Ithien said. He seemed to be taking it as a personal betrayal after the kindness he'd shown her. "She'll get there ahead of you and the damage will be done."

"There's also no way to get there at the moment," said Telesta. "That was the last manta going in that direction. Even once we've got her away from those grasping churchmen, the *Lodestar* will take weeks to repair. Ravenna's got a long head start."

"We'll have to ask the other clans," Mauriz said, with bad grace. "Discreetly."

"Cathan, I'm afraid after this we'll have to keep an eye on you," Mauriz said, unapologetically. "We're not sure of your commitment and we can't risk you being abducted by someone else. Like the Pharaoh's people, if there are any."

"No argument," said Ithien, to Palatine as much as to me.

She nodded reluctantly. "Remember he's an honored guest, not a prisoner. This will all depend on him in the end."

Would it really? I had been right, back in Ral Tumar, thinking that in not making a choice I'd forfeited the chance. I could see where this was going now, the inexorable way they'd bring me around to their cause, whether I wanted to or not. Oh, I could refuse, perhaps, but I was more or less in their power, and they'd secure my cooperation in the end by fair means or foul.

I was tired of being a pawn, caught up in one scheme after another. Even if there was no way out, I could at least try to make my own choices.

"Guard me if you will," I said, pulling myself up straight. "Don't worry about my commitment. I will help you."

Telesta looked hard at me for a moment, then nodded in satisfaction.

"A little delayed, but a good choice," she said, pleased. "And I think it's time we introduced you to some of the others."

I'd made the decision too late for it to mean anything, but at least I was involved of my own free will. I couldn't really have been thinking what I was committing myself to, but Ravenna's words and deeds of the night before were still fresh in my mind. I felt as if she'd betrayed me, even though it had probably been the other way around. But there had been no need to drug me, surely? Better for her just to have slipped away in the night.

But it might not have been enough. *Sometime, if you can escape that name of yours, we'll meet again. Not before. Never before.* She'd had to say that, and, clumsy as it was, I knew what she meant. It was small comfort to know that she hadn't been able to go without an explanation, or even that, quite obviously, part of her had wanted to do something else. But then . . .

Thetis, I wasn't even sure what was going on anymore. She was gone, that I knew. Gone to take her place as Pharaoh of Qalathar, to make sure that I wouldn't be the one to lead her people against the Domain, if it ever came to that. She hadn't trusted me enough to ask me to come, which I would have done without hesitation. I would have done everything I could for her as Pharaoh, but now I had no option left except the one she'd so bitterly opposed.

Days wore on in Ilthys, and mantas came and went, none of them going to Qalathar. One was expected soon, the harbor master had said, but it belonged to Clan Jonti, and they weren't to be trusted. They were as religious as any Thetian clans got, Palatine explained, and strong supporters of the Exarch—and thus the Emperor—in the Assembly.

Although I was gradually brought into their councils, watching their plan take shape as Mauriz grew ever more irritable with the days of enforced waiting, I remained lonely and isolated. Palatine was so much a Thetian now, in her element with her equals, people who were almost her disciples. Listening to them speak about the republic, on the occasions when they did, was almost as alarming as hearing Domain fanatics preach. I might have trusted her, and her relationship with me didn't change. But she was too closely linked with Mauriz now.

As were most of the other people I met. Of the nine consuls, three were staunch republicans: those for Clans Canteni, Scartaris and Rohira. As representatives of the factions headed by each of those clans, they had chosen their staff, as far as they could, to match their own ideals.

Of the six others, three—including the harsh-faced woman, who turned out to be the Jontian representative—were older, more concerned with pleasure than work, people who were unlikely to rise any higher. I didn't often meet any of those, and the Jontians especially weren't welcome in the Scartaris consulate. Then there was the spokesman from the first day, and the Salassan gourmet, who seemed to have been assigned to Ilthys because it was the place where he could do least damage. He was inclined to wax lyrical about the delights of Selerian Alastre, and the difficulties of getting any good food in uncivilized Ilthys. But despite his disdain for the supposed provincialism of the Archipelago, he could be good company.

And while the Polinskarn consul, plain-faced and unsmiling, was a stranger, she had Telesta as a guest.

Telesta had held herself apart from the republicans since we arrived, staying with her clanspeople in the austere atmosphere of their consulate. She'd come over to visit a few times, sitting in on discussions but rarely saying anything. There were too many unanswered questions about her now.

I went to see her a few days later, only to find her waiting for me to ask the questions.

There were no servants in the Polinskarn consulate, and it was a staffer who led me along the upper gallery of the courtyard to a library complex that seemed to extend far beyond the limits of the consulate itself, a warren of cubbyholes and suites all leading off the central rooms.

Telesta was waiting in one of them, a somber figure sitting in a wooden chair, surrounded by bookshelves. So many books! Rooms and rooms of them, shelves floor to ceiling. And this was only a small library in a provincial city.

Maybe not so provincial, on reflection. Ilthys was where the Archipelago and Thetia met, almost halfway between Qalathar and Selerian Alastre. A crossroads in summer, although with the coming of winter it was as isolated as anywhere.

"Cathan," she said, standing up and coming forward. "I've been waiting for you." She nodded to the staffer, who withdrew with a rustle of cloth.

"Waiting for me?" I said.

"Yes. No one likes being left in the dark, and there are many things my esteemed colleagues haven't bothered to tell you. Come into my study."

I followed her across the carpeted floors to a recessed door in the next room. The library didn't have an enclosed, musty feel to it, which was refreshing and unusual. The windows were shut, of course, so that the books didn't get too damp, but I could feel a slight breeze on my face. Were those ventilation shafts set into the white-painted walls where the bookshelves stopped?

"I thought you were only a guest here," I said, as she led me into a large, high-ceilinged study with two wide, arched windows.

"I'm a full Archivist." As if that explained anything. "The equivalent of a level below Mauriz in my clan," she elaborated. "It doesn't mean much, but there are three or four of these suites kept for visiting Archivists. Some people stay here for weeks or months, and they need room to work. Take a seat."

I was more or less used to sitting on divans by now, so I took a place without looking too graceless or feeling as uncomfortable as I originally had.

"It's late enough for wine—will you have some?"

I nodded, looking around for some indication that somebody was occupying this room, something that marked it out as Telesta's place, at least temporarily. She seemed so reserved, colorless even, that she was impossible to assess. But, aside from a few writing implements on the desk and some books on a shelf above it, there wasn't much sign of habitation.

I didn't have time to read the titles on the books before she gave me a glass and sat down, cross-legged, on the other end of the divan.

"What do you want to know?" she asked simply.

I was surprised at her bluntness, which could only mean she had something to gain from it. Well, I would make the most of it.

"Why, for a start." She knew what I meant.

"Why I've helped Mauriz and his circle? Why I would be concerned about it when I'm not a republican?" I'd suspected she wasn't for quite a while, and now she'd confirmed my suspicions—unless there were more layers here than I could see through. It seemed too elaborate, though, if she wasn't: why bother with a masquerade? What would she gain by deceiving me like that? As far as Mauriz was concerned, my worth was my existence, my name. Not what I knew, or wanted to know. Heavens knew, he'd been indifferent to that so far.

"Among other things."

"One at a time." She smoothed back her hair, an entirely unconscious gesture I'd seen before and been comforted by. She didn't have the precise control of, say, the Sacri, although she always seemed very still. It made her more human. "How much do you know of Polinskarn?"

"You're historians, chroniclers, you collect books and keep yourselves apart from the other clans."

"That's how we're seen. Collectors of knowledge, not just of books. Our archives are bigger than the Great Libraries, because we've been collecting for longer and more efficiently. There are few books we don't have, maybe a couple of dozen in all the world. Mostly because they're on the Domain's High Index and even their existence is heresy."

"The archives of the War?"

She fixed her gaze on me for a moment and I held her stare, uneasy as it was. "Later. As far as Thetia is concerned, we're a source of information for the other clans. Always for a price." She smiled faintly, which reminded me unaccountably of Ravenna. There was a similarity there to the old, emotionless Ravenna, something in her general manner, but nothing more. Palatine's vitality and her quick, impulsive movements and judgments were absent in Telesta.

"So you sit on the sidelines, always separate, and flap like birds of ill omen in your black tunics?"

"Mauriz has a way with words. I don't agree with him on a lot of things. You're one of them."

"The same way you'd disagree on whether the *Elexiad* cycle glorifies war or not?" I wasn't going to let her talk about me as if I wasn't there. Not now.

"No. The *Elexiad* may mean something in the courts of Thetia, but not here. To everything there is a season, and this is a time for war, not poetry. Not that you can separate them entirely, or forget poetry entirely in wartime."

"*I sing of arms and the man, 'who came forth from the walls of Tir.*" The opening line of the *Elexiad*, setting the tone until the last words: "*And his spirit fled, sighing and angry, to the shadows.*" It began and ended with war, but Thetian poetry was never one-dimensional. Even the bad verse pretended to be more than that.

"So I'm more to you than just an intellectual distraction?"

"You seem to think we're ivory-tower scholars, like you find in the Great Libraries. Unlike them, we live in the real world. We have clanspeople to support outside all this; they are the people who will suffer if Mauriz fails."

"Or if he succeeds."

"If you become Hierarch, you mean?"

"That's only part of it, the part I know. There's more, which I'm not considered trustworthy enough to hear yet."

"You won't hear it from me." Impassive as ever. Outside the windows, the sky was darkening, the clouds growing grayer.

"I didn't expect to." She did know, I was sure, but there was no reason for her to tell me. I was the one at a disadvantage here.

"You didn't come here just to find that," she said, matter-of-factly, after a moment's pause. "Palatine could have told you. There's something else, something that you think only Polinskarn can help you with; the clan, not me in particular."

She was more perceptive than she seemed. Even a Polinskarn librarian, as reserved as she was, couldn't afford not to be. I couldn't tell how much a daughter of her clan she was; there was no way that all the Polinskarn hierarchy would hold the same neutrality.

"There might be," I said, sidestepping the issue. "Your library here is supposed to be the best one in the Archipelago outside Domain control."

"You want to use it."

I nodded. "If you'll let me."

"It won't be free," she said. "We wouldn't have got where we are by letting just anyone use our libraries. And you have more to offer us than mere gold."

I'd known there would be a price, of some kind, and also that it would be something other than money. "Then what?" I said.

Telesta paused for a moment, her watchful gaze fixed on my face.

"Something unique, that only you can give us."

"Aren't I something unique anyway, as far as you're concerned? You helped rescue me in Ral Tumar. Surely your clan's not going to sit by while Mauriz takes over? You must have a plan of your own, or is it enough to watch Mauriz plunge everything into chaos?"

"Chaos isn't good for historians," she remarked. "It makes waves in the inkwells, and we have to mop it up."

She said it with her usual detached seriousness, but it sounded almost like a flash of humor. What passed for humor among historians, at any rate.

"What, then? Mauriz's plan can't fail to make waves, so unless you actually want everything to fall to pieces . . ."

"You're a pawn as far as everyone in this is concerned. You're not rich, you're not well known yet, and most importantly you don't have a power base. We all have our clans—the Emperor his agents, the Domain their priests and Inquisitors. From what I've heard, there's nobody outside Oceanus you can rely on, no group of people following your cause. Am I right?"

She was, which made admitting it even more galling. Even if I'd had a power base of my own, I wouldn't have told her but, as it was, I didn't. Only an unreliable, slippery Cambressian admiral and a cautious Merchant Lord. Both with their own followers, their own agendas. I didn't include Marshal Tanais—he was a force of nature, an unknown, whose price could well come even steeper than Mauriz's.

"Everybody's help comes with a price tag, including yours," I said, before she could continue. "That's what you're saying. But I don't know your price, because you haven't told me what I am to you."

"You can work it out for yourself," she said, uncrossing her legs and going over to fetch the wine flask. I'd drunk my glass without even noticing, and wondered if she knew how little I could take. Two would have to be the limit.

What did she mean? What did I have that would be valuable to Polinskarn—or what might I have, if Mauriz was successful? My gaze followed her across the room, then I took the chance to look over at the books on the shelf above the desk, as if they could give me any inspiration.

I was too far away to make out more than a blur of lettering on most of them. I thought some might have been Thetian histories, and on the spine of one the word *Alastre* caught the light. Only on the nearest one could I read anything else, the title *Ghosts of Paradise*. I knew that title, knew it very well, but I couldn't immediately place it.

I couldn't make out the author's name, though, and once again Telesta got in the way, handing me another glass of wine. I wasn't sure if she'd noticed my scrutiny of the shelves.

"You want knowledge, books, something like that?" I hazarded. "A kind that would make you much more powerful."

"Very cynical, but quite right," she said, unperturbed. "Never believe a Thetian who tells you he's working for the common good. Or a Tanethan."

The Tanethans were more blatant about their ethos of pure profit, though, and lacked that irritating sense of being a people apart. Lord Foryth looked down on everyone and everything, but it was because he was rich, powerful, and could afford to. For the moment.

I thought for a moment, wondering what they could get out of me. I didn't know the locations of any secret libraries, nor did I have access to any hidden knowledge. Except the heretic collections, and surely they were too small.

"The Imperial Archives in Selerian Alastre?" With any luck, I'd never be in a position to control access to those.

"We can get into those ourselves once the Emperor's gone," she said, with a faint smile. "There is another place, somewhere that no one has seen for two hundred years."

Two hundred years. A city lost since the usurpation, a city that moved with the tides. She was demanding *that* as payment for a few hours in a library?

"Too much," I said flatly. "I don't know what was in the Sanction library, but it's worth more than what I'm asking."

"It's a fair exchange." She didn't look ruffled by the refusal. "You spend some time in our library, we spend some time in yours."

My library. The absurdity of it. I laughed, not seeing it as funny at all. "You want me to let your clan loose in the Sanction library? What gives me the right to do that?"

"You're the Hierarch, Cathan. Sanction belongs to you, as it always has. You may not have any power at the moment, but one day, perhaps, things will be different. We're asking something that you might never be able to grant."

Sanction belongs to you, as it always has. Her words seemed a bitter mockery, true though they were. The ancient residence of the Hierarchs, something else that was much older than the Empire it had been a part of. Carausius had loved the city, though he'd never fully described it in the *History*. To even think that it belonged to me felt like arrogance of the worst kind. I didn't even have the Hierarch's title, and probably never would. Sanction was unreal, a city that might not even exist, and hardly something I'd thought about.

It was unreal. I bit off what I was about to say and looked over at the bookshelf above the desk again. *Ghosts of Paradise*—I knew what the title meant now, what it signified.

Telesta looked at me questioningly. "What is it?"

"That book," I said, pointing at it. Trying to keep my voice calm despite a sudden rush of excitement. "Why do you have it?"

"Do you think we take any notice of the Domain indexes of banned books?"

"That's more than just banned."

"Salderis was one of us. A Polinskarn. That still matters."

"Could I have a look?" That she carried a copy around seemed unbelievable. There couldn't have been more than a dozen or so copies left, especially when so few had been printed originally. The book was on the High Index, and I'd have thought any copies Polinskarn possessed would have been sealed away in the central clan library. To find one here . . . I just hoped she wouldn't immediately demand something in return.

To my surprise, she didn't, and a moment later I was holding what had to be one of the rarest books in the world.

"First-generation copy," Telesta said, sitting on the edge of the couch beside me. "Printed in a hurry, so not as good as the originals, but more than adequate."

It was a plain volume, bound in treated bark like most Archipelagan books, and quite slim. Just a title on the cover, *Ghosts of Paradise*, and the author's name, Salderis Okhraya Polinskarn.

I opened it almost reverently, feeling the same way as the first time I'd seen the *Histories*. There were no elaborate titles, no dedications or endorsements by one authority or another. Not even a publisher's symbol, because no one would have dared admit to publishing this.

The typeface was heavy, irregular, as if the text had been printed by an apprentice. But it was readable. That was all it needed to be.

It was a lifetime's work in less than two hundred pages. I knew so little about it that my ignorance was frustrating. But if this was all it was supposed to be, even without the Domain's hysterical description of it as a work of the blackest deviltry and the foulest paganism—*paganism*, for Thetis's sake, they had descended to that level to blacken Salderis's name—then I had to read it.

Telesta caught the expression on my face and smiled.

"I think I'm beginning to understand some things now," she said. "How much do you know about Salderis?"

"As much as anyone, or as little as anyone," I said. "More of the oceanography than most people." It had been Lepidor's Master who'd told me and Tetricus about her, as much a cautionary tale as anything else. I'd never been sure whether he respected or loathed her: respected her for her ideas or loathed her for the damage she'd done to the Guild, ending the era of cooperation between Domain and Empire that had reached its height with the *Revelation*. Salderis's book had been published less than a decade later, while the memory of the ship's loss had still lingered.

"She's not widely known anymore." Telesta stared down at the book, looking regretful. "The Domain have demonized her, altered the records. Witchcraft, paganism, heresy, debauchery—there was nothing they didn't accuse her of. Children can't even be named after her."

"An extreme reaction, even for them. She said that the storms were made by humans and they could be understood, even unmade, by us. Yes, it's dangerous, but not that bad."

"You haven't read it, have you?"

I shook my head.

"What you just said is what it seems to be about—on the surface. But it isn't just the idea that threatens them. The Domain doesn't depend on control of the storms, although the protection they give is very important."

Just how important was something not even she knew—but Salderis might have done. I *had* to read this book.

"Why, then, did they try to destroy every copy? Surely that's bound to bring it to the attention of the few people who might be able to use it."

"It was the rest of the world they were worried about." Telesta's voice had an uncharacteristic fierceness. "It's obvious to anyone who reads it. There's nothing we can do about the storms; what she proposed needed far more energy than all the mages in the world could provide. But she proved that a religious problem could be solved using science. That the Domain weren't the only people qualified to deal with the world."

I stared at her for a moment, nodded slowly, realizing what she meant. People would question—if the storms could be explained by science, then what about *other works of Ranthas*? The Domain knew the power of ideas, a power they had used better than anyone. In the wrong hands, it could be devastating for them.

"So the book isn't so much about storms as science itself?"

"Not for Salderis, it wasn't. It was her life's work, although she was only forty or so when she finished it. She was writing about the storms— she doesn't seem to have seen the danger."

"How could she not?" I didn't believe that. A Thetian, not knowing what she was doing in researching the storms? It was hardly a political nicety.

"It's a failing of my clan that we can lose touch with reality sometimes, closeted in our fortresses. She seems to have lived in a world of her own, not caring about politics or religion. Science was what mattered to her."

I was about to reply, but I cut off the words before I said them. I could bring this up another time. I didn't want to annoy Telesta by challenging her view—and for all I knew, it could, conceivably, be true. Polinskarn was a strange clan.

But then, they had their own myths, their own reputation, and what better way to defend without insulting anyone the blemish Salderis had left on their reputation? A genius in a different reality, who hadn't meant to cause the furor she did. A martyr, even, to the cause of learning, although they'd never say so in as many words.

It was clever, and it served to exonerate themselves at the same time. Salderis had been a maverick.

"Could I read it?" I asked hesitantly. "That, and explore the rest of your library, in exchange for letting you have limited access to Sanction one day?"

"How limited?" Strange she might be, but she was still Thetian. Ever the merchant.

I almost certainly conceded more than I should have, but she'd found my weak spot and she knew it. In the end we came to a deal that didn't give too much away, didn't leave me feeling as if I'd thrown the secrets of the universe open to the highest bidder.

"You'll have to read it here, though," Telesta said apologetically. "We're not likely to be leaving anytime soon, so if you come over here for a few hours every day, that'll be enough. Mauriz mustn't think we're planning something separate."

"So you're going along with him now, to get into Sanction?"

"More or less," she replied, almost offhandedly. "There are other things here and there, but that's the most important."

I stayed with her to eat supper in the Polinskarn consulate, where they served food at all hours. It was much later than I'd thought, in fact, and the Scartaris embassy would be closed down for the night. My escort was bad-tempered when he was finally rousted from the guardroom, obviously preferring his own mess to the company of the Polinskarn marines.

But I left with more hope that I'd come with, going back through the rain with the certain knowledge that it didn't take magic or armies to hurt the Domain.

Chapter XVI

On either side walls of gray and green were rising up out of the water. Knobs of rock, all of them weathered by wind and water, protruded here and there from the vegetation covering the cliffs. The strait couldn't have been less than seven or eight miles across, but it felt much smaller. The mountains surrounding it towered over everything, obscured by the layer of mist that mirrored the gray water.

And the spray—the Jayan Strait was even rougher than the open sea, a funnel for the waves that crashed over the galleon's bow, drenching everything in sight. Already soaked to the skin as I sat in the waist, I didn't care. I wasn't going to sit below decks now, and the overbearing Mauriz wasn't going to come on deck. A perfect arrangement.

I scanned both shores for signs of life but saw nothing, only more cliffs as the straits curved around and opened out into calmer water, protected from the fury of the ocean. Not the Inland Sea, at least not yet. But still no buildings, settlements, signs that people lived here. Only a wild, primeval forest like a shadow over the slopes of the mountains.

It was ominous, as Ravenna had said, but not depressing. The sky and sea might be dull, lowering, but the sheer impact of Qalathar was too much for them to obscure. To me it seemed a world apart from the paradise islands of the rest of the Archipelago. There were no palm trees, no gentle, sloping beaches, no rounded hills, no white cities clustered by the shoreline.

Qalathar's cities weren't white. I knew that from the descriptions I'd heard. But as with Qalathar itself, no description came anywhere near the reality.

As the galleon tacked its way into the open water at the center of the strait, I finally got a glimpse of the city of Jayan, sprawled along the shoreline under an out-thrust promontory of the mountain. It couldn't have been much bigger than Lepidor, but it seemed to be from a different planet. Jumbled terraces of low, columned buildings rose up from the gray water, broken here and there by trees and gardens, ever-present in the Archipelago.

But Jayan was a world away from Ral Tumar. I stared in amazement at the vibrant reds and blues of the city, almost like a potter's creation. There was no white, no gray, no gold; the stone itself seemed to be that incredible shade of red, like burned terracotta, adorned wherever possible by blue like the sea in a fairy tale.

Jayan was no metropolis, just the city guarding the strait. I was to see other and bigger places in Qalathar, but here was the first tangible evidence of just how different the Island in the Clouds really was. And of why Ravenna had done what she'd done, for the sake of this strange, alien land wreathed in mist.

Oddly enough, though, as I kept my lonely vigil during the long passage through the Jayan Straits, going below only when I had to, it never felt too strange. Not in the way Taneth had, the first time I'd seen it—an immense, crowded, hostile place. Qalathar had something else, an other-worldliness that I couldn't put into words, or even into coherent thoughts. But I wanted to know it better.

Jayan slipped by, and two smaller towns along the coast whose names I didn't know, clusters of red buildings under the lee of the forest. The strait widened gradually, the shores falling away on either side. Still close enough to be a presence, though, sharply defining the edges of the strip of gray water we were sailing over.

A sudden squall reduced the land to a gray blur through sheets of water; the rain drumming on the sails and the deck drowned out all other noises, even the seabirds with their lonely, desolate cries. But it cleared as quickly as it had come, the scudding clouds sweeping across the surface of the water like the shadow of a kraken.

There wouldn't be any kraken here, or in the shallow waters of the Inland Sea, which in many places was barely deep enough to operate mantas. One place where the *Aeon* wouldn't be hidden, at least, which only left the rest of the planet to search. And no oceanographers here to speak of. There'd been a huge station in Poseidonis before the Crusade because of the uniqueness of the Inland Sea and the creatures in it. But now that was gone, razed to the ground, and the oceanographers had been burned as heretics. The creatures living in the sea were Ranthas's creation, the priests had declared. It was not the oceanographers' place to study them, just to assist sailors and fishermen.

The shadow of the Domain was never far away in Qalathar.

It was in the early evening, the leaden sky darkening without a hint of a sunset, that the galleon passed the line where the shores fell away into murky distance, and entered the Inland Sea.

At last there were more ships here, dark silhouettes against the water and the gray line of mountains surrounding everything. Not as many as I'd imagined, though that was hardly surprising on an unpleasant winter's evening, but more than there would be anywhere else at this time of year. Ringed by the mountains, Qalathar was protected from the fury of the storms, whatever direction they came from.

I was still left alone as the galleon beat its way around to port, setting a course through the uneven mass of the Ilahi Islands for Qalathar's capital. Ravenna would be there somewhere, unless she'd been hidden away by her loyalists. But I doubted that. I couldn't see her letting herself be trapped in the mountains while others did the work.

The mountains. I looked back over the ship's quarter, back toward the west, but there was only water and cloud. Too far to see the titanic cliffs of Tehama that Ravenna had described. Just a darker line of purple cloud in the distance, with occasional flashes of lightning.

We had the wind in our favor now, so it wasn't long before we were sliding through the outer channels of the Ilahi Islands, huge masses of rock rising sheer from the sea, a few of them with towns perched below their peaks. I wondered how anyone could get to them; there didn't seem to be any harbors to speak of, and some of the islands had vertical cliffs nearly all the way around. Very defensible, but probably uncomfortable places to live.

I rather began to wish that somebody would come to join me, at least for a minute. Not Mauriz, because he was more than I could take at the moment. But I wouldn't have minded Telesta or Palatine. I would especially have liked to see Telesta . . .

I'd had too short a time in that library, only three or four days after Mauriz's temper finally ran out. There'd be no mantas going to Qalathar for another fortnight, the harbor master informed him. A terrible undersea storm between Ilthys and Thetia had made travel from the north impossible.

Mauriz wasn't used to being thwarted like this, and nor were most of his companions. Even Palatine seemed to have fallen back into Thetian ways, expecting things to go right simply because of who she was.

Escaping from the air of mutual recrimination that hung over the Scartaris consulate, I had spent most of the next couple of days with the Polinskarn. There were never many people around, and I had the time, the peace and quiet, to read Salderis's book.

I'd always thought it had a strange title for a scientific work. *Ghosts of Paradise* sounded like a ballad, or maybe an old Thetian oratorio. But as I read it, working my way through Salderis's theory, it didn't seem so inappropriate anymore. Any mage worth his salt knew that the atmosphere was contaminated with residues from the Tuonetar magic used toward the end of the War. Despite their advances the Tuonetar had been overstretched, forced to rely more and more on magic to help their exhausted troops.

What Salderis, not a mage, had realized was that the residue was something more than that.

Her theory was so elegantly put together that it was hard to believe how long it had taken her to develop it—and that nobody else had ever duplicated the feat. She wrote well for the ivory-tower academic that she was supposed to have been, and there were passages that seemed blatant contradictions of that view.

Not to mention the fact that she'd obviously been a field oceanographer for several years.

On the very first day of the Worldsend expedition we were trapped inside by the sheer force of the wind, which made it impossible to open the door. This wouldn't have been so bad if there had been any food in the building, but unfortunately there wasn't. The Worldsenders are used to this, and make provision for it, but as a group of ignorant offcomers we were totally unaware, and so spent an unpleasant few hours waiting for the wind to die down. It is a sad ruin for an archipelago dubbed the "Isles of the Blessed" by the first explorers to land there.

As far as she knew, no one had ever attempted to explain why Worldsend had been so devastated when seemingly identical island groups such as Ilthys had survived intact. She offered a few theories, a comment that the storms' effects on life on the islands should be looked into in at least as much detail as the storms themselves, and went on. But she'd left a trace of herself behind, the way that Thetians writing books always did. No matter how scholarly the work, the character of the author always came through.

There was very little mention of the Domain, except at one point.

It has long been suspected that the Domain have ways of predicting the storms and somehow warning their temples across the planet, although few actually know how this is done. Imperial Intelligence was most helpful in telling me (involuntarily) what little is known about the facility in the mountains north-west of Mons

Ferranis. It is heavily guarded, but it would seem that not all Sacri are immune to the urges that plague the rest of us, and can be persuaded to loosen their tongues on occasion.

As far as I can tell, the Domain have access to some kind of flying observatory, or at least its pictures, and can gain views of the whole planet from above, thus seeing the storms while they are forming. The scientific value of this is incalculable, but the Domain is not interested in science, or in the original builders of this flying observatory, whatever it is. It was there before the storms, which raises another question: are the storms and the observatory linked somehow? The Tuonetar were undoubtedly the catalysts of the storms, but was their ability to view the world from above a factor in the storms' original appearance? Most crucially, given the date of Midsummer 2559 for the first recorded superstorm, is it possible that the Tuonetar used the system to watch the storms unfolding?

She didn't mention the *History*, or even the alternative account of the War that it represented. Not even the Domain denied that the storms dated from the Tuonetar War, the after-effects of unspecified weapons. In their version, the Tuonetar had been defending themselves against unwarranted Thetian aggression, but the result was the same.

When I finally finished reading Salderis's book late that evening, I sat back in my chair and stared at it, still open at the last page. My body was stiff and aching from sitting in the same position for almost the whole day; I hadn't spent more than half an hour away from the library and there weren't any comfortable chairs in it—not for one still unused to Thetian furnishings, in any case.

It didn't matter. My head was swimming with a confused mass of ideas that I was still trying to grasp properly. I simply hadn't had time to absorb all of Salderis's theories, but I'd read her words.

The book's title had been entirely appropriate, it turned out, but I was still struggling to come to terms with the terrifying concept implicit in the last few pages. It wasn't until the end of the book that Salderis revealed exactly what she meant by *Ghosts of Paradise*. It was almost as if she'd crossed the line separating the genius that had inspired the rest of the book from a form of insanity. All that was left of a better world . . . had she been saying what I thought, or was my tired mind seeing things that weren't there?

I wasn't in a condition to decide at the moment. There was no doubt what the book itself said, and why it was so dangerous to the Domain. But what she'd outlined was dangerous for me, too, and the idea of interfering with the storms suddenly didn't seem such a good one anymore. I was dealing with things far outside human experience. The Tuonetar mages who had set off the storm cycle had been using human magic on a planetary scale. What I wanted to do was the opposite of that: to use planetary magic in an arena that was much too small for safety.

"Cathan?" I hadn't even heard Telesta come in. I looked up wearily.

"You're exhausted."

"How can I be?" I protested. "I've done nothing."

"Mentally exhausted. You've hardly moved all day, and you've read the whole of that book in a few hours. Most people take days to finish it, however hard they try."

"I haven't got that much time."

"It's still remarkable. Here, I'll give you a hand up." I closed the book and let her help me stand up. I staggered, felt a wave of dizziness, but managed to retain my balance.

"Thank you." It was dark outside the windows, and raining again, though the storm wasn't as bad in Ilthys as it would have been at home.

"Have you always been involved in oceanography?" she asked, extinguishing the aether torches as we left the small room I'd been working in for the relative comfort of her study.

"Just the sea, until I was fifteen or so." Not my only interests, by any means, but I'd spent far more time in the sea than had any of my friends, whether diving, sailing, or swimming.

"I wondered for a long time whether we'd made a mistake with you, that you weren't a Tar'Conantur. Everyone in your family's always very intense and single-minded about some things. Perseus was supposed to be like that about his music and his art. Palatine hasn't stopped thinking about establishing a republic since she came of age, while Orosius . . ." She paused, staring off into empty space. "Orosius takes everything to extremes. You never seemed to have that kind of passion for something, the way everyone else in your family does. Today, I've realized yours was just hidden."

"Have you met Orosius?" I found it impossible to call him my brother.

"A few times," she admitted, folding up some papers on her desk. "I worked in the Imperial Archives a few years ago, just after his illness, and he occasionally came down there. The Archives are a creepy place—I think he felt it was some kind of spiritual home. None of his ministers ever came in, in case they got lost. But sometimes I met him in the more remote corners. He was . . . unsettling. Very cold."

Her voice was calm, but it sounded to me like her feelings had been slightly stronger than those of mere unease. She was five or six years older than me, and he'd been thirteen when he fell ill. There was an obvious explanation for how he could inspire fear in a woman six years older, but I didn't think that was it.

"Don't worry," I said. Telesta didn't want to talk about it.

"I don't. I know he's your brother, Cathan, but there are few people in Thetia who'd mourn him if he died now. Certainly none of his own family would. Palatine hates him, Arcadius would crow with delight and rush back to make himself Emperor, and Neptunia wouldn't bat an eyelid." Neptunia was Palatine's mother, Orosius's aunt.

I found I didn't want to think about Orosius, not while I still had Salderis's words etched into my mind. I said goodbye, and went back to the Scartaris consulate in the pouring rain, my head full of current bands, storm cycles, whirlwinds, coriolis cycles and images of the desolate islands of Worldsend, barren rocks where there had once been green jungles and plantations. That was the effect the storms could have in the wrong place, used the wrong way.

Two days later, Mauriz paid the captain-owner of a cargo galleon an exorbitant sum to take us across to Qalathar. The man refused to take more than ten of us, so the marines who'd survived the *Lodestar*'s destruction were left behind in the care of the consul.

Sarhaddon and Midian would already have arrived and made their triumphant entry, I thought, watching Tandaris, Qalathar's capital, take shape on one side of the humpbacked hill ahead of us. The sun must have set, because the sky was a uniform dark gray, the breaks between clouds no longer visible. It was raining again, and I was beginning to feel the effects of having been out on deck so long in wet clothes. I'd been below an hour or so ago to dry myself and change, and I was now standing on the quarterdeck, wrapped in a storm-cloak, watching the lights of Tandaris in the darkness ahead.

"It would have been good to see it in daytime," Palatine said as she stood beside me. "Do you suppose it's always like this?"

I was in a more sociable mood, having temporarily lost my desire to be alone, and I was glad of her arrival. Like me, she was wrapped in an enveloping cloak and hood, almost like a priest's. The difference was that our garments were heavy and ungainly, whereas priests were usually given lighter ones, tailor-made for them and the climate.

"What about the tropical diseases?" I asked. Qalathar looked like the kind of place heavily populated by vicious, biting insects.

"You're so depressing sometimes. Besides which, you're Thetian—you won't catch anything serious."

It *was* a rather gloomy thing to say, really, but it had been worrying me. The island with the Citadel on had been free of mosquitoes and dangerous fevers, but almost everyone except Palatine had spent a few days wishing they'd never come when they'd contracted some unnamed illness or other. Palatine, of course, never caught anything.

"Fine for you to say. When was the last time I was in Thetia?"

"It's inborn," she said, with the irritating tone of somebody giving a lecture. "If we caught all those diseases all the time, we wouldn't survive."

Yes, I thought, *but that's Thetia. This is a different climate.* I wouldn't be much use as a Hierarch laid up in bed with any of the various unpleasant illnesses the island was probably plagued with. There'd be no way to escape in that state, which worried me more than the thought of the actual illness.

"Our ambassadors here are usually fine." Palatine caught my train of thought. "You will be too."

Thankfully the sea wasn't choppy, or we'd have had to anchor offshore and come in at dawn. As it was, the captain steered his ship into Tandaris's outer roads, until a harbor galley came gliding over the black water, flamewood lanterns burning at bow and stern, to take us in tow. One of her officers and a few men came on board, pulling himself up the side to make a check.

"Why have you come?" the officer asked, one of a group of figures huddled in the lamplight on deck. He'd asked the formal questions. "It's not safe here."

"We were chartered," the captain said, a hint of unease in his voice. "Thetian high-ups."

"How high up?"

"High enough, I hope." It was Mauriz, emerging from the companionway. "Just how dangerous is it here, Centurion?"

"A new Inquisitor-General arrived five days ago with a decree from the Prime. They've already started arresting people and hauling them in front of the tribunals." The officer turned slightly. His characteristic Qalathari face was unnaturally pale, and he looked haggard and tired. "They'll be burning people again soon, heretics they've taken on their way here. I have to ask, sir, who are you?"

"Mauriz, High Commissioner of Clan Scartaris."

"Ah, you're not in very good odor, then." The officer looked almost terrified now, and I saw a look of alarm on the captain's face. "I've got orders to alert the Domain authorities if you arrive."

"How exceptionally tiresome," Mauriz snapped. "Thank you for telling me, Centurion. I assume the Thetian Viceroy is still here?"

"Yes, he is."

"And a Fleet representative?"

"I honestly don't know. There are no Imperial ships anywhere in Qalathar."

Palatine and I looked at one another. *Why not?* I wondered. Had the Emperor withdrawn them to give a free hand to the Domain, or was there some other reasoning behind it?

We didn't get the chance to speculate, though, because the officer went on, "There are Sacri watching the docks, and two or three Inquisitors."

Although Mauriz pressed him, he refused to say any more. Just then the discussion was interrupted by some of the sailors, who took the captain aside. Away from Mauriz and the officer, they didn't seem to notice the two of us in the shadows.

"Captain, is it going to be safe going in? The crew don't like the sound of this Inquisition thing." It was the bosun, a short, powerfully built man with a shaved head. Very ready with his fists, I'd noticed during the journey, but not a bully. "I mean, it was fine back home, but they take it seriously here."

"Not if there's burnings, and tribunals, and things." I wasn't sure who that was, but he sounded nervous. "Ilthys is one thing, but this place isn't a joke."

"Not with these Inquisitors around." The bosun's gaze darted around as if he was afraid of being overheard. "And if these Thetians are wanted . . ."

"You mean you want to go straight back, without even spending a night here?" the captain said.

A third man, perhaps the sailing master, voiced his assent.

"We've got enough supplies, we can stop at Methys for fresh water. Passengers can go in on the galley, and we'll be out of the Inland Sea before dawn."

"I'll put it to them," the captain said, and walked back to Mauriz and the officer. "Centurion, my crew won't come on shore, so could we transfer our passengers and go straight out again?"

"We chartered *you* to take us to Tandaris, not the Qalathari authorities."

"I'm sorry, Lord Mauriz, but this is a private ship. If they don't like what I do, the crew can remove me, and you won't be any better off. And we won't take a pay increase, either."

Mauriz glanced over at the three sailors responsible, then back at the captain. There was silence except for the continual pattering of rain and the dripping of water on the decks. One of the Qalatharis fidgeted with his knife-hilt.

"Very well," he said, with bad grace. "I'm docking one-fifth from what I agreed to pay because you haven't delivered us safely to Tandaris. Go back home and spend it in Ilthys, where all the Inquisitors are paragons of virtue."

The captain looked as though he might argue, but the bosun shook his head. In the few minutes since the centurion had come on board with his news, a merchant crew willing to brave the terrible conditions of winter without complaining had become like frightened rabbits. There wasn't even an Inquisitor in sight.

I had an all too familiar feeling in my stomach as I went below decks to get my bag. Even before we'd set foot in Qalathar, the Domain's shadow had fallen over us again.

The ship's crew watched in silence as Mauriz handed the captain the remainder of his fee and then followed his luggage down the side of the pitching galleon into the harbor galley. One by one, the rest of us followed, taking up almost all the free space. The galley seemed dangerously overloaded, but none of the swarthy Qalathari oarsmen complained as it pulled away from the galleon's side and headed for the inner harbor.

Sheets of rain soon reduced the galleon to a large, indistinct form behind us, the captain's shouts and the creaking of its timbers barely carrying above the noises of water. Then only the lanterns were visible as the ship slowly turned about and vanished into the night.

"Centurion, do your orders consist of anything more than alerting the Domain authorities?" Mauriz asked tersely, keeping his balance despite the motion of the boat.

"No, but I'll have to detain you," the officer said.

"You don't have the authority. Send a runner up if you want, but that isn't a warrant to arrest me."

"Things aren't the way they were anymore, Commissioner. The whole of Qalathar's under Domain rule now. We have to do what they ask or the Inquisitors accuse us of being heretics too."

"The Domain comes before the law and the Empire, then?"

"Depends on your interpretation of the law, sir, but in reality it does. The Domain is the power in Qalathar, not Thetia. We're not protected by secular law."

"It has come to this at last, then," said Telesta sadly. "The Domain no longer bothers to recognize any law but its own."

"Who else's law is there in Qalathar?" the centurion demanded. "The Emperor doesn't care, the Pharaoh doesn't exist. Perhaps if you lived here you might understand how it is, instead of watching from your airy palaces in Thetia and demanding to be given rights when it suits you."

"Nobody's *given* rights. You *have* them. Including the right to law, which the Domain so carelessly ignores." Mauriz's tone was, as so often, contemptuous. "And the Emperor will care about Qalathar soon enough, because if he doesn't, he might find himself losing his throne."

I wondered at that—was Mauriz getting overconfident? But the officer only took it for Thetian noble's empty talk, and didn't bother to reply.

There were ships all around us now, mostly lateen-rigged Qalathari vessels, low and sleek, designed for fast passage across the relatively calm Inland Sea. But there were lots of berths empty, and very few bigger ships, Archipelagan galleons. There had been one riding at anchor farther out, its stern windows brightly lit and shapes moving within, but that seemed to have been an exception. Perhaps a Domain guardship of some kind, or owned by somebody who collaborated with them, like Lord Foryth in Taneth.

Taneth. I wondered how Hamilcar was getting on in his attempt to bring Lord Foryth down, in that sunlit city on the other side of the world where the Domain was a religion, not a government. He wouldn't expect to hear from us yet, and I didn't think he was going to. We'd promised to sound the dissidents out for him a long time ago, but that had been with Ravenna as a guide and before the Inquisition arrived. And Elassel, who'd gone with him to see what life in Taneth was like, free of any Domain interference—was she enjoying it?

I was still thinking about them when the galley drew up alongside its quay by the harbor master's office. The centurion and one or two of his men climbed out, then indicated for Mauriz and the rest of us to follow them.

I set foot in Qalathar for the first time in the driving rain of a winter evening, on the wet stones of a deserted, darkened quay. The ground underfoot felt just the same, but somehow everything was different. Whatever the circumstances were, I was in Qalathar at last.

Part Three
The Ashes of Paradise

Chapter XVII

Flamewood lanterns burned around the gates of the Viceroy's palace, casting a ghostly light through the driving rain. Set into niches in the monolithic gateposts, three on each side, they gave the whole scene an unreal quality, like a scene out of some ancient past. On either side the towering walls stretched away into the darkness, their huge stones stained a dull red that seemed almost black. The Tuonetar color.

But the last remnant of the Tuonetar empire lay many miles away, shrouded in the clouds, and we were standing in a rainswept street in Qalathar on a winter's night. The small group of people around me, huddled inside their cloaks, had none of the grandeur or power they'd possessed in Ral Tumar a few short weeks ago.

A small door swung open and another Qalathari officer stepped out, enveloped in a black cloak.

"What is this, Centurion?" he demanded of our escort, obviously unhappy at being disturbed. Predictably, the centurion didn't get a chance to answer.

"I am Mauriz, High Commissioner of Clan Scartaris, and as a Thetian official I request an immediate audience with the Viceroy."

I didn't actually know who the Viceroy was. There had been three, none of them actually Thetian, as far as I could remember, but the centurion's cryptic remark earlier, about the weakness of Thetian power here, was worrying.

The officer paused for a moment, studied Mauriz carefully, and nodded his head. "The Inquisition want a word with you, but that's not my problem. Come in. You too, Centurion."

One by one we stepped through the small door into a narrow gatehouse, out of the rain for the first time in what seemed like an eternity. Beyond it, a few more scattered torches illuminated a gloomy courtyard with a few palm trees and a silent fountain. Around the edge, a lighted colonnade wound its way upward, dry and welcoming.

It had been more or less inevitable that we'd end up here after landing, as the centurion was quickly worn down by Mauriz's abrasiveness and threats to call in the Viceroy anyway if he wasn't immediately taken up to the palace. After a quarter of an hour trudging up from the harbor, the land seeming to sway almost like the deck of a ship, I was thankful for the relative warmth and the roof keeping the rain out. I still felt slightly out of balance, but it wasn't too bad.

As the door closed behind the centurion's guard, there was a whispered conversation between the guard officer and his deputy, almost drowned out by the endless hissing of the rain. A moment later, the deputy ran off into the colonnade, a shadow against the painted walls as he made his way around and disappeared inside the palace.

"Who is the Viceroy?" I asked Palatine as quietly as I could.

"No idea," she said. "There was a good one for ten years or so—he kept the Domain vaguely in check—but the next one was useless. I think he got thrown out by the clan presidents. I'm not sure who replaced him."

The centurion was asking the guard officer, who'd taken off his black cloak to reveal a tribune's insignia on his otherwise plain uniform, what to do next. More soldiers appeared from the guardroom, their expressions very different from those of the men who'd escorted us. I guessed these were Thetian-Qalathari troops, protected by the Empire from Inquisition persecution.

A moment later the door on the colonnade opened again and the under-officer emerged on to the balcony.

"The Viceroy will see you in a few minutes," he called down to the courtyard. "Come up at once."

Palatine and I looked at each other questioningly as we followed the tribune out of the gatehouse and into the gently rising colonnade. The light here was warmer, without the unearthly pallor of the shielded torches outside, and the inside of the colonnade was painted in the vibrant reds and blues of the rest of the city. We left a trail of water on the dry stone floor as we went, but I was glad to be back in civilization after what felt like an eternity on a perpetually damp galleon.

"Can you smell spices?" Palatine said, just as the door was opened again and fragrant warm air wafted down the gallery toward us. More attendants spilled out and helped us take off the sodden cloaks. I couldn't feel much difference, because I seemed to be fairly wet underneath as well, but it was a relief to be rid of the weight, if nothing else. From the dye-stains on it, the rain had removed what was left of my disguise. I very much hoped there would be no more need for it, since Matifa was still in Ilthys.

Then we were ushered through the wide doorway and into a spacious, brightly lit antechamber with a marble floor.

Why the welcoming committee? I wondered as I gratefully accepted a cloth from someone to dry my face with. We seemed to have stepped through a door into a completely different world, a world that was almost overwhelming in the sudden shock of arriving there.

I felt a momentary dizziness, almost certainly tiredness, and squeezed the cloth against my head for a second. It passed almost as quickly as it had come, and I looked around to see the others, except for Mauriz, looking relieved to be inside. The Scartaran, of course, just looked as if this was what he expected.

As the servants withdrew, two more people appeared from one of the corridors leading off, and I stared at them blankly for a moment. Only for a moment, because then one of them cried "Cathan! Palatine!" and rushed forward to give me a crushing bear hug. Then, before I'd recovered from Laeas's enthusiasm, Persea gave me an equally warm but less painful embrace. It was more than a little bewildering to see two of my old friends from the Citadel here, although it was only to be expected, given their connections. How wonderful, though, to see some friendly faces at last!

"What are you doing here?" she asked, with a delighted smile. "We come to meet this dangerous high-ranking Thetian on the Viceroy's behalf, and we find you here."

"That's the dangerous high-ranking Thetian," Palatine said, indicating Mauriz who was watching us, an amused smile on his face, the first I'd seen there in a long time.

"My apologies, Lord Mauriz," Laeas said, turning to the Thetian. "I'm here to convey the Viceroy's greetings."

"Not very sincere, given the trouble I'm causing."

"Perhaps. But he'll definitely see you." Both Laeas and Persea were wearing the white of Viceregal service along with their Qalathari clothes, and were looking very official.

"It's good to see you again," Laeas said, turning back to the two of us. "The Viceroy will be very pleased."

"Why?" Palatine asked, but the Viceroy himself answered her, appearing in the archway ahead of us. He looked haggard, but his face lit up when he saw us, and he strode forward with a smile. Like his men, he was in uniform, unadorned except for the admiral's stars—Archipelagan stars, not Cambressian. My second surprise of the night, almost too much for my tired mind to take in. Perhaps one of the Elements was watching over us, after all, to bring us at the end of this long journey to the one high-ranking Archipelagan whom we knew, and—to some extent—could trust.

"Mauriz," he said, nodding to the High Commissioner. The tension in his voice disappeared when he turned to us. "Cathan, Palatine, I'm glad to see you."

"You've risen in the world," Mauriz said, almost exactly echoing Ravenna's words to this man when I'd met him for the first time, just a few months ago. "Viceroy of Qalathar, no less."

"And of a whole world of trouble," sighed Sagantha Karao. "But, all of you, do come in."

As we walked with him through the archway and along another brightly lit passageway, I still found it hard to believe that Sagantha was Viceroy of Qalathar. Ravenna had called him a true politician, someone who knew when to change sides, whose sympathy with the heretics was a flexible commodity. Had we—and she especially—died in Lepidor, he would never have forgiven the Domain and kept faith with his wardship of the city. But it wouldn't really have changed his political alignments, and I doubted he would even have considered revenge.

But just how flexible were his morals? Cambress, notoriously secular, was one of Thetia's two mortal enemies, and here was an admiral and ex-Suffete of Cambress serving as Thetian Viceroy in the Domain-controlled Archipelago. It would take a real logic-twister of a philosopher to justify that.

At least we had arrived safely here in Qalathar, and there could have been many worse people living in the Viceroy's palace.

Sagantha led us through a side door and into a reception chamber, thankfully furnished with chairs and sofas instead of couches, although all the furniture was in a Qalathari style. It was a diplomatic reception room, a point aimed very obviously at Mauriz. And the paint on the walls was unmistakably real gold.

"Do sit down," Sagantha said, instructing one of the servants to bring drinks. He didn't sit himself, but stood in front of one of the windows and surveyed the group. Mauriz stayed on his feet, too.

"I'll be quite frank, Commissioner Mauriz, and get this over with now. Then perhaps we can work something out," the Viceroy said, not waiting for the wine. "Your arrival here is unwanted, disrupts Imperial policy, and goes expressly against the wishes of the Pharaoh."

"As I've said before, Ad—Lord Viceroy—" I wasn't sure whether it was a deliberate slip of the tongue or not "—I'm a Thetian citizen and an official of Clan Scartaris. I can travel where I want."

"Quite true, but planning rebellion is generally frowned upon."

"Are you openly suggesting I'm a revolutionary? My republican views are well known, but only a priest would consider the two to be the same."

"I'm not *suggesting*, Mauriz. I know," Sagantha said coldly. I saw Laeas and Persea's uneasy looks as they sat nearby, watching the rest of us. There would be time for proper reunions later, I hoped. As soon as possible. I wanted nothing whatsoever to do with this, although I knew that was a forlorn hope.

How much had Ravenna told him of the Thetians' scheme? She must have been here, there was no other way for him to even suspect what Mauriz was up to. For a second, I found myself almost hoping she'd told him everything, that he'd be able to nip this whole thing in the bud. But it meant more to me than an undesirable complication now: it was a chance to strike back at the Domain and at my brother.

"From your many spies?" Mauriz demanded, evidently planning to bluff this out as far as possible. "You play a dangerous game yourself, Viceroy, and are in far more danger of breaking your loyalties than I am."

"That isn't the issue. I am the authority in this land now, and only Ranthas and the Emperor can remove me." He sighed, fixing his gaze on Mauriz. "My position may be far from secure, but the Emperor is the least of my worries at the moment. It's in my best interests to keep things that way."

"Far be it from me to comment on the appointment of a rebel and a foreigner as Viceroy."

"As you're so fond of saying in Selerian Alastre, Cambress is part of the Empire. It has its uses. As do the laws of Qalathar and Thetia, which are fairly specific where treason is concerned."

"On whose evidence?" Mauriz said, with a curl of his lip, and strolled around the back of the sofa I was sitting on, glass of wine in hand. I was holding one too, which I hadn't really noticed and didn't want to drink. I was too tired. "You're accusing me of treason against the Pharaoh of Qalathar, for which you would be on fairly shaky ground even if I was Qalathari. As far as Thetia's concerned, republicanism isn't a crime."

"I echo your sentiments entirely on the second point, but there's a difference between republicanism and revolution."

"I say again, *where is your evidence*? Who told you this?" Mauriz said, very intensely, pointing accusingly at Sagantha.

"The Pharaoh did," said Sagantha, after a short pause. "She considers her informant reliable, and as regent for her, I act on her behalf. The rightful ruler of Qalathar has charged you with high treason and conspiracy, Mauriz Scartaris."

"So much for your friend," Mauriz hissed, rounding on me.

"I wasn't the one who let her listen to everything," I replied, jumping to my feet. "She hasn't betrayed anyone. You didn't take any precautions, or bother to check who she was. I thought deviousness was second nature to any Thetian."

"Are you implying I'm incompetent?" Mauriz said, his expression tightening the way it did when he was angry. "You knew all along."

"Yes, I did, and of course I didn't tell you. I have a lot more regard for her than I ever will for you. You've just relied on arrogance and your position to get you out of tight corners. It's not going to work here or anywhere else that your clan doesn't own."

Mauriz looked furious, but I stood my ground, helped by the fact that I knew I had everyone's support while Mauriz didn't.

"*Tace, tace!*" Sagantha said, moving in between us with an air of genuine authority, quite different from the force of personality that Mauriz used to get his way. "Calm down. Mauriz, you will answer my charges."

"What charges? Forgive me for thinking this is a reception room, not a court of law. I am accused of plotting to replace the Pharaoh," Mauriz said, ignoring me totally as he turned back to Sagantha. "Viceroy, you have no case, no witnesses, no *proof* that I am plotting anything against anyone. If we can end this pointless debate and move on to something more fruitful, we'll all be a lot happier." Still standing myself, I watched the two of them confront each other, Mauriz's challenge hanging in the air. He was daring Sagantha to accuse him officially, to produce Ravenna as the witness and have her seized by the Domain.

And Sagantha was well aware of that. His words, when they came, were very soft and very deliberate.

"I can equally well have you turned over to the Domain, who'll be very happy to talk about your actions in Ilthys. Their case might have no basis in law, but they can make life very difficult for you. Remember, I'm the final court of appeal in Qalathar. Only the Assembly or the Emperor can overrule me."

So Sagantha knew. He was inviting Mauriz to play his trump card and use me to try and better that claim. But the Thetian was too clever.

"The Domain don't have a monopoly on making life difficult. So I suggest we stop threatening each other, Viceroy, and talk about other things."

"I think not," Sagantha said, very deliberately. "I hold all the cards here. The Domain want revenge for being humiliated in Ilthys. I'm the only one who can protect you from them. The clan consuls on their own can't do it. Not here. We discuss what I want to discuss."

"Which is what, exactly?" Telesta said. We'd almost forgotten she was there, sitting quietly over to one side.

"Why you're here," Sagantha said. "No one will believe a business trip, not with the company you keep. Scartaris and Polinskarn together? Oh, I think not. I know what you're doing, who your traveling companions are. I bear them no ill will at all, and I'm happy to call them friends. Nor do I want you or Lord Mauriz to suffer in any way."

"So if you know all this, why accuse us? You've still given no proof." Mauriz said, drinking down his wine and putting the glass on the table.

"I don't have time for this," the Viceroy said wearily. "I met the Emperor just a few weeks ago. For the sake of the spies who infest this place, wherever they are at the moment, I won't reveal any more. You don't have a monopoly on intelligence."

Anyone who'd met the Emperor would see the resemblance between us.

"So, then?" Mauriz said, not confirming or denying the Viceroy's implication. "What of it?"

"It will stop." Sagantha spoke absolutely flatly, in a voice that carried a heavy weariness in it. The tiredness had been there in Lepidor, I realized with the benefit of hindsight, masked behind his politician's façade. "You want to displace the Pharaoh and put in your own leader to serve the interest of Thetia. No, I lie. Not even Thetia. The republican movement."

"If such a plot existed, it wouldn't threaten your Pharaoh at all. There is a rightful Emperor, and a rightful Hierarch. The Hierarch was—is—a religious leader."

"Mauriz, have done," Telesta said. "You're not a credit to Thetia tonight, and you're just digging a deeper hole for yourself."

"So what's your part in this?" Sagantha asked, turning his attention to her and ignoring the furious Mauriz. "Resident weathercock?"

Telesta lifted one thin eyebrow. "If we're going to talk of weathercocks, I can propose better candidates than myself. I'm not a republican and I'm not fond of the Emperor, either. But, for my own reasons, I want the Domain out of the Archipelago. In the two years since she came of age, the Pharaoh's failed even to show herself and Qalathar has done nothing. If you had, we would have helped."

Scorn showed plainly on the faces of the three Archipelagans.

"Of course—like you did twenty-four years ago," Laeas said derisively.

"You just get rid of your worthless Emperor and help us when you're ready."

"Four ships my clan sent to help you. Four ships that were destroyed in harbor through the treachery of an Archipelagan President. No one sent any more."

"A strange version of history, if we've never heard it," said Persea.

"It's true, actually. Some reinforcements did come from Thetia during the Crusade, although I never knew which clan sent them," Sagantha said. "Ral Tumar switched sides and destroyed them."

"Archipelagan unity at work again," said Mauriz dismissively. "Did you send for help beyond Worldsend? Could you even muster an army? As I recall, Viceroy, that was when you discovered your Cambressian heritage and took yourself off for the duration."

"I went to try and get help, since you obviously weren't going to provide it," Sagantha snapped, shaken for the first time. "It doesn't matter whose fault the last Crusade was. What matters is your attempt to replace the Pharaoh with a Hierarch, a religious leader who'll see us just as a means to overthrow the Emperor."

"I didn't come to discuss details of this spurious plot."

"No, you came to implement it. Here it counts as treason, and I can't allow it to proceed."

"You're wrong," Mauriz said flatly, walking toward the door, then stopping and turning just in front of it, arms crossed. "The plan is to restore the Hierarchate, illegally abolished by religious decree two hundred years ago, and force Orosius to abdicate his powers in favor of the Assembly. This will of necessity involve driving out the clerical carrion who've infested the islands for far too long. The Pharaoh is in fact subordinate to the Hierarch as far as religion is concerned, but the Hierarch doesn't have any secular powers. This is treason perhaps, but only against the Emperor."

"Except when it comes to leading this holy rebellion," Sagantha said scathingly. "I'm sure there'll be room for Archipelagans in your little Thetian cabal. I find it hard to believe you've convinced the Hierarch that his services will be needed for a moment longer than absolutely necessary. *Abdicate his powers*, indeed. You want an end to the Imperial line, to the very idea of an emperor, and before that can happen, three people have to be dead. The Emperor, the Hierarch, and their cousin Arcadius. Because until they are, Mauriz, you can never be safe."

"We aren't murderers, Sagantha," Palatine said furiously almost jumping out of her chair in which she'd been quietly sitting, seething. "How stupid do you think we are? Thetia might tolerate Orosius's death, but no more. We need a Hierarch! We need Arcadius! Do you honestly think a Thetian republic would be favorable to the Domain? They can control monarchs, as you know, but not republics. You're Cambressian, for Ranthas's sake—you virtually threw them out."

"My apologies, Palatine, but Thetia never looks to any interest but its own."

It was a strange tableau, caught at a moment in time: an aloof Mauriz watching with those glittering, calculating eyes; Palatine glaring at Sagantha, who stood, his face set, hands clasped behind him; Laeas and Persea watching tensely; Telesta detached and emotionless in her corner. The torches were flickering ever so slightly, a sign of inferior-quality flamewood.

It was Telesta who broke the silence, oddly enough. "And you do, is that what you're saying? All our views are relative, of course, but we're doing something we believe in, to help Thetia, because we're Thetians. Mauriz is, Palatine is, I am—and Cathan's more Thetian than he thinks. Either you want our help or you want independence, but you can't criticize us for being isolationist *and* imperialist."

Sagantha picked up a full wineglass from the table and held it up in front of one of the torches, casting an elongated silhouette on the far wall.

"The Thetian Empire is an illusion. It appears to be far more than it is, a shadow over the rest of the world, but it is nothing more than that." He brought the glass down again. "Beautiful, like this, but fragile." He tapped the glass with his finger, making an insubstantial, off-key sound. For a moment I thought he'd drop it, but that wasn't his kind of gesture. He put it back on the table.

"And after two thousand years of history, what is left of Qalathar?" Telesta asked, in the same quiet tone. "You had your empire once, in the days when Tehama still meant something. Two thousand years ago, before anyone even lived in Thetia, there was nothing but Tehama and Tuonetar. The Tehaman Commonwealth, stretching for thousands of miles in every direction. Thousands of miles from your center, the island of Qalathar. What had started out as just another part of the argument was different now." I saw everyone's eyes fixed on her, as she told us something I'd never heard before.

"The world was empty then. It's still very empty now, outside the areas that we know. There are only endless miles of uncharted ocean. But in those days Qalathar was the heart of an empire—Qalathar and the plateau of Tehama. Because they were peoples of the reefs and the ocean, the inland seas were sacred to them. So they built cities here, and lived as rulers of the whole world they knew.

"The Commonwealth has been gone for nearly a thousand years. There's hardly any record of it anywhere and none of its original people are left, except for the Exiles. When the Thetians arrived here three hundred years ago, Qalathar was an autocracy, the Pharaoh was a god-king, and not a single record of the Commonwealth remained.

"Qalathar has had its days of glory, and so has Thetia. The difference is that we still have the empire, we can still set an example. The Domain is as foreign to us as it is to you. We're a people of the sea, not the land. Everything is centered around the ocean, the sea, and everything in it, and nowhere in that is there anything remotely resembling fire. What does it have to do with us?"

What does it have to do with anyone? I wondered. Why Fire? It was obvious in the Archipelago that everything was dependent on Water, that everything came from the sea. If I remembered rightly, there was almost no farmland anywhere in the Archipelago, unless the orchards and gardens clustered around the cities counted as such. Nothing except forest, and rock, and sand, on hundreds of thousands of islands that reached far beyond the known world. It was so easy to forget that there was a place where the Archipelago ended and the unknown world began.

That wasn't what I was trying to think about, but I was tired enough for my mind to be drifting off in all directions, and I was still standing up.

"I hope you weren't saying what I think you were," Laeas said grimly.

"I'm saying that both our nations have to save themselves," Telesta finished, "but that Thetia can bring the rest of the world with it. The Archipelago will follow the Pharaoh, but it'll also follow us. And we have the resources, the money, and the ships for it to be possible. Quite simply, you don't."

"As smooth an argument for empire-building as I've ever heard," Persea said angrily, speaking for the first time. "Did Aetius have any of those things when he defeated the Tuonetar? All your wealth, your resources—what do you spend them on? So that the President of Decaris and the Emperor can have their harems. You're no better than Halettites. Make Thetia a power again and the world will respect you, but until then we'll treat the Empire with the contempt it deserves. I serve the Pharaoh, her Viceroy, and *no one else.*"

Laeas nodded approvingly, and I saw Sagantha flinch slightly. I wasn't sure when I'd started noticing those tiny signs, but I had. He hadn't wanted Persea and Laeas to join in or say that, but it was too close to the line he'd taken for him to disagree.

"Thank you for your contribution, Persea," he said tightly. "Some of you are very tired. May I suggest that we adjourn for the night? You've been given rooms, and we'll continue our discussions in the morning. Please don't try to leave the palace—my men are under orders to make sure you stay inside." He struck a chime hanging unobtrusively by one wall, and the door opened.

"Laeas and Persea, show my guests to their rooms, and arrange anything they need."

He remained where he was as we filed out, standing in front of the window, a worried look in his eyes. This was the real Sagantha Karao, not the man we'd known in Lepidor.

Once we'd left, Laeas and Persea fell in with Palatine and me, studiously ignoring the two Thetians. Neither of them seemed to have much diplomatic finesse, so I wondered why he was employing them as aides.

"I'm so sorry we had to have that," Persea said, visibly relaxing. "You look exhausted, both of you."

"And we should know," said Laeas, more familiar now that he was smiling, but with less of the openness that had always marked him out. They'd both subtly changed and I wasn't sure whether it was for the better. "We've all seen each other at dawn after blundering around in the forest all night, looking like the living dead dragged up from the bowels of the earth."

"Some people look like earth elementals anyway," Persea said, scrutinizing Laeas.

"Some people know how to exhaust others without going near a forest," he answered, sounding very like the Laeas of old for a minute. But the banter was slightly strained, without the easiness it had once had.

Half an hour or so later, having eaten a quickly prepared meal and washed the salt from my body, I sat down at the small writing table in my room. I was unwilling to go to bed just yet because of the faint thought that had been niggling at the edge of my consciousness ever since Telesta's impromptu history lesson. My bedroom wasn't very grand: it was painted in a fiery russet and had yellow rugs on the tiled floor, but it was better than anything I'd been in since leaving home. Perhaps my accommodation in Ilthys had been all right—but I didn't want to remember Ilthys.

I wasn't surprised when Persea knocked on my door a few minutes later, no longer wearing her Viceregal white but just a plain green tunic.

"Hello." I smiled faintly, stood up and offered her the chair.

"I've been sitting in chairs all day, so I'll use the bed—if that's all right?"

"You don't need to ask."

"Always polite." She paused. "I'm sorry about my outburst back there, but it's what I believe. You don't want to have anything to do with this, do you? You're not really sure of anything."

I hadn't realized I was that easy to read. But then, we knew each other well—once we had even been lovers. Did she have a political agenda now, I wondered, like everyone else seemed to?

"No, I'm not," I admitted, sitting down again.

"I haven't come to convince you to join my side, don't worry. I don't have a side, but I don't like Mauriz. Or Telesta, actually. She seems innocuous, but she's not."

"I wouldn't have called her innocuous, but . . ."

"She's a historian, and a good one, which we should respect. But she uses that to further her own cause, brings history in to bolster her argument. She does that so well that you don't notice it happening."

"I thought you didn't have an agenda."

"No, I don't. She appears to have a more balanced view than Mauriz, to be more neutral. I'm not saying that she isn't, just that she's not as impartial as she claims to be."

"And you are?"

"I'm your friend, Cathan, first and foremost. I'm not involved, really. I can see you're unhappy."

I paused slightly—though for too long to hide my hesitation—before answering.

"Do you want to be Hierarch?" Persea asked bluntly. "Just tell me."

The fragile commitment I'd made in Ilthys wavered and fell apart. I slumped back in the chair, once again ashamed of my weakness. Since Ral Tumar I'd been pushed around, too indecisive to achieve anything, to come down on either side. I despised myself for it, but I seemed to be incapable of changing anything.

"No." I forced myself to look up, and said, very clearly, "Not at all."

"Why not?"

"What do you mean, why not?"

"Exactly that? Come on, tell me. Why on earth would you rather stay an obscure escount and a mage than be Hierarch of the Thetian Empire?"

"Why do I need to be Hierarch, Persea? I'm not a religious leader. I'm not a very good leader of any kind. How can I convince anyone of anything when I don't believe it myself? Why do I deserve that, just because of an accident of birth?"

"Is Lachazzar any better for being elected?"

"I'm not a religious leader!" I repeated, frustrated that she didn't seem to see it. "I'm not a messiah, and I shouldn't be. I was born into a peculiar family who have strangeness running in the blood, but I nearly escaped from it. I haven't been brought up as a Tar'Conantur, and I'm never going to be one."

Persea kept her calm green gaze fixed on me as I spoke, a mix of sadness and sympathy in her look.

"Cathan, would you truly benefit from a life as an oceanographer somewhere? Doing experiments, trips up the coast, squabbling with your colleagues, forging the budget requests? Is that a life you really want?"

"Yes, it is," I said fiercely. "Emphasize the negatives all you like. Does everything have to be political, in the end?"

"And will you be able to sit back and watch things happen, watch the Domain rise or fall? Another Crusade in the Archipelago, more Inquisitors? Be a distant observer when Orosius sends his fleet against it, starts a war? A mourner at the funeral of another republican leader, murdered by the Emperor's men on the Assembly floor? What when you hear about the death of the last Pharaoh of Qalathar?"

"Does everyone in the world have to be involved?"

"Everyone in the Archipelago is. And however you've come by them, not everyone has your gifts. I don't enjoy saying the things I did earlier about anyone, certainly not the Thetians. They need a restoration, a renaissance. We need a liberation. You don't need to do this on your own, and you can't. But because of what you are, you can help." Persea was very rational and even-tempered. Her reasoned argument was the complete opposite of the tongue-lashing that Ravenna would have given me, which perhaps I really needed to stir me out of self-pity. But Ravenna had abandoned me: she hadn't trusted me enough to take me with her when I'd gladly have gone.

"Help by going along with Mauriz and Telesta's plan? If they win, I end up with a life of empty ceremony and ritual, shoring up their republic."

"Help by doing what you came here to do," Persea said ingenuously. "Your idea, your plan, nothing to do with Mauriz or Telesta or Sagantha or anyone else. Ravenna's not going to be able to find the *Aeon* on her own, and Palatine's too busy plotting republics again." Serious again now, she went on, "Laeas will help you, and we'll find a few other people who can be trusted and might know something. Oceanographers, sailors, anyone else useful."

"Find the *Aeon*?" I echoed stupidly. Laeas must have told her about it; I'd mentioned it in my letter to him.

"Yes. If you have it, it gives you independence. It might be hard to use, and it'll be even harder to find, but no one in charge of something like the *Aeon* can ever be a puppet."

It sounded easy, a lifeline. But I could just see, once I had it, the wolves closing in and taking over, swarming over my weakness and indecisiveness. It would only raise the stakes.

"No, it won't," she replied, when I said so. "How can you be so negative? The ship stands for everything you love, and it doesn't pin you down anywhere. At the moment you don't have a chance to assert yourself, because you're always in someone else's power. There's no way Mauriz or Telesta can stand against the *Aeon*. And before you say it, they *won't* seize it. Please, Cathan, start your search again. You were planning to anyway, but do it for yourself, and all of us . . ." Persea tailed off, almost despairing at my expression. "I'm sorry if I sound like another politician, but . . ."

"But you don't," I said, pulling myself upright, thinking of those tantalizingly brief descriptions of a ship, a jewel in the ocean. "I'll try." And with that, I wanted to believe I'd crossed another barrier, had made a decision for myself for the first time in months. Only time would tell whether I had the will to keep on with it, but at least I'd have tried.

"And everyone from Lepidor and the Citadel will help you as much as we can. Not Sagantha, not yet—it'll be your decision whether to tell him or not." She got up from the bed as I stood up and looked questioningly at me.

"Could you stay?" I asked her, not caring whether it was right or not anymore.

"Of course." Persea gave the lopsided smile I knew so well, pulled her sandals off and went over to extinguish the torch.

Chapter XVIII

The next morning Sagantha was gone. Called away to trouble in the mountains, Laeas said, but we all knew the real reason. He wanted Mauriz to cool his heels for a few days and be forced to wait for the Viceroy to give him another audience at a time more convenient for Sagantha.

"How did Mauriz take it?" Palatine asked as the four of us ate breakfast together in a small, beehive-shaped room in the guest wing. Persea had done us a favor by making it clear to the other Thetians that this was a reunion, and not a gathering they were invited to.

"Surprisingly well, I thought," Laeas said, working his way through a giant melon. "Do you know if he has other plans?"

"He probably expected it. Gives him time to think."

"Forgive me, Palatine, but I hadn't realized before that Thetians were quite so arrogant," Persea said, frowning. "He's unbelievable. Telesta's fairly bad, but Mauriz seems to think everyone else is a menial."

"Clan Scartaris are like that. But he's not so bad when you get to know him."

"Of course he isn't, because you're Thetian. Patronizing fool." She'd been angry about that when we'd talked later on in the night, and I hadn't cared to defend him.

"He *is* rather bad that way," Palatine admitted. "And he's not at his best at the moment. Things keep going wrong, and he's not used to it."

"Unlucky for him," said Laeas shortly. "Just so long as he doesn't get worse while the Viceroy's away."

I listened without saying anything, relishing the chance to eat fresh food again after weeks on that galleon, its stores taken on in an emergency and not really adequate for the long crossing. The bread in particular, brought from the kitchens by Persea, was delicious.

"Does Sagantha spend most of his time here?"

"He's only been Viceroy since we got back. His excuse is quite legitimate, actually; so far he hasn't been able to leave the city. Too many problems, and he's got the Domain to deal with now. Midian's commandeered half of Sagantha's buildings to quarter the Sacri."

"Yes, leaving Sagantha with about two hundred people and one manta to govern Qalathar," Persea said, in disgust. "They tried to take all the ships, but we kept the *Emerald*. They won't keep her even if they manage to take her."

Laeas looked across at Persea levelly. "Why? What exactly did you do to her?"

"I'm not telling you in case someone's listening. Even if they know, they won't be able to stop it."

"Are your friends trying to get us in more trouble?"

"No, we're trying to keep the balance. Sagantha doesn't need to know, and there won't be any problems so long as the *Emerald* is still ours."

"Please, Persea, one of these days you'll go too far."

"Nothing we're doing is a crime."

I looked from one to the other, worried by the implications of what they were saying. Even within the Palace, between these two, there was a division? It sounded like Sagantha had no control over anything.

"You've seen what the Domain defines as heresy; they're just as good on crimes." Laeas was concerned, I could tell from his expression, and guessed this was a bone of contention between them. "Some of the others don't have your sense."

"What's made you such a voice for reason since we got back?" Persea demanded. "You still won't tell me why you agree with Sagantha all the time. He's a good man, but is he ever going to stand up to them?"

Although Sagantha was good company, it was hard not to agree with Persea on that. He'd got where he was by never provoking strong opposition, and I knew he'd been elected Cambressian Suffete two years ago because of his reputation for leaving stones unturned. And, perhaps, because of bribery: Dalriadis, my father's admiral in Lepidor, had hinted at that once or twice, and Sagantha could certainly afford the occasional bribe. Not that it mattered greatly, since Cambressian elections were frequently won that way.

"He'll be able to accomplish a lot more if you don't back him into a corner," Laeas replied. "The more problems the Domain has, the more pressure Midian will put on him."

"We're not going to see eye to eye on this, Laeas," said Persea, sighing.

"Just leave it. You can trust my people, and as many others as I have any hold over. But some of the other groups have friends in places too high for me to deal with."

Like me, Palatine had remained silent, but she didn't look as worried as I felt. She probably saw this as an opportunity. "Does Sagantha know these groups exist?"

"Probably some of them, but he hasn't been here long enough to know everything that's going on, or to call in all the people he knows. Things might be better when some allies get here."

"Does *people* include Cambressians?"

"Thetis forbid," Persea said quickly. "Yet another world of trouble."

"Having a few Cambressian warships here wouldn't do us any harm," Laeas said. "Cambress isn't going to stand by and watch the Domain take over—"

"And the Emperor's just going to allow the Cambressians to interfere?" Palatine interrupted. "Come on, it would do more harm than good. Orosius hates them: if they come here, he'll be furious."

"When did that worthless non-emperor last do anything at all?" demanded Persea. "He doesn't act on anything—he's too scared that the military will just ignore him."

"Is that what they tell you?" Palatine seemed to have forgotten about breakfast, as had the other two; I'd already finished because I hadn't been talking. "That he's afraid of being ignored?"

"He is," I said, the words slipping out before I could stop them. I didn't want to give the others any hint that I knew more than they did on this subject. "The rest of the world calls him a paper Emperor: the military don't respect him so he feels that he *has* to intervene personally or he'll be forgotten."

"Last time I looked the military were behind him."

"You were arguing the other way in Ral Tumar, and what I've seen over the last few weeks just confirms it. The only person they'll all follow is Tanais."

"How do you know this?" Palatine fixed her gaze on me, more commanding and magnetic than Ravenna could ever be.

"I've listened while you and the Thetians have talked. Orosius has his agents, yes, but they're the only people he trusts."

Which might be true, but his fear of being forgotten was something I'd only come to realize in the last few days. The idea of a twin, somebody as similar to him as I was, with a claim to almost the same eminence, made him afraid of being thrown into the shadows.

"The military are sick and tired of being thought of as feeble. They'd welcome the chance to assert themselves."

"Would they?" I persisted. "People are still afraid of the Navy, but the admirals know they're not as good as they were. If the fleet goes into action, they have to get everything right or it would destroy their reputation."

"The Emperor won't start a war," Laeas said confidently. "Sending ships here against the Cambressians would do that, and he knows he could lose it."

"I think you underestimate us," Palatine said, looking at all three of us in turn. "Cambress will never defeat Thetia. You believe we're in decline, and some of us may be. But the sailors are all recruited from the clans, and every one of them is a better sailor than any Cambressian can be. Cambress can never win a naval war in the Archipelago because it's a Continental power. It's as simple as that." She had the utter confidence she'd always possessed, the confidence that had brought her to prominence at the Citadel and that she'd backed up with talent.

"They're descended from your own navy," Laeas said, rather weakly, after a moment's pause. "They have the same traditions . . ."

"But they aren't us. They just grafted the experience we brought to them on to what they already were. They're people of the land, as we're people of the sea." I remembered Palatine saying exactly the same thing back in Lepidor. The idea of being "people of the sea" was the oldest of the Archipelagan beliefs, Telesta had said once, and the one that made them a people apart. The Continentals might outnumber Archipelagans by three or more to one, but the sea kept them out. Maybe it was the same belief that gave the Thetians their arrogance.

Or it had, once upon a time. But all the thousands of miles between Equatoria and Qalathar hadn't kept the Crusaders away. Whoever had mantas could cross the sea, no matter where they came from.

I said so, and earned a glare from Palatine.

"Perhaps they can cross the sea, but that doesn't mean they can beat us." She sounded disappointed. She'd probably expected me to agree with her on this at least.

"Palatine, just stop to think for a moment," I said. "Cambress and Taneth are still expanding—they're still moving forward. If they weren't, we wouldn't have come. The whole Archipelago, including Thetia, is living in the past, and the Emperor knows it. At the moment his only chance is to keep up the façade of imperial power—and not act until he can be sure of winning." *Once he has me*, I thought even as I said it.

"Do think Tanais would agree with you?"

"Tanais is more than two hundred years old. He saw the Empire as it was, and he's seen it as it is now. There's no comparison."

"Keep the Cambressians out of it for now, Laeas," Persea said before Palatine could answer. "Whether it leads to war, or the collapse of Thetia, bringing them in isn't going to be Sagantha's first thought. He's more experienced than we are."

And less principled, I added silently. Would Sagantha call the Emperor's bluff in an attempt to destroy his credibility? And would it be such a bad thing if he did? Orosius would have to act, and if the gamble failed, his reign would be at an end. The republicans would have their chance to rebuild, and I wouldn't have to be involved.

We stayed off the topic while the others finished their breakfast. Laeas and Persea passed on what they knew of the others from the Citadel, mostly the Archipelagans. Mikas had begun his obligatory service in the Cambressian Navy, they'd heard, but they had no idea where he was stationed. There was no news of the Citadel itself—why should there have been? Another group of novices was training there now, learning what we'd learned, being taught the traditions so the memories wouldn't be lost. It was a vital process but, in the end, sterile. All they did was to preserve the true past; it wasn't getting the heresy anywhere in the present.

Once we'd finished, Laeas and Persea went off to work, leaving Palatine and me to our own devices inside the palace. We weren't allowed outside, and there seemed very little to do within the walls.

I declined Palatine's invitation to go to weapons practice with the garrison, and regretted it almost as soon as she'd gone. There really was nowhere else to go—Telesta would probably have taken up residence in the library, and I had no desire to see her. Little hope in any case that there would be a lead here. The Pharaonic library had been in Poseidonis until the Crusade, when it had been burned or stolen. What was here would just be a shrunken relic.

My wanderings took me eventually, a while before sunset, to the map room. It was linked to the library by a door, I was told, but was not part of it. I could at least hope Telesta wouldn't be there.

She wasn't, thankfully, and I breathed a sigh of relief as I looked around the empty room, whitewashed and vaulted like a catacomb, with the deep map cupboards set into alcoves in the walls. It looked very old, with narrow, poky windows letting in the filtered gray afternoon light from outside: the aether table in the center looked peculiarly out of place.

I'd told the room's watchman that I needed to use it for oceanographic research, which was at least partly true. The question was how much of the collection had been aether-recorded, and how much of it was on paper. Aether-recording was still hideously expensive, given the time it took to map every part of an island above and below the waves, and there was a virtual Thetian monopoly on the technology.

The sound of my footsteps on the floor made a slight, dull echo, like tapping a hollow stone wall, and when I lifted the latch on the reference cabinet there was another muted, odd resonance. The room seemed to soak up sound.

Inside the cabinet were the indexes to all the maps, which I flicked through impatiently, hoping there would be one of the whole of Qalathar. There were three, but the reference numbers all referred to paper maps, none of which would have the underwater topography I needed. The aetherized section was even smaller than I'd feared, limited to Qalathar, Thetia, and a few of the larger island groups. No use for finding the *Aeon*, then, but I thought it could be worth having a look at the one of Qalathar later on.

Faced with the prospect of further boredom, I decided to try something I otherwise wouldn't have bothered with. I had the *Histories* with me; Persea had said that copies were quite common here, so I sat down with a large map of the Archipelago at one of the tables around the edge and tried to trace the *Aeon*'s movements during the final days of the Old Empire.

Two hours later, trying to pick out useful fragments from what had been written essentially as a dramatic work was proving even more frustrating than I'd feared. Carausius's *History* ended six months before the usurpation, but an unknown chronicler writing at least a decade later had continued the story. He'd been a mage of Water, that much was certain, but not as senior as Carausius, and his emphasis was very definitely on the religious chaos of the usurpation. His finishing point was what he took to be the final death knell of the old religion, when the mages from the last stronghold fled south into the ocean. To found the Citadel and its sisters, I suspected, given some of the names he mentioned.

The Continuator, as someone with a total lack of originality had dubbed him, was also unbelievably depressing to read. He had a right to be: he'd been chronicling the fall of the world he knew, the death of all his friends, and the ascendancy of a man he loathed. And he'd almost certainly committed suicide after he'd finished his account.

So all I'd achieved after those two hours was to be certain that the *Aeon* had been in Estarientian, south of Selerian Alastre, when Tiberius was murdered. My notes had got more and more spidery as I'd gone on, and once or twice I'd pressed right through the paper. It was sickening to read of Valdur's duplicity—what he'd had, what he'd thrown away—and I wanted somebody, something, to rail at. The hunts, the deaths, the proscriptions, they had ripped apart a world still recovering from the war and let loose the Domain on Aquasilva. I'd never believed that reading a book could make me this angry, but it did. Worst of all, deep down there was the awful knowledge that I carried the blood of the man who'd done this. I was Valdur's three-times great-grandson.

Your family destroys everything it touches, even their loved ones . . . even the blood that runs in your veins is tainted. Rotten to the core. My mind drifted back to a day I'd rather have forgotten, the day the invasion of Lepidor had begun, the day of Ravenna's fury and her attack on the Tar'Conanturs. She'd seen me as nothing more than one of them. Palatine and me both, in fact. And all the time in Ral Tumar and Ilthys, Mauriz and Telesta had been talking about the Tar'Conanturs, playing on my heritage, and I hadn't refused them outright as I should have done.

Another black wave of depression hit me, and I buried my head in my hands. Something else I'd never realized, been too caught up with my own misery to see. That was why she hadn't asked me to go with her, or even forced me to; my behavior had confirmed many of the things she'd accused me of. I wouldn't have minded either way, in truth, but she hadn't been able to trust me.

"Do you spend your whole time in libraries, brother?" someone said behind me, not bothering to conceal the sneer in his voice. "Perhaps that's why you're so small and weak. There's nothing to be learned here, nothing I don't already know, so why bother? I might give it to you, in the right circumstances."

I jumped up, deliberately kicking the chair backward at the place his voice had come from, and rounded on him, trying to match his tone.

"Is there nothing more than this in your life, pathetic excuse for an Emperor?" Orosius seemed hazy, insubstantial somehow, but I pressed on. "Your Empire is a laughingstock, a rump sitting in the middle of the ocean, while you haven't even risen to the level of Valdur yet. He destroyed a world, and I can't recall you ever having done anything." I tailed off weakly as I saw him step *through* the chair toward me. I only had time to see the anger on his face before he touched me, and I felt something like an aether surge hit me.

The last time I had felt this, it had been bad. This time, it felt as if every nerve in my body had been scraped at once. I screamed with the shock

of it, only my howl came out as a gargle, and my legs gave way. As I hit
the stone floor, everywhere on my body touched by the hard surface
seized up excruciatingly, an agony only made worse by movement. For
a second I thought I would simply black out, but I didn't—nor did
Orosius release me. He must have just stood there, looking down, as I
writhed on the floor in agony, unable to breathe, my skin feeling like a
mass of flames.

I didn't register the moment when he finally let go, because my whole
body was throbbing with pain. I could only breathe in gasps, deliberately
trying to draw in enough air. My eyes showed nothing more than a maze
of colors and shadows that hurt my senses as much as everything else.

"We may be brothers, but you are my subject and I am your Emperor.
Remember that always." Orosius's voice came from very far away, but
so much of the pain had remained, and I was too weak to move or
respond. "No matter how strong you may think you are, I will always be
better than you."

I managed to open my eyes and saw a blurry image standing a foot or
two away, looking down dispassionately. *Ravenna was right*, was my one
clear thought, *absolutely right*.

"I hope you're in a more tractable mood now, brother," he said,
moving out of my line of sight. I tried to turn my head, but my limp
muscles refused to cooperate. "I'm perfectly within my rights to execute
you for high treason. It would be inconvenient, of course, but you need
to keep it in mind."

Once again I was powerless, although he hadn't been as subtle this time.
There was no question of using magic after what he'd done. It wouldn't
have worked on a non-mage; in fact, it wouldn't have worked as well on
anyone else. It was only because our magic was identical that he could do
it, effectively earthing my magic for . . . who knew how long?

"You're wondering why I'm here, aren't you?" Orosius's dislocated
voice came now from somewhere over on the other side of the room.
"How I can still track you down when my Voice is on the other side of
the world?"

I tried to shake my head in a feeble gesture of defiance, but I wasn't
sure if he'd seen it.

"I have been watching you since Ral Tumar," he said, after a pause.
"I know all about Mauriz's pitiful little conspiracy and his attempts to use
you as part of it. Our esteemed cousin Palatine is still making trouble, still
too blinded to see what a fool she is. They couldn't even get from Ral
Tumar to Ilthys without running into trouble. Not even with you

disguised as a servant. A nice touch, that, although it shows you how petty Mauriz really is."

He moved back into my line of sight again, still looking slightly fuzzy to my stinging eyes, a commanding figure in white. It was a projection of some kind, but a remarkably solid one, without a trace of transparency. Another thing I couldn't even begin to understand how to do.

"You can't hide from me, Cathan," he went on. "Not all the scheming of the little people like Mauriz and Telesta can conceal you. I know more about their plans than any of you do. Oh, and you really ought to change your eyes back. They don't look anything like as good when they're that color, although it's probably more suitable for you."

"Are you afraid I'll eclipse you?" I croaked, my throat aching with the effort, and immediately gasped for breath. I felt my chest spasm and a renewed agony all down my back.

Orosius looked down with a condescending smile. "You could never eclipse me, brother."

"Then why bother?" I managed to ask, finally.

"You should know." He turned away again, tracing a complete circle around me. "They are little people. They don't realize how difficult it is to overthrow an Emperor. They think it's just a matter of raising a few revolts, getting the fleet to desert. None of them really know, they're just fumbling around at the feet of giants. Reinhardt could have told them. Maybe he was a traitor, but he put them all to shame. Even his daughter."

He kept pacing around at the edge of my vision, my eyes straining to follow him. Did he really admire Palatine's murdered father, or was this just another game?

"They think that they can use you as a puppet, give you a meaningless title dredged up from one of Telesta's books, and that Thetia will fall to them like a house of cards."

The fringe of his white cloak brushed through my foot. "Have you stopped to think about how they'll do this? There aren't even any true republicans in the Assembly. The clan leaders are fat old philosophers, nymphomaniacs and lechers, windbags who'd rather argue about poetry than run a country." The contempt in his voice was chillingly unemotional.

I swallowed painfully, gathered up as much courage as I could muster and said, "And your own achievements are so dazzling, after all. Do you dictate policy to the two luckless concubines who have to share your bed each night? Run your harem according to the best traditions of Cupromenes?" Three hundred years ago, Cupromenes had written a series of brilliant poems about life in a harem. He'd been the chief eunuch.

It was a wild shot and not a worthy one, but it struck home. Orosius abruptly stopped, and stared down at me again, cold rage showing on his face.

"Spoken like one of the little people, brother. You know so little about magic, there are a few things I'll have to explain. One of them is that when you earth a lot of magic it leaves a residual trace behind that takes longer to fade the more you've used."

"Coward," was all I managed to say before he touched me again. It felt like he'd rammed a stake down through my chest, and my whole body convulsed.

I blacked out before he'd finished, but only for a few seconds, too short a time. It was worse than it had been last time, as if I'd been seared by a flamewood cannon. My left hand was locked in a rictus around the leg of the chair, but somewhere at the back of my mind, despite all the pain, the single fact that I'd managed to bait him persisted. And there was no way I was going to try it again.

"You'll see what I'm capable of soon enough," he said, seemingly unchanged by the effort of pouring that much magic into me over such a distance. "All of you will. This self-pitying little land of Qalathar, the rest of the Archipelago. We will purge the islands of the heretics, the republicans, the corrupt nobles, the little people, and leave only those who deserve to remain.

"For two hundred years the Empire has stayed its hand, left the world alone. Weaklings like our father, wretches like Mauriz and Telesta, they have had their day. My fleets will remind the world what Thetia really is, and why they built cities and we built an empire."

Orosius squatted down beside me, turquoise eyes shining.

"You'll only have one more warning after this, Cathan. You will come to Selerian Alastre and prove to me that you are my loyal subject. Not the Hierarch, not the Escount of whichever provincial clan you come from, but a subject of the Empire. You will submit to me even if I have to drag you across the ocean in chains, and there is nowhere in the world you can hide from me or my helpers. Do not let my people find you here, or you will regret it."

He stood up, then turned back to me, a slight smile on the all-too-familiar face.

"Oh, I almost forgot. They must have mazed your mind, my brother, for you to dream of finding the *Aeon* and claiming her as your own. She belongs to me and I will find her. I have the Imperial Archives here, the records of the fleet, the last will and testament of Admiral Cidelis. My people can find her without even leaving the city, while you trail across the Archipelago clutching at straws. Remember the *Revelation*, Cathan."

Then he strode out of sight, and didn't say any more. Lying nerveless on the floor, I had no way to tell if he'd gone or was still there watching me, gloating.

I stared up at the ceiling, seeing the rough edges of the bricks not entirely concealed by whitewash, the faint streaks of dirt here and there. It was more comfortable than turning my head, because almost any movement hurt—still. Then the lights went out, leaving me in darkness.

Even over ten thousand miles Orosius had reduced me to helplessness without a struggle. All of my plans, my hopes, had been laid bare before him as if I'd shouted them out to the world. There was nothing in the writings of the Continuator that could have made me feel as desperate as I did now, powerless before a brother, an Emperor, who seemed almost omniscient.

He'd spoken of a purge of the Archipelago, and I wondered what he'd meant. Had it been mere bravado, the imagination of a man whose control was supposedly limited to those he had physical power over, like those concubines who in more than four years had failed to bear him a single child? Or did it really mean something this time? Orosius was still the Emperor, and he had the authority to order the legions and the fleets into the field as Palatine had predicted.

Chapter XIX

No one came.

I lay on the floor of the map room for an eternity, unable to move and aching from head to foot. I couldn't hear any noises from outside except the distant screeching of gulls through the narrow windows. After a while it began to rain, and rivulets of water streamed down the glass, blown by the wind whose keening drowned out even the screech of the gulls.

The pain only seemed to get worse the longer it went on, and as soon as I'd recovered enough energy to move again, agonizing cramp hit all of my muscles at once. If Orosius had wanted me to hate him, he couldn't have done better. He'd been aware what the effects of his magic were, and he'd waited until just the right moment to provoke me into attacking him.

But worst of all was that he knew. What chance did I have against the resources he could command in finding the *Aeon*? He could discover its location—the information had to be somewhere in the Imperial Archives—and once he'd found the vessel he could order an entire fleet into the field to protect it. Doubtless the Exarch of Thetia, his Domain puppet master, would go with him, one step behind as always, to persuade him that it was a discovery to be shared.

Once they had the *Aeon* there would be no point in us going on. Unarmed the *Aeon* might be, but there was no telling what powerful technology it might have on board. Carausius had used the ship itself as a weapon, and Orosius commanded power far beyond that of Carausius—Heaven only knew how. Orosius would use the ship as an instrument of terror, like a monstrous artificial kraken, roaming the ocean at will because no one would be able to stop them. Not even the Cambressians.

Had we never thought of it, the Emperor would never have remembered and we might still have had a chance. But all I could see now were roads leading in the same direction, toward a final victory for the Domain. Even if they killed Orosius, it would be too late for the rest of the Archipelago, and House Tar'Conantur would end with him.

I was beginning to think that would be no loss to the world.

A depression blacker than any I could remember engulfed me, and I would have cried if I'd been able to. This was far, far worse than capture by the tribesmen in Lepidor, or even the capture of Lepidor itself by Etlae. They had been flesh-and-blood enemies, but their power had had a limit. The Emperor was more than just flesh and blood, he had to be. It wasn't anything I could explain or would even have wanted to know as I lay there—but then, his abilities went beyond the limit of the explicable. No matter how weak he might appear, he ruled the whole Empire, and he had channeled raw magic through me without even the slightest effect on himself.

My own brother, a true scion of the family into which I'd been born. How could we be excused? Valdur, with all the monstrous evils he'd committed. Landressa, his great-grandmother, who'd murdered three Emperors in ten years, all close relations, to get herself on the throne. Her son Valentine's execution of thousands of Tuonetar prisoners in cold blood. Ranthas, it went on and on! Catiline the Mad, Valdur's younger son, who'd run amok through the palace until he'd been accidentally killed by his daughter, the future Empress Aventine. My weak, vacillating father Perseus II, too stubborn to let others control the Empire for him, ignoring the Archipelago's pleas in the months before the Crusade.

There was only that one generation who were held up as examples by the heretics, execrated by the rest of the world. How did anyone really know Aetius and Carausius were paragons of virtue as the *History* said they were? *How could they be?*

I would not go to Selerian Alastre. Not if it was the last place left in the world. The thought of putting myself in Orosius's power was both abhorrent and terrifying. Where was there to hide from him, though, if he could find me this far? I couldn't escape my Tar'Conantur blood unless I hid, as Ravenna had done, for the rest of my life, somewhere so far away that the name meant nothing. And there was no such place. Desolation overtook me again, and I closed my eyes wearily.

But all I could see in the quiet of my mind was the *Aeon* hanging in a black emptiness, a titanic presence in the utter darkness. It was from there that the thought came to me, thrown up from the depths of my mind.

Admiral Cidelis had been running from the Emperor, from the Domain. The one place on Aquasilva where there would be no mention of the *Aeon*'s final location was the Imperial Archives. Of course there wouldn't be.

My eyes opened abruptly and the *Aeon*'s image vanished. Cidelis would have taken her somewhere beyond the reach of the Empire. Somewhere she could never be found by Imperial searches. I hardly noticed my shift into thinking of the ship as *her*, the way the Emperor had spoken. If he could have located her by looking in the Archives, she would have been found long ago. But she hadn't been.

There had been a deafening silence on the subject for two hundred years: a total and complete absence of any information about the *Aeon*. It was the Guild's job to survey the oceans, to report anything unusual. Our probes could go six miles down, but all those surveys made down the generations had produced nothing. It had to be that way. There was no one alive to protect the secret. She had to be hidden somewhere so deep, so remote that no one could ever find her by accident.

Orosius wouldn't find her by looking. As long as Cidelis hadn't destroyed her—and I couldn't imagine the Admiral doing that to his beloved ship—he *must* have intended someone to find her one day. Someone who wouldn't be under Imperial control. How could he have done that?

My mind was racing now, the despair pushed aside for the time being as I tried to keep track of this train of thought. There was nothing to distract me, nowhere for my attention to wander except back into bleak depression.

If an Emperor decided to search for her, he'd take the approach I had. Search the libraries, the oceanographic records, mobilize the legions of archivists and chroniclers at his disposal. It wasn't inconceivable that in Cidelis's day Valdur would have mobilized the whole Empire to find the ship. After meeting Orosius, it was so clear. The Emperor believed he would find her if he looked long and hard enough.

Cidelis must have known that. There had been oceanographers in his day, so he must have reasoned that there always would be, and that their techniques would get better as time went on. They might be controlled by the Emperor, so the *Aeon* couldn't be concealed anywhere that they would discover.

Where, then, did that leave? Or, more importantly, who did Cidelis want to find the ship? She was so ancient, probably so dangerous, that he couldn't possibly allow her to fall into the hands of the wrong person.

Not an Emperor, because he didn't want Valdur to have her. Nor anyone who could come across her by chance. No one who could use her against the interests of the Empire. Which left only Imperials who could be trusted. From his own day? Had he intended the *Aeon* to be found by a few people, to whom he'd passed the message?

No, that was too risky. There were too many unknowns during the usurpation, too many things that could go wrong. And Cidelis couldn't rely on the trustworthiness of those who might end up with the message. It had to be aimed at a position, not a person.

Hierarch. Valdur had proclaimed the Hierarchate dissolved, abolished. The Hierarch could only be a follower of the old gods, the gods Cidelis had believed in. If there was a Hierarch again, it would be a sign that the Empire had returned to sanity. And surely it had to be the Hierarch, not simply the Emperor's twin. What was the difference?

I sighed and tilted my head to one side, suddenly wondering whether my brilliant chain of reasoning was so clever after all. It was improbable beyond belief that I was the only one to have worked this out. So was I looking for hope where none existed? Surely not.

But what if the ship was somewhere the Hierarch would find her, somewhere only a full Hierarch would be?

And all my reasoning had led me from a place where the Emperor could find her to a place where I couldn't. I knew the *Aeon* had had something to do with the mages' city of Sanction; was it conceivable that Sanction was where Cidelis had put her in the end? Sanction had been lost for two hundred years, and was beyond anyone's reach.

I had enough control over my body now to turn myself over, gasping at jabs of pain in a dozen new places. I gritted my teeth and tried to push myself up, but my protesting arms wouldn't support me. How long would it take for someone to come? Surely they must be missing me by now?

I started inching over to the nearest table, to use it as a support, but stopped when I remembered something else.

Sanction was gone too, closed, vanished from the seas. The Continuator had recorded its disappearance, mentioned specifically that it had been Carausius and his wife Cinnirra who, unaided, had put the city beyond Valdur's reach. And they had done it on the third day of the usurpation, after the murder of Tiberius but before Cidelis could conceivably have reached the city.

So Sanction was as remote as the *Aeon*, and presumably separate. Where else could a Hierarch be expected to look?

Here, finally, I ran out of ideas. There was nowhere else associated with the Hierarch. His realm was everything mystical, unworldly, concerned with things beyond mortal experience. That was the way it had always been, the Emperor master of the body and the Hierarch ruler of the mind, a balance to keep the Empire from ever sliding too far into tyranny or decadence. As it had without the twins, in the past two hundred years. Where did Orosius's unnatural powers fit into that?

But as I pulled myself up, trying to ignore the fact that every muscle in my body seemed to be screaming, and collapsed into a chair, Sanction was still the only answer I had. The Hierarch had no need of places other than Sanction. The *Aeon* had come and gone in the last few years before the usurpation, a transient device that had been shared between Emperor and Hierarch. The old religion had had no centralized structure, no sacred places in common except for Sanction, dedicated to Water. And although I believed my reasoning had been right for a while, it had led me to a dead end.

I was still sitting in the darkness, staring off into nothingness, when Palatine found me. I wished, in a way, that it had been Persea or Laeas, because although they knew less, they'd also not have inquired too closely. Oh well, at least Palatine would believe what I told her.

I closed my eyes instinctively as light lanced in from beyond the cautiously opened door, and heard the rushing sound as the room's lights were switched on.

"Cathan, there . . ." Her voice trailed off, and I heard her shut the door again behind her, showing a presence of mind I would never have had. "What's happened? Why is the room like this?"

I heard her footsteps crossing the room, stopping just in front of me. It was still too early to open my eyes, and the glare was painful even through their closed lids. I'd have to explain—there was no way I could pretend nothing had happened, not this time. Which meant that Mauriz and Telesta would both be asking me questions, demanding to know exactly what the Emperor had said, blaming me for not having told them of the first time he'd manifested to me.

I had to keep to myself what had happened between us.

"Palatine," I said slowly, my throat terribly dry and sore, "is everyone looking for me?"

"Not yet. Just me and Persea—Mauriz and Telesta have shut themselves away in a temper. Nobody has seen you for hours, and Persea and Laeas are supposed to be keeping an eye on all of us. You look awful, and your skin's gone white. Is it more magic?"

"Can you help me back to my room, tell the others I'm ill? Please? I'll tell you what happened, but . . ."

"Only if you *do* tell me." She came around beside me, touched my sleeve and then jerked her hand back. "Thetis! What is it? This whole room feels like there's been an aether surge."

"Worse," I said. "Could we leave?"

How we managed to make it back to my room two corridors away without collapsing, I had no idea, but we did. It was agony every step of the way—bad for Palatine too since my skin seemed to be painful even for others to touch. I was acutely aware how easy it was to reduce me to this state: even though magic was independent of the physical world, exhaustion still affected my use of it. I didn't have the strength and weight to take a lot of punishment, such as I had received in the icy river in Lepidor, or even from the raw power channeled through me by Orosius.

We didn't see anyone I knew, only a few servants going to and fro about their business. Palatine gave one the message that I'd been on the receiving end of an aether surge and asked them to summon the palace healer.

When the healer came there was very little he could do for me, unfortunately, although he didn't suspect the cause was anything more than an aether excess. What he did do, thankfully, was administer some very powerful painkilling concoctions, and he left by the bed a glass of the most potent soporific he had.

"Now, tell me what really happened," Palatine said when he'd gone, sitting down in a chair beside the bed. "The others may believe it was a surge, but you say it was something worse. I need to know in case this is a threat to all of us, another piece of Domain trickery."

I shook my head. "Not Domain. You remember the mage-testing at the Citadel?"

She nodded, waiting for me to go on.

"Whoever does it draws up from a reservoir of power, I can't explain how, and channels it through you. If you're not a mage it just goes straight through, but if you are, then—"

"I know, I felt something like it. This is the same, but worse?"

I nodded.

"Who?"

I looked away for a moment, wishing I'd told her back in Ral Tumar before all of this had started, before it became so difficult. "My brother."

"How?" she demanded, but I turned back, cut her off fiercely.

"You have no idea how far he can reach. It was a projection, an image of him. Enough to do this, though."

"So he knows who you are, and that you're here." She paused. "What else? There's something else you don't want to tell me."

It was futile trying to hide anything from her, and I gave up. "I've met him once before, in the oceanographers' in Ral Tumar."

"You've already met him and you never told us? *Why?* Once he's found you he can follow you, and he must have been tracking us all this time."

The lack of reproach on Palatine's face only made it worse, and I couldn't meet her gaze.

"He has been," she said, after a moment. "He knows everything we've done."

"Of course he does," I said, in an instinctive effort to defend myself. "That henchman of Mauriz's—Tekla—works directly for him. That's how Orosius found me in the first place."

"Althana keep and preserve us, Cathan. He's the Emperor's right-hand man. I should have made the connection, but because you didn't tell me we've put our heads in the lion's mouth." Her brutal frankness was easier than false sympathy would have been, but it didn't make things any better. "Is there any reason why you didn't say anything earlier?"

I shook my head very slowly, wishing with all my heart that I'd had the courage to tell her the first time, even after what had happened. "Both times he . . . crushed me," I finished lamely, not wanting to use any words that were more precise. Why had I been such a coward this whole journey, unable to decide for myself, letting Mauriz and Telesta pull me along as they wanted to? Everything I'd done was so pathetic, so weak; I was no better than my real father had been. "He's so far beyond me, there's nothing I can do against him."

"Cathan," Palatine said slowly, "I think it would be the least you could do to tell me exactly what happened both times. I know it will be painful, but it may help. I'm still your friend, whatever you've done, and I'm not going to pass this on to Mauriz, Telesta or anyone."

So, haltingly, I told her, in the end not sparing myself any of the details because I felt I owed it to her. She didn't say very much, and her expression didn't change. She was the one who should have been Emperor or Hierarch, not Orosius, and certainly not me.

And when I'd finished, finally, she looked very sad and took one of my hands, which must have hurt her more than it did me, with the residue of Orosius's magic still deeply ingrained.

"I was wrong to judge you so harshly for not telling me, Cathan. I'd assumed that because you were his twin, his brother, there might have been some semblance of humanity in his treatment of you. I should have known better—he's a monster whoever he's talking to, and probably the closer we are to him, the worse we suffer. That's why Arcadius is out in Oceanus, because it's as far away from Thetia as you can get.

"The others won't understand. They can't, because they're not Tar'Conanturs, so they just see him at a distance," she went on. "He did . . . something similar to me. That projection of him, it was the same thing he used to replace me at my funeral, when everyone thought I'd been murdered. What he actually did was kidnap me—maybe because the Exarch told him to, I don't know. He took my clothes and left me in a freezing cold cell for several days, never taking me out except to drug me and use my projection at the funeral. And after that he came to tell me that as far as the world knew I was dead and buried, and that the republican movement was breaking up. I think he was going to keep me there indefinitely, but the next day something had changed. He had me chained up, then gave me another drug . . . and I don't remember anything more until I woke up in Hamilcar's fortress."

I stared at Palatine for a moment, hardly believing what she was saying, and felt my skin prickle.

"I've never told anyone else and I never will, because it was as bad for me as it was for you."

"*As* bad?" I shuddered. What she'd described was ten times worse than anything he'd done to me. She'd told me without even having been asked, whereas I'd kept silent and endangered everyone.

"He never used magic on me, never tampered with my mind. I wouldn't have been brave enough to mention the harem, though. You got off lightly there."

"It's true, then?"

She sighed and sat back in her chair. "Absolutely. He's desperate to ensure the survival of the line. Either someone's making the concubines infertile, or he's just barren, which wouldn't surprise me. Still. Questions remain, like what to do now."

"Do we have to tell Mauriz and Telesta?"

"We can't, really, without explaining it, and I know you don't want to do that. Nor would I." She looked around the room suspiciously. "Laeas and Persea assured me that no one's eavesdropping, and I blocked up a listening hole here earlier, but you can't be certain. It is a palace, after all, and Sagantha will want to keep an eye on us. That's certain. I should have thought of this earlier, it's too late now."

"Do you think someone really has been listening?"

"I hope not. No way to tell. Sagantha does have a sense of honor. A selective one, perhaps, but it's to his credit that he has one at all."

"And the Emperor's people? Orosius must have someone here to have known where I was."

"I don't know how he found you," Palatine said, shrugging. "I know Orosius can't listen in to conversations—we set a trap once to find that out—so whatever he knows about us he's found out from his agents. Enough of this. He's cornered us now, and he's obviously planning something. It looks like he wants us to feel trapped, to believe that he can pre-empt anything we try."

"He can. It's not as if we have a lot of choices." I shifted position, slightly, my body feeling very leaden. The healer's draught had worked, partially at least, although there was still no position I could feel really comfortable in, and it felt stiflingly hot under the sheets in the enclosed room. "Could . . . wait, I'll whisper." Palatine leaned over and I said, "Could we persuade Tanais to depose him?"

"It would take a lot to convince him," she said doubtfully, staying close enough to whisper still. Perhaps it was melodramatic, but I didn't want to take any chances this time. "He believes in the monarchy more than anything else, and always has. He wouldn't accept a republic."

"There are other candidates."

"Don't go there, Cathan. Valdur did this once before. I shudder to think what Tanais would say."

"Tanais has a loyalty to the Empire. He said himself that Orosius isn't a credit to the family. Would he really stay loyal to such a man?"

Her green gaze fixed on me again, although this time I could meet it. "You know who you're proposing to replace him?"

"I know there are supposed to be three people in line. You tell me."

"My mother wouldn't, I don't believe in it, and Arcadius is too distant. And unmarried."

"Palatine," I said softly, "Orosius is a monster. What he can do to us, his closest relatives, he can do to anyone—and he will, if he's given the power."

"You're deadly serious about this, aren't you? Not just a wild idea."

"Did you expect anything else? I'm afraid of him, of what he can inflict on me, on you, on anyone. My war wasn't with him until today, but now it has to be. He and the Domain are allied, I know, but that isn't really what matters. If we achieve anything here, how long will it last before he steps in and crushes it? It doesn't matter whether it's in the Domain's name or his. We're a threat to them both, and they realized that before we did."

Palatine sat still for a long time after that, then moved the chair as close as she could to the bed. "Tell me what you're proposing, exactly."

I took a deep breath, aware that I'd need to take the sleeping draught soon, and told her what I'd worked out in the darkness of the map room, after Orosius had left me lying there like a trapped animal. That the Emperor wouldn't be able to find the *Aeon*, and that I might, if luck was with us for once, be better able to do so.

"Controlling the *Aeon* will help break the Domain's control here, because the protection they can provide from the storms is their main hold over people," I said at last. "It might give us a safe place as well, until they launch a crusade. But if we're to survive that, Thetia has to be on the right side. I want to find Ravenna, convince her that the only claim over Qalathar is hers, get her help. She might be able to put the final pieces of the puzzle in for me."

"While I ask Tanais to lead a military coup against the Emperor and put me on the throne instead," Palatine finished. "Do you really think it has a chance?"

"What other chance is there? If we just ignore Thetia, then all we do is build houses on sand, and sooner or later the tide will come in and destroy them. It would be all right if we could rely on neutrality, but I don't think Orosius will do that. He'll intervene, to restore his reputation and maybe to capture us as well."

"I will think," she said, after another long pause, "while you sleep. We don't tell the others what's happened or what we're planning. And whatever we do, you and Ravenna have to see each other as soon as possible, before you dig any more holes between you. I've been as guilty as either of you, but we have to trust each other. Sorry, I know it's a lame thing to say, but I'm thinking."

She handed me the sleeping draught, which for once didn't taste foul, and waited until I'd finished it.

"If it's any help, I think you do yourself too little credit," she said, pausing before she opened the door. "I think you'll be able to match Orosius with the *Aeon*. And to be there on the day he meets someone as powerful as he is, especially if it's you, would be a great privilege. Goodnight."

Palatine turned out the light as she went, and the door clicked closed behind her. For the second time in a day I was left in the dark, but there was no comparison with the previous occasion, and I was half-asleep this time anyway.

Despite the drug, I dreamed, a dream of the *Aeon* hanging in the shadows, a black bulk against a deeper blackness of the ocean, always hidden just out of sight.

Chapter XX

" 'In the name of Ranthas, His Grace commands you to deliver up these fugitives and sinners to justice, that they may atone for their sins against Ranthas and against the Domain, His servants on earth . . . They are guilty of the crimes of heresy, blasphemy and refusal to acknowledge the authority of His Holiness Lachazzar, thrice blessed of Ranthas . . . By the authority vested in all servants of the Domain by the Edict Universal and at the request of *Domine* Abisamar, Inquisitor-Captain of the Province and Islands of Sianor . . . Within the third hour after sunset on this sixty-third day of winter in the year of Ranthas 2775.' That's more or less what it says, not that you didn't already know." Laeas rolled the letter up and threw it on to the table in front of him. "Since no one's empowered to act in the Viceroy's absence, there's nothing I can do about it."

Standing stiffly off to one side, against the large windows of Sagantha's reception office, the Guard Tribune said, "Unfortunately, they won't take no for an answer."

"Well, they'll have to, for Ranthas's sake." Laeas leaned back in the large chair, looking pointedly at Mauriz and Telesta. "You got us into this trouble. Do you have anything useful to say?"

Mauriz wasn't used to being spoken to like that by anyone, especially not when they were not Thetian and were several years his junior.

"It's your duty to keep us safe, nothing else."

"Very helpful." Laeas rapped his knuckles on the desk, looking very authoritative, I thought. He, rather than Persea or Sagantha's secretary, was doing this simply because he was more imposing than either of them. I hadn't realized until this morning just how skeletal the Viceroy's staff was. Apparently several of them had taken to the hills or returned home when the Inquisitors arrived. "Diplomacy seems to be an alien word to you, despite your ostensibly being an envoy to someone. Of course we'll protect you, although in the event of Sacri storming this palace I can't guarantee your safety. There's nothing more I can tell you now."

"I wish to ensure that I can contact the Scartaris consul at any time of day."

"Talk to the Tribune here. He's in charge of all the runners."

Mauriz and Telesta spun on their heels and walked out, directing glares at Palatine and me as they did. I'd seen very little of them since we arrived, and they obviously resented the fact that we had more allies and sympathizers in Qalathar than they did. They must have been counting on protecting us, not the other way around.

After a quick discussion with Laeas about guards' leave, the Tribune also left. Laeas got up from behind the huge desk with a sigh of relief.

"Just my luck that the first time Sagantha goes away he leaves me with those two. Persea, you've been out. What's it like in the city?"

"Not good." She got up from her chair against one wall, next to where the Tribune had been standing. "The Inquisitors haven't caught many people, so they've issued another decree saying that they'll withhold blessing from the fishing fleets unless they have absolute cooperation. They can use *cooperation* to mean anything."

"Superstition," Laeas muttered. "The fishermen won't go out without a priest's blessing and his assurance that they'll be safe from storms. It's the second that's most important, really, but they're a superstitious lot."

"Come now, it's not as if *you* aren't," said Persea.

"Only to a point," he said crossly. "The idea that some mumbo-jumbo from a priest who has nothing to do with the sea will protect them and give them a good catch is ludicrous."

"You said it yourself, that's not what's really important. They have to consult the oceanographers to discover what the sea's like, and the Domain for the weather. And it's the Domain that holds the power there. It's a tradition as old as the Domain is, and nothing short of a miracle's going to change it." She glanced over at me as she said the next words. "Maybe you're our miracle."

It was said with such deadly seriousness that I didn't know how to reply. Persea's sense of humor was very direct, and I could tell when she was joking. This time she wasn't.

"I told them what you worked out yesterday, before the aether surge," said Palatine apologetically. "We need more help."

I wondered what else she'd told them, to make Persea come out with a comment like that. But the others didn't seem to find it ridiculous.

"Is the same thing happening on the other islands as well?"

"You know as much as we do there, but I presume so. Everywhere in the Archipelago works on the same general principles. Except the

Citadels, and all the people there have probably still got their heads in the clouds."

"Only at the Citadel of Wind," Laeas pointed out helpfully, and I couldn't help smiling. There'd been so little to joke about lately.

"How do people feel about the Inquisitors?" Palatine asked a moment later, breaking the brief moment of levity.

"They're not popular," Persea replied. "People resent the way they work, but they're usually too afraid to say anything openly. The city's changed in the last few weeks—I know it well enough to see the difference. Oh, and the other thing, I should have mentioned it earlier, is that there are a lot of rumors going around. Many of them are about the Domain, what Midian's going to do, but there are a lot, and they're fairly consistent, saying that the Pharaoh has returned. Now we know that she has—" my gaze met Palatine's for a second in a brief flicker of alarm, dispelled by Persea's next words "—because Ravenna's gone to join her."

"What are they saying?" Laeas asked, suddenly more intense than he'd been all morning, his overworked-aide look vanishing.

"What you'd expect, really. The Pharaoh is back on the island, she's in hiding somewhere, she's going to return and deal with the Domain, even that she's raising an army. I've heard these rumors before, so it's too early to tell whether they're being spread deliberately or not, but people want to believe them. They want to think that the girl they've waited twenty-four years for is finally going to step into her grandfather's shoes and drive the Domain out."

"And so do you," Palatine said.

"It's totally irrational, knowing how bad things are, but you're right, I *so much* want it to be true. Mauriz and Telesta don't understand it."

"But do you believe in the Pharaoh herself, or just in someone who'll get rid of the Domain? That's what everyone wants most, to see them thrown out of the islands and never come back. I think they'd even put up with the storms for that. They're not as bad here as on the Continents, we might just be able to manage."

"We—the people of Qalathar—could throw them out ourselves, theoretically. But then we'd just be a disorganized mob. Everyone here has grown up with our parents telling us how brilliant Orethura was, how he kept the Domain in check for so long, how he resisted them until the end. They lived through the Crusade, and they're the ones who told us about his granddaughter."

"I don't think this is an argument you can win, Palatine," I said from my armchair over in a corner facing the desk. I felt like an old man, still having to be helped around, but Orosius's magic had been a lot more pernicious than I thought, and still weighed very heavily on me. I ached to my bones all over, in my arms and legs especially, and I felt renewed sympathy for Carausius, attacked in the same way during the last battle of the War, so badly crippled that he'd thought he would never work magic again. In the end he had, one last time, to take Sanction out of Valdur's reach and himself out of history. I couldn't see how he could have survived. "Orethura was the first Pharaoh in three hundred years to be born an Archipelagan. His granddaughter's the same."

"I see the point," Palatine admitted. "But if she *is* back, *what's she going to do*? None of you seem to have thought of this. Midian controls the harbor, nearly all the military, the city walls, and the towns. Not to mention a large number of mages. The Pharaoh doesn't have any force to speak of. And what about Sagantha?"

"If the Pharaoh comes back, Sagantha doesn't have to take responsibility for anything," I pointed out. "He keeps his position but is no longer the chief scapegoat. Why in heaven's name did he take this post in the first place? He must have known it would be a minefield."

"Sagantha flourishes in minefields," said Persea. "He's a born survivor."

According to Ravenna, that was simply because he knew when to change sides.

Midian had left Sacri in front of the gate to remind us of his demand, but they disappeared after two days when a howling storm descended on the city. The clouds were so thick and dark that night effectively fell hours early. I watched it from the window of my room for a while, looking out over a dark gray sea and brooding bruise-colored thunderclouds that stretched all the way to an obscured horizon. The only relief was the lightning and the white of the breakers crashing against the sea wall, but even that disappeared around the time sunset would have been.

It was impossible to discover anything simply from being inside the storm. My scope was too limited, bounded by the steadily narrowing visibility and the oncoming night. It was a cyclonic storm, I could tell, moving along the storm band like a mobile timber knot; the wind was coming from the north, not along the east-west axis of the storm band itself.

Worse than not being able to tell was not having anyone to discuss it with. The oceanographers were all too afraid of the Domain, and the one other person who ever seemed to have investigated had been dead for—

how long? I actually had no idea when Salderis had died; nothing had been heard since her exile forty years ago. I didn't even have a copy of *Ghosts of Paradise*; it belonged to Telesta and I had no desire to talk either to her or to Mauriz. For the first time in weeks I felt I had a sense of purpose and knew where I was going again. Talking to either of the Thetians would only destroy it.

In any case, Telesta wasn't an oceanographer. Maybe she had an interest in the history of oceanography—I wasn't sure—but she wasn't a scientist. Tetricus? It was a pity he hadn't come, really; he had none of the loyalties that kept getting in the way. But then, I wouldn't have wanted to drag him into this situation.

If Sarhaddon had been an oceanographer . . . I felt a deep twinge of regret and sadness. All that intelligence and wit, and he'd ended up as a fanatic and an Inquisitor.

I didn't know any more oceanographers, which was not surprising given how much of my life I'd spent in Lepidor. A few passing acquaintances from a group who'd visited Lepidor and Kula once . . . I seemed to remember they were from Liona, in the northern Archipelago, on the same current system as home. If I ever managed to find the *Aeon*, I'd need help. Help to man her, help to understand what the SkyEyes told me, help even to keep her provisioned. Something else I hadn't thought of. The ship could produce its own food somehow, strange as that sounded, but after two centuries everything inside would be dead.

And Ravenna . . . Ravenna was a mage, not an oceanographer, although she'd had a few lessons from the Master of Lepidor's oceanographic station at her own request before we'd left. I missed her dreadfully, especially knowing that the last time we'd seen each other she'd viewed me as a rival, a threat to her heritage. Persea and Laeas were passing on messages through their contacts, hoping that sooner or later one would reach her—they still thought that she was a companion of the Pharaoh. And I was hoping that she hadn't turned against me again as she had in Lepidor.

A line of palm trees was silhouetted against the lights just beneath me, bent nearly sideways by the force of the wind, and every so often there was the occasional sharp crack as a branch broke loose. Tiles fell from a house over the street, shattering as they hit the roadway, and a moment later a loose shutter crashed past. If this was a large storm, it had barely begun; surely the city couldn't take damage like this every time?

"Worse than usual," Persea said when I found her much later on, working behind the desk in the reception office where we'd been this morning. The curtains were open to give her a view out on the city, and all the lights were on full. "I've had reports of damage from all over, and we're nowhere near the eye yet."

"Is there a shield up?" I perched on the edge of the desk, warming my hands under one of the ornate reading lights; for some reason it was very cold in the palace tonight.

"Yes, but it's only a weak one by your standards. Storms aren't usually as bad here. It won't help if this continues." She scrawled something at the bottom of a piece of paper and put it to one side.

"All the Domain mages must be useful for something."

"That's the problem. They can stop it, yes, but only as long as they want to." She shivered, looking around in irritation. "It's freezing in here. What's wrong with the hypocaust?"

I got off the desk and touched my hand to the floor between two of the Ferratan rugs. The stone, which should have been slightly warm to the touch, was cold.

"The fire must have gone out hours ago, and no one's noticed," Persea said after testing it the same way.

"It's past midnight—they're all in bed."

"Why not you?"

"I slept too long with that potion. I'm still not tired at all."

"I wish I could have too much sleep. The whole palace will freeze if we don't do something about this, so let's go and have a look at the generator."

I headed for the door, but Persea called me back and drew aside a curtain in a corner behind the desk, revealing a smaller entrance and a poky hallway. A narrow spiral of stone steps led down to one side, lit by a painfully unshielded aether globe.

"You lived in a palace, you must have had passages like these," she said as I followed her down the steps. "I used to think secret passages were terribly exotic, now they're just useful. And not very secret."

We came out into a wider hallway with a few doors leading off. The walls were painted rather than being the unadorned rough stone of the traditional warren, but this was more a convenient route to somewhere than a genuine passageway. We had a couple in Lepidor that everybody knew about, and so did some of the larger Houses. One had saved my life during the occupation.

"Where does the main passage go?" I asked, following Persea through another door and into a long, narrow room with locked cupboards along one whole wall.

"It connects everything on this level. This is the lower floor, the level of the gardens. The generators are down below."

"Why so far down?" My voice boomed suddenly as we left the long room and went down another flight of stairs, wide and straight, leading into the generator room. It was even colder than it had been upstairs.

"It's safe this far below ground, so . . . Where's the engineer?"

The flamewood generator that should have powered the palace's heating system was a cold, lightless bulk taking up most of the room. Crystal slits that should have glowed blue with aether were dark, and there was a total silence where the hum of the reactor should have sounded.

Persea reached out her hand hesitantly, touched the outer casing of the reaction chamber and jerked it back instinctively, hardly touching it. Then she laid her palm on metal that should have been blisteringly hot to the touch, and said, "Cold."

There was no sign of the engineer whose duty it was to keep the system in working order, nor of his night-shift deputy. The whole palace depended on this set-up—heating, hot water, cooking fires, all the lights that weren't run off stored aether.

"We have four hours of reserve lighting," Persea said, walking around one side of the reactor. "We must have nearly exhausted it. No time to linger here." She stopped on the far side, hidden from me. "Um, Cathan, could you please look at this?"

Written in glowing, insubstantial letters on the back of the furnace was a passage from the *Book of Ranthas*.

Fire is the gift of Ranthas. He brings light and warmth to those who fear him, darkness and death to those who turn their face from him. When they cower all alone in the night, shivering with the cold of the mountains in winter, they will know the true power of Him and His righteous warmth.

"Interdict," I said, my heart sinking. "No fires will light in the palace until they lift it." Fire was the Domain's element, and they could give it and take it away at will. Making us completely helpless.

Persea clutched her arms around her chest. "I should have remembered they could do this."

"No point in wasting time down here. It's warmer up above."

"Nowhere will be warm."

We ran back up as fast as we could, back up to the room we'd come from where Persea extinguished all the lights and summoned the night steward. His face was ashen in the pale glow of the single aether lamp as we told him what had happened, the noise of the rain against the window-panes providing a sobering accompaniment.

"I can't keep the house running, Ma'am," he said bluntly. "I'm sure my superior will agree, we can't feed everyone like this. It'll get worse tonight, much worse, and no lighting or heating tomorrow. Especially if the storm goes on."

"We'll have to keep on for now," Persea said. "Go around, tell all your staff what's happened, work out something for tonight. Turn every light out as soon as you can, and find all the spare blankets we have. Pass on the same instructions to the guard, and I want everyone assembled in and around the courtyard at what would normally be breakfast time tomorrow." When he'd gone she turned to me. "We're going back to my room to find more clothes, then we'll tell the others. Don't bother with Mauriz and Telesta. It's their fault—they can suffer."

In the event we did need, both of us, more clothes before we went to wake the others. Laeas had to know, and Palatine couldn't stand the cold. Not surprising for a Thetian.

We held an impromptu conference in Palatine's bedroom, sitting on the side of the bed that she'd refused to get out of. I was the best off of the four of us, used to snow and cold northern winters. But I'd never slept in an unheated building during a storm before, and the Viceroy's Palace was a tropical building, not designed to keep the heat in.

"There's really nothing we can do?" Palatine asked.

I shook my head. "We can't even relight the fires until they lift the ban. Which, presumably, won't be until we're all handed over."

"I'll send to Sagantha first thing tomorrow," Laeas said, his voice getting deeper the way it did when he was angry. "With any luck he'll be able to sort them out. Bastards. Putting us under interdict because we refuse to recognize those pathetic trumped-up charges. Mauriz is a pain but, and I hate to admit it, he's completely in the right here."

"But Sagantha won't be here until evening at least, and I'm not sure we'll be able to hold on to the staff until then."

"The staff all hate the Domain as much as we do. They'll stay with us as long as they can."

"Which will be until about lunchtime tomorrow, when we have fifty people and no way to cook anything. No one will want to eat fruit for weeks on end."

"And without the lights, everything has to stop at sunset," Palatine added. "It's so dark during the day anyway, with this storm."

"We have to hope the storm's a short one, but I agree with you on that. It'll be black every night once the sun goes down—there's no way we can keep going. Fine, if only the main power had failed, but the rest of the lights have gone now. Mine stopped working before you came. I thought it was just drained." Laeas stared out of the window, its curtains open to admit the faint light from outside.

"Do you really think Sagantha can get Midian to lift the interdict?" I asked doubtfully. I couldn't see his expression as he answered. "Sagantha can usually manage that."

"Without handing us all over?"

"He won't."

"Yet," said Palatine.

Laeas turned toward her for a moment, probably with a black look, then looked away again. "He wants you for some other reason. Firstly, he won't give you up so easily, not when it means execution. Secondly, it's not in his interests."

"Why?" she demanded. "He wants to stop Mauriz plotting against the Pharaoh. What better way than giving him to Midian? Mauriz's plotting is stopped, Midian's happy, Sagantha gains favor, life goes back to normal. Or as normal as it gets here."

Laeas ignored the last comment. "And Sagantha loses favor with the people. He's playing both ends against the middle. If he gives you and the Thetians up, the ordinary Qalatharis see him as a weak-willed collaborator, he loses their support, and if the Pharaoh ever comes back, he'll be out. They've put up with worse themselves—I can remember the whole city being under Interdict for nearly a week. Six or seven years ago, when my parents lived here for a while. We all ate fruit and leftovers, and when it got dark, it got dark. Fine by me," he added. "I got to spend more time with my girlfriend without anyone noticing."

"That was high summer, Laeas," Persea said, a note of humor in her voice. "You can sleep outside without any blanket then. You probably did, in fact."

"We'd probably find this wonderful if we were that age," Palatine said. "Or children. Parents distracted, everything in the dark—as long as things don't get too inconvenient it's great fun."

"Play murder games and sit around with candles. Although, of course, they wouldn't work either."

"Pretend to be pirates in caves, gloating over booty," was Persea's suggestion.

"And when the stable cat appears, it's turned into a huge demonic tiger," I said, speaking from experience. The one we'd had when I was a child had been huge, and black, with yellow eyes like some terrible creature of the night. Much given to prowling around in dark places and giving people a fright when it appeared from nowhere.

"I don't know why you needed an actual cat," Laeas said with mock reproach. "We could conjure anything up out of thin air—a whisper of wind in the trees and we were all searching for forest demons."

"Owls," Persea said firmly. "They're the worst. When I was outside, at night, however many people I was with, the owls always got me. They hoot, and it's so eerie, then they swoop down out of the trees and they look so big. Ravens and crows make horrible noises, but they're not as menacing as the owls."

I smiled, as did the others, silent for a moment. Probably the others had the same thoughts that I did, looking back through rose-tinted glasses and thinking how much simpler things had been. When all there was to be scared of was parental retribution, and things that went bump in the night.

Someone had to break the spell eventually, but it wasn't me, and Palatine did it as gently as possible.

"Time to relive all that, I think, for tonight at least," she said. "And until the storm finishes."

Despite the situation, though, the mood had lightened. We were cold and facing a night without heat or light, but somehow it seemed more bearable after remembering nights spent in tree houses. After all, I'd even managed to sleep on a rock in the middle of the Citadel's rainforest for a night, a few paces away from a waterfall.

"He's gone for the wrong tactic, I think," Laeas said suddenly. "Deprive us of light and warmth, and it just gives us a hard time. The city isn't affected. If he'd done it the other way around, put everyone under interdict except for us, we'd have had a mob at the gates inside two days screaming for us to give him what he wanted."

"You really think so?" asked Persea.

"It wouldn't be worth his while. If it was the Pharaoh Midian wanted, it'd be a lot harder, and I think the mob would be at his gates, not ours. But for a few Thetians, why put up with all the inconvenience?"

"Don't go giving them ideas. I hate mobs. Even when you're part of one, it's horrible, because you simply lose control."

"Lots of experience, Persea?" Palatine said.

She smiled faintly. "Here and there. I don't ever want to be in that position again, unless it's in the market square in Poseidonis, waiting for the Pharaoh to come out on her balcony and announce the refounding of the city."

"I'd drink to that, but I don't seem to have anything to drink."

"Brilliant idea," Laeas said. "Back in a minute."

He was, with a small, heavy glass bottle and four tiny glasses. I couldn't read the label on the bottle, but guessed it was one of those lethal spirits the Archipelagans were so fond of drinking.

I was wrong. "Thetian spice brandy," he said, pouring a small measure into each glass. "You'll be fine, Cathan, it's not actually as strong as it tastes. You have to drink it in one draught."

"To the Pharaoh," Persea said, when he'd put the bottle away again, "and to Poseidonis."

"To the Pharaoh," we echoed, and drank.

I nearly choked on the alien taste of it, but once I'd got it down, and felt the warmth in my chest, I had to admit that it wasn't that bad.

We looked at each other uncertainly, then slid off the bed and gave the glasses back to Laeas. I threw Palatine a bundle of extra clothing before we left and went out separate ways. I could see well enough to find my way back to my room, so I parted company with Laeas and Persea outside, and went back to my room to try and make myself as warm as possible. I slept a troubled sleep, with the wind and rain howling outside and a terrible chill in the room, and awoke to an even more troubled day.

Chapter XXI

I was shaken awake by Palatine, and opened my eyes to see her swathed in a military cloak, a scarf wrapped around her head. Where had she got that from?

"Only a northerner could sleep through this."

I glanced over at the window, and my heart sank as I saw rivulets of rain running down the panes against the backdrop of a leaden sky outside. There was a crack of thunder, followed by a rolling barrage that went on and on as the dark room was lit up by successive flashes of sheet lightning.

I pushed back the covers reluctantly and grabbed my own cloak, unfortunately not a military one. I'd slept fully clothed every night for the two weeks since the reactor had gone dead, but getting out of bed was still a shock.

"Why so early?" I asked her, pulling fresh clothes and a towel from where I'd left them the night before. She was holding hers rolled up under her arm.

"Not that early—dawn was three hours ago."

"What dawn?" My words were drowned out by another deafening roll of thunder. "No sign of an end to this yet?"

She shook her head. "Our hot water supply's very limited this morning: our friends outside the walls are too busy making sure their house doesn't fall down. Had to get you up or you'd miss it all."

"Thanks."

I followed her through the corridors, where isolated aether lights burned here and there, down to the small room on the ground floor that was serving as an impromptu washroom. A hole had been hacked in the wall and a copper pipe put through to the nearest friendly house, across the street to one side of the palace. They piped up what they could heat every morning, but it wasn't nearly enough.

"Just in time," Laeas said, as I nearly slipped on the damp stone. It was marginally warmer in here than it was anywhere else, but only the water had any real heat in it. "I've been holding some for you. We're the last; all the servants were up ages ago."

I put my stuff down in the roughly curtained-off cubicle to one side that served as a changing room, a space barely large enough for two people to stand up in, let alone change.

"You two go first." Persea's voice came from the other side. "And for Thetis's sake hurry up. The water's getting colder all the time."

Laeas and I were as quick as possible with the improvised shower—a hose attached to a drum on the end of the pipe, which stored up water and then delivered it in short bursts, usually with just enough time between bursts for the person showering to feel cold. The water was only lukewarm this morning, and we were limited to two bursts each, about enough to get wet all over but no more.

Once I'd finished, I wrapped the towel around myself, shivering while I worked the apparatus for Laeas. Then we dashed into the cubicle and changed as quickly as possible, without drying ourselves properly. It was uncomfortable, but not unbearable. Everyone's motto during the past fortnight.

Used to this routine by now, I was fully dressed in half a minute or so, and gathered up my clothes, waiting until the women had finished. Then, as the last people to use it, we tidied the room as much as we could before depositing our old clothes in the laundry bag and heading upstairs, hoping to find something for breakfast.

"Not many deliveries this morning," Laeas said gloomily. "Storm's too bad."

"Can you remember a winter like this?" I asked.

He shook his head. "This is the worst I've known, and it sounds as if the rest of the island is getting it too. Another roof came off in the middle of the night, injured quite a few people. No one dead, thankfully, but we couldn't get anyone to the infirmary."

"And the Viceroy?"

"His usual self. He's decided to go back to full lighting again, now that we've restored the connection to the city network. We're to turn everything on tonight, send a message to that bastard in the temple that there are a few loopholes in his mages' powers. Thank heaven whoever built this pile was too mean to put in direct flamewood lighting."

"Wonder what the theological significance of aether is," Palatine remarked, as we arrived at the kitchen.

The fruit remaining was mostly oranges, and we took a couple each as well as whatever else we could get. Which was not very much after everyone else had taken their share, but at least the servants were now being fed by helpful neighbors. They were eating a lot better than we were, actually, although twice in the last fortnight the Viceroy had taken us to dinner at a restaurant nearby, with a massive escort to prevent Midian trying anything.

I'd been looking forward to today, until the storm had hit. Last night the guards had finished reopening a tunnel—a genuine secret passage, this one—that led downhill to a small house overlooking the harbor. It gave us an escape route as well as, more importantly, a chance to go out into the city. The Viceroy was even allowing the two Thetians out, properly disguised, on a kind of parole. If neither came back at the specified time, he'd lift his protection. There were no ships leaving the harbor in this weather, so they couldn't get away.

But with the appalling weather, I couldn't see us being able to go. Few shops would open on a day as bad as this, and it was so miserable outside that none of us really felt like braving the elements. We could see just as much—and get just as wet—in the palace garden.

On the other hand, there was so little to do in the palace that Palatine and I had been getting more and more restless and irritable as the days passed. The palace felt like a prison, a dark and gloomy one with a regime of austerity. And outside, a mob baying for the Sacri, who'd kept watch on the gate every day they could. Midian hadn't lessened his demands, hadn't given in to Sagantha's diplomacy. He held all the cards here in Qalathar, and he knew it.

"There you are," a voice came as I finished my second orange. I looked around to see the Viceroy's secretary standing in the doorway. "He wants to see you as soon as you've finished."

"Fine," Laeas called back. I wondered what it was this time. Not more dire news, I hoped. There had been more arrests: over two hundred people were now incarcerated in the temple prison, awaiting or undergoing trials for heresy. Some of them would burn, which made me sick every time I thought about it. Was it really worth it? The priests almost always offered a way out, but many didn't take it. This time, as in Lepidor, it would be worse: they'd give their victims less of a chance. And they were using torture. That was a flagrant contradiction of their own laws, not to mention a flouting of numerous earlier Imperial decrees that were ignored by the current Emperor as well as by the Inquisitors.

Nobody in their right mind wanted to face torture or the stake, so those arrested gave in, gave more names when threatened again, and more people were apprehended. Fishing fleets couldn't leave until the

Inquisitors were satisfied that none of the crews were heretics. And still there was no hope on the horizon, except for the (by now) old rumors about the Pharaoh.

That was not, as we discovered when we arrived in Sagantha's office, the case anymore. Grander than the room that we'd used while he was away, with a high ceiling and expensive rugs on the floor, the faint lighting didn't do it justice. His desk stood in a pool of brightness in an otherwise rather dark and dull room, and at his invitation we all pulled up chairs around it.

"Palatine, Cathan, you and the others need to leave," he said without preamble, sitting back in the plain but cushioned chair he used. Governing an occupied country from a dark and unheated palace was taking its toll, and there were lines on his face that hadn't been there before. I still had no idea why he'd accepted the Viceroyalty. "I've allowed you into town as a temporary measure, but this can't go on forever. Things are getting too bad here, and you're a source of tension. I'm not throwing you out or anything, but you're achieving nothing here, and I think the rest of the island is too dangerous."

Palatine and I looked at each other uneasily. Neither of us wanted to stay penned up in the palace, but to leave the island, Ravenna, probably any hope of finding the *Aeon*, sounded just as bad.

"Neither of you are happy about it, I can tell."

"Can we just disappear?" Palatine asked. "No protection, we'll take our own chances."

"Yes, but doing what? You came here with a plan to supplant the Pharaoh."

"We came as part of *Mauriz's* plan to supplant the Pharaoh," I corrected him. "I'm the pawn, remember?"

"You are, Cathan, but wasn't Palatine heavily involved in it? From a political point of view, you're both wild cards with no loyalty to anyone concerned."

Not sure how high his opinion of me was, I decided to take a risk and try focusing his attention on something else. Although even if it worked, I wasn't sure whether it would backfire on me.

"Not true," I said defensively. Then I added, lamely, "For either of us."

"Ravenna." He rested his chin on his fist for a moment, giving me a searching look. I'd told him the truth, but only part of it; I hoped that would be enough. We'd agreed that we shouldn't tell him about the *Aeon* because we couldn't trust him not to call in the Cambressians. "You know she left because she didn't trust you?"

It was a bitter blow, hearing it from Sagantha, but it was something I already knew.

"She didn't trust me over Mauriz's plan." *Because I was a Tar'Conantur*, I added silently, and wondered if there would ever be a way to get around it.

"Do you think she'll have changed her mind?"

"Am I going to end up as anything other than a puppet Hierarch? I decided to go along with them after she left, when it looked as if theirs might be the best way to get rid of the Domain. What chance do they have now?"

"Realistically, there isn't any way to get rid of them," he said heavily. "No troops, nothing to counter their mages, no protection from the storms. Yes, I know you and Ravenna managed that incredible thing in Lepidor, but that was against one mage and a handful of Sacri, on friendly territory. All the Pharaoh can do is hide out in the countryside. If she starts killing priests, there'll be more arrests and trials."

He would have been right—if it hadn't been for the *Aeon*. The Sacri weren't the decisive factor here, well trained as they were. They just protected the Inquisition while it went about its work. And the Inquisition had the whole island at its mercy. Would people still support Ravenna if even mentioning the Pharaoh was declared heresy?

"If you ship Mauriz and Telesta and their staff out somehow, preferably back to Thetia," Palatine said, "all we ask is to get safely out of the palace."

"Will your friends help them?" the Viceroy asked Laeas and Persea.

They looked at each other quickly, then nodded. "If we get rid of some of Cathan's disguise, it should work. Leave the eyes, make his skin darker, he'll still be Thetian but not distinctive."

"I'll think about it," Sagantha said shortly, making a gesture of dismissal. "Laeas and Persea, I need your help with this correspondence."

"How on earth is he planning to get us out?" Palatine said when we'd shut the doors behind us and were safely out of earshot. "They search every ship that leaves, even the fishing boats. He's up to something, no question about it. Yesterday he was talking about us staying for weeks more here, which was very depressing. Now, suddenly, we have to go, and especially Mauriz and Telesta have to go. He doesn't seem that concerned about the two of us."

I shook my head. "Normally I'd agree with you, but that doesn't ring true either. We're more use to him than Mauriz or Telesta, surely. Aren't we?"

"Yes, you're right." We emerged into the main courtyard with its rising colonnade, now dull and gray in the pouring rain, and ran three doors along. One of the main corridors was closed because of a skylight that had been broken the day before, and the tribune's men were busy repairing the damage. "You especially. As Hierarch you're too valuable to let go, especially for a Cambressian, and as the one person Ravenna feels any real affection for, he can use you in his dealing with her. You're not through being a pawn yet."

"I know. But I will be. The longer we stay here, the more chance we have of hearing from Ravenna."

"It's been five days so far. Even if you hear from her tomorrow, every exchange of messages will use up more time."

I smiled at Palatine and shook my head. For once I'd managed to come up with something entirely independently. "When the message goes back I'll be able to trace it."

"Magic?" She frowned.

"Of a kind."

"Won't that attract the Domain mages' attention?"

"It only works because we've linked minds before, no other reason. And when I find her she'll make me tell her how, so I won't be able to use it on her again. Just this once, I'll know how far away she is, in what direction. It should be enough."

"Your mind's taking a worrying turn, Cathan," Palatine said, smiling slightly. "If I didn't know better, I'd say you had an idea of what you're going to do."

"Yes, I do," I said curtly, my momentary good spirits vanishing in an instant. Despite the humor, she made it sound as if my having an idea was unprecedented. Did everyone really have that low an estimation of me? Or was it just because she was Palatine, the one who always had the ideas?

"I'm sorry," she said, putting her hand on my arm as a placatory gesture.

I pulled away from her and deliberately turned back the way we'd come. "No, you just regret having said it out loud. No sympathy required."

I walked back along the colonnade, ignoring the biting wind, and headed through the gray corridors to the library. Telesta would probably be there, but what did it matter? She had the same opinion of me the others did, only—like Mauriz—she didn't hide it. I knew I was a hopeless, indecisive leader, but did that make any ideas I had freakish in their rarity?

Telesta was, as I'd expected, already in the library, standing in front of a light with a massive black-bound volume propped up against one of the shelves.

"Cathan. Good morning." She glanced out of the rain-streaked window. "Or maybe not. I haven't seen you for a while."

"I don't come in here very often," I said neutrally.

"Time passes at a different rate in here. The days don't drag so much."

Time passes at a different rate for Clan Polinskarn, was my private thought, but I didn't voice it. I'd been intending to come and see her for several days, but had kept postponing it through an unwillingness to talk to either of the Thetians. I'd only really come here through a spur-of-the-moment decision in any case, and might have gone on putting it off forever.

"Could I borrow some of this time, then, if you can spare it?"

"Depends whether I can help you." Telesta closed the book and slid it back into its place on the opposing shelf. "If our contract still holds, then I owe you more answers. Is it historical?"

"Partly. At least, the *question* is historical. I'm not sure about the answer though."

"Go on."

"Tanais Lethien. Do you know who or what he is?"

She pulled two chairs up to the table nearest the light and indicated for me to sit down. "To explain that, I'm going to have to tell you a fairly long story. Have you the time?"

I nodded and sat down.

"You know that the Tuonetar Wars went on for centuries, in fact for the whole of Thetia's existence until the usurpation. The Thetians always knew that the Tuonetar were there beyond the outer islands, an enemy there could never be peace with. No one ever considered a treaty with the Tuonetar, although there were periods without fighting. We were a warrior society in those days. The women fought alongside the men, as they still would if it were allowed, but there was always a distinction between the time for war and time for peace. Thetia itself, until the very end, was sacrosanct, a place for pleasure, music, dancing. All the greatest operas, the greatest poets, the greatest philosophers, are from that time.

"We fought for centuries with the clans, using a levy of ships and marines that served for a campaign before going home again. There was no standing army except for the Imperial Guard, who we still call the Ninth Legion despite there being no other legions anymore. There were only a handful, even in those days. It wasn't until the time of Valentine, Aetius's father, that the Navy was formed, a time when the Tuonetar suddenly started appearing in greater numbers.

"The clans were very reluctant to give up ships, so the Navy started off with a collection of reject mantas, manned by misfits and opportunists. Most of the marines had to be lured away from fishing villages to serve for a pittance, until the Emperor could persuade the Assembly to give him some funds. But they didn't, and the fleet had to subsist on what it could plunder from enemy strongholds. Valentine was an old man by this time, and he was directing all his energies into winning battles. The clan forces were tried and tested, if unreliable, and, as the clan leaders had hoped, the Navy was sidelined." She shrugged. "Things don't change, except now it's the other way around." She was still wearing black, her body almost indistinguishable in the general gloom, only her face properly visible in the pale aether light.

"I suppose the Navy would have died a slow death in time," she continued, "just being used for mopping up unimportant outposts, had it not been for a young marine on the flagship. He was a centurion, promoted from the ranks as they always have been. His name was Tanais Lethien, and he came from the mountains inside Canteni territory. You give up your clan name when you join the Navy or the Guard, but he was originally Canteni."

I'd never realized that, but it made sense. The warrior Canteni, they called themselves, even now when their martial spirit was only remarkable when compared to that of the other clans.

"When the flagship was boarded during some minor skirmish, Tanais managed not only to repel the Tuonetar but also to capture the ship they'd boarded from. He used it as bait to lure the rest of the enemy into a trap. And because of the way the Tuonetar navy worked, using a few carrier ships and a lot of smaller ones, he'd managed to strip the defenses from one of the carriers. The clan forces under an Imperial admiral told him to stand off until they could catch up with the Tuonetar carrier and destroy it, but Tanais feared that it might get away. So he convinced the flagship's senior surviving officer, a lieutenant called Cleomenes Cidelis, to disobey orders and give chase."

Cidelis, the future admiral. This must have been twenty-five years before the end of the War; I'd had no idea that Tanais had known Cidelis for so long.

"They destroyed the carrier, but when the admiral got there he was furious and demanded the arrest of both Tanais and Cidelis for disobeying orders. They resisted—possibly not a good idea—and the two fleets escorted each other back to port. Tanais and Cidelis were taken to the capital and court-martialed, but a sixteen-year-old called Carausius persuaded his twin brother, the Crown Prince, to intervene. Emperor Valentine pardoned the two officers and actually promoted them."

"The point of all this was that it marked the first time the Imperial force was taken seriously. Tanais and Cidelis gave it a sense of pride, and the Emperor stopped ignoring it. In a decade they turned it from a joke into what we now know; Tanais founded the legions and Cidelis made the Imperial fleet bigger than the clan one—they even had clan ships deserting to go over to the Navy.

"The two of them founded the Imperial military, the military Aetius used to win the war. The army never forgot what Tanais and Cidelis had done, and they never forgot Aetius's intervention. Clever Carausius let his brother take the credit, and that was something his son would despise him for.

"Tanais ended up as Marshal, a post Aetius created specially for him, and fought all through the war. He never lost a battle, not once in all those years. You know what happened during the War, how in the end the army followed the four of them into Aran Cthun. Every year on the anniversary of Aran Cthun's fall the Navy and the legions hold a service for the dead, to remember that march, and Aetius's death, and the fact that Tanais and Cidelis saved them. They see Tanais almost as a god, even now.

"I'm not sure what happened during the usurpation. Both of them were away from Selerian Alastre on the night that Tiberius was murdered. Cidelis was never heard of again. He's not on the list of Valdur's victims, or among those who went over to the usurper, or on the roll of the Founding Fathers of Cambress. It's as if he disappeared off the face of the earth; I personally think he committed suicide.

"But Tanais didn't. He's not on any of the lists either, but during the first five years of Valdur's reign someone killed every member of the high command who'd gone over to Valdur. You know that from the Continuator as well, but Tanais didn't reappear until after Valdur was dead. He was murdered too, though not by Tanais. A religious maniac cut him down at the palace gates. Such a fitting end.

"Since then Tanais has appeared once or twice a generation for a few months at a time before he vanishes into the shadows again. Just enough to keep the legend alive, for enough of the officers to see him, for the Emperor to know who he is. He's come to the Imperial funerals, my father saw him when Perseus was buried. He's never interfered in the succession, but if he told the military to make him Emperor, they probably would."

"It doesn't sound like something he'd do."

"Who knows? How can he live for over two hundred and fifty years?"

"Centuries to us, but to him?" I said, wondering. "When was his last appearance?"

"In Thetia, about four years ago. He spent three months at the military academy, which was when he tutored Palatine. But you've met him, so obviously he spends time in places other than Thetia."

"It's still perfectly possible that in two centuries he's only been active for ten years or so, though?"

"That was my thought as well. Yes, if you add up the time he's known to have been active, it comes to only a fraction of those centuries. And there's a lot of magic we know nothing about, not since the purges. The Domain mages might be able to explain it, I suppose."

"So you believe he *is* Aetius's marshal."

She looked surprised. "What else could he be? Everything else is absolutely consistent. Isn't it a principle of logic and of science, that all other things being equal, whichever explanation is the simplest will be correct?"

"Do you think it's an existence any human being could tolerate?"

"I believe human beings can tolerate anything, given hope. It's an old idea, of course, and if you've read enough Thetian philosophy you'll be familiar with the opposite argument."

"I'm afraid not. I've read some philosophy, but I only really paid attention to the scientific works."

"Manathes's *Natural History*, Bostra's *On the Nature of Things*?"

"And others. Yes, they were always more interesting."

"I never got on with Bostra. Too dull, too pedantic. Cathan, why exactly do you want to know about Tanais?"

She said it in exactly the same tone she'd used for the sentence before, springing the question on me without warning. I thought I'd got away with it, that she'd assume Tanais was relevant enough to need no explanation.

The real reason—that I'd asked to find out his link to the much more obscure Cidelis—was something I had no intention of revealing. "He's important. And I wondered how you can talk about him and never question who he is."

"Why did you ask me instead of Palatine?"

"You're a historian." Weak, perhaps, and Palatine's connection with Tanais might mean she knew much more. And because I felt Telesta would have been more likely to be interested in the details. "Is there really no record of what he did during the usurpation?"

"Not that I've seen. My guess would be that he was incapacitated by

assassins, poisoned maybe, and got out of the way so that he couldn't
cause trouble."

"But what could he have done? Once Tiberius was dead, Valdur was
the last remaining Tar'Conantur."

"You forget that Valdur wasn't acting with hindsight. He murdered
his cousin, the rightful Emperor, and he might well have been afraid that
Tanais would simply kill him and seize the throne. Tanais couldn't have
been attacked openly, he was too important, but if he was out of the way,
then Valdur would have time to consolidate. Cidelis could have been
quietly murdered at the same time. If any excuse was needed, Valdur
could say that he—and maybe Tanais as well—went down with the
flagship."

"You mean the huge ship, the *Aeon*?" I said, doing my best to feign
ignorance. "How could he have explained that? By saying it was blown
up?"

"It wasn't," she said, looking at me curiously, and for a moment I felt
an icy stab of fear that I'd given it away. But then her skeptical expression
disappeared, and I heaved an inner sigh of relief. "That was a fabrication.
He made up the story because it was an embarrassment not to have the
Aeon. I think it probably *was* destroyed in the end, by Cidelis, because
there's been no more mention of it, and something so big would be
impossible to hide. Too much time since then for it still to be unnoticed.
Maybe—"

She never finished that sentence, because there was a sharp knocking
on the door and Persea came in.

"Sorry to disturb you, but we have more problems. Sarhaddon has just
arrived from Taneth with some kind of a warrant from the Prime, and
he's at the gates."

"To arrest us? With the Sacri?" I'd been so sure nothing would happen
in this appalling weather—why had the Sacri even ventured out?

"No. No guards at all, just a pair of priests. He wants to see you,
Cathan."

Chapter XXII

I waited for Sarhaddon in the room just off the atrium where Laeas and Persea had met us on the first night. The lights had been turned on full at the Viceroy's orders, giving some welcome brightness, and the floor had been perfunctorily cleaned to give the impression the palace was in better shape than it really was.

Because of Sarhaddon's relatively unimportant status, Sagantha had ordered that none of us should be there to meet him when he was ushered in, and I stood out of sight around the corner. Sagantha himself was still in his office and didn't intend to see Sarhaddon, who might have primarchial authority but was unimportant as far as the Viceroy was concerned until he specifically requested a formal audience.

There was a sudden flurry of activity: I heard the door open and guards ushering people in—or was it only one person? The door closed again, far too quickly for three people to have entered. Maybe the other two had had to wait outside. Water dripped on the floor; someone took his cloak.

"Someone will be along in a minute, *Domine*," one of the servants said. "Wait here until then." He must have left then, because after that there was silence except for the sound of rain falling on the skylight.

Why had he come? Did he think I could possibly forgive him, that any of us could forgive him, for what he'd done in Lepidor? I had wanted to simply turn him away, but Sagantha had insisted that I see him, to find out if he offered a peaceful resolution of some kind.

Peaceful resolution! Where was the Viceroy living? An Inquisitor, who Sagantha knew had been involved in the invasion of Lepidor, bringing a message of peace? Sagantha just wanted to use me to pursue a possible avenue of escape, something that might benefit him. Ever the politician, he got others to do his dirty work for him.

The servant who'd greeted him so coldly came in through the door at the far side of the room I was waiting in.

"What of him?" I asked.

"He's wearing robes that I've never seen before, but other than that he looks like any Inquisitor. There's that look in his eyes, what I can see of them under the cowl. The other two were the same, wolves in sheep's clothing. Or whatever these new robes are. They're in the guardhouse— Sarhaddon's the only one allowed to come inside."

"Anything else?"

The man shook his head. "Nothing more I can tell at a glance."

"Thank you."

He went out again the way he'd come in, but I waited a little while longer before going out to find Sarhaddon standing quietly under the skylight, wearing the robes of an Inquisitor—in white and red, though, not white and black.

He turned to look at me as I came in, eyes hidden inside the crimson cowl. "Cathan," was all he said.

I stopped a few feet away from him.

"Whatever you have to say, say it now, before my patience runs out," I said, with a coldness that hid my anger. How dared he stand here and greet me as if we were old friends parted by circumstance?

"You have a lot to forgive me for, Cathan," he replied. "But—"

"There is no question of forgiveness, Sarhaddon," I cut in savagely. "I haven't forgotten, and I never will. Nor can anything you do conceal what you've become, a mindless fanatic for your twisted faith. If you've come in some inspired attempt to convert me, then you can save your breath."

"I wouldn't underestimate your intelligence so drastically. You've fallen a long way, though, Cathan."

"With a stake and a few faggots hurled after me to help me on my way, of course. Listen to yourself, Sarhaddon. I can remember what you said about the hardliners, the fundamentalists, how scathing you were about them. How long did it take you to change your spots? A year? Or just a few days, when you realized which way the wind was blowing and jumped on Lachazzar's bandwagon?" I wanted to know what had happened, what they had done to turn him into a zealot. Or whether it had been there all the time, and the man I'd known on that journey had been an illusion all along.

"You forget." He pushed the hood back, and I was shocked at how drawn and tight his face had become, as if all the zest for life had been drained out of it and replaced with—what? He was the only Inquisitor I'd known as a person beforehand. His expression wasn't like that of someone for whom life itself had become a dead weight, more like—an addict's? An obsessive's? Both of those, really, if one thought about it. "I had no choice, as you did. I was sent into a seminary, cut off from the world for nearly a year. I studied theology under some of the most brilliant minds I've encountered, and I realized just why the world has one Faith, why that Faith has to be adhered to. Every one of those fathers in the seminary could have been a leading light in the Great Library, but they'd realized that theology was more than just dry formulas recited at prayer. So few people truly believe, Cathan, so many see only the ritual and the ceremony."

I stared at him for a moment, surprised by the emotion in his voice, as if that should have been drained from him too. They hadn't needed to do that, though, because hate was just as strong a tool as love and even more useful from their point of view. Had he known what love was like? I wondered, although my experience hardly qualified me as an expert.

"Our paths mirrored each other's. On that manta, Etlae sent you one way and me the other, but what happened to us in that year was much the same. You would have come to the Holy City too, but for Ravenna. Twice, in fact."

That manta. The *Paklé*, the ship that had taken us from Pharassa to Taneth but was waylaid by Etlae and the *Shadowstar*. Because we'd recognized her, Etlae had to keep us quiet, binding Sarhaddon over to silence and me to a year in the Citadel. That had been Ravenna's idea, and with the Provost of the Citadel, Ukmadorian, present as well, Etlae had had no choice but to agree.

"Etlae didn't want to rely on my silence, nor on yours. You were to have joined me, but the heretics interfered and spirited you away to their island."

Stunned into silence, I stood there looking at him uncertainly. Palatine and I had been abducted, briefly, at the end of our stay in Taneth. Our kidnappers had been Foryth men, we'd thought—or had they? Had that been just a blind, to make it look as if Palatine, then Hamilcar's secretary, had been the target of one more pointless blow in the feud between the two Great Houses?

If Sarhaddon was telling the truth, and I had to admit it made a lot more sense now, then the kidnappers had been Sacri, ordered to take me to the Holy City. It was not unusual for the heir to a clan or House to spend a year under religious discipline, and in the Holy City I'd have had no escape. But Ravenna had been following me, together with two crewmen from the *Shadowstar*, and had intervened in time.

"Before you call me a fanatic again, Cathan, look at yourself," Sarhaddon said softly. "While I was in the Holy City I changed my views, I realized that it *is* important for there to be one Faith throughout the world. And you went through the same in reverse."

"That's not true," I said automatically. "They showed me what the Domain has done over the centuries."

"Your mind is as closed as you say mine is." There was no rancor in Sarhaddon's voice, no hectoring. "During that journey, your view of the Domain changed, but you still thought it was essentially a force for good. Now you're sworn to its destruction. Isn't that just as extreme?"

"Did I try to kill you?" I demanded. "Your logic and your words are fine, but what about your actions?"

"Midian, Lexan and I all tried to dissuade Etlae from condemning you. *Think*, Cathan! What would Lexan have gained by your death? Your father would have declared blood feud with him and, once Moritan had recovered, that would have been the end of Lexan. He wanted Lepidor eliminated as a rival clan, not a feud that could lead to civil war."

"How dare you claim that!" I almost shouted at him, roused by his incredible arrogance, the monstrosity of his lies. "You tell me that you had no part in that, that you weren't going to kill that Archipelagan, Tekraea, if the fight didn't stop, weren't going to light the fire? You're beyond contempt if that's what you're trying to claim."

"I was ordered to give you one last chance."

"I don't believe you."

"Etlae didn't want to believe she was wrong. I'm sure she was still convinced that the Pharaoh was there."

"Etlae was a treacherous bigot. She should have joined the Imperial court instead of the Domain. She and Orosius would have got on well."

"Treason as well, Cathan?"

"Treason, heresy, what's the difference in the Domain's eyes? Lachazzar believes all other rulers should be subject to him, although I'm sure he conveniently forgets this when dealing with the Emperor. I suppose you admire him now. A true, unbending defender of the Faith, an enlightened Prime."

"A Halettite," said Sarhaddon evenly. "I don't agree with his desire for a Crusade. He's true to what he believes, but not all of his supporters agree with his use of the Sacri. Most of those the Sacri killed during the Crusade were innocent of heresy. We lost an entire generation to the Domain because of that, and now we may lose another. You've said it yourself: there are those in the hierarchy who want the Domain to rule the world. Why rule a wasteland?"

"Those wise men taught you to dissemble and lie as well," I said bitterly, stepping away from him. "All I see standing before me is an Inquisitor, a fanatic, surrounding himself with webs of deceit to draw me in. In Lepidor, you were prepared—glad, perhaps?—to set light to that pyre on Etlae's orders and burn twenty-three people alive. Without a trial, even a travesty of one, without a confession, in defiance of even the Domain's laws. You knew at least half of them were innocent, but you didn't even tell Etlae that you wouldn't do it, that she should let one of the Sacri carry the torch. You might forgive yourself, but none of us ever will. And it never will be just, however you cast it."

"It wasn't just. I know that. When I arrived there, I didn't know what Etlae was going to do. I thought you'd be charged with heresy and brought back to the Holy City with us. She even said your family could continue to rule as long as they swore allegiance to the Domain and allowed Midian free rein."

"And you believed that?"

"I had to. I was only a month out of the seminary. You and I were the only two people who knew of her double life. You are an enemy of the Domain, a heretic, but you're also an immensely powerful mage, and you—Ravenna as well—could have been retrained as mages of Fire. That's what I wanted to happen, what I was told would happen."

"But you still can't explain it, can you? All your flowery excuses, your explanations, your comparisons, can't disguise the fact that you were about to light that pyre."

"As I said, Etlae wanted to give you one last chance," he said, visibly shaken for the first time. "I will tell you this because I must. She used terror as a weapon. She gave you no real choice in the hall, because she was furious at how near you'd come to destroying her, and because you could still defy her." His gaze bored into me, alight with a kind of unholy fervor.

"We all disputed her decision. She relented, told us what to do. I was to light the pyre and let the flames spread around the edge. The mage was perfectly capable of controlling them, as you know." He gestured toward the darkened corridor off to one side. "Don't dispute that, you're a mage too. You'd spent a night in the cells, waiting to die, and you were tied to a stake watching the flames come toward you. I would offer you a chance to save not just yourself but all the others, because I was the only one you really knew. You would have accepted because it meant saving all the others. You'd have agreed to anything she asked of you to save their lives."

I felt as if I'd been winded and took an involuntary step backward, reaching out to steady myself. "You . . ." I had been ready to withdraw into my mind, to shut out the outside world and the pain of dying. I wouldn't have been able to hear him, and Etlae would have taken my silence as an answer. None of the others had the luxury of magic to soften the agony, and my readiness to use it, without Hamilcar's intervention, would have cost all their lives as well as my own. I swallowed uneasily, unwilling to believe the magnitude of what he was telling me. "And she would have doused the flames and marched us all in again? She'd have looked a fool."

"You wouldn't have been burned, Cathan. The Inquisition didn't want her to kill you either. They have to be seen to be doing Ranthas's will, and summary execution wasn't part of their plans."

"You stepped forward—with that torch—ready to light the wood, but not burn us? How can I truly believe this?"

"Because you're rational and intelligent. It was brutal, yes, and wouldn't have happened with anyone other than Etlae. Terror only breeds hatred, Cathan, and you're living proof of that. If the Inquisition starts burning heretics in the Archipelago, thousands will die—and all for nothing. Lachazzar will send in his crusade, and this time they won't leave the destruction unfinished."

"But there'll be no more heresy. No one will ever resist you again. The Archipelago will be ashes, but you'll have rid yourself of the opposition."

"Have you ever read Carinus, Cathan? The Thetian historian? *They make a desolation and they call it peace.*" I doubted those words would be forgotten even if Carinus himself was. There would always be someone, some event to whom they applied. "We do not serve Ranthas to turn His world into a desert."

"*His* world?" I demanded. "We float on the surface of an infinite ocean, and you speak of the world belonging only to Fire? The world is made up of *all* the elements, not just your chosen one."

"But without His holy fire there would be no life, no cities, no civilization. Just a huge empty desolation." *Fire is the spark that gives life in all things.* "But I wander. I don't want to see these islands laid waste. Why should I?"

"Why should anyone? Because the population hates you, because some of them believe in the old gods whose worship you've made heresy. Because some of them refuse to forget the Domain's betrayal."

"Past history," Sarhaddon said dismissively. "What happened two hundred years ago is, of course, important but if it comes to dominate our lives, then we'll never go forward."

"Forward to your promised land where there's no dissent at all."

"It is the Domain's *methods* that have created the dissent, not its *message*," he said, his voice fired by conviction. "There are millions of souls damned for all eternity because they lived before we came, there are hundreds of thousands more who have refused to recognize our truth. And if the Crusade comes, how many more will join them?"

Whether or not Sarhaddon truly believed what he was saying, I'd never heard an Inquisitor talk like this before, and into the back of my mind came the faint suggestion that, for all his participation in Etlae's crimes, he might be different. So many of the Inquisitors were cunning, subtle, clever in their own way, but they were also bigoted, stupid even. I knew Sarhaddon was intelligent, and I felt a faint surge of hope. I couldn't forgive him, but I wanted to believe that he was unique. Not a copy of Lachazzar.

"We come to preach, to save," he finished. "To bring souls back to the light. If the Prime sees that most of the Archipelago has returned to the fold, he won't launch the Crusade."

"To isolate the heresy so that it can be hunted down?"

"I will preach to the heretics as much as to the alienated. Cathan, there *will* be a crusade if things go on. The Inquisition will carry out its sacred duty with far too much zeal, there will be risings, and Lachazzar will send in the crusaders. This time they will stay, they will kill anyone suspected of heresy, and there will be so much death, so much killing."

"And why are you telling me this?" I asked him finally. "Why do you come here?"

"Because you are a prominent heretic, a man I know, and you quite possibly know the Pharaoh. She could be reinstated. I have been asked about it, and have talked to the Exarch, even the Prime. She would be allowed to protect her people as long as she supported our efforts at conversion. We won't be using force and coercion this time, but persuasion, as we should have done from the beginning."

"You want me to talk to the Pharaoh? Persuade her that the Domain—which murdered her family, which has forced her to hide all her life—wants her cooperation? That's more than a leap of faith."

"I would like you to try. Even without that, I'm asking you to let me try. Give me a period of grace, and I'll do what I can to lift the Inquisitor-General's interdict on you. I have a warrant from the Prime himself that gives me a mandate to preach that not even the Inquisitor-General can overrule." He withdrew a heavy roll of parchment from the fold of his robe and handed it to me.

I unrolled it and started reading the heavy lines of text, my eyes straying to the massive primarchial seal at the bottom. I read quite quickly at first, then slowed down, stopping to reread sentences I could hardly believe, that hardly seemed real.

By express order of His Holiness the activities of the Inquisition authorized by the said Edict Universal are hereby suspended within the territories and islands of the

Thetian Dominion of the Archipelago . . . all members of the Venatic Order are hereby given the power to intercede on behalf of accused heretics if such accused can show to the Inquisitors that they fully recant their sins and will be accepted back into the fellowship of man . . . all such penitents to be spared the mark of shame as long as they faithfully obey all decrees and canon law of the Holy Domain . . . brothers of the Venatic Order are hereby given the authority to preach in public spaces. Furthermore the Venatic Order is authorized to preside over and engage in religious debate with such notable heretics as shall come forward, the said heretics to be given a safe-conduct during and for a month after any such debate . . .

Why? Why had Lachazzar done this? It all sounded so alien to his usual ways, the idea of preaching and religious debate, something Primes had authorized in the past but not for many years now. Lachazzar believed in fire and the sword, he had sent the Inquisition into the Archipelago—and now he was suspending its activities to allow a couple of dozen preachers a free rein? He had to be up to something.

"Why has he allowed this?" I asked Sarhaddon bluntly. "Is it your plan, or his?"

"I had the idea for the Venatic Order, and I persuaded some of my instructors to apply to the Prime for approval. I will be frank with you, Cathan, we suit his purpose very well. He told me why he was letting us do this. He has sent in the Inquisition, and the population is in terror of what they'll do. You've already had some burnings, and there will be many more if the Inquisition has its way. We offer hope, a way out without more suffering. If we are given free rein, not opposed by the heretics, then the Inquisition will be ordered to persecute only those heretics who openly defy us."

"Stick and carrot."

He nodded very slightly. I stared down at the parchment, signed and authorized by the Prime himself. I'd seen the primarchial seal before, and there was no way Sarhaddon would have forged it. "All I ask is that period of grace," he said, after a pause. "For you and the other heretics to allow this to go ahead. This is a beautiful island, even in such foul weather, and I don't want to see it devastated by the Crusade. Lachazzar wants to be remembered as the Prime who ended heresy, although you and I both know that won't happen. But I would like to know that the Domain gave you a chance to stop the storm that's coming."

"I don't have the authority to grant this. You should be speaking to the Viceroy."

"Have I convinced you? If the extremists among you take advantage of the truce to launch attacks on us, the period of grace will end. You do nothing, and the Inquisition will do nothing. Meanwhile we will try. The Archipelago is the only place in the world so bitter about the Domain that hatred has overwhelmed all reason. We both know that there are heretics elsewhere who live closet existences, but terror is not the way to deal with them. And it isn't the right method to tackle the problem here."

I rolled the parchment up carefully and gave it back to him again, turned away from him to look down the side corridor and out of the storm-lashed window at the gray sky. If this was genuine—could it be? Could it possibly be? It was an olive branch, and I so wanted to believe in it—but if Sarhaddon succeeded, then our dreams of ending the Domain's power were over.

Or were they? Cambress had defied the Domain without straying from religious law. They upheld the principles of Ranthas but there was no Inquisition there, had been no burnings or even heresy trials in six decades. Mikas had told me that anything was tolerated in Cambress so long as it didn't impinge on the State or the Navy—which were the same thing, really, in Cambress. He might have been exaggerating but I knew his father only attended one ceremony a year, far less than the absolute minimum. His father had been Suffete and was now a full Admiral and senior member of the Kanu council.

And in the last few weeks I'd realized just how fragile our dream had been, with the Emperor's hostility and the undeniable fact that the Archipelago couldn't win a war. But Ravenna . . . she would never, ever cooperate. She had lost almost everything to the Domain, she hated them with a passion that I could never match. And she only knew Sarhaddon as the man who'd been going to light our pyre.

"I would like to talk to the others," I said finally. "What you're saying gives me hope despite Lachazzar's signature, but without their agreement my word is no good to you."

"Do they include the Viceroy?"

"Do you want to request an audience?"

"I think it might be a good idea, and perhaps inspire trust, if he could grant me a hearing with you and whoever these others might be present. Then I'll withdraw and let you discuss it."

"I suppose so," I said reluctantly, wondering whether this was a good idea, or whether I was giving him the opportunity he sought for . . . what? Aside from depriving us of a base of support that could only offer sentiment, I couldn't see how his plan could be anything other than genuine. Even Lachazzar's agreement made sense, given how much a

Crusade would cost. The last one had drained the primarchial coffers, I knew, despite all the booty they'd taken. The seizure of Lepidor was to have saved money for the coming Crusade. "What part does Midian play in this?" I turned back to him.

"He'll see the Prime's logic. There are rewards in it for him, too."

"And his being deprived of slaughter?"

"You go too far. If this works, his participation will be well rewarded. A senior Avarchate in Equatoria, probably."

"And all those in the Inquisitorial prisons awaiting execution? What of them?"

"My brothers will offer them the chance of recantation. That's what we're trying to get across, that the Domain will accept those who have lapsed. Some will refuse to give up their faith and will be burned, but only then will there be any more executions."

"Will you be able to change their procedure, though?" I insisted. "Guilty until proven innocent. That's what provokes the hatred."

"Remember I'm not a senior figure. I can't move the earth."

Not too many promises, then: he wasn't going to lie—at least not obviously—to gain my support.

"If you'll wait here, I'll go and see the Viceroy now, outline what you've told me."

"Impartially?"

"Impartially. You'll have to wait here—this isn't my palace and I won't presume to invite you in any farther."

"That's fine. It's dry in here, at least," he added, with a trace of the old, wry humor.

I left him standing there and went out the way I'd come in through the back passages to find the Viceroy, by the longest route I could take. I had to give myself time to think.

Could I believe what he'd told me about those final moments in Lepidor, that Etlae had been going to spare us—spare us the stake, at least? She and her fellows, who must have included Sarhaddon, had invaded my home, poisoned my father, almost killed my adoptive brother. She'd sentenced me and the others to death and had had us tied to the stakes. Was that as far as she would have gone?

But Sarhaddon had been only a junior priest, someone whose loyalty she surely wouldn't have counted on. And now he'd come with a message of reconciliation and peace. Would the Prime do that simply to trap me? To believe that was the height of arrogance, that I'd thought of it at all showed how malign Orosius's influence was. I wasn't a leader of the heresy, and as far as I knew they weren't even aware of my ancestry.

And if his proposal was an extended trap, to bring in more of the heretic leadership, there were more efficient ways to do things. Sarhaddon had come to ask me to be a messenger.

"I'll see him," was the Viceroy's answer.

Chapter XXIII

Two days later a pale, washed-out sun shone down through the clouds on to the city of Tandaris, for the first time in weeks. Too faint to cast shadows, it nevertheless gave the buildings a new aspect, the reds and blues standing out more strongly from the white, the green of trees much more prominent. Tandaris was a city of warmth and light, and the grayness of winter didn't do it justice. It had been built before the War, when there had been little change between seasons, and the damage we saw as we walked down from the palace testified to how ill-suited it was to withstanding the storms.

We stepped around a pile of rubble and branches where a fallen orange tree had crushed a garden wall. A man was standing on top of the trunk, hacking at branches with an ax while an older, white-haired man and a boy dragged away the ones he'd already cut. They looked up curiously as we went past, not greeting us but not hostile either.

The sound of hammering came from a house across the way; somebody had erected a barrier in front of it, surrounding a pile of smashed tiles.

"Be careful there, or you'll get splintered," someone called. "The roof still isn't safe."

"Thanks," Persea called back. "I've never seen it this bad," she said, turning back to us. "Every house, look. I'm glad they didn't cut the whole city off, it would have been appalling."

She was right, I thought, as we came to a junction. Every building had signs of damage—broken windows, loose or missing shutters—while up the street, across the junction, there was another heap of fallen masonry being piled up by half a dozen people.

"What happened to Agathocles?" she asked as we took a left turn downward, passing a tiny square with a boarded-up taverna on the other side. A broken sign hung drunkenly from its support, the words *Taverna Agathocles* just legible, while the mark of a flame appeared to have been branded on the wooden door.

"Arrested," said Laeas grimly. "A week ago. You don't come down this way very often, obviously."

"It's not the quickest way," Persea replied, as we lost sight of the taverna around a corner.

There were signs of life here: shops open, one or two awnings up, and more people than I'd seen in the whole three weeks of my stay. Chatter and the smell of fruit and bread drifted up into the morning air. We were still a few streets away from the market square, one of the disadvantages of being in the palace. It had been the town's fortress once, before the now-ruined Acrolith had been built a hundred feet higher, and the outer walls were still thick enough to withstand siege weaponry.

There was a tense, expectant atmosphere, I thought as we walked down the wide, curving street that led to the market square. Not a feeling of impending doom, it was more as if the city was holding its breath. Waiting to hear if Sarhaddon's message really did offer an end to fear.

"We forget that what people want most is to get on with their lives," Persea commented, as we passed a mother shepherding six or seven children, some of them clearly not her own, through a gateway bearing the pen symbol that indicated a school. "Politics should be harmless as far as they're concerned."

"As should religion," Telesta said. "There's nowhere else in the world where ordinary people are so afraid of the Domain as they are here."

"I wouldn't go that far. There are places where it's edgy, but this is where the real problem is." Persea gestured around her. "If there's another crusade, Tandaris will go the way of Poseidonis: everyone butchered or carted back to Haleth to serve as slaves. That's why we're giving Sarhaddon a chance."

"We still have Orosius to deal with."

"Orosius is in Selerian Alastre. The Inquisition is here. If Sarhaddon stays true to his word . . ."

"Then what?" Mauriz demanded. "What exactly will he do? If they repent, join him in prayer, that makes it all fine, does it?"

"He's offering an amnesty, as you might have noticed," Laeas said, probably curbing his irritation because he knew this was the last time he'd have to put up with Mauriz. "It's his business how he organizes it."

"And have you thought what happens if he succeeds? It'll isolate you, take away your base of support. Fine, let him call off the Inquisition. But don't just sit around waiting for everything magically to be all right, because that's not going to happen. Have you considered how much power he'll gain if he succeeds?" He'd been like this during Sarhaddon's audience, annoying the Viceroy to the extent that he'd been told to shut up or leave. For some reason, Mauriz loathed even the idea of what Sarhaddon was suggesting.

But Mauriz had a point. Palatine had seen that coming, and in two days of discussion we'd failed to agree on anything except that I should talk to Ravenna as soon as possible. There'd been no word from her messenger yet, though, and I was afraid she'd recalled him when we agreed to Sarhaddon's terms. The idea of cooperating with the Domain, as Sarhaddon had hinted at, was repugnant, but what other avenues did we have? The *Aeon* would knock away a pillar of the Domain's power; would that matter, though, with a population calmed by Sarhaddon's speeches?

If they were calming. Today would be the first time one would be delivered to the people: Sarhaddon and one of the wise instructors he'd rhapsodized about would alternate their orations, passion and logic together. Did he really carry a message of reconciliation? And if he did, was it anything more than just words?

"The Domain has kept power for two hundred years," I remembered Ravenna saying, that terrible night in the cells below my father's palace. "They've changed history, they set themselves up as has never been done before. There have been holy wars, I know. But in all that time there's only been one really serious breach, in the Archipelago about twenty-five years ago, because they got a Prime who was too hardline. They were never as popular here, but life went on. People didn't mind them as long as they confined their quarrel to the rulers. But in the Crusade they didn't, they tried to teach the population a lesson. *That* is why they're so hated."

The road doubled back on itself now, again running parallel to the slope to give a gentle descent rather than the steep one a direct route would have taken—too steep for comfort. There were more shops here, and a gap between two buildings over to the right, a small paved open space with benches and a balustrade that just topped the dome of the building below it. The paving was littered with fallen leaves from the two trees that stood there, both still intact, and beyond the stone railings I could see the sea.

The morning mists had cleared, and it was more blue than gray for once, stretching in a cerulean expanse to a horizon more distant than I'd ever seen it before. Its surface was dimpled by small waves, but there were no whitecaps—there wasn't much of a wind in this lull between storms.

I realized the others had left me behind. But Laeas glanced back and stopped, glad of any excuse to avoid Mauriz.

"Beautiful, isn't it?" he remarked. "You should see it in summer. Incredible color, like it was at the Citadel. A lot of it is shallows, and you can see the sandbanks."

"Are those the Ilahi Islands?" I pointed to an arc of low black shapes in the distance, looking almost flat from here even though I guessed they were hilly. "We passed them on the way in, I think."

"Yes. The big one on the left is Lesath, then Poros and Chosros, Ixander, Iuvros, Peschata. I can't remember the smaller ones, like that group of three in the middle. Oh, the Aetian Islands."

"Aetian? After the Emperor?"

"Yes—some Imperial officers put up a memorial to him there for some reason. I'm told there's another group called the Tiberian Islands actually inside the Desolation, exactly on the equator. Someone built a lighthouse there as a monument to Tiberius."

"Why inside the Desolation?" I asked, my attention caught. *Why? Why would anyone go to that trouble to build a lighthouse so far beyond any known shipping lane?* Especially one that couldn't be maintained.

"No idea." Laeas shrugged, then his brow furrowed, as if he was remembering something. " 'Those who keep their eyes on the earth will never see the beauty of the stars. They walk in their light without seeing, hear their music without listening.' That's supposed to be the inscription. It stuck in my mind because it's such a strange thing to write. There're two more lines, something about a mirror of heaven and hell, but I've forgotten those."

"Come on!" someone was calling from farther down. We stayed there for a minute, then set off reluctantly after the others. *Why those two shrines?* I wondered. *Why would Imperial officers do that, build monuments on barren islands? More to the point, why should one of them be dedicated to Tiberius?*

The others were waiting for us at the bend, standing by a stretch of blank wall between a café and a weaver's. Just ahead and below us, I saw as we joined them and set off again, was what had to be the market square; we were coming in from one side, slightly above the level of the square.

The first thing we noticed was how full it was, a sea of dark hair and bright colors with a few islands around trees or statues—even then, there were people perched on the plinths of the statues, or balanced on the trees' lower branches. There was a hushed chatter and a feeling of anticipation, focused on the empty speaker's platform in front of the impressive, columned Agora.

"I had no idea there'd be so many here," Persea said as we went on down, losing sight of the square itself behind the rows of people lining the edge of the road. "Look at all those faces in the windows. I don't think I've ever seen it this full."

Every window around the square was packed with people, too, almost as if this was a huge fiesta. But the mood was too serious for that, too uncertain. They'd come in the hope that this really was a new start, but none of them were sure. The looming temple walls over on the far side held dozens of Sacri, not to mention Inquisitors and their prisoners.

"We're staying here to watch this now," Persea said to Mauriz and Telesta when we reached the level of the square, stopping at the outskirts of the crowd. "Laeas will take you the rest of the way before he comes back to join us."

We said goodbye to them without any particular warmth, Mauriz for once passing up the chance to capitalize on the occasion. Perhaps he felt he'd already got his message across. Then Persea led us along the back wall of the square and down a narrow, almost invisible alleyway with plants growing up the white walls on either side. There was a tiny, enchanting courtyard at the other end with more plants spilling over and up in every direction, and four large, ornate doors. One of them belonged to a "friend" of Persea's who was letting us watch from one of his balconies, out of the way of the crowd in case it turned ugly.

She stepped up to the door and rapped the knocker, but it was a while before we heard footsteps inside and the door was swung open. A man a couple of years older than Laeas or me greeted Persea with the familiarity of an old friend, and ushered us up a flight of curved, sweeping stairs. It was a very grand house, rather like Hamilcar's in Taneth although less ostentatious in its decoration, because the man who owned this was a native Archipelagan, not a connoisseur.

"Whose house is it?" I whispered to Persea as our guide's attention was momentarily distracted by someone appearing in the hall.

"Oh, didn't I tell you? He's Alidrisi, President of Clan Kalessos, who live in the eastern section of Qalathar."

Alidrisi: why did that ring a bell? I didn't have time to recall it, though, as we were led into an airy, high-ceilinged sitting room where six or seven people were already out on the balconies.

"Persea and her friends, Cousin," the guide called, and the people watching turned their attention away from the square.

"We're glad to see you," said one of them, coming inside. He gestured to some bottles on the cane table in the center of the room. "Please have a drink. I'm Alidrisi Kalessos." He was strikingly tall and swarthy, and could easily have been Southern Archipelagan. Hamilcar's age, I guessed. Maybe older, though, perhaps in his mid-thirties.

"My friends Palatine Canteni and Cathan Tauro," Persea said, introducing each of us in turn. Alidrisi raised his eyebrows and looked briefly at Palatine, then very closely at me. His expression was searching, changed in an instant from politeness to a disturbing intensity.

"I had no idea I'd meet you so soon," he said at last, abruptly. "You're not what I expected."

Persea looked at him questioningly.

"Pour yourselves a drink and we'll join you on the balcony in a minute," he said, his gaze only moving to her for a second or two.

A woman in an oceanographer's tunic waved a bottle at Persea from the balcony, and I suddenly remembered. Alidrisi. One of just six or seven people in Qalathar who knew Ravenna's real identity. Which meant he'd been in contact with her, I was sure.

"How is she?" I asked, once the others had taken their drinks and moved out of earshot. I had an uncomfortable feeling about this.

"Who?" An instant shift of expression, back to the generous host, belied by the fire in the brown eyes.

"You know," I said warily.

"She said you were untrustworthy. I've no obligation to tell you."

"She said I couldn't be trusted," I said, hoping I'd read it right.

"Same thing."

"How is she?" I repeated. "You've seen her within the past few weeks, maybe less. Did she come here when she landed?"

"Your arrogant presumption isn't welcome. I'm not required to answer your or anyone else's questions."

"Yes, you are," I snapped, anger battling with a surge of hope at having met, so unexpectedly, someone in contact with her. "You greet a total stranger like that in public, then instantly deny all knowledge of what you've just said. I'm not asking where she is, what your plans are, or even whether you're treating her as she deserves or just as a pawn like the others. *How is she?*"

"As well as can be expected, given what's happening here," he replied tightly. "Untrustworthy isn't the first word for you that springs to mind. Rude, perhaps, since I've known her all her life."

"You visited her in the Citadels, did you?" I shot back, amazed at myself for acting like this, as if I was drunk or talking to an enemy. "I got the impression she knows the Viceroy better." I felt an inexplicable surge of hate toward him, an urgent need to strike out at him, to hurl him across the room by using my magic.

I forced myself to stop, to bite back what was on the tip of my tongue. Why was I doing this?

I took a deep breath. "Lord President, I apologize for that. I'm being unforgivably rude."

"Apology accepted," he said, after a moment. Then he smiled warmly, a smile that this time did reach his eyes. But a faintly troubled expression stayed on his face. "I apologize, too, for greeting you like that. I'm frequently accused of being tactless—not a good trait for a clan president." I couldn't believe this man was a clan president at all. In Thetia, perhaps, but not in Qalathar. "She's worried, even depressed, actually. It hasn't been a happy homecoming, and she's not happy about this either. And no, we're not treating her as a pawn, just keeping her somewhere safe."

"Is she unhappy about this because of Sarhaddon's plan, or just because she doesn't trust the Domain?"

"You're the one he persuaded into this, aren't you?" A guarded expression now: this man was so mercurial that I kept being thrown off balance.

"He was a friend of sorts a while ago. I'm the only one of us he knows."

"And you trust him, even after what he did to you?"

"Did she hear his version of what happened?"

"She did, but she wasn't convinced. Nor am I, nor is anyone here. You come from somewhere where the Domain is rational, just a part of life, where it doesn't torture and burn and persecute as it does here. Here . . . they've never tried anything like this, and it's almost certainly just another trick."

"If he succeeds, no Crusade. Lachazzar gains credit, saves money."

"Lachazzar isn't interested in money," Alidrisi said with a sudden surge of venom, another instant shift in his demeanor. "He wants to feed the fires of Hell, stoke them higher than any of his predecessors have. If they reach up and singe the world from below, so much the better. It'll be a warning. He doesn't want to win this way."

"Can we take chances on that?" I wasn't sure why I'd got embroiled in this, but Alidrisi was a hard man to ignore, too forceful to tear myself away from. And he had spoken to Ravenna recently. I was suddenly so tantalizingly close, I *had* to get a message to her somehow. "Everyone knows Lachazzar wants a Crusade, and they don't want that to happen. If Sarhaddon gives them a chance to stop it, won't they seize the opportunity?"

"I think the hatreds go too deep." Alidrisi waved a hand over at the window, toward the invisible but very audible crowd. "He'll sway them with honeyed words and then strike—we have to find out how." He must have seen my skeptical look, because he went on: "He seems to have convinced you, which surprises me. Trusting a supposed friend who was ready to execute you seems . . . dangerous. They've broken every promise they've ever made, they'll betray anyone if it gains them more power. Kings and emperors do it all the time, but they don't pretend it's the will of God."

"But Qalathar can't defeat the Domain. Has anyone, ever, come up with a way to do that, or do you just struggle from one crisis to another, trying to avert them as they come?"

"Are you implying that we're a conquered people?" he said, face darkening again.

I held up my hands as a gesture of placation. He seemed as quick to calm down as he was to anger, but I couldn't be sure of that. "No more than Oceanus. But you don't have any way to strike back decisively, anything that will protect you when another Crusade comes."

Alidrisi relaxed slightly, but there was a troubled look on his face and he didn't answer for a minute. "I have this conversation so often, and never get an answer to that question. We have no central authority except the Viceroy." From his gesture of disgust, I guessed his opinion of Sagantha wasn't very high.

"But the Pharaoh will just be a Domain puppet, won't she? No army, no fleet, no way to protect her from them or their magic."

"If you imagine for a second that she'll ever cooperate with them, you've misread her completely."

"I know that," I said levelly, resenting yet another insinuation that I somehow wasn't worthy of her. He must guess what I felt for her, and it rankled for some reason, enough for him to seize every opportunity to attack me. "Everyone wants her to return as a conquering hero, throw the Domain out just by looking at them, restore freedom and peace and all of that. Fine, she's more than capable, but how?"

"There are allies waiting out there for enough incentive."

"Willing to risk interdict, excommunication? People obey the Domain because it's supposed to speak with the voice of Ranthas. Only the Domain can stop the storms, allow us to have fire. That's even without the Sacri and the Halettites."

"So we should give up and accept defeat, try to come to a compromise? Is that what you're saying? That we're never going to defeat them any other way, so if we beg them hard enough they'll give us a token independence? That's fine for an Oceanian—you probably didn't know what a Sacri looked like until a year or two ago. Persea and the rest of us have grown up seeing them every day, knowing that they have the power of life and death over us. Are they really going to surrender that power as easily as Sarhaddon says?"

"No, you're right, I didn't grow up with them. But does that disqualify me from being able to oppose them? They've destroyed my homeland too, only there they didn't use fire and the sword." It rang false in my ears, calling Thetia my homeland, and it sounded pompous as well. It wasn't my home, it was just where I'd been born, and I didn't feel Thetian.

"A very pleasant destruction, isn't it?" Alidrisi commented sourly. "Parties, nights of music and dancing, opera. You can't blame the Domain: your own people started getting lazy as soon as there was nobody left to fight. The Domain is just a convenient scapegoat."

"And who's *your* scapegoat?" I demanded, anger flaring up again, although it wasn't my place to say this. "You've had twenty-four years to prepare for this day and you've done *nothing*. The Pharaoh has no more chance of assuming her throne than she did after the Crusade. These alliances have never materialized, the pathetic fleet you had was lost the moment the Inquisitors appeared, and you're just as powerless as you always were. And despite that, you've rejected this chance before you've even heard what it is."

I stopped suddenly, with a dreadful feeling that I'd just cut the tenuous connection to Ravenna. I watched Alidrisi nervously. Why did it have to be this man? I still had another contact—but maybe this was it anyway? Thetis, why had I opened my mouth?

"And you're going to take the credit if this works?" he asked very softly, menacingly. "Because he came to you first with the proposal?"

"Have you ever been condemned to death, Alidrisi? The whole of Qalathar is under sentence, as you say, but Sarhaddon's giving it the right of appeal. Will you stay here if the Crusade comes and suffer along with the rest of the island?"

"I do not recognize the authority of this court. None of us do, not me, not Persea or Laeas, not those people out there. Until the Domain is gone, destroyed and driven out, there is no justice here. All we achieve is a suspension of that sentence. Yes, we have to have a plan instead of simply responding to their actions. That's exactly what you've done— you've let them take the initiative again and distract us while they prepare their next move. I'm not going to go along with it. None of us are, especially not the Pharaoh you claim to love. Either that's only a claim or you're as much of a fool and a madman as the rest of your race. You choose, but don't entangle her in this."

Alidrisi turned away deliberately, took his glass back out onto the farther balcony and started talking to two people already standing there. I stared after him for a moment, biting down hard on my lip. He held the only bargaining chip, and he'd put me decisively in my place.

"That didn't go well," Palatine observed, appearing behind me. "I take it he's opposed to Sarhaddon."

"He's opposed to everything," I said savagely, unable to hold back my anger any longer. "He thinks it's just a distraction while the Domain prepare for the Crusade, and he's never going to accept anything less than their defeat. Of course, he doesn't have any idea how to do that, but he's quite sure that I'm not worthy to speak to Ravenna. She's unhappy, he said, which doesn't surprise me with people like him around."

"*Tace, tace!*" Palatine said, looking around with a worried expression. "Too many can hear us."

"Too many are always listening," I said. But I kept my voice down this time. Alidrisi's last outburst had worried me; it did sound very much as though they were keeping Ravenna under control. But in that case why tell me she was unhappy? Had that been deliberate malice?

"I can remember her saying she was a pawn in the nobles' power games. I think I understand now. Sagantha isn't like this—I think he genuinely cares about her—but Alidrisi seems to regard her as . . . as a possession. I couldn't hear what you said, but I saw his expression. I can see why you're concerned, but he's one of the few really powerful Qalatharis, Persea says. It's not a good idea to make an enemy of him."

"It felt like he'd already decided to go that route when he heard my name."

"Yes, it did. Wait a minute." She went back to the window, pulled Persea away from the others for the moment, and asked her something. Persea looked puzzled, gave quite a long answer, then Palatine came back. "She says he's quite easy to read, which means he *is* hostile to you. It must be something that Ravenna said."

"Do you think he knows about my family?"

"Did he mention it?"

I thought for a moment, then shook my head, quite sure that there hadn't been anything like that. "He knew I was Thetian, insulted Thetia once, but never my family."

"Odds are he doesn't know, then, so he thinks you're a fairly unimportant Oceanian who happens to be of Thetian birth somehow. If Ravenna talked about you with affection or something more, they'd get worried. They may want to use her to buy help."

"Buy help?" It took a moment for me to realize what she meant.

"It's a barbaric custom, I know. You probably do it in Oceanus. We don't."

"But most of the places they could get help are republics, like Taneth and Cambress. Family connections aren't enough there: they don't even like their leaders to have royal connections."

"That's what worries me," Palatine said, moving around to look over at Alidrisi where he stood on the balcony, his back turned to us. "Could you just tell me more or less what he said to you?"

I did, as best I could remember, while she stood there and listened.

"It sounds like he really didn't have a plan, but that's too much to believe. He might be more subtle than we thought."

"Why does it worry you?"

As the noise of the crowd outside suddenly died, the people on the balcony stopped talking. A profound silence took hold.

"Marriage alliances tend to be made in Hell," Palatine whispered. "At least, that's what most Thetians think. The ones who don't belong there anyway."

Chapter XXIV

I found myself squeezed into a corner of Persea's balcony between the ornate iron railing, a massive glazed flowerpot and a petite, almost elfin woman in an oceanographer's tunic. Not the one who'd waved the bottle at Persea a few minutes ago; there was another female oceanographer there, her heavier build and light brown hair setting her aside from the Qalatharis. I thought there was a male oceanographer, too, on the other balcony, a gray-haired man who'd been talking to Alidrisi when we came in. It was the first contact I'd had with any of the Qalathari oceanographers, but there was no time to talk as, in tense silence, we watched the temple gates swing open.

After so much waiting, it was almost anticlimactic to see half a dozen Venatics, resplendent in red and white, process out of the temple. There were no Sacri to be seen, no Inquisitors, only a thurifer in an acolyte's habit, clouds of incense wafting from the censer he waved at the crowd. A gap opened up as if by magic in front of him, people moving instinctively to one side or the other.

The Venatics wore their hoods down, the pointed cowls looking far less sinister that way, and I couldn't see any decoration or embroidery on their habits. Sarhaddon was easy to spot, in the middle pair, with a patrician-looking older man beside him. Presumably one of the instructors he'd talked about so much. The other four were all older than Sarhaddon, though not by much; three of them, I thought, had the look of ascetics.

The six Venatics reached the far edge of the crowd and the gap closed behind them. The temple gates had closed again, leaving only the two Sacri who'd been on guard there all along. I glanced up at the sky, reassuring myself that it wasn't about to rain. The sun was still a washed-out point of light in an almost painfully bright, featureless sky.

People below us stifled coughs as Sarhaddon and the man beside him climbed the stone steps on to the speaker's platform. Sarhaddon stood aside at the top and let the other man cross the two or three yards to stand near the front of the platform, by the stone balustrade that separated the speakers from the crowd. The older man raised a hand, and the people below bowed their heads, a ripple moving out from the center point of the crowd.

"In the name of Ranthas, Giver of Life, Lord of Flame, who was at the beginning and shall be at the end. May He who guides all things mortal look on us with favor at this day's rising, noon and setting and accept us all with His infinite mercy."

There was a pause after he'd finished. Then we looked up again, to see the two of them exchange places. I was surprised that they'd chosen Sarhaddon for what must be their inaugural sermon—surely there were older, more experienced priests they'd have preferred?

Perhaps it was the image. The thought came unexpectedly as Sarhaddon began speaking. Despite the changes, he didn't look like an Inquisitor, an inflexible old fundamentalist. Whether that was the truth or not didn't matter; it was the appearance that counted.

"Citizens of Qalathar," he said, standing with both hands on the balustrade, surveying the crowd with a thoughtful expression. "I am Sarhaddon, a brother of the Venatic order. I'm not an Inquisitor, I don't come with fire and the sword. Nor do my brothers whom you see here, or the few others who make up the Order. We have dedicated our lives to the service of Ranthas, and we bring nothing more than words.

"Too many times the pen has failed to be mightier than the sword. When conquerors come with fire and blood, words cannot be used against them. All they provide is a legacy, a remembrance so that what was spoken and done is not lost but will echo down the centuries. Your people, the people of the Archipelago, have a long and glorious history. From a time when my own people on Oceanus still lived in the darkness of savagery, you have the writings of Tehama. For your ancestors, nothing was more important than words. Their great leaders were orators and advocates who gave such brilliant speeches in a lost city a thousand years ago that your children still learn them and study them.

"When my teachers at the seminary wished to give us an example of divine inspiration, they brought out the *Book of Ranthas*. When they wanted to demonstrate human brilliance, we read Ulpian, Claudina, Gerrachos. They lived at a time when there was no higher honor than to be called *Orator*, when those who rose to the heights were those who could debate, argue, speak. And those who could put into their speeches the passion of their hearts were remembered as the greatest of all. Tehama wasn't primarily a literate society, but their speeches were still recorded for all time.

"You all know the story of Ulpian's Defense of Postumio better than I do, so I won't patronize you by retelling it. He saved an innocent man's life against a lamentably corrupt jury solely by the power of his words. There are other examples, too—the Plea for Peace, the Address at Midnight—of which you'll have heard. My own people, the Pharassans, once followed the same path, although none of our orators are as celebrated. We gained a reputation for wily diplomacy, for being able to negotiate our way out of any trouble, no matter how terrible, and for bringing an end to wars that seemed set to last forever.

"I know what you're thinking, that this was a long time ago. When, during the last few centuries, have words proved their value? They haven't stopped fire and conquest, they haven't prevented the evils that we, among others, have wrought in your land. Words too frequently work the other way, to corrupt a pure purpose, to insinuate, to deceive. They have negative power as well as positive, and evil counsel can be far more destructive than good guidance is beneficial. Sometimes.

"I'm not an Ulpian or a Gerrachos, and as I'm sure you've noticed I'm certainly not a Claudina." There was a faint ripple of nervous laughter at that, but none of us broke our concentration to turn away from him. "Nor am I here to win a case or speak for peace or war. I came with the words of Ranthas that you know, to give a call for reason, for reflection. There are those of you who follow different gods, for whom there are Eight instead of One."

He pointed up into the white sky, at the point where the weak sun lurked behind its curtain of clouds. "Do you feel the warmth, see the light coming through the clouds for the first time this winter? For weeks the world has endured the most appalling weather, far worse than previous winters. There are places where the clouds are so dark and thick that it is dusk at noon. Trees grow sick, unhealthy, animals die, the darkness saps men's spirits.

"For three months the sun has stayed hidden, except on rare days such as this when Ranthas shows us His favor. The sun's fire is concealed from us by the clouds, and we only survive by His gift to Aquasilva." He pulled a flamewood branch out of his robe and waved it high, a brilliant melange of reddish-orange wood and gold leaves that was a thing of beauty even without the sun's reflection shining off it. "Where would we be without this? Huddling in the deepest caves, confined to the mountains and the continent, unable to keep ourselves warm, to cross the seas, to give our cities light and heat. In fact, we wouldn't have any cities of stone, monuments like the ziggurats, the Hall of the Ocean or the Acrolith."

A curious combination there, I thought, still watching the glitter of the flamewood branch, wondering if I'd ever see a real tree. A normal priest would have listed the ziggurats and temples, but he'd mentioned the Thetians' and the Qalatharis' greatest achievements as well, not reminding them too closely of the Domain. I doubted there'd be another mention of the Hall of the Ocean, Selerian Alastre's greatest monument, which had been very conspicuously dedicated to Thetis.

"Look back through history, and you see how it is those gifted with flamewood who have built the greatest cities, the greatest empires, made the biggest mark. Three hundred years ago the Thetians had a monopoly; only they knew the secret of flamewood. They used it to glorify their name and their cities, to construct great monuments, to send their ships to every corner of the earth and bring the world under their rule. All others were pale shadows by comparison.

"But when Ranthas made known His gift to others and the secret ceased to be a secret, the whole world rose beyond those primitive times. Other great cities were built to rival those of the Thetians: Taneth, Cambress, Pharassa, Raneveh, Poseidonis."

There was a collective intake of breath, a few gasps of shock, from the square below. Sarhaddon was in dangerous water here. Many of the people of Tandaris had lived in Vararu or Poseidonis before their destruction in the Crusade. Some might even have seen their fall. And no one would forget who had done it.

"Remember that we live in buildings quarried by flamewood, transported over the sea by flamewood mantas, that through His grace we gain aether from it. The aether which shields you from the storms, from enemy attack, which lights your homes.

"What other protection is there from the fury of the elements? Fire to keep you warm, to keep you safe against the fury of water and wind and shadow. It is more than an element. Would you compare it with the wind which howls through our cities with every storm, a destructive product of the sky? With the water which surrounds us, which the oceanographers map and chart, understand by means of experiments and instruments? Can there be a deity in something so easily understood by us? These fragile platforms of earth and rock, inert, dead without the light of the sun, which we call continents and islands, and which serve as a platform for our feet? Or even shadow, the absence of light, of heat, a darkness? Who is there among you—aside from those newly wed—who would wish for endless night? Thure has that for months at a time, and what is Thure? A desolate wasteland of ice and rock where nothing grows, nothing lives.

"Fire is beyond all those, not a mere part of what makes up the world. We have the sun, the source of all fire, vast beyond our imagining, the embodiment of Ranthas in His purest form, while on Aquasilva He has given us a fraction of that for when His face is turned from us. Imagine a world without the sun. No life, no spark of anything, just a ball of dead, lifeless liquid and rock. There would be no life in sea or on land then, just a whole world of glaciers and unimaginable cold. The other elements would be there, of course. But what good would they be, what power would they have? What power can make life from frozen ice without heat?

"Or a world with a sun where He had not given us His gift. Where there was no heat to keep us through the night or the winter, where the spark of life was absent. All the other elements might be present, but without fire to show and guide us, there would be no intelligence, only the beasts of the forest and the monsters of the deep.

"Fire overcomes all the other elements: it flickers, changes without rhyme or reason. It turns water into steam, takes the chill from the air, consumes the things of earth. And it banishes the shadows. No one can feel safe in darkness; it gives shelter to thieves, murderers, assassins and worse. Evil cannot flourish in plain view—it seeks out all the dark corners and can only be banished by fire and light.

"If these other gods exist, why do they ignore their worshipers? We are assailed on all sides by the sea and the storms, blanketed in shadow for months of the year. Can any of you truly say that you prefer winter to summer, weeks and weeks of half-light and terrible weather to calm seas, blue skies, light and warmth? *This is a hostile world*, but by the grace of Ranthas *we can survive*. More than that, we can build and flourish, raise children and live lives secure from the fury of the elements because of one thing: the gift of Ranthas.

"Many of you hate the Domain because of what it has done. But remember, in the generations since the First Prime we have kept at bay the fury of the storms, we have protected you from this world, we have brought Ranthas's gift to every corner of the earth. We have saved you from the chaos and the lies which went before.

"Two hundred years ago the world was hanging over an abyss, in a time of darkness, of war, of slaughter. Clouds of dust blocked out the sun and whole continents burned as armies fought to the death. Not a corner of the world escaped the war, from the Desolation to the ice cap. It had been centuries since the world had known peace, as the combatants carried their struggle farther and farther from the homeland.

"But then came the real destroyers—Thetian monarchs and their twisted mages who by their savagery stained the name of their race with blood, and escalated the conflict. Worshipers of fire fought against them, helped to secure their fall, and assisted better men to lead us out of those dark times. After the slaughter, we supported, we rebuilt, we banished the last of those mages from the earth. And we brought peace. Yes, there have been wars since then, between islands, states and empires, because the baser nature of man is to make war.

"Those mages who caused the catastrophes drew on the power of the other elements, which some say have their own gods, citing these mages as evidence of these gods' power. But because they draw from the primal, unadulterated forces within them, they cannot bring anything more than destruction. These mages are overwhelmed by the baseness of their magic, which twists their minds. They cannot build or protect, only destroy. The power they released was beyond their ability to control, and so there were endless wars, an era of chaos when no one, nothing was safe."

We listened in silence as Sarhaddon told the crowd the Domain's travesty of history in all its appalling detail, a history that they already knew but which he and his companion then spent more than an hour reinforcing. It was all the more sickening, in a way, because they used logic and reason instead of mere fervor. Many of the crowd would have heard stories from the *History*, the real one; a few might actually have read it, although possession of a copy was virtually a death sentence.

Both intelligent men, compelling speakers, they held the whole square silent as they talked. I couldn't and didn't tear myself away, nor did anyone else standing beside me. We listened to the story they told, the points they made, and I felt the seeds of doubt beginning to worm their way into my mind. If Thetia's real history was so different, then why had even they forgotten it? Clan leaders over the centuries must have read the book that offered them a chance to avenge the stain on their past, yet they'd never taken it. Only their deep-seated hate for Shadow and the Tuonetar remained, and that was part of the Domain's history too.

It wouldn't have affected me so profoundly had it not been for my encounters with Orosius. Only in the *History* and the Continuator's work were Aetius, Carausius and Tiberius heroes, because they and their most loyal followers had written those books. I thought of the others down the centuries, as I had too many times before, and wondered how they could possibly have been seen in that way.

Sarhaddon and his companion's descriptions of them were so like portrayals of Orosius and Landressa! Aetius a competent commander, but how profligate with lives against an enemy not nearly as strong as the *History* had made them out to be! He had sacrificed thousands and thousands in his battles, killed and tortured prisoners without mercy to make the enemy fear him. And in the end, in those final months, he had deliberately stripped Selerian Alastre of most of its garrison. The *History* had never explained why the city was so weak when the Tuonetar attacked, but despite the horror they conveyed, Sarhaddon's words made an awful sense.

"Aetius used his own capital, his own people, as bait to lure the Tuonetar legions and fleets away from the north. They descended on the city in their thousands, put it to the torch and killed or enslaved all who lived there. The city we know today was rebuilt after that, despite the destruction," Sarhaddon continued. "While their armies were occupied his brother led their own fleet up to the north, the homeland of the Tuonetar that today is so barren nothing can survive there. They took revenge for an atrocity that need never have happened, but in the fighting, finally, some unnamed enemy soldier put an end to the Emperor and his reign of terror.

"You may hear that the Tuonetar drifted away, fell apart because their capital had gone. That is only half the truth. They did indeed, but only because Carausius, in vengeance for his brother's death, raised the elements against them and threw Aran Cthun down into the darkness. He used the destruction of the city's sacred talismans to unleash slaughter across the world, a magic so powerful that, despite its success, it crippled him too.

"This is a man, remember, who admitted to causing the deaths of thousands with his primeval magic *because they were the enemy*. Who else had the power to cause the tidal waves, the surges, the floods that took so many lives, on both sides? The submersion of so much land at that time is a matter of history. The storms made it worse, but could they have done that on their own? Could the Tuonetar have accomplished it? Their magic was twisted, but it was Shadow. Ask yourselves who else it could have been, all you who believe in his story: who else had the power to use the sea as a weapon?

"Finally we come to the 'usurpation' that those who walk in the shadow of this book see as the end of freedom and the beginning of terror, the exact opposite of reality.

"Two cousins, one a son of Aetius, the other of Carausius. They had fought and commanded in the war, seen the blood, the massacres, the torment. One father was dead, the other crippled, but the war was over. The Tuonetar had been all but exterminated as a people and as a race, those who survived had been rounded up and butchered, enslaved, banished to the farthest miserable ends of the earth. The capital was in ruins because of their fathers' stratagem, one that Tiberius had helped to plan, and their country's resources had been drained. The mages who had caused so much suffering and terror during the war were still at large, their power not curbed.

"They began to rebuild, yes, but on the old foundations. Tiberius, who revered the memory of his father, raised monuments to him in the new city, conscripted new legions to keep the peace in the lands his father had taken. Thousands upon thousands were forcibly drafted in to return Selerian Alastre to its former glory, working without reward from a depleted treasury simply so that Tiberius could have his palace, his city, a place of beauty while the world lay in ruins.

"No one knows how many perished from the storms, whose fury had been exaggerated by the tyrants' magic, yet was anything done, were shields built as a protection? The mages were honored, raised to positions of power and influence, as were the officers who'd been loyal to the tyrants at the expense of their country. They had known what would happen if Selerian Alastre was taken, yet they hadn't protested against it.

"But there were those in the new generation who abhorred what their fathers had done. Valdur despised his father, seeing him for what he really was, and he gathered around himself those who thought likewise, many of whom had lost loved ones in the War. Many of these people had been involved, yet they loathed the memory of it and sought to prevent such things ever happening again rather than build a new order like the old. They taught Valdur the true magic of fire where before he had known only the savagery of the other elements. Ranthas spoke to him and he listened, as his family never had before.

"And so he committed a crime to prevent a greater one repeating itself. It is a terrible thing to usurp a throne, yet Valdur's own life was in danger because of his association with those who opposed the magic. People who had sworn loyalty to him, friends and relatives, threatened him because he had seen the light where they had not. They were the false ones, who had raped and murdered their way through the War and had knowingly taken part in its horrors.

"And they were the only ones to suffer, because they were condemned in the eyes of men and gods for their actions. All Thetia acclaimed Valdur, and all the Empire turned on those who had mutilated it so. Thetia finally had a leader who set his face against the past horrors committed by his family, and what they had led Thetia into. Men saw for the first time what they had done, but no matter how bad their sins, Ranthas allowed them to repent, granted them absolution through His priests who could now speak freely as never before.

"The butchers and the accomplices of the tyrants were hunted down and brought to justice, the twisted mages put to death because they were beyond redemption. Theirs is a path that corrupts the mind gradually, and as more and more magic is used, it takes them over: they become husks, mere vessels for the savage power they channel. Those who were young and could be saved were, but most could not.

"The Continuator calls it a bloodbath, a reign of terror, without mentioning that these were the architects of the War, of ruin and famine, many of whom had themselves killed far more than died at this time. And since then the world has remained stable, as empires come and go without ever tipping the balance to the extent that these mages were allowed to. There was no more such violence, and since then Thetia itself has known internal peace and tranquillity as never before.

"Apart from the dissent of a small minority, and it is those I have been seeking to convince today, more than any others. Words, as I said, are powerful, whether spoken or written. They have led many along paths they would not otherwise have taken, and words handed down with authority, with the weight of so-called history behind them, can be the most persuasive of all.

"Tradition is what gives these words their weight, but not the tradition of successive generations examining and understanding the legacy of their forefathers. I mean the blind following of tradition, of what we are told by elders who themselves have no true understanding. The doctrine of the Domain has changed over the centuries, as we discover new aspects to Ranthas, new ways of seeing him that have come from looking at the past and the present. We have not obediently parroted what we were told by old monks in the seminaries: they made us understand why things are as they are.

"For those who follow this book there has been no such evolution of ideas. The young are taught what the old believe with all their hearts because they were told it in their own youth, and so on. You may say, if the *History* is as false and misleading as I say, why is it believed? Why was it *ever* believed? Why, if we already have the true record of the times, does this other record exist?

"The answer lies in loyalty, people of Qalathar. Loyalty is one of the strongest forces, one that binds the world together, but those who have been corrupted and refuse to turn can be blind to the true nature of what corrupted them. After everything that had happened, after all the horrors of the battlefield had been revealed to the world in their fullest extent after the War, there were some few who remained from the retinue of the Tyrants. People whose crimes had been justly revealed before the world, but whose cunning and guile had allowed them to escape the punishment meted out to their fellows.

"For the Continuator, who saw the tyrants as heroes despite the rivers of gore they waded in, there was hope in the tale that some few mages and officers of the fleet had fled south from Thetia into the Desolation. Hope that perhaps some might have survived.

"That we shall never know, but what is sure is that some did not go that far. Some who still commanded influence and respect among those who had only seen the War at second hand. The Archipelago was the least affected area of the world, rarely visited by one side or the other, its people then as now few and hardy, not numerous enough to be seen as a source of recruits.

"These people who fled justice turned around at the edge of the known world, and didn't venture south into the ocean to meet their deaths as did their comrades. They founded settlements somewhere in the south of the Archipelago's ten thousand islands, settlements hidden by the old magic from the eyes of the world. There is a great deal of ocean out there to hide in.

"And these refugees stayed, in time made themselves known to the world through secret means, recruiting from across the world those who, in a lesser way, still believed the propaganda of the Tyrants. The refugees taught them this distortion of history, and in time their children learned it too. They were misled by the criminals, the murderers, who had served the tyrants, and as men and women died and the world moved on, the people who had fled became forgotten, and generation after generation in all innocence believed the lies they had been told.

"We live in the present, and the problems of the past are always more immediate than those of the present, and so over the years in the minds of those who had been—and are still being—misled, the Domain came to represent an evil, an evil that had destroyed the world before. One's grandparents always look back to the golden age of their youth, and so generations of heretics have been led astray from the true path. They see us as having destroyed a world that never was, blackened the names of those who were, indeed, tyrants and butchers.

"Too often this view has been answered with intolerance, suspicion, and outright persecution. We seek to fight evil in all its forms, not remembering that there will always be leaders and followers, and we look back at the accounts of the age of anger and terror and persecute those who follow its forms. Too rarely does it occur to us to wonder why these are still being followed after such vast expanses of time, or why these voices from the past can still haunt the world today.

"I call to you, to all Qalathar, to all the Archipelago, to think, to consider, to listen to what I have said and to hear me again in future. I offer a safe-conduct signed by the Prime himself, as you have seen, to any who would argue this with me and my brothers. You may choose the place, the time—I only ask that you allow an audience, as many as may want to come.

"And I say also that for those who have been misled, by our blessing you may return to the true path and put your past behind you. Countless thousands have turned their face from us, but we will not turn away from you. Those who come to us will be absolved, and those who confess their faith before witnesses—as is the custom, as no heretic will consent to do—will be judged true children of Ranthas. All those known as heretics who we receive into the body of the Domain shall be safe from any persecution all their lives, as will those who wish to affirm their faith whether they have previously doubted or been doubted in the sincerity of their belief.

"I offer forgiveness, peace and redemption in the name of Ranthas who brings light and life to the world, now and forever. May He go with you, now and forever."

Chapter XXV

We all stood in silence as Sarhaddon made the sign of the flame and followed his companion down from the speaking platform to join his brothers. The crowd, seemingly stunned into silence, didn't move or change at all as the clerics formed up into a little procession again, led by a thurifer whose censer had long since cooled. Then, suddenly, as if released from a spell, the throng moved. In all directions at once, it seemed, and all talking simultaneously. It was almost painful, so much sound after hours of nothing but Sarhaddon's voice.

Some people at the edge headed away and began to disperse, but some headed toward the middle, and there was a rush toward the Venatics. For a tense moment I thought they were about to be torn apart, and glanced over at the temple where surely there were Sacri poised to spring.

But that wasn't the crowd's mood, and the conversations we could hear coming up from below were hushed and intense, not angry or accusatory. Gaps opened up in the swirling mass below us, and the Venatics, heading not toward the temple but to another road from the square were suddenly surrounded by a huge cluster of people. At a word from Sarhaddon's companion the procession dissolved again and the Venatics separated. A moment later there were six white islands surrounded by people gesturing excitedly.

It was a moment before anyone on the balcony moved. Then I felt the pressure on my leg released as somebody stepped backward, opening up a space. Everyone started talking at once, the same excitement in their voices as that I could hear below. I stared out across the square for a moment longer, watching the crowd mill around.

Then the oceanographer next to me shifted along the rail as more people went inside.

"Sorry, I didn't leave you any room there," she said, an uneasy expression on her face. "You don't agree with him?"

"I'm Thetian," I said, for the second time that day, not wanting to complicate matters too much. "If you look at our Emperor now, it's hard not to believe Sarhaddon."

"It just . . . goes against everything I was taught. I'm not sure what to believe anymore."

"Were you at . . .?" I deliberately left the question unfinished, and she understood.

"Yes, I was at Water three years ago. I don't know if you've seen it, but it does look very Thetian. I think about what he said at the end there. He turned everything on its head." She waved her hands in a typically Archipelagan gesture of frustration. "I always thought Carausius was someone I'd have liked to know, but the things they say about him are so horrible. And the thought that Aetius would destroy his own capital, all those people, like that—could anyone be so monstrous?"

Every year on the anniversary of Aran Cthun's fall the Navy and the legions hold a service for the dead, to remember that march, and Aetius's death. Telesta's words rang in my head, words that had to be the truth because she wanted me to trust her. Would they do that for a man who'd condemned so many of their families to death as a gamble?

But he was a Tar'Conantur—why shouldn't he be like the rest of his accursed family? Why should there be those three exceptions in the litany of death and blood that accompanied us down the centuries? Part of me knew that Sarhaddon was doing this only as a means to an end, and probably two months ago I wouldn't have believed a word he'd said. But that had been before I met Orosius.

"There you are." It was Palatine again, but her face showed worry rather than doubt. Less numbed than I was, she introduced herself to the oceanographer, whose name was Alciana.

"Cousins?" Alciana said, after I'd given her my name as well, and Palatine nodded. "You don't seem as worried."

"I don't believe Sarhaddon," Palatine said. "Not the way he looks at things, anyway. Probably the Citadels were founded that way, but does it automatically mean the founders were these butchers he talked about? The military still think of Aetius as a hero, and they wouldn't if he'd wasted so many lives."

"Aetius was a Tar'Conantur," I said. "Why should he be a paragon of virtue when the rest of his family are so twisted?"

"You only hear about the ones who are," she said intensely. "The normal ones aren't interesting, can't be used as propaganda."

"Then why do they never become Emperor?" I demanded. "Or do

you just mean the ones who don't have power, so can't make a name for themselves?"

"Princess Neptunia may not be very warm, or a very good mother, but she's not a monster. Not in the slightest way. Nor was the old Emperor."

"The old Emperor abandoned us to our fate," Alciana said softly, looking from one of us to the other. "The new one may do much worse. I think Cathan's right."

"You would believe Sarhaddon, then?"

"As I said, I don't know what to believe. The Domain are the ones who burn people for disagreeing with their religion. Did Aetius or Carausius ever do that?"

"No, they didn't. Sarhaddon's trying to convince the ordinary people, I think, the ones who never went to the Citadels. Their indoctrination is far more severe than ours was, if you can call ours that. Are there any people you know of who could debate with him, who wouldn't be afraid and would put a good case?"

"People are scared," said Alciana regretfully. "Diodemes over there, the oceanographer with gray hair, might have done it, but what if he does? The whole of Qalathar will know he's a heretic, so the moment the Venatics' amnesty ends, he'll be arrested. Whoever debates really has to lose the argument and convert to save himself."

"Someone from one of the Citadels, perhaps?" I suggested. "No fear of retaliation, since they can disappear again afterward."

"But whoever comes will take weeks to get here, and then they might still be able to track him when he goes back."

"It looks like people are taking notice of Sarhaddon." Palatine gestured over the fast-emptying square; we were the only people left on the balcony. The Venatics were still down there, near the platform, with a substantial crowd circling each of them. "This must be what he wants."

"I think I agree with them," said Alciana. "Everyone's been talking about a crusade for months, even more so since the inquisitors arrived. I see the Sacri every day when I walk from my home to the Guild station, and my parents have told me what happened last time. The rest of my family are heretics, but they don't want to die. Nor do I, but that's what will happen if there's a Crusade. I'm not the stuff martyrs are made of."

It came down to that in the end, I thought as I'd thought before, whether faith was more important than living a normal life, or living a life at all. History was important, yes, but the Domain's greatest wrongs were in the past, and was that something to die for? A past that might not even be what we thought it was?

"I think things are clearer now," said Palatine thoughtfully. "We wondered what Sarhaddon wanted, now I think we know. He'll separate the martyrs from the rest, because everyone now has a chance to concede without cost, save themselves from more inquisitors and the Crusade. Those of us who remain outside are the ones they can hunt down."

"Sarhaddon said he was only trying to save those who wanted to be saved," I said.

"I thought it would be impossible to win over so many, that it was just his dream. Now I see even you doubting, Cathan, and it's become very real."

"You're friends of Persea, so you're probably involved with the dissidents," said Alciana, and paused for a minute. "And you're not Qalathari. People will have told you this already, but you have to realize that if there's a crusade it will be the end of the Archipelago. We'll lose what freedom we have, this city will be captured. Everyone knows that. We cannot resist them, we simply aren't strong enough. Anything we do is no better than a gnat's bite. Even if we fought and won, they have a whole world to give them more troops and try again, including the Emperor." She fiddled with the hem of her sleeve, a gesture that went oddly with her urbane, cultured look and reminded me of Palatine.

"I hardly know you, so I don't know why I'm saying this, but it's people like Persea and Alidrisi who'll cause the problems. I try never to think about what will happen if the crusaders come, but sometimes I can't stop myself when I'm depressed. They'll turn this city into a charred wasteland and pitch their tents on what's left of it. And they'll kill or enslave everyone I know, including my whole family.

"And because I'm young and pretty, I'll be sold as a concubine in Haleth instead of being killed, if I survive the fall of the city. You have no idea what it's like, knowing that such a thing could happen and that there's really no way you can stop it. I'm not sure what to make of Sarhaddon and his message, so I'll listen to more speeches, but I don't believe in Thetis strongly enough to die for her. So please, if you don't believe him, don't tell everyone and try to refute it. Let *us* decide for once."

"In all fairness, he already has," Palatine said, as Alciana again fixed her very grave gaze on both of us. I didn't try to say anything. "Sarhaddon knows Cathan—he came straight to see him when he arrived here. Cathan helped convince the Viceroy to allow it."

"So that was you, was it?" Alciana said to me. "I heard someone had done that, not from Persea or her people either. Why, when you're not even one of us?"

"Ask Persea," Palatine said, again before I could reply. "She'll tell you."

Did Persea know? I wondered. *Did anyone?* It had been for the same reason Alciana had said, except that I didn't stand to suffer.

"I will," Alciana said, "but thank you." She turned away without saying any more. I saw Alidrisi's face over to one side for a moment, watching us. Then he too moved in the other direction. Everything was the same as it had been before the speech: the light, the room itself—and the people were still uncertain. But the mood was more serious.

"Why did you bring that up?" I asked Palatine. "There was no need to tell her."

"We don't want them to see us as interfering foreigners."

"And they won't now?"

"They may still, but they'll also know that you did them a favor, and if we ever have real trouble that could be a lifeline."

"Still calculating political advantage, even after that? It only works if this isn't a trick."

"What's wrong with you, Cathan? You've hardly said anything since you saw Sarhaddon two days ago. And surely you don't believe what he said about Aetius and the others? Could the monster he was talking about have written the *History*? No one can write a book that long about things they've experienced without their character coming through. Carausius wasn't a crazed butcher, so why do you have this view of our family? Even my mother, as I said, she's not really a very good mother, but she's not cruel. Is this the way you see yourself? Me?"

"No. I'm Perseus's son, aren't I?" I stared at her for a moment. "He was always more concerned with his art and his poetry than with ruling an empire. My other father—Count Elnibal, that is—said that marrying my mother was the only decision the old Emperor ever made for himself. Much good that did him."

"Will you scorn her as well?" Palatine asked quietly, very calm. "She isn't Tar'Conantur, there's not a trace of that in her. She loves the sea like you do, and she's a lot braver than your father was. You may think the Tar'Conantur part of you is the only one that matters, but we all have two parents and you've never asked about your mother."

The rest of the room dwindled into insignificance, and I felt a mixture of guilt and shame, realizing how true that was. People talked about my brother and my father, but only my adoptive father, the Count, had ever mentioned the Empress. My mother was the Countess of Lepidor, as far as I was concerned, and always would be. Perseus would never be my father: he was more like a grandfather who'd died before I was born.

"Did you know her?" I said finally. "And why does nobody talk about her?"

"I last saw her when I was fifteen. Perseus died young—he was only thirty-seven. Orosius was three. She stayed on in Selerian Alastre after that to raise Orosius. I think she tried her best to bring him up vaguely normal. But the Exarch couldn't stand her, and in the end he forced or persuaded Orosius to banish her. I think she was alone in the last few years, and Orosius was turning into a monster, so she must have been desperately unhappy. Glad to leave, perhaps, and she cursed the Exarch before she went. He's still there, actually, growing old and never promoted.

"She was too lively for that court, except Perseus, I suppose, and she was better at being a mother than my own was. She had coppery red hair, an incredible color, and green eyes. And although she laughed a lot, she was never really happy there. You know she was an Exile; she belonged out on the ocean, far away from land and cities."

"What happened to her, after she left?"

"I don't know. She was younger than Perseus. I think she went back home to the Exiles and is probably still alive. I'm sure Tanais would know. Maybe one or two of the clan rulers who were her real friends there, like Aelin Salassa, would be able to tell you. Aelin's father was the Chancellor who was executed when you were born."

There I knew otherwise. Baethelen had died in Ral Tumar, trying to carry me out of the clutches of the Domain.

"Cathan, what's important is that you're not like them. You look like your brother, your father, every Tar'Conantur who's ever lived. But that doesn't mean anything. No one can be totally evil, certainly no family. Forget whether or not Aetius and Carausius were heroes or murderers, or, if you must, follow your mind, not your doubts. You still haven't found either of the things you're looking for, so concentrate on them. There's nothing we can or should do about Sarhaddon except watch." Palatine's tone was brusque now, but it worked. I was too susceptible to doubt and worry with every new thing I heard, and all of it only served to distract me from the *Aeon*. Only at night did I remember that, because the ship hung in my dreams, a vast presence forever out of reach, shrouded in darkness. I still didn't know what she looked like.

"*Either* of the things?" I asked.

"Yes. I just hope you aren't in love with both of them."

Only a Thetian would make a comment like that, even a Thetian as normal as Palatine. "What about Alidrisi?"

"Ask Persea if he's your contact. If he's not, we keep on as we've been going. If he is," she moved close to whisper, "we follow him. Are you up to that?"

"Of course." I looked around and saw Alidrisi in the middle of a group of people over on the far side of the room. No one seemed to have left yet, and most of them were holding full or nearly full glasses. He probably wanted to hear everybody's reaction, judge the best course of action; I had the feeling he'd be another one not influenced by Sarhaddon's oratory.

Persea. Where was she? Not over near Alidrisi, or behind me on the balcony. She seemed to have disappeared. Laeas caught my eye and waved me over.

"If you're looking for Persea, she'll be back in a minute." He introduced me to the two men he was talking to, obviously people he knew well. One, very dark-skinned, had a name that sounded Cambressian, so perhaps they were here to represent another part of the political spectrum. There seemed to be representatives from several of the heretic factions here: Alidrisi and probably some other Pharaonic loyalists, the oceanographers. The more I heard of her, the more Persea sounded like a hardline dissident. I guessed Laeas was essentially loyal to the Viceroy and I knew he favored Cambressian intervention. I wondered if there was a pro-Thetian factor. "What did you think?" He had an expression of careful neutrality; his two companions were thoughtful. I wasn't about to second-guess him.

"Disturbing," I said, which was the truth, if not for the reasons I'd given. "After all they taught us—"

"But what about here and now?" the Cambressian interrupted. "I'm not going to decide whether or not to change my faith on the basis of past history. What matters is whether you think Qalathar will go down his route. More important, whether what we heard today is as open as it seems?"

"I think the message isn't what's important. He has to sway them, and it's an effective way to do it. I've only talked to Palatine and Alciana so far, so I can't be much more help."

The Cambressian rolled his eyes in exasperation. "You might be, Alciana isn't. All the oceanographers are the same, terrified of offending anyone at all."

Laeas made a noise that was probably a polite cough but sounded more like a rumble, coming from him. "You're not being very diplomatic today, Bamalco."

"You're an oceanographer?" He said some things in Cambressian that I took to be swear words. "My sincere apologies."

"Be fair to them," the third man said. "They can't just disappear like the rest of us if the Domain gets on to them. If they have to run from the Inquisitors, their names get circulated and they can't go back to being oceanographers."

"Bamalco," Laeas said, "I can probably repeat what Alciana said word for word; I've heard it from other people. If there's trouble here you'll get recalled to Cambress. You don't stand to lose anything."

"Except a lot of friends," Bamalco said, bristling slightly. "Everyone's said the same thing, more or less, because everyone stands to lose if there's a Crusade. It's just that when one looks at the rest of the world, there are so many people who could help but won't. Like the Cambressian government, of course. I warn you—they held elections for next year's magistrates a few weeks ago and the two new Suffetes hate each other with a vengeance. Whatever one does, the other will block, even if it's a proposal to raise their stipend. My people are going to have their work cut out." Not Cambressian, then: he had to be Mons Ferratan, probably a half-breed.

"The joys of a republic," Laeas murmured.

"Ah yes, but this doesn't happen every year. It's just bad luck that this is one of the times nothing will get done. And maybe they have a republic, but they get outside Cambress itself and all that 'rule of the people' stuff goes down the drain."

"Does anyone except the Viceroy have a real say here?" I asked.

"There's a clan assembly, technically, which can't do anything. The Viceroy's government is so skeletal that you can hear the wind whistling through the gaps. It's individuals, really, people like Alidrisi and one or two of the other Presidents. Everything's done in the Viceroy's name, and he's working for the Pharaoh."

"I think pigs might fly," said Alciana, suddenly appearing with Persea to my left. We moved around to make room for them. "Admiral Karao, working for anyone other than himself? There's a non-starter."

"That's a bit extreme," Persea and Bamalco said at the same time, and stopped.

Laeas smiled. "Very predictable."

"No, I'm serious," Alciana said, looking at me although she was talking to the others. "How many of those people are really working for her? She's, what—twenty-one, twenty-two, now? And she's been kept hidden all this time, while people supposedly work for her return. Clan presidents can do what they like at the moment, although they have to watch out for the Domain. If she comes back as anything other than a puppet, they lose power."

"But she'd make a very good puppet," Bamalco said. "They are working for her, and probably for her return too. She'd make a great figurehead for anyone."

"I don't think she'll want to be a figurehead," I said. "Would you?"

"I think she has to appear very soon, or people will start to wonder if she really exists. Oh, *I* believe she's real, but this is a bad time. If she doesn't come back now, when things are really serious . . ." Bamalco shook his head. "She's not in a good position."

"Do you ever predict anything but doom, Bamalco?" Persea asked, making an exasperated gesture. "Is that why you're here and not in Cambress, because nobody there would believe you?"

"If you don't want my help . . . I can take myself and this doom you talk about somewhere else. Thetia, perhaps. No military ethos there."

"Bamalco's too much of an individualist to enjoy serving in the Mons Ferratan navy," Persea explained. "Or so he says. We think it's actually because he was so much trouble they wouldn't have him."

"Their loss," Bamalco said dismissively. "Anyway, our fleet always ends up helping the Cambressians, which would be fine if we didn't have to put up with their engineers as well. They have the best fleet engineering academy in the world there. They'll admit anyone, but only people who went there ever get to be chief engineer."

"So why didn't you go?" I asked.

"Bah! You think I want to spend three years square-bashing? They run the place under military discipline."

Laeas's other companion immediately objected to this opinion, and they launched into an argument that sounded like it was covering familiar ground. I pulled Persea aside as Alciana joined in, and looked around to check that Alidrisi wasn't nearby. He was still talking to those same people, thankfully, so his attention wasn't focused on us.

"Persea, is Alidrisi your contact with the Pharaoh's people?" I asked her in as quiet a voice as I could without actually whispering and so attracting more attention than I was trying to avoid.

"Yes, he and his staff. Why?"

"He doesn't like me. We've already had an argument today—he thinks that I'd be a bad influence on Ravenna and thus on the Pharaoh, or that she might tell me where the Pharaoh is." I wondered if we could keep the pretense up forever, or whether they'd realize sometime.

"Well done. If he won't help, there's nothing more I can do."

"Thank you, anyway. Do you know if he's left the city in the past couple of days?"

"He's only just arrived from Kalessos . . . Cathan, why are you asking me this?"

"I need to know."

Persea sighed. "You're mad. Look, I know you want to see Ravenna, but this is going too far. If she's with the Pharaoh, they'll be heavily guarded, and Alidrisi won't be pleased if you discover where that is."

"I need to see her, not just because of that. I've got no further with the other search, and she might be able to help me there."

"On the other hand, you might just end up being locked up by the guards. Cathan, I can't help you here. I'm not from the inner circle, I'm not a player on the same scale. Alidrisi has some of the few good soldiers left in the Archipelago, and if he's told them to guard the Pharaoh and her entourage, they will. If the Domain finds her, there's no telling how bad it could be, and he won't take my word that you're one of us."

"He isn't a mage," I said flatly. "Could you just tell me when Alidrisi's next leaving the city, if you know? I'll take my own chances."

"This is Palatine's idea, isn't it?"

"It doesn't matter whose notion it is," I said, sidestepping the question because it wasn't one of Palatine's ideas. People had more confidence in them. *When does he leave?*"

Persea looked around warily. "He came back yesterday because of Sarhaddon. As far as I know, he's staying until the end of the week, in five days' time, when he goes back to Kalessos. It's six or seven hours on a fast horse."

"He doesn't sail?"

"To Kalessos, in this weather? The coast west of here is a killer: there are no safe harbors on the north side at all. It's bad going by land, but no one would take even a battle cruiser to Kalessos in winter."

That was the coast where the *Revelation* had been lost, I remembered now. Funny to have tried for a record dive in such a notorious patch of sea, but they must have had their reasons.

"So how does he travel? Surely not on horseback in this weather. By carriage?"

"Yes, but don't push your luck. And please, Cathan, if you must follow him, don't use magic. It'll bring every mage in Qalathar down on you like a ton of bricks. You heard Sarhaddon today, it's one of the things they won't forgive."

And it would lead them to the Pharaoh, was the unspoken next sentence. And make life more difficult, although I really didn't have a clue how I could follow a carriage for a twelve-hour stretch in the middle of winter. It didn't seem like such a good idea after all. I could probably use a *little* magic, out in the countryside away from the mages' area of influence, but no more than a little. The more I used, the more likely they were to detect it, and not everybody would be able to slip away from the hiding place in time.

"I know you don't want me to interfere, but you've heard what people have been saying today. The *Aeon* is a wild card, and if nobody else finds her, there's nothing they can do about her when we do. She's an asset they haven't planned for."

"I know. But if they're the ones who get the ship—"

"They won't be. She'll be a refuge as well, remember. A place where the Domain definitely can't follow us."

"The Domain will follow us to the ends of the earth, Cathan, if they think it's important enough."

"The ends of the earth aren't under their control, though. And nor will we be, if I can find the *Aeon*. It was Ravenna's idea to look; she might well have found some clues I haven't."

Persea gave her lopsided smile, one that I saw so rarely these days. She had changed in the six months since we'd left the Citadel, as we all had, but it was hard to see her as everyone else did, as one of the Domain's most dedicated opponents. "You don't need to make excuses. I know you're serious about finding both of them. Now, better for us not to stand here whispering too much. People will begin to listen. Talk to people, find out what everybody thinks. That's why we're here."

Not quite right, I thought as we split up. We were here so that Alidrisi could discover what everybody thought without him having to make an effort. But if he could make use of the opportunity, so could we.

Chapter XXVI

"This is all our work," Alciana said, waving her hand over the island of Qalathar, green and verdant in a blue sea as it would look in summer. Beneath the water's surface the bedrock of the island was a dark, indistinct shadow. "We surveyed it on a shoestring budget: the Guild said Qalathar was a low priority for an aether model with this much detail."

"Impressive," I said, resting my hands on the aether table's edge and examining the image. The detail was incredible, even for land that would only have been given a cursory survey, using balloons—one whole area in the west was blank, but I knew why that was. Underwater . . . we'd had nothing this precise in Lepidor even from visiting ships, because our coast had never been a priority. Or it hadn't been until recently.

"The Guild has only done Thetia, Taneth, and the main routes so far," said her fellow oceanographer Tamanes, the only other person in the station's spacious map room.

"How did you get hold of the equipment?"

Tamanes smiled. "We got the prototype once Headquarters had finished with it. It has a habit of exploding in our faces, but it works."

"Watch this." Beside me Alciana sank her hands into the control pads and the image flickered and grew larger as we swooped in on the tiny white patch that was Tandaris. I saw the city swell from the merest trace to a near-perfect representation, complete with parks and trees, before she tilted the view and we sank underwater. The light in the room changed to a soft blue glow, and I saw on the table a huge, dark cliff complete with its irregularities and openings, sweeping away to either side of the city. They'd been able to see a long way down, one of the advantages of the new surveying equipment the Thetians had developed a few years ago.

"How deep does it go?"

"Eight or nine miles around most of the island, less along Perdition's Shore. No one was going to risk losing the surveyor there, and in any case people keep well away from that coast." She moved out again, the island rotating wildly, and then narrowed in on the north-western coast.

The island was mountainous here on a Continental scale: there was an almost continuous wall of cliffs, broken every now and then by coves that I could see would never be safe harbors. The image faded out almost immediately inland, as if covered by a veil of mist. The mountain fastness of Tehama and the Sacred Lake lay somewhere in there, and on the map I could see the bay, facing open ocean to the west, where the great waterfall plunged more than a mile from the plateau above.

Below these dark cliffs the rock was a nightmare of sheer walls and spurs that was oddly fuzzy compared with the rest of the image, as if they'd been charted with a first-generation imager. At the very bottom of the scanner's range and several miles offshore there were upthrust pinnacles of rock like the summits of submerged islands, standing out from the surrounding emptiness.

"Why on earth did they send the *Revelation* here?" I wondered aloud. It was probably a question that they were used to hearing, but I still knew very little about it. It was nothing to do with the *Aeon*, but I was still curious.

"Who knows?" Tamanes said with a shrug. "Perhaps they thought it could find out why this whole area is so evil. Those rocks and cliffs look impressive, but they're only a danger to sailing ships. We lose mantas here as well for miles out to sea, and nobody knows why."

"Maybe they thought it was the back door of Tehama," Alciana suggested. "There were priests involved, after all, and we all know they're longing to get into the place."

Tamanes gave her a quick warning look that he thought I didn't see. "A strange back door if ever there was one, trying to get on to a plateau via the seabed. I think they were just trying to find out why the place is so treacherous. A couple of Imperial ships had been lost there a few months before, and the Emperor was funding the other ship, in one of his more lucid moments."

That had been my grandfather Aetius V, an old man by then and spending his time experimenting with various substances thoughtfully provided by his Exarch. What a credit to the human race our family was.

"Is that long inlet there part of Perdition's Shore as well?" I pointed to a deep, cliff-bound crack in the coast near one end of the image, at the very edge of the high mountains. "There don't seem to be any settlements on it."

"Yes, that's more of the same. People have hideaways along our side of the inlet, because they can't be reached from the sea and it's almost as difficult by land. We've no charts of the inlet, but for some reason there's a strong current coming out of it, stronger than the three or four tiny little rivers draining into it can account for. Since our side's pretty inaccessible and the other's Tehama, we can't have a look to see why. It's not very important."

Looking at such a realistic map of Qalathar, I could see how Ravenna's homeland—birthplace—could remain cut off, bounded as it was by Perdition's Shore, the inlet and a range of impenetrable mountains that seemed far too big for Qalathar. It was a strange island anyway, thinking about it—by far the biggest in the whole Archipelago, outstripping Beraetha and the biggest Thetian islands by a long way, mountainous where all the others were mere bumps on the sea, and surrounded by turbulent waters and shallow seas. Bostra in his *Geography* had said little about it, describing instead in great depth how Thetia was like a huge crater, a ring of mountainous islands around an incredibly rich, shallow sea. Qalathar, unfortunately, hadn't been interesting or important enough to merit his attention.

I thanked them for showing me the image-map, and we left the room, turning off the table before we went. Tamanes excused himself to finish some work, but Alciana invited me to have lunch in a café across the road. It was like dozens of other such places in the city, with room outside for seats in summer and a few tables inside for coffee and light meals. It belonged more to the harbor than the town, I decided, catching the smell of cooking fish; there were antique oceanographic instruments on the walls, and a fishing net slung part-way across the beamed ceiling.

The proprietor obviously knew Alciana and nodded to her as we came in; I caught sight of two older men in blue tunics eating in a far corner, and guessed that this was probably a favorite eating spot and watering hole of the oceanographers. Other than the men and two sailors quietly drinking coffee at the bar, it was empty.

"What'll it be?" the proprietor asked, regarding me suspiciously with his deep-sunken eyes.

"Cathan's an oceanographer too," Alciana said sharply, then turned to me. "Do you like stuffed vine leaves? They do them with morsels of fish here, very tasty."

I nodded. "Fine."

"A large plate of those, please, and two coffees." Everybody in the Archipelago drank coffee of some kind; it was taken for granted.

We waited for the coffees and then sat down away from the bar at a table with high-backed wooden seats, below a venerable brass tube-rack with several polished glass chemical tubes that was mounted on the wall. It was much quieter than any café I could remember, and for it to be this empty at lunchtime on a working day didn't seem like a good sign.

"Some of my friends may join us later, if they can get away," Alciana said, sipping her coffee. It wasn't remarkable, I discovered when I tried it, but not bad either. "No one from the station, though—they're all busy today."

"How many of you are there at the station?"

"Twenty-one at the moment. The Master sent two apprentices off to the university in Thetia when the troubles began, to keep them out of harm's way."

There was no university in the Archipelago, not as we knew it in the rest of the world. Poseidonis had had one, on a level with the best Thetian ones, and so had Vararu, but both of them had been destroyed, so there were no universities nearer than Mare Alastre and Castle Polinskarn, both in southern Thetia. There were no great archives, either.

"Does he think the Guild will be in the line of fire?"

"I have to admit, Cathan, that's why I asked you to lunch. I've never left Qalathar, and you've been all across the Archipelago since the Inquisition began, not to mention that you seem to know what's going on."

"I haven't seen as much of it as I'd like to."

"Nor have I. But we haven't heard anything from Guild Headquarters about this, and they must know by now what's going on. Did you visit the stations in Ilthys or Ral Tumar?"

I paused, remembering the part I'd played in Ral Tumar. Alciana deserved to know, especially now when things were so uneasy. "I only went to Ilthys briefly. They thought they had the protection of the Thetians, which counts there."

"It counts everywhere except here. And Ral Tumar?"

"Not good. I spent a couple of days in the library there. The Inquisitors came on the last day and arrested all except one of the oceanographers. She got away to Thetia, as far as I know, to tell the Guild what had happened."

The look of horror and fear on Alciana's face was chilling; of course, she'd had no idea. I hadn't seen any more persecution since then, but that mind-mage had warned Amalthea in Ral Tumar that there would be a purge, and had ordered her to tell the Guild. Had she ever got there, or had she been just one more victim of his duplicity? They must have heard by now from ships' crews, merchant mantas that had passed through Ral Tumar in the intervening six weeks. But there had been no arrivals from Thetia here, no word from Guild Headquarters to its most threatened outposts.

"Are you serious?" she said.

"I'm afraid so. They were doing some research with dolphins, using them with the fishing fleets, I think, and some zealots denounced it as unnatural. I'm afraid I don't know how it went after that."

"I thought until now that they were going to leave us alone—none of us have been arrested yet—but if they could be arrested for that . . . there are so many things we've done."

"Are there zealots in the city, strict observers of all the rites and things?"

"Not like Ral Tumar. Here we all suffer from what the Domain does; I don't think anybody would denounce Guild members. At least, I didn't. You know, the Inquisitors came for one of our neighbors yesterday, dragged her out of her house in the early hours. She worships Althana very devoutly, but not many people know. One of her friends must have informed against her, and that's never happened before. It's enemies usually, people who are business rivals or unfriendly Houses."

Was it Palatine who had said this whole Inquisition would be a chance for some to settle scores? I hadn't believed it until now, not having met those in the line of fire. Only the committed heretics, those who'd been to the Citadels, would resist Sarhaddon's appeals.

"Why would anything have changed?"

"Have you listened to the second and third sermons that Sarhaddon gave?"

"Of course, we were in Alidrisi's house."

"I know, there was no time to talk after he finished last night. I was talking to Tamanes and Diodemes outside—you know Diodemes, someone said he might be willing to debate—and they weren't very happy. Sarhaddon talked about sacrilege a lot, of how magic can appear in many forms, be hidden well."

"He's trying to blacken the reputations of our mages, turn people against them. Especially Shadow."

She smiled faintly. "How can you blacken a mage of Shadow? You were at that Citadel, someone said, which is strange for a Thetian."

"I live in Oceanus."

"You must be important, from the way people look at you. But anyway, that's not the point. Since that second speech things seem to have changed: people I don't know look suspiciously at me when I pass them in the street. It's only been three days, but there's a difference and it worries me."

"People think you're mages as well."

"Not that bad, but you know that we're always considered a bit apart, something special. Sarhaddon was right the first time: we analyze the sea and try to understand it with alchemy and strange tests that no non-oceanographers can understand. We can tell what conditions are going to be like far out to sea, the way the Domain can see the storms in advance."

"Which *can* seem like a kind of magic." The Guild had been persecuted before, although usually it was individual members who got too involved in the wrong kind of research. "But they can't do without us."

"If they can arrest a whole station in Ral Tumar, what about here? People know Diodemes is a heretic, and that a lot of us are—about half, in fact, and none of the others are very ardent believers in Ranthas. None of us would have chosen to be oceanographers if we didn't want to work with the sea."

We broke off the conversation as the gaunt proprietor came over, carrying a dish piled high with stuffed vine-leaves and the flat bread that they were usually eaten with. He didn't say a word when Alciana thanked him, just stalked away again.

"He's an old grump," she whispered, "but he's all right really. He won't denounce any of us, it would lose him half his customers. He helped someone get away about ten years ago."

"What have you been doing that they might not like?" I bit into one of the vine leaves, which was as good as she'd said it was; I hadn't tried them with fish inside before.

"Hard to tell, really, but if trying to train dolphins counts as unnatural, I don't know how we can be safe. We've put tracers on seals and followed them in a ray before now: they tend to be more single-minded about finding fish than the dolphins. There's some other work, more technical, that they might not like, but if they come after us they'll think up an excuse anyway. That's not really what worries me so much as the way Sarhaddon mentions us in every speech and then five minutes later starts talking about sacrilege, hidden mages and how dangerous all the heretic magic is. I think people are connecting them, which is the worst thing that could happen."

"But they still need you—the city won't function without a station."

"The city can function with only a few oceanographers," she said gravely. "Stop trying to reassure me. You're staying in the Viceroy's palace and you seem to know everyone—I wonder if you could help? Pass this on to the people you know, ask them if they think the same. Tamanes and Diodemes agree with me, by the way, so you can mention their names as well. Everyone thinks I'm too nervy and flighty to be trusted."

"I'll do what I can," I promised, "although I'm not sure whether anyone can protect you if they do come. The Viceroy could protect us because we were inside his palace surrounded by his guards, but you have to be in the station, and men outside won't help."

"We can't leave, either. If anyone does, the Domain will see it as admitting guilt."

I heard the sound of the door opening and felt the cold air from outside wafting into the room. It was colder than it had been this morning—the few days of lull seemed to be ending. Another storm on its way. I was just glad we'd had the chance to see the city in better conditions, however briefly.

"Alciana, there you are." It was Bamalco, the Mons Ferratan engineer, with Tekraea, who'd been one of the Archipelagans in Lepidor. The one Sarhaddon had threatened to kill if the attacking sailors weren't called off, in fact. "How's your date going?" Their arrival shattered the quiet, and both of them seemed very loud and big.

She gave him a wintry smile and we moved along to give them room to sit down.

"Are those the fishy vine leaves you've got there?" Tekraea asked hungrily, reaching for one.

"Yes, but you can order your own, there's not enough here for four," Alciana said, batting his hand away. He got up reluctantly and went to order some.

"Seriously, has she told you?" Bamalco asked me. When I nodded, he said, "Good. I told Laeas as well. He'll tell the Viceroy, but whether that will help or not remains to be seen."

"I thought you supported him," I said.

"He's still a Cambressian, you have to remember, and he's very good at jumping ship when he needs to."

"And he's not the Pharaoh," Tekraea said, slipping back into his seat. "He needs to bring her out of hiding."

"I'm not sure he knows where she is," I said, and could have kicked myself. Well, it was too late now. Persea hadn't been very helpful; perhaps these two would be.

"Come on, he must."

I shook my head. "Alidrisi does, but the Viceroy has never mentioned it."

"They don't see eye to eye," Bamalco said. "He's too moderate for Alidrisi's liking. Bad news if you're right and Alidrisi does know where the Pharaoh is."

"Is Alidrisi popular?" I asked carefully.

"In some circles, but he's difficult to deal with. I'd support the Viceroy any day: he's more experienced and not so extreme. Even if he is a Cambressian."

"Half Archipelagan," Tekraea reminded us. "Perhaps if he got hold of the Pharaoh again she'd be able to come out openly. He's the Viceroy, after all, and he's got more real power than any of the others."

"There are a lot more Kalessos clansmen than viceregal troops. At least now they've seized all his forces."

"Kalessos have feuds with people. There'd be trouble if just one clan, like Kalessos, got hold of her. She's independent, not a puppet—I wish they'd stop treating her like one."

"She has no one else to rely on," Bamalco reminded him gently. "They've been hiding her all her life, so she owes them for that."

"And they owe the rest of us a ruler who can do something about those jackals out there," Tekraea said fiercely. "Dragging people away in the night, hauling them before tribunals of men who wouldn't know justice if it bit them. Power-hungry fanatics, all of them. And Sarhaddon's no better, Cathan, whatever you might think. He's poisoning their minds: people are seeing mages in every corner. That's what he's doing. He's creating this vast conspiracy of evil mages—any heretic could be one—who corrupt everything they touch. He can't come straight out and attack the gods like he did on the first day, so he has to attack us instead."

"But if he stops the Crusade . . ." Alciana began, as Bamalco put a finger to his lips, a sign for Tekraea to lower his voice.

"How? By persuading us that it's better to lie down and let them walk all over us?"

"Would you rather they came and butchered everybody?"

"Why did they come last time?" Tekraea demanded hotly. "Because they tried to ban our customs, and when we resisted, they invaded. Now, because everyone's so afraid, no one fights anymore. They just have to tell us not to do something, arrest a few people, and everyone falls into line. The Assembly never meets, we have to burn our dead, the Festival of the Sea has been turned into a Festival of Ranthas.

"And because we've opposed them in the last few months, they send

these Inquisitors, the red and the black. The black ones come and drag
people away, then Sarhaddon and his red brothers come to offer us a
chance at salvation." There was a whole depth of bitterness in that last
word. "Salvation if we do as they say, because we'll do anything to
avoid a Crusade. They will destroy what's left and claim it's for our own
good."

"But the alternative is being dead or enslaved, don't you understand?"
Alciana said. "I heard what happened to you and Cathan in Lepidor,
when the Prime was trying to get weapons for a Crusade. It's not just a
cloud on the horizon, Tekraea, it's covering the sky. People live with
different customs, but if the crusaders come, none of us will live at all."

"And is life always worth living? We've been powerful before, we can
be again. Ships can be built or bought, can't they? So can weapons.
Orethura was too peaceful to allow it, but he had the chance. If he'd built
a fleet, we might still be our own masters. If we were strong, people like
the Cambressians would see the point in helping us."

Bamalco shook his head sadly. "I admire your ideals, Tekraea, but you
have to live in the real world. We don't have the shipyards to build a fleet
that could destroy theirs out at sea, and who's going to sell us weapons?"

I had come to the Archipelago to offer weapons to the dissidents, but
somehow this part of my mission had always been pushed into the
background. I was wary of speaking to Persea about it now, because if we
sent arms and they all ended up in the hands of Alidrisi, it probably
wouldn't be an improvement.

I glanced over at the bar, but the proprietor was nowhere to be seen.

"Are there a lot of people who think like this?" I said.

"What do you mean?" Bamalco's face was suddenly inscrutable.

"Tekraea, you're not really attached to any of the leaders in particular,
are you?"

"Not really." The others shook their heads.

"If you are, you're very good at hiding it," Alciana said.

I said, "There are people like Alciana who can't really act because
they've got too much to lose, people who simply won't, and people
attached to Alidrisi and his friends. But all the rest of those people—in
Lepidor, for example—what about them? Persea's wary of Alidrisi. She
seems to believe the same things, but I get the feeling she and her friends
are working on their own."

"Everyone's splintered, if that's what you mean," Bamalco said.
"Alidrisi uses various groups and gives them some help in return, but he's
not really a leader any more than the Viceroy is. The trouble is that even

together we'd still not be a fighting force, or even good guerrillas if that's what you're thinking of."

"I'm not sure what I'm thinking of," I said, finishing the last of the vine leaves. "It's not really my place to interfere, either."

"If you can help, it is," Tekraea said. "I know you're not Archipelagan, but after Lepidor you count as one of us anyway. And you're Thetian, which puts you halfway there. Half the trouble is that we don't have friends in high places in the rest of the world."

"Do I come under that heading?"

"You've got connections to Great Houses, you're friends with Palatine and you're related to a senior Thetian family of some kind. That's high places as far as we're concerned: it means you can help. If you have any ideas."

"I'll have to talk to Palatine," I said. "She's better with ideas than I am, and she can make sense of the rambling ones I do have."

I stayed with them while Bamalco and Tekraea demolished another plate of vine leaves, then we got up to go. The two sailors had gone, although the oceanographers were still sitting in their corner.

As we passed the end of the bar the proprietor emerged through the beaded curtain that covered the kitchen entrance and tapped me on the sleeve.

"A word of advice to you: if you're an oceanographer, don't wear Guild colors while you're here. I won't ask why you aren't wearing them anyway, but don't start now. People know our oceanographers, but they might be a bit more hostile to a foreign one." Then he vanished back the way he'd come as we exchanged uneasy glances.

"I don't like the sound of that," Bamalco said, as we pulled the hoods of our cloaks over our heads and stepped outside into the rain. "Alciana, take care. You too, Cathan."

Alciana and Bamalco headed off in the opposite direction, but Tekraea walked with me part of the way back to the palace.

"I've seen you and Palatine in the last couple of days, but where's Ravenna? I thought I saw her a few weeks ago, but nobody's mentioned her."

I turned my head abruptly and looked at him, but there was no smile on his face. He was very open, his red hair a match for his fiery personality. Not one to ask questions with a sting in the tail.

"We had an argument," I said briefly and semi-truthfully. "I don't know where she is."

"You're both mages, I know; how many of our mages would it take to deal with the Domain ones they've got here?"

"I don't think we've got enough." I knew only the two of us and the older mages of Shadow, in fact: Ukmadorian had said the other orders had more, but hadn't told us how many. "Why?"

"The Domain mages are half the reason people are so afraid. We all saw in Lepidor that Sacri are only flesh and blood. Your father's guards and our sailors were nowhere as good as the Sacri, but we killed all of them. The mages are more than that—you know yourself how hard it is being deprived of fire. With them out of the way, I think people might be a bit bolder."

"We'd need about the same number, I think."

"Even if you used the storms again?"

"I can only do that with Ravenna, and it's a bit indiscriminate. We wrecked half of Lepidor with that storm, and Tandaris isn't as strongly built."

"That butcher Sarhaddon's been going on about evil magic. Perhaps you ought to remind him what it's like someday. Why did you let him do this? I mean, surely you hate him as much as we do?"

I wasn't going to tell Tekraea what Sarhaddon had told me, because I'd never been entirely convinced myself, and Tekraea was one of the few people I'd met here whose conviction was genuinely stronger than his doubts.

"He was my friend once, and I'd like to believe he's different. Even after what he did there, I can remember him calling all the zealots madmen. I hoped he'd be one of the saner priests. There are some."

"He's not one of them," Tekraea said, shaking his head as we parted and went our separate ways. "You'll see."

Chapter XXVII

"Weapons? Your weapons?"

"My father's weapons," I said firmly, looking around at the circle of people sitting down or perched on various items of furniture. The room was really too small for nine or ten of us, but it was the best we could find outside the palace where no one would be listening in. "The weapons that Lachazzar was so eager to get his hands on, that he invaded Lepidor for."

"Why didn't you tell us?" Persea began, but Bamalco interrupted her.

"That doesn't matter. What I want to know is why anyone would sell us weapons when it's so dangerous. Especially since you'll have to do it through a Great House."

"How many of you know House Canadrath?"

Most of them nodded; only Tamanes and one other shook their heads.

"They're the House who trades most with us," said Laeas. "About the third biggest in Taneth, aren't they? I know they've got several satellite Houses."

"Red and white are their colors," Bamalco said, nodding. "They've got a lot of contracts out here and some in Oceanus. Are they your contract partners?"

"No, that's House Barca, but they were planning to sign an alliance with Canadrath when I left. Barca are too small to branch out yet."

"Can we get back to these weapons?" Persea called, as several people started talking at once. "Whose idea was this?"

"We've only just started making the weapons," I explained, once everybody was quiet. "Under the original contract Hamilcar would take them to Taneth and sell them there, but apparently now most of the weapons sold there are going to the Halettites. Canadrath don't want there to be a Crusade because it'll ruin them, and neither they nor Barca want the Halettites to be any better armed than they are at the moment, especially since Eshar's been making threatening noises at Taneth."

"So, it's in Canadrath's interest for the weapons to go elsewhere?" Bamalco asked.

"Yes, of course," said Palatine.

"That's good," he said emphatically. "But why here?"

"So that if there *is* trouble the Archipelago has more chance of survival. And," I went on carefully, "if it damages the Domain, it'll be good for Canadrath, because the Domain isn't good for business."

"And what about the ban on selling weapons in Qalathar?"

"The plan was that if we got an agreement here, we'd look for a middleman in Thetia. One of the more active clans not worried by the illegalities. I'm sure you can arrange a little smuggling."

"A little smuggling? Really? You call tons of weapons a little smuggling?"

Tekraea's expression was almost happy.

I wasn't sure I felt comfortable as an arms dealer, even though the intention was for the weapons to be used against the Domain. It was still trading in death, eventually—but then the Domain would inflict just as much death if we did nothing about it.

"And payment?" Bamalco said, raising one eyebrow. He was the commercially minded one, it turned out, having grown up in the mercantile atmosphere of Mons Ferranis. "I hate to point it out, but we don't have large amounts of ready gold."

"That was to be agreed."

"Where do they think we're going to find the money from?" Tamanes asked. "It's a good idea, but only people like Alidrisi have enough resources to finance this kind of thing. Or the Viceroy—have you talked to him?"

"If people like that find out about the weapons, they'll take over, or not approve the idea in the first place," Bamalco said. "But we still don't have the kind of money your father and Canadrath will ask."

"No, you don't," Palatine said. "But there's one person who might be able to get it for you, given enough leverage to influence those people."

"Who is?"

"The Pharaoh." We were taking a risk here, but Palatine had spent the whole of last night thinking it through after I'd talked to her, and had decided that it could be done. If Ravenna agreed. That wouldn't be a problem, I hoped, because of what the Domain were doing. Concealing the fact that Ravenna was herself the Pharaoh, not just the Pharaoh's companion as everybody thought, would be much more difficult. I was determined to keep her identity secret as long as possible, and she'd made me promise to, which was why I still hadn't even told people I knew as well as Laeas and Persea.

"None of us has a link to the Pharaoh," Tamanes protested, but he was cut off by Persea.

"We do. Cathan, I have to ask, do I detect an ulterior motive here?"

"Yes, but it's not the main reason. She was going to be our link to you anyway, being an Archipelagan—that was why she came originally."

"Ravenna?" Tekraea said, a puzzled look on his face. "What do you mean?"

"She's a close friend of the Pharaoh." It was Laeas who spoke this time, given one of the few proper seats because he was too big to perch safely on tables or the arms of the sofa. It was beginning to feel quite hot, even though the room was at the very top of a building and drafty with it. Probably why Tekraea's House never used it. "That was what misled the Domain in Lepidor."

Bamalco held up his arms for silence as another burst of conversation broke out; everybody was very excitable and twitchy. Nervous, actually. We weren't protected by guards or palace walls here, and the Inquisitors had the right to search private houses for concealed heretics. "So you think this Ravenna person can persuade the Pharaoh to do what, exactly? The Pharaoh doesn't have any money either."

"But she has influence," Palatine said. "She's of age, so if she gives a command it should be obeyed. The trouble is that she's always in the power of others, people like Alidrisi and the Viceroy. Now I know that some of you approve of and support them, but can you honestly say the Pharaoh's better off being controlled by one of them? They both have their own agendas, and would any of you want her to come to the throne because Clan Kalessos put her there? That would leave far too much power in Alidrisi's hands. And Sagantha—sorry, the Viceroy—would be in the same position if it were his people who acted."

"Us?" Tamanes said incredulously. "Is that what you're getting at—you want us to be her base of support?"

"Not just you. All of you have groups of friends who favor one faction or another, but everyone is dedicated to the Pharaoh no matter how abstractly. We know there are people who can't do very much—the oceanographers, for instance—because they're so exposed, but if everybody was working to the same ends, through people in contact with the Pharaoh, she'd have her own supporters to rely on."

"This is entirely in character, by the way," Laeas said to the rest of the Archipelagans in the pause that followed; I could see several skeptical faces. "She was lethal at the Citadel, made the rest of us look like amateurs."

"You're serious, though, about . . . creating, becoming . . . a faction for the Pharaoh?" Tamanes said, in the tone of one trying to make something clear for himself.

"Absolutely. Why else would I tell you? Are there any of you who wouldn't like to see her on the throne? She has the whole of Qalathar behind her, it's just that no one is doing anything directly on her behalf. Everyone works for Alidrisi or Sagantha or whoever, but after so long in exile she doesn't have followers of her own."

"But how can we trust so many people with such a close link to the Pharaoh?" said a friend of Tamanes whom I didn't know. "What about informers?"

"And what can we actually accomplish with this, if we can get it together, if the Pharaoh can give us the money for the weapons? What then? Do we take on the Sacri?" The speaker had another unfamiliar face.

"We have a chance to strike back!" said Tekraea, eyes flashing. "To make them hurt."

Three or four other people started to speak all at once, more than drowning out the noise of the rain beating against the small windows at each end of the room. Palatine shouted for some kind of order, but everyone seemed to feel that she'd finished and it was time for a general debate.

"See what I mean about Archipelagans in general?" she whispered to me, throwing her hands up in defeat. "We Thetians are just as bad."

It was only Laeas crashing his fist down on the table next to him that cut off the noise, abruptly. Palatine was too polite to do it.

"It's the first ambitious idea anyone's had here in ages," he said bluntly, standing up and coming to stand between Palatine and me. We moved to either side to give him room. "So stop finding problems with it. In case you didn't know, this woman is Palatine Canteni. Her father was President Reinhardt Canteni, the only decent Thetian clan leader in thirty years, and she's been personally tutored by Marshal Tanais himself. And as if that wasn't enough, she's a descendant of Carausius. Everyone shut up, stop arguing and listen to her."

Palatine inclined her head in thanks as Laeas sat down again, the room very quiet now. "We take things a step at a time, first. We don't rush in all directions, telling everybody we can. The first and most important thing is to find Ravenna. She may be with the Pharaoh, she may not, but Alidrisi thinks she's important and is keeping an eye on her somewhere. Does anyone have the faintest idea where she is?"

There was a long silence, during which Laeas and Tekraea both fixed their gazes on Persea. I saw her fidget uneasily, looking uncomfortable, but nobody said anything. Finally she burst out, "Yes, I think I do. Only for the past couple of days, though—Cathan, I didn't know when I talked to you."

"Where? Kalessos?"

"No, that's too far away. I know Alidrisi owns a ruin or two along the edge of the inlet by Perdition's Shore, high in those mountains where nobody in their right mind would go. His grooms and stable hands were complaining about the state of their horses' hooves every time he comes back from Kalessos, and they were surprised that he's managed to lame two of them even though he's a good horseman. Now, even an incompetent can ride from here to Kalessos on one of those horses without laming it, but the mountains are a different matter."

"How far away are his places?"

"You can see the mountains from here. The main road goes east through the hills and then veers south when it hits the edge of Tehama. There are side roads all along that stretch, most of them very bad because no one really lives up there. I'm not sure exactly which one he takes, but it'll be three or four hours' ride, I think. Would be much quicker by sea, except that you can't go that way."

"It must be within reach or he wouldn't go there so often," Laeas said. "Even in foul weather."

"Normal weather, you mean," Bamalco said, looking out of the window. "I think some of the storms we're having at the moment are too bad to try a long ride in. Is there really no access from the sea?"

"There must have been once," Tamanes said, "because there are the remains of a Tehaman port near the head of the inlet. There may have been a safe channel some time ago, but when the Thetian fleet destroyed the port they blew up the opening as well, to stop anyone using it again."

"Vindictive bunch sometimes, the Thetians," someone commented. "No offense to Cathan and Palatine."

"How did the Thetians get past Perdition's Shore?" I asked, momentarily distracted. "Tamanes, you said the Shore is on both sides of the inlet, so there must have been a way in, marked by the Tehamans."

"Carausius acted as a guide, apparently," Tamanes said. "I don't know the significance of that."

"Is there or is there not a way to get into the inlet and up the cliffs from the sea?" Palatine demanded. "That's the important thing now."

Tamanes shook his head firmly. "If there is, it's too dangerous to try it now."

"Fine, then it'll have to be by land. A villa or crag fort on or near the cliffs, high up and easily defensible—am I right?"

Persea nodded. "It'll be guarded, probably by Kalessos clansmen."

"How much of a guard will this Ravenna have if she's not with the Pharaoh?" Tekraea said. "If I was Alidrisi, I'd put them together, no question—and do remember, she's not a prisoner."

"But having two places would be much safer. If someone comes, the person they're guarding can be spirited away to the other."

"We're not talking about ballads here, are we?" Palatine said firmly. "Two houses need more guards, that means more explaining, more food, more pay. One house, as few guards as are safe, a couple of staff. They'll have to get supplies somehow, which means taking either a wagon or a couple of mules up every so often. It has to be somewhere well built and warm, if people can live in it at this time of year. And somewhere with no other people in the area, because he's guarding the most precious thing in Qalathar.

"We have to find out where it is exactly," she went on. "We can't go wandering around in the mountains. Most of his people, maybe all the ones who are here, won't know about it—that would be too dangerous."

"I think it's rather unlikely that we can just find the Pharaoh or her companion so easily," Bamalco spoke again. "I followed your reasoning, but would Alidrisi really hide her somewhere so obvious? It's too neat—some half-ruined castle above Perdition's Shore, in the wilds and miles from anywhere."

"Where is there that's safer? Not the city, because there's too much danger from the Inquisition and other people. And the advantage of the mountains is that there are lots of ways out; if someone tries to snatch her there are paths, goat-tracks, and a thousand places to hide. There are no hiding places in the city, or on a ship, or even on a small island."

"So if they're together, why don't we get hold of the Pharaoh as well?" Tekraea demanded. "Ravenna will know us, she can explain to the Pharaoh that we're on the right side, and then we can hide the Pharaoh ourselves."

"But can we?" said Persea. "Maybe you don't like Alidrisi being in charge of her, but he can protect her. He has safe houses of whatever kind—he's a powerful man. If we take the Pharaoh herself, he'll move heaven and earth to get her back, but would he do the same for a companion?"

For a second time the meeting descended into general chaos, and Laeas shook his head in resignation as Palatine glanced over at him. Tamanes and Persea were arguing fiercely, Bamalco was trying to get two others to talk sense, and Tekraea was telling anyone who'd listen that the obvious thing was to rescue both of them from the corrupt hands of Alidrisi.

Palatine grabbed my sleeve and pulled me as far away from the others as she could, wedging us into a useless corner between the door and a large wooden chest with cobwebs surrounding it. The air was very dusty there and I couldn't help coughing.

"We're digging ourselves deeper and deeper into a hole, Cathan; this is not going well. They like the idea but it's all very academic: let's rescue the Pharaoh's friend so that she can talk to the Pharaoh to persuade Alidrisi to give us some money. So we can buy weapons to do what?"

"You know . . ."

"Of course I know, but these are intelligent people: in Thetia they'd all be at university or on their way up through their clan hierarchy. Because this is Qalathar, everyone's energy is focused on the Domain."

"What are you trying to say?" I asked her, dreading what her answer would be.

"*Tell them*. She is what she is, and we can't change that. She has to come out of hiding sometime, and soon."

"You're always working on the principle of telling people what they need to know. You were the one concerned about betrayal in Ral Tumar, not me, and you were right."

"You've gone from being too trusting to being too untrusting." Still nobody was listening, but there seemed to be a little more order, with Bamalco presiding over an impromptu debate between three or four of the others.

"If I tell them, I break my promise to her."

"And she's already broken your trust by running away in Ilthys," she said bluntly.

"Palatine, we don't know half of the people here. If even one of them gets captured, or, Thetis forbid, is working for Sarhaddon or Midian anyway, the Domain will have found what they've been looking for these past twenty years. She's survived because it's a secret."

"And because of that she's in the hands of men like Alidrisi. Cathan, if Ravenna helps you find the *Aeon*, that'll be a place so safe that no Inquisitor will find her in a thousand years. But she has to participate in this, and she won't forgive you if you put her in an even more difficult situation than she's in now."

"I've broken her trust too many times," I said stubbornly. "Not again."

"Neither of you really trust each other, and you know that. We can't afford this. Whether you love each other or not, you're our best hope. Both of you. You agreed to be partners, the first mages of Storm, and while it doesn't make any difference what else happens between you, that has to go on."

"Fine. Tell them, then. Let them spread it around."

"That was a remark worthy of your brother," Palatine snapped, and turned back to the rest of the room. "Can I say something?" she asked Bamalco, interrupting the debate.

"You're overdue for another turn," he said with the trace of a smile.

"Sorry about that, everyone. We have a confession to make, which should clear some things up, and we're sorry to have misled you on this. You're doubtful about everything we've said, especially going to all this effort to rescue the Pharaoh's companion but not the Pharaoh herself. What I'm about to tell you is breaking a very solemn promise Cathan and I both made, and I want everyone, individually and with the rest of us as witnesses, to swear that they won't pass it on to anyone. Is that agreed?"

There was a general murmur of assent, and we went around the room, listening to each person in turn swear on all eight of the Elements to keep the secret. It wouldn't protect us from a traitor, but I hoped for all our sakes it would seal the lips of anyone who wasn't a Domain agent. We did it very slowly and as solemnly as we could in a hot room full of so many forceful personalities. As we did so, the mood grew quieter, people sat back, and an air of calm descended.

Not a single person swore only on the eight elements; many added a promise by their clan honor, some by their city—one or two, very soberingly, gave their home as Poseidonis—and in Tamanes's case by his allegiance to the Guild.

For the first time that night, there was total silence as Palatine finished her oath, reaffirming the one she was about to break—although she hadn't really promised as I had. Then I made my oath.

"I swear in the name of Thetis, Mother of the Sea; by Tenebra, Lady of the Shadows; Hyperias, Lord of Earth; Althana, Mistress of the Wind; Phaethon, Bringer of Light; Ranthas, Master of Fire and One among Eight, and by Ethan of the Spirits and Chronos who watches past and future; by the honor of my clan that I will keep secret what is told tonight from all other souls living or dying. And I call all of you to witness that in doing this I break a promise made to the dying, and will be forsworn until you see her whose trust I broke forgive me."

I finished speaking and stepped back to let Palatine occupy the center space again, profoundly grateful that I didn't see condemnation on anyone's face, and wondering why only Persea had realized the import of what I'd just said.

It had been an oath sworn to the dying, rudimentary as it was, because those condemned to death were considered to be dying. I could remember every word from that terrible night in the cells, and I had lied to my friends and my family to keep Ravenna's oath. Now I was going to stand by while Palatine broke the oath for me in a room with people I'd never met before. And it was to protect Ravenna, exactly why she'd made me promise it the first time. I could still taste ashes in my mouth.

"The Pharaoh does not have a companion," Palatine said simply. "Some of you have met Ravenna, some of you haven't. She is the Pharaoh of Qalathar and Orethura's granddaughter. We want your help to rescue the Pharaoh of Qalathar both from her enemies and from those who pretend to be her friends."

This time the uproar was so loud I was afraid we'd be heard in the temple.

"So she was there," Persea said wonderingly. There were stunned looks on people's faces. "She would have died rather than let the Domain use her as a puppet."

"As will we," Tekraea said fiercely. "I will pledge my life to her as well as my service! Why shouldn't we serve her as the Guards serve their worthless Emperor?"

"Give her your pledge when we find her," Laeas said gently. "For now, you have sworn the oath. Does anyone have any doubts left? If not, then listen to Palatine. We're all agreed on *what* we're going to do. What must be decided now is *how*. Palatine?"

"We can do this two ways. Either we try with one or two people, trusting to stealth, or everyone comes, which gives us more opportunities but is harder. And we do have to assume they've an escape route handy, so that if they see enemies approaching they can evacuate."

"Alidrisi leaves tomorrow; he's going back to Kalessos," Persea volunteered. "Cathan was going to follow him on his own, but maybe we could all go."

"Too obvious. He'd notice a crowd of horsemen following him. We can't draw attention to ourselves. Even a single horse trailing him has to have a good excuse, and if we don't keep him in sight all the time we risk losing him."

"Someone lying in wait?" Laeas offered. "I don't know how many roads there are, but it can't be more than half a dozen. If we have somebody hidden at each turning, who can then trail him as far as they can up the valley, would that work?"

"It might," Persea said thoughtfully. "But it's harder to explain a horseman up there. On the main road, perhaps, but not in the mountains. And if he goes up he'll have to leave the carriage. He'll be on known ground while we're floundering around, and he may leave people at the crossroads."

"What if we just watch to see which road he takes?" I suggested. "Yes, it means we'll have to do more searching, but there's no risk of being detected. When we know, we can send everyone up to find the place."

"You forget we'll probably be seen. They mustn't know we're searching for them."

"Steal Alidrisi's horses and pretend to be him and his Kalessos heavies," said Tekraea. "The guards won't notice until we're very close."

"We have to know where the place is for that to work," Bamalco pointed out. "If someone who's supposed to be Alidrisi starts searching for his own hideaway, his guards aren't going to be convinced."

"Cathan, didn't you once say you knew how to find her?" Palatine asked. "A week or two ago—something about magic, I think it was."

"That would only have worked with a letter. When she touched it I'd know where she was. But we can't get Alidrisi to carry a letter."

"Is there no other way? Nothing else you can try to find her?"

I thought for a moment: there must have been something they'd taught us in the Citadel. But they'd been absolutely emphatic, with good reason, that we should never use magic where it could be detected. It left a faint residue on us and on the place we'd used it, a residue that, if it was strong enough, could be detected from miles away.

"How far are the mountains from here?"

"Twenty-five miles at their closest, maybe forty to the last road."

"Then if we can find which turning it is," I said carefully, aware that I was more or less committing myself, "I can probably find the place in the dark. I'm a mage of Shadow, the dark isn't a problem."

I saw a few stunned faces then; obviously Persea and Laeas hadn't told many people. Something I had to be thankful for, given Sarhaddon's lambasting of all our magic and its attendant evils. Especially Shadow. People were afraid of the dark.

"But how many of us can come with you?"

"That's the problem. I can find my way there in pitch blackness, but I'd have to guide you, and it would be tricky when we reach the place and have to climb in."

"That's manageable," Palatine said. "And I know you can climb up vertical walls and things, so you can get in. And out again. If the rest of us were to wait below for you . . ."

"Some of us," Bamalco said. "We need a safe place to take her afterward, and that needs to be arranged too. If we do this at night-time, the weather will be appalling, which means the fewer of us on the road the better. Lightning flashes will light it up and they may be watching. Where can we use as a safe house? Short-term or long-term, doesn't matter, but it has to be somewhere protected from Alidrisi and the Viceroy."

"We may be able to help for the long-term," Palatine said, "although we have to talk to Ravenna first. As for the short-term, maybe House Canadrath would help us? She doesn't have a sign saying "Pharaoh" on her head, and she's only in danger from people who'll recognize her. Alidrisi won't put her in danger by launching a general hunt, he'll have to be careful. And quiet."

"What about that night, though? The city's closed at sunset—we won't be able to get back in until the next morning."

"No villages, no hostels," Persea said immediately. "People will talk. Unless anyone's House is out in the middle of nowhere?"

Nobody came from a farming family, which wasn't surprising given the small area of farmland in Qalathar.

"Woodsmen's lodges," said one of the people I didn't know. "The tree-cutters don't work in winter, their lodges will be empty and no one will be there to ask questions."

"Thank you," Palatine said. "Now it's just the little details we have to work out, like the horses, the supplies, and exactly what everyone will be doing. We have to plan this properly: there isn't a margin for error. And Perdition is not a kindly mistress."

Part Four
Perdition's Shore

Chapter XXVIII

We left Tandaris in the rain, a soft, all-penetrating drizzle from dark clouds that promised worse to come. Six riders, wrapped in heavy cloaks against the rain, on nondescript bronze-maned horses, our departure wasn't questioned by the Inquisitors or the guards watching the open gates. It was the dead of winter, true, but there were still people coming and going along the island's main road; they didn't have time to interrogate everybody, much as they might have liked to.

None of us could carry swords, which worried me slightly. There were no bandits to speak of in Qalathar, so we had no legitimate reason to be armed with anything more than Archipelagan fighting staves, which the Domain considered useless. I was out of practice with the stave, as I hadn't touched one since I left the Citadel.

We rode parallel to the sea at first, along the side of the hill the city was built on, crashing waves a few yards below the sea wall on our right. A stiff breeze was blowing in from the sea, dragging our cloaks around and occasionally carrying spray far enough to get us wet. The stones of the road were slippery and the cliff above looked in a bad state; I could see places where it had given way quite recently, leaving scars where the vegetation hadn't had time to grow back. This road had been unusable for much of this winter, Persea had said, and I could see why.

Tandaris disappeared from sight almost as soon as we rounded the first corner, obscured by the uneven bulk of the cliffs. Ahead of us the shoreline curved around, flat for a while, then becoming steeper and steeper, gentle hills quickly giving way to towering crags whose peaks were lost in the clouds. The headland at the end was forty or fifty miles away, invisible in these conditions; Perdition's Shore began this side of the headland but was hidden as well.

The hill beside us fell away, terrace farms lining its slopes as soon as they were shallow enough, and I looked back to see the city again, white walls running unevenly along the slope. It looked much the same from the land as from the sea, although I was seeing the other side of the spur leading up to the citadel so that most of the town center was hidden from view. The red-brown of the temple's tower was glaringly out of place among the white and blue houses; there were probably half a dozen Sacri there watching the city and the surrounding countryside. I wished them no joy of it.

Not that I'd get any joy out of the long ride ahead. It had been months since I'd last ridden, back in Lepidor, and I was setting out on a fifty-mile round trip in horrible weather. I hoped I'd be in a fit state to be creeping around and scaling walls when I reached my destination in four or five hours' time.

Inevitably, everyone had wanted to come, but cooler heads had prevailed. Palatine was with us, of course, along with Persea and one of her friends who'd also been in Lepidor. Tekraea and Bamalco were with us, too. Laeas was on duty at the palace and responsible for allaying Sagantha's fears; he was also in charge of the arrangements for hiding Ravenna. Tamanes, unable to escape from his oceanographic duties, would be helping him. Of the two others who'd been at the meeting, neither of whom I knew, one was watching Alidrisi and the other had already ridden on to survey the road and the turnings.

We turned away from the sea wall, following the road between empty fields and rows of trees that reminded me of home. The plain seemed much bigger now than it had when viewed from the city, although the hills that ringed it were still very close, their slopes terraced or covered with forest. Qalathar must have been beautiful in summer, but it was foreboding now. I didn't know if it was the weather or the atmosphere. Or the lack of movement out here in the fields, a stillness broken only where white villages clustered on the hillside.

"Does this plain ever flood?" Palatine asked Persea as we entered an avenue of cypresses, a windbreak that in one form or another seemed to stretch all the way from the city to the opposite foothills, branching off here and there between fields. They seemed to use trees here instead of walls, maybe because the winds weren't as strong. Cypresses wouldn't have lasted through a really big storm at home.

She nodded. "Once or twice, and the water's quite high this year. But there are only little rivers, not big enough to cause much trouble."

"So you can't flood it as a defense?"

"I suppose you could, but it would drain away fairly quickly. Anyway, it wouldn't help. Tandaris can't stand a siege, the walls have been weakened. It's the same all over the island: they wanted to make sure we were never confident enough to resist them again. That's why they destroyed the Acrolith—they didn't even take it for themselves."

"They didn't need to, with the temple."

We met no one else until the road and the avenue of cypresses joined with the main highway, coming out from the city's Land Gate, about three miles from the walls. There were a few horsemen and a wagon or two, no pedestrians that we saw. People had their hoods tightly pulled down, their faces sometimes swathed in cloth, and they didn't look at anyone they passed. An official clan carriage clattered past, its windows curtained and the coachman huddled under a small awning at the front.

"Are there Inquisitors out in the countryside?" I asked Persea, moving forward to ride alongside her as Palatine dropped back slightly. "Or are they all in the city?"

"There are some in each town, and roving tribunals going through the villages. They always arrive in the middle of the night and prevent anyone from leaving suddenly. That's why we can't be safe staying anywhere there are people."

"It's not a problem up by the Shore, though."

"No, that's one thing we don't have to worry about. Cathan, don't you think Ravenna would have got out by now, if she'd wanted to?"

"No," said Palatine from the other side of Persea, very definitely. "She's not a prisoner, we have to remember that, but, all the same, Alidrisi can't let her out of his clutches. She's wanted by Midian even though he doesn't know she's the Pharaoh. That, I think, is the best reason for keeping her out in the middle of nowhere. And if she can't get hold of, say, proper boots or a heavy cloak, she simply can't get out. It's as simple as that."

"What about taking them from the guards?"

"Think about the practicalities. Would you want to be scrambling over the mountains in torrential rain, wearing boots that were far too big for you? And she doesn't know those mountains, they'd be easy to get lost in. No, in her place I wouldn't try it. There are other ways, like winning the guards over, which would work if she was anyone else. But they're not imprisoning her, they're protecting her, and if they know who she is, they'll be very scrupulous."

"We have to hope she *wants* to get out of their clutches," I said, as we crossed a small, fast-flowing river, too narrow to be navigable but swollen by the rain; the water was almost at the top of the bridge's arches.

"Cathan, you worry too much," said Palatine firmly. "This is Ravenna we're talking about—do you really think she wants to be cooped up out there at Alidrisi's whim? He's one of the people who's been using her as a chess piece, and he still is. Of course she'll want to get out of his hands."

"How did she end up there, though? When we arrived, Persea, the Viceroy knew what had happened. He must have talked to her. How come he's not the one keeping her safe?"

"I was wondering when you'd ask that." The road curved around a hillock, bare brown earth with a row of figs planted as a windbreak on the seaward side. "Yes, she came to see him the night she arrived. Laeas and I didn't see her, we'd both gone to bed, and we only heard about her next morning. They talked for a while, and he decided it wasn't safe for her to be in the palace, since it would attract Midian's attention. I don't think Midian knew you were here until Sagantha arrived: it was Mauriz and Telesta he was after. Anyway, I'm wandering. Sagantha arranged for her to stay somewhere that night, and the next day he was going to have her moved to a safe house outside the city. She didn't want that, and I think she slipped away from his men. Sagantha launched a search, but one of his guards who was a Kalessos clansman told Alidrisi, and he managed to get hold of her."

"She didn't have any better luck than us, then," Palatine commented. "Probably a smoother journey. I'd rather know how she managed to escape in Ilthys. She got out of the consulate grounds and on to that manta without anyone noticing."

"So much for Scartaris security," Persea said scornfully. "They wear that armor which makes them look like fish, and they're about as useful. As for Polinskarn, their idea of secrecy is probably braining intruders with their books. Actually, no. They brain you with their books and then produce a historical reason why they had to do it, justifying everything."

"Didn't Sagantha try to get her back?" I asked.

"No. He said Alidrisi could look after her for him because he didn't have enough soldiers to do it himself. It sounds as if he doesn't care, but it isn't that way. I think he knows where she is, and that he's been planning to get her back at some point."

"Why didn't you tell us this last night?" I asked.

"Because it's not time yet and, if you remember, we're trying to keep Ravenna out of everybody's hands. Sagantha is better than Alidrisi, but she doesn't trust either of them. I hope that won't be the case with us, because we're her friends."

"Don't pin your hopes on it," Palatine remarked. "Getting her to trust anyone could take some time."

"No, it won't," I said, suddenly angry, with myself as much as with her. "She didn't rely on us because she couldn't, because you started planning a republic again the moment you got a chance, forgetting everything we were supposed to be doing, and I was too spineless to object. Maybe she thought she could object, after Lepidor, I don't know, but we both let her down. Why should she take the risk again?"

"Because even if we're as untrustworthy as you say, we're the best of a bad lot."

"*If* we are. She'll just think we've come back because the last scheme went wrong and she's useful again, and because I couldn't bear to be away from her."

"You know, it is possible that she wants to see you as much as you want to see her," Palatine said. Then she fell back a full length and started talking to Bamalco.

I spurred my horse on enough to draw in front of Persea, and watched the hills ahead draw slowly nearer through their curtain of rain. The horses were bred for endurance, but we'd have to stop and rest sometime, and we couldn't afford to ride fast now and wear them out later. Whether they'd be in a condition to carry us back tomorrow I didn't know. There were so many uncertainties in this, and it seemed such a mad plan, especially when we had no confirmation that Ravenna was there. In an hour or two Alidrisi would set out for Kalessos. If he didn't stop or make a detour up into the mountains, but went straight on to Kalessos, what then? We'd have been wrong, and that would be that unless we told Sagantha what we were doing.

I hadn't answered that question for myself by the time the road began to rise and we neared the edge of the plain. The city was now a sprawl of white buildings in the distance, and we were coming out of the cornfields into the olive groves. All the slopes around us, terraced or not, were covered with neat lines of gnarled trees, broken here and there by heavy lines of windbreaks. They looked bare and drab now; the thin soil they stood in kept from washing away by the terraces. Beyond the first hill there were more, a whole small valley of them with a swollen stream running down the middle. I saw one or two stone-built huts on little paths that led off the road, but nobody in them. Why should there be? This was the middle of winter.

Or was it? How much of winter was left? It seemed to have gone on forever, a sterile time of waiting, hiding, and shivering in Sagantha's palace. Before that there had been the misery of the boat journey, weeks in Ilthys, Ral Tumar . . . not to forget that we hadn't left Lepidor until a fortnight after winter began. I counted up carefully, even the individual days here and there. It was nearly three months since we'd been sitting on that hillside looking out over the sea and Palatine had come to tell us it was the beginning of winter. Three months of appalling weather and cold, and winds.

It had to end soon. I felt my spirits lifting as I realized we couldn't have much more of it left, maybe two weeks, four if we were really unlucky. It had been a bad year, though, and that might mean winter would drag on. And we hadn't yet had an announcement from the Domain or the Guild.

But it didn't feel as though winter would go on forever anymore. A few days of bizarre weather and we'd be out of it: the clouds would dissipate and temperatures would rise. And I'd get to see Qalathar as it should be seen, not battered by the vagaries of the planet's weather, a pattern of winter and summer that no one understood.

It had been much more simple and less dramatic before the War, according to the *History*, and why should Carausius have lied about that—if, that was, he had lied about anything? In those times there had been a few months of slightly cooler weather, when there was a lot of rain, but nothing more. The sun had still shone for much of the time, and in tropical Thetia, as in Qalathar, there had been days indistinguishable from summer. How that mild cooling had become the demonic, light-deprived months we knew now was anybody's guess. I didn't think the Domain knew, or the Guild. Perhaps that was a secret the *Aeon* would be able to uncover.

I was still thinking with longing about the onset of summer as we left the olive valleys and passed into the next level, of forests and pastures, the hills now rising steeply on both sides of the road. The stonework of the road wasn't as good here: there were occasional holes and the edges were irregular in places. We had passed the last turning off to any of the plain's villages, and there was less traffic now: we'd overtaken two horsemen and a carriage was coming into view around the next corner, but I couldn't see anyone else. It wasn't very impressive for Qalathar's main road, and I wondered if this was because of winter or the Domain. We would see in a few days, when winter ended.

I talked to Persea for a while, until the road veered sharply around a huge promontory of rock and we had the rain directly in our faces. The hills on the right were thrusting higher and higher, becoming rockier and rockier, but as yet there were no turnings.

"Is it my imagination, or is the wind getting up?" she yelled as we rounded the corner and could look up again.

"No, it isn't your imagination." I glanced up at the sky and saw dark gray, menacing clouds. Another storm, and it was still only about midday, by my reckoning. There were no aether clocks out here to tell the time.

"Rain's harder, too. Typical. It's going to be a horrible night."

"Worse for them than for us, I hope."

We stopped to rest the horses about half a mile farther on, in the ruins of what might once have been a small wayside hostel, abandoned for many years. There had been many such, Persea's friend said, built by Orethura as post-houses, but they had gone the way of so much else in the Crusade. This one didn't look like it had been burned down, and I didn't think the crusading armies had come this far. The Archipelagans had surrendered before any enemy had even set foot on Qalathar itself; the ravaging of the Ilahi Islands and the sack of Poseidonis had been to teach them a lesson and give the army its booty.

Bamalco handed out provisions, which, because he'd kept them in an oiled bag, were thankfully dry, and we ate a kind of lunch while the horses rested and were fed. They'd have another chance later on as well, while I was trying to get into the villa, crag fort, or whatever it was. *Please, Thetis, let Ravenna be there!* It didn't matter if she didn't want to come, because I could deal with that. But she *had* to be there. After all these weeks of waiting and doing nothing, jumping at the Inquisition's shadows . . .

Then we mounted and rode on, passing valley after forested valley to the left, the south. There were higher hills in the background, but they were still hills. What we finally saw, as we crossed an almost torrential river by a battered stone bridge and looked up, were mountains. Huge, dark silhouettes against a dark sky, towering over us indistinctly. Their peaks were shrouded and I could only see grayness behind them. Maybe on a clear summer's day I could have looked through the gap immediately ahead of us all the way through and across the inlet to the edge of Tehama. But not today.

With the mountains in sight, we quickened our pace for a while and rode around the edge of a high meadow with goats grazing in it—the first signs of life away from the road that we'd seen, except for the screeching birds that seemed to be everywhere. I didn't see the herdsman, but I assumed he was there somewhere; an irregular pile of stones on the other side above the stream might well have been a hut.

We passed another small party traveling the other way, the first for quite a while, and they were obviously hurrying to make it through the mountains before the storm broke in earnest. And then, in what at first seemed a twisting gorge like any other, we saw the gray line of a road heading off to one side, up a small hill. I followed it up with my gaze and saw a hairpin bend a couple of hundred yards farther on, and then another flash of it as it crested the next hill. Even at this distance it looked rough and patchy, but there was no doubt about where it was heading. We'd reached the first turning.

We slackened our pace, at last, and made our way slowly down and around to the turning. I could feel muscles in my legs beginning to ache, but not nearly as badly as I'd feared. Still, there were many more miles to ride tonight, and it would only get worse. Palatine had removed some ointment from the palace stores, which she said was very good after too much riding; I hoped she was right.

Persea looked around as we stopped by the turning, checking that no one was in sight behind. I looked around at clumps of bushes and the edge of the forest a few yards to the left of the road. Where was the advance party? Even setting out with two horses at dawn, the scout would have had farther to ride than any of us and might very well not have made it yet.

But then there was a shout, and a man emerged from a cleft in the rocks below the road.

"There you are!" Palatine called. "Successful?"

He nodded tiredly. "Come off the road in case you're seen—there's a cave-room back here."

It was another of Orethura's improvements, a cave that had been enlarged, tidied up and turned into a place where people could stop and shelter from the weather. There was room for the horses in a side chamber. This was an unexpected break for all of us.

"How many roads are there?" Palatine asked, as we sat down on the wide stone ledges that lined the cave. There was even a fireplace, although the flue had been smashed and there was no wood to burn.

"Five turnings," he reported. "This one, then two more quite close together about four miles away, another one nine miles away, then a last one at eleven miles or so. If he's coming by carriage, as Persea says, he either leaves it somewhere while he goes up, or it goes on without him."

"How does he explain the coach arriving in Kalessos without him?"

"Exactly." The scout nodded, curly hair falling over his eyes. He brushed it back with a gesture of annoyance and went on. "So I looked for places to hide a carriage. There's no way you could do it at the farthest turning for a mile or two either way, and the side road is too steep. The nine-mile one and both the four-mile ones have places, and carriages have certainly stopped at the nearest one of those recently, in the past week or so. All the roads go up into the mountains: I didn't follow them very far because I didn't have time. Oh, and this turning has got nowhere you could leave one. More interestingly, I found hoof marks, recent ones, a few dozen yards up the first of the four-mile turnings."

"Let's have a look at the map," Palatine said. Persea handed her an oilcloth map, borrowed from the Palace map room, that showed this area. We unrolled it on a dry area of the cave floor.

"We're here," the scout said, pointing to a spot where no offshoot road was marked. "The next two and the last one are on the map here and here, the one nine miles away isn't but it's by a little lake here."

"Sidino Valley's this one . . . Matrodo . . . the one at nine miles doesn't even have a name, the last one is Prothtos."

"We can't really cover them all," Bamalco said. "It looked possible back in Tandaris, but just think about it now. If we send someone to the farthest turning and Alidrisi comes off here, someone has to go and tell the person at the end, and they have to come back. So two people would have to ride an extra twenty-two miles. That's about as far as we've already come. One person would have to do another eighteen to the nine-mile turn, which is almost as bad. I say unless we've got a good reason we have to leave those two out."

"I've done it, and I tell you it's no joke," the scout said.

"I suppose you're right," Palatine said, scrutinizing the map carefully.

"No, he's *definitely* right," said Persea's friend firmly. She was taller and more muscular than most of the Qalatharis; I thought that she, like Laeas, was probably Southern Archipelagan. "Unless we're just going to leave people, and tell them to start back at a certain time."

"Even then it's impractical," Bamalco said.

"His hideaway can't be in Prothtos Valley," Tekraea said suddenly. "My clan has some crag-places up there, and we border on Kalessos. It's too open, and we don't like them very much. I don't think Alidrisi would risk it."

"Thank you," Palatine said. "The next one in looks more attractive. Nothing's marked here—there doesn't even seem to be a place for a road. Very hard to get to."

"There are limits," the scout said. "That one's very steep and rocky. Since we have to ignore some, we might as well rule it out because of getting horses up there."

"Fine, fine," said Palatine testily. She wasn't pleased about not being able to watch all the roads, but I agreed with the others. It was too far to

go. If Alidrisi didn't take any of the first three turnings, we'd be able to
assume it was the next one. And if he and Ravenna weren't there, then
we'd been wrong, or as a last resort Tekraea could ask his clanspeople for
help. With a little more time we could have done this thoroughly, but
last night everyone had felt that we didn't have much time. The day after
tomorrow was Ranthasday, and to be riding around would have been
very suspicious. We had to do this now or risk another three days of
waiting.

In the end we decided that four of us would jointly watch the double
turning—the scout said the two roads were within sight of each other.
Palatine, Tekraea, Bamalco and I would take that one, while Persea, her
friend and the scout stayed here.

"Unfortunately not in this warm cave," Palatine said. "If they stop
here they're sure to search, so at both places we'll have to find a vantage
point. Somewhere we can see and not be seen, and where we can send a
rider on without the carriage people noticing."

"Maybe the forest is best, then."

"Not if it gets dark, it isn't," said the scout. "We don't want somebody
blundering around in the trees, trying to find their way back on to the
road. They could get lost."

"We'll worry about that if it happens," said Palatine. "If they go past
the first turning, Persea, you and others wait. Then ride on and stop out
of sight. Otherwise, you'd better send somebody on through the forest to
the next bend in the road."

"I'll do that if we need to," the scout said. "On a different horse. Both
of mine need a long rest."

"Aren't you exhausted?" she asked.

"Not that exhausted." He grinned. "Don't often get a chance to do
something as worthwhile as this."

"How far behind will Alidrisi be?" Palatine said, still staring at the map.
"I don't know much about carriages traveling long distances."

"If he left when he was supposed to, half an hour or so after us . . .
then he'll be an hour, an hour and a half behind us."

"But they won't have stopped for a rest, so we'd better get a move on.
The next few hours are going to be miserable for everybody, and the
weather's going to get worse and worse. Be careful not to get cut off by
these streams. Does anyone know how long the valleys are here?" She
was pointing to the double junction four miles away, where the roads
from two of the side valleys converged at the same point on the map.

"Matrodo's about ten miles long. It ends at the sea," Tekraea said. "I think it does, anyway. Above the cliffs. The other one looks longer on the map, though I'm not sure whether it is."

"That one ends at the sea as well," Persea's friend said.

"Are we certain the inlet's not navigable?" I asked. "If everyone thinks it is, mightn't that be the best defense of all? To have a sea-ray moored at the bottom of the cliff, ready to slip away?"

"You haven't seen Perdition's Shore," Tekraea said. "Tamanes was right. It would take a brilliant pilot, in summer, and in a big ship."

"Still, let's keep it in mind," Palatine said, folding up the map again. "Do you mind if I keep this?"

"No, go ahead. We'd better move now. You've got another four miles to ride in the rain."

"Don't remind me."

The rain was hissing on the stones outside, and, dark and gray as it was in the cave, we were reluctant to step out. Only when Palatine pulled her cloak and hood tightly around her and led her mount out did I hear the hoof beats of several horses—very close.

I saw looks of horror on people's faces, grabbed Palatine's arm and pulled her back behind the shelter of the rock.

"Fighting staves ready!" she hissed as the sound of the hooves slowed, then stopped. Someone dismounted only a few yards away, and I thought I heard a voice, although the words were impossible to make out against the noise of the rain and the wind.

"Too late," Palatine said. We moved out into the open to see five cloaked and hooded figures still mounted and one, a bow slung across his back, standing by his magnificent silver-maned stallion.

"Oh no," Persea said softly.

"You're getting slack, Palatine," said Mauriz calmly.

Chapter XXIX

"What are you doing here?" Palatine demanded, as Tekraea and the others came out of the cave behind us. The nearest of the mounted people had to be Telesta, smaller and slighter but riding another splendid horse. As for the others—well, they were probably guards; each one carrying a bow slung across his back and a quiver of arrows by his saddle.

"You were careless," Mauriz said, handing the reins of his horse to the nearest guard. "Someone was following you."

"Following us?" Persea said. "Who?"

"Sacri. Maybe several. We killed two, but that doesn't mean they were alone. Midian knows you left the city. What in Elements' name are you doing?"

"Trying to remedy your mistakes," Persea replied before Palatine could say anything. "This is nothing to do with you."

"But it is, I'm afraid." Mauriz moved toward us, and I saw the gleam of metal under his cloak. Thetian scale armor, about the only armor in the world that was actually comfortable, according to Palatine, but very difficult to make and hideously expensive for foreigners to get hold of. "Palatine is my friend, I don't want to see her or Cathan fall into the hands of the Domain. Nor, I think, do you. What are you doing out here?"

"Persea was right," Palatine said testily, but I could tell she wasn't as furious as she'd have been if anyone else had turned up so inconveniently. Was her friendship with him going to get in the way again? We were supposed to be neutral, dedicated only to the Pharaoh and to no other. What was the point if people from the various factions started edging into it? Especially these two, whose plan had been the reason why Ravenna had fled in the first place. "We're trying to put your mistakes right."

"We're doing the same," Telesta said, speaking for the first time. "It's perfectly possible that the Domain will be following you out here, and they outnumber you quite considerably."

"There *is* such a thing as secrecy," Palatine said, irritated. "I don't think killing people who are following us is the way to keep what we're doing secret. What are the Inquisitors going to say to Midian? 'Oh look, we lose Sacri all the time in these mountains, Your Grace, let's not bother finding out why the ones you sent out haven't come back.' Were you watching us in the city?"

"We've had you watched since we left the palace," said Mauriz. "I'm sorry about that, but I'm sure you don't trust the Domain any more than we do." There wasn't a trace of apology in the expression on the elegant face half-hidden under the hood.

"But you trust Tekla," I said scathingly. "A mind-mage you *know* is working for the Emperor, and you believe him when he says he's with you? That's a very good idea, of course."

"He helped us get you out of Ral Tumar."

"And he's helped the Emperor by telling him all your plans. Don't come out here telling us we're in danger when there's probably an arrest warrant waiting for you in Selerian Alastre."

"We shall see," Mauriz said shortly, then turned back to Palatine. "What are you doing out here in this—" he glanced up at the mountains and around at the gray landscape "—godforsaken wilderness? This is something to do with Alidrisi, I know, but what?"

"It's none of your concern," Tekraea said, and I saw heads nodding in agreement.

"You seem totally incapable of understanding," Mauriz said, a slight testiness in his voice. "We've ridden all the way out here to eliminate anyone who might be trailing you, and we've killed two Sacri doing it. We're involved now whether you like it or not."

"The whole point of this," said Palatine, with a sigh that echoed my own thoughts, "is that no one else is supposed to be involved. All you've managed to do is incriminate yourselves, and our plans won't help you in the slightest."

"But if, as Cathan says, the Emperor knows what's going on, it's not safe to stay in Tandaris doing nothing."

"That's sophistry," Persea said flatly, coming to stand on the other side of Palatine, facing the Thetian. "You came here to make trouble, and you're still making it. Nobody trusts you, least of all those of us who know why you came and what turmoil you've caused."

"Be that as it may," said Mauriz, "whatever you're planning has already gone wrong. You can't get rid of us, but we may be able to help you."

"Help us with what? You're unpopular with the Domain, the Pharaoh, the Viceroy and the Emperor. You've managed to offend everyone on this whole island with any power or importance and a lot of other people without accomplishing any of your original goals. All you'll do by being here is attract attention. All you *have* done is attract attention."

"Yes, and in a day or two the Domain will start to wonder what's happened to their people. They've disappeared off the face of the planet and, for the time being, whatever you're planning won't be interrupted. We're here to stay: there are six of us and we're better archers than you'll find in the whole of Qalathar. Furthermore, from what we saw of the preparations you were making, this is quite important, and something you don't want the Domain to know about."

"As you've pointed out, we share many of the same enemies," Telesta added.

"Let's not stand out here in the rain," said Palatine. "Bring the horses in, if there's room."

Amazingly, there was room for everybody, just about, although it was a little squashed sitting on the now-wet ledges. The four guards sat quietly in one corner while the rest of us argued.

"Listen," Palatine said, "I'm going to ask everybody whether they want to accept this help, so please keep quiet, Mauriz."

"Fine." He leaned back against the rough stone of the wall, watching with a cool, expressionless gaze. Palatine ignored him and talked to the rest of us.

"You've heard what the two of them have said. For those of you who haven't met them, one is Mauriz Scartaris and the other is Telesta Polinskarn. They're Thetian republicans whose main aim is overthrowing the Emperor by whatever means. Mauriz is an old acquaintance of mine. They aren't working for the Domain, I can assure you. Cathan is too valuable to them, and they won't risk irritating him or me any more than they already have." Mauriz looked faintly amused at this, but said nothing.

"Unfortunately they're not popular with the people who interest us, either. In fact, they're part of the reason we're out here instead of sitting comfortably in Tandaris." She was being deliberately elliptical here, not giving away anything if she could help it.

"What she means," Persea said, interrupting, "is that one person in particular won't trust them and dislikes them intensely."

"True," Palatine admitted. "But they are here, as they said, and we can't do anything about it. And even if they do exaggerate, they're still Thetians and demon archers."

"Palatine, it won't work," I said. "What happens if we arrive in their company? Remember why we are here in the first place."

"We shouldn't tell these Thetians," Tekraea said, looking angrily at Mauriz. "As you said, they're exactly what we're trying to get away from. They may be on their own now, but in time they'll outnumber us and be able to take what they want."

"Is this to do with that friend of the Pharaoh's?" Mauriz asked. "We have no interest in Qalathari internal politics."

"Except when you want to use them to further your own plans," Persea said. "As you did before, which was why Ravenna ran away."

"Don't tell me you've given up that plan," said Palatine.

"No, we haven't, but I'll accept that support for the Pharaoh is a lot stronger than we thought it was. You were helping us, Palatine, don't pretend you weren't. So were you, Cathan."

I saw Bamalco and one or two others look suspiciously at us then, before Persea said, "Stop it! If you're here to help, then help. You're just starting more arguments. Cathan and Palatine are both with us; they could have gone with Mauriz and Telesta but they didn't. Cathan would never do anything to hurt Ravenna, so don't listen to this. Mauriz, Telesta, if you swear to secrecy and help us, we may be able to help you in the future."

"Fine," Mauriz said. "Do you all agree?"

There was some more resistance, but Persea had been the Thetians' harshest critic so far, and when she came around, it more or less ended the argument. Mauriz, Telesta and their guards, probably finding the whole business highly melodramatic, swore on their clan honor to help for as long as we needed. Maybe all the oaths were childish in their way, but even when the Domain claimed to be able to absolve anyone of oath-breaking, a promise like that had to hold more weight than a simple agreement.

"Mauriz, we don't have much time," Palatine said, when that was over. "We're waiting for Alidrisi because we think he's keeping Ravenna in a stronghold up one of these side roads. We're going to watch this one and the next two to see which one he takes, then when he leaves we'll go up that road and try to get her out. Understood?"

"We passed Alidrisi on the road about two hours ago," Telesta said. "That doesn't give us much time."

"Thanks to you," Tekraea muttered.

Since they'd just ridden harder and faster than we had, there was no question of sending them on to watch one of the farther turnings. Mauriz and two of his guards would ride the remaining four miles with us; Telesta and the others would stay at the cave with Persea and the scout.

This time nobody hesitated. We brought the horses out as quickly as possible and mounted. The rain had got worse, or at any rate it felt like it after being out of it for a time. And we had another four, maybe eight miles to ride in it, with conditions deteriorating.

"We'll be over in the forest there," the scout said, pointing at the dark, gloomy trees across the road. "You use the forest where you are, there might even be a dry patch or two—some huge trees there."

"Thank you! Good luck!" Palatine called as we turned our horses along the road and cantered off. I heard a faint echo of her last words from Persea, then we were too far away and the noises of rain and hooves were too loud for us to hear anything else.

Four miles of riding along the slippery, desolate road between the hills, the forest and the mountains, as the sky grew steadily darker and more ominous, seemed like an eternity. I'd forgotten what it felt like to be out in a storm, and this one looked as if it was going to be very bad indeed. Footing would be treacherous farther up in the mountains, and the thought of scaling walls or whatever else I might have to do was a lot more daunting now I was here. Uncomfortable reality had caught up with the previous evening's plans, as it had been bound to do, and now we had the two troublesome Thetians with us.

How could I persuade Ravenna to trust me even for a moment, when Mauriz and Telesta were with us? She'd left because of them, and now they'd be there when we rescued her, if "rescued" was the word. Alidrisi might well have woven a fabric of lies about me, saying I was still in league with them—and why shouldn't I be? I'd been too weak to decide one way or the other in Ral Tumar, and they'd won more or less by default. Since then she'd heard nothing except from Alidrisi.

I tried to distract myself by thinking about the *Aeon* instead, hidden in such a way that only one person in the world would ever be able to find it. Or maybe concealed somewhere in such a way that even if people knew where it was, they couldn't reach it. In that case, though, how had the crew got out? Even a skeleton crew would have had to be able to leave, and if the vessel was hidden by some magic or in a place where only the Hierarch could go, then there had to be some way out. And if a skeleton crew could get out, then perhaps I'd be able to get in.

Two minds had to be better than one on this problem. And without Ravenna there really wasn't any point. I could see the storms and predict where and when they would hit. But there was nothing I could do to control them on my own.

Come to think of it, how was I to reach the ship anyway, once I knew where it was? Always assuming it was just hidden in some obscure corner of the ocean, I'd still need a manta to reach it. And a manta would have to be crewed . . . such a voyage couldn't be kept secret. I'd have to find people who knew how to control such a monster but who could be trusted, and who would be able to hide it from the prying eyes of the Emperor and the Domain.

I'd heard nothing more about the Emperor's search, but then, I hadn't really expected to. It would be a secret matter, only the Navy's high commanders or maybe just the Emperor's agents being allowed to know what they were looking for. Orosius didn't want anyone else getting hold of it, and the Cambressians or the Tanethans would mortgage whole cities to get control of the *Aeon*.

Still, I was no closer than I'd been two weeks ago, and I didn't even have an idea where to look next, only the hope that Ravenna would have looked at it in a different way, and might have realized some things I hadn't. Her mind didn't run on the same tracks as mine: she was more of an abstract thinker.

It took about an hour to reach the next turnings, both leading off from the outer edge of a wide curve where the land sloped gently upward on the mountain side. A vast crag towered over us, bleak and imposing. Beyond it I could see yet more mountains, their peaks lost in the gray mist. There were two valleys; one of them going more or less due west, I thought, toward the inlet; that must be Matrodo. The other led off at an angle from the first, separated from the road about half a mile away by a rampart of cliffs and scree.

I looked the other way, toward the forest, and saw what the scout had meant: there were huge old cedars lurking behind the brush at its edge. The wide, shallow stream that we'd been riding beside the past couple of miles separated the trees from the road; the water was fast-flowing but we had to hope that the current would not be too strong for the horses.

"We should have a few minutes before Alidrisi arrives," Palatine said, halting and dismounting at the base of the second road. "This was where the scout said he found hoof marks, so we'd better go and have a look."

"Where's this place for hiding a carriage?" Tekraea asked.

"You could drive a carriage up this slope," Mauriz said, looking around critically. He swung down off his horse and gave the reins to one of the guards. "Well, come on."

We walked up the road, careful to stick to the stony bits where possible so as not to leave footprints. The marks were where the scout had said, although there were none on the road leading up.

"You could hide a carriage there," Mauriz said as soon as we crested the hill. The road dipped a little below us, and on one side, partially hidden by trees, was an open space covered in loose stones. Here and there beside the edge of the road there were hoof-marks, once even something that might have been a carriage rut.

"They must have come back along here to brush away the prints," Palatine said. "Hide the carriage there, and then . . . go on up that road."

No more than a dirt track, it climbed quite steeply for a while, tracing a wide zigzag up the side of the hill. The valley behind didn't seem anything unusual, the sides and far end lost in rain and clouds. Maybe we had something to be thankful for; even if the people in the hideaway could usually see this far, the prevailing conditions were too bad for them to see us coming.

"No sign of anything close by," Tekraea said. "And we've another ride ahead of us, if this is where they are."

"We'd better get back into the forest. Alidrisi could be here soon."

We rejoined the guards and turned the reluctant horses toward the river. Mauriz overtook me on his stallion, splashing my legs as he rode across easily. The rest of us had more difficulty; my horse was uneasy but kept its footing, and I reached the muddy bank on the other side without getting too wet. It was dark here and water seemed to be dripping from every branch, malevolently directed by some unseen force to hit places that my cloak didn't cover.

"In here," Mauriz called, although I could hardly see him.

A couple of dozen yards inside the forest there was a kind of shelter formed by two tall, dense trees and a thicket of smaller ones that made a roof of sorts. It was still wet, but not quite as wet as it might have been. I caught the faint smell of damp cedars.

"Tether the horses to this tree," Mauriz said, kicking a fallen branch out of the way. "They won't like it, but then nor will we."

I'd already dismounted, and I led the horse over to tether her to the low branch he'd indicated. My boots squelched in the wet mulch, and my cloak snagged on a splintered branch.

"I really am a glutton for punishment," Bamalco said, as we stood in the driest patch we could find and stared out toward the road. "Food, anyone? I wish we had something that could keep coffee warm—I could really do with some of that."

"Thetian spiced brandy?" Mauriz offered. "Strictly for medicinal purposes."

That was what we'd drunk in Palatine's room the night the aether generator went out, I remembered, and I was glad of a gulp: it warmed my throat and chest. I'd have to be careful to wait a few hours before I had any more; with the spices in it masking the taste of the alcohol, I couldn't tell how strong it was.

" 'Strictly medicinal,' " Palatine said, when we'd eaten and the flask had gone the rounds. "You carried that in Selerian Alastre; how can it be medicinal there?"

"It's medicinal for me, all right," said Mauriz. "Keeps me awake while the President's droning on. Thetis, he gets more boring with every month that passes. Sometimes I wish we'd chosen one of the eccentrics. I think if he played funeral marches for us at meetings it would be more lively."

"Is Flavio Mandrugor still quoting poetry on the Assembly floor?"

"I'm afraid so, although he's been a bit woebegone since his sparring partner President Nalassel died. I rarely go near the place anymore, except when they're debating something that's in my area. I have to talk to the President for a sustained period of time, which isn't a good idea. And nothing really happens anymore: all these motions come up and get talked into oblivion." He sighed. "Your father must turn in his grave every time the Assembly meets. I think even you'd be surprised by how bad it is."

"I doubt it." Palatine's expression was sad. "I think even when I was there it had reached the level where that stops mattering, where it can get worse and worse without any change, because everybody ignores it."

"Maybe. Perhaps there's a good side to being out here in a forest in the rain—it feels like real life again. There might be a Council meeting right at this very moment, everyone politely telling the President that this and that will get done, and in about half an hour it'll be over; they'll stuff their papers in their bags and run off in search of earthly delights. Another evening of pleasure, everybody!" he said, like the narrator in some comic puppet show. "The president of Decaris is throwing one of his famous orgies, although there's strong competition from Thamharoth and Vermador! A shipment of vintage Tanethan red's just in, and the tavernas around the bay are trying to use it all up in a single night! A certain bald-headed military incompetent from the Northern Fleet is funding a lavish new production of *E Pescliani* with a cast of hundreds, on for a month at the SeaSky Opera House, or if you prefer religious spectacle, the Khemior Dervishes are performing in the Hall of the Ocean."

Suddenly he had the same passion and sadness in his voice that Palatine had on the rare occasions she spoke about home, and an intensity that bordered on self-loathing. It wasn't themselves they hated, though, but what they were. Neither Tekraea nor Bamalco leaped in with a cutting remark, I noticed.

"You're better off away from Thetia, I have to admit," Mauriz said, after a long pause. Then he turned to me. "It must sound incredible to you, the way we go on about Thetia, but I hope you can see why we want your help. I look at the Assembly and I think, why am I bothering? But then, any change has to be for the better, because I don't see how it can last like it is." It was strange how Palatine's accent had stayed with her in the two years she'd been away, while Mauriz, who'd lived his whole life in Thetia, had a much more polished Archipelagan accent.

"Mauriz, I think a lot of your problems were because you didn't know who you were talking to," Palatine said, raising her voice to be heard above a sudden gust of wind that rustled the trees in every direction. "We couldn't have told you, but every time you met us you dug yourself deeper into a hole. Cathan resented what you were doing, and Ravenna . . . you were involving her in a plot that would have deprived her of her own throne."

"She . . ." For the first time Mauriz looked stunned. So much for his clan's power and all his posturing; none of that could wipe out the mistake he'd made. "*She's* the Pharaoh?"

"Yes. That's why we're here, to get her out of Alidrisi's clutches." To the others, she said, "Better to tell him now than later—he has to know, anyway."

Bamalco nodded, his expression unreadable; Tekraea looked sullen.

"And you're trying to rescue her. I see why you were objecting to the whole concept. Thetis, you didn't even warn me."

"Because if we had you'd have sent her somewhere else," I said. "You'd have done exactly what Alidrisi has: you'd have shut her up somewhere in the back of beyond where she wouldn't be a problem. She won't be very happy to see you."

"No, I expect not," Mauriz said, his mask of assured aloofness back in place. "We did rather underestimate the strength of feeling here, as I said. But we've got a chance here that no one has ever had before, and I'm not going to throw it away."

"*I'm* your chance," I said angrily. "I don't want or intend to be Hierarch. You have my support if you want to remove the Emperor, but you can do it another way. You were going to treat me exactly the way everyone's treated Ravenna. The difference is that her people need her. Yours don't need me or mostly even remember what I'm supposed to be."

"You're wrong there," Mauriz said. "You heard what I was saying a few minutes ago. *Our* country deserves every chance we can give it. Telesta will agree with you that the Domain have to bear a lot of the blame. But can't you see that a strong Thetia would be able to do something about that? Be able to protect the Archipelago for a change?"

"Why should you protect the Archipelago? All you'll do is use me against Orosius, and once I've done everything I can and Thetia is a republic, I'll be expendable. There'd be no need to keep your promises and help the Archipelago. Maybe you'd be justified in arguing there was too much to restore at home, but whatever your excuse, you wouldn't do anything."

"The Domain doesn't like republicans," Palatine said. "They hate the very idea, because it's so alien to their way. A Thetian republic would have to fight for survival at home and abroad. That includes the Archipelago."

"I'd like to believe you," I said, "but I don't think it would happen that way. It's not in your interests to throw the Domain out of the Archipelago unless you come to conquer. In a republic, you'd probably be too busy arguing."

"Like everyone was last night? We're here, aren't we? And you're the one who wants to remove Orosius. Would you rather have another Emperor whose son or grandson could go down the same path? Or a republic where that can't happen?"

"Remember what I said about the Suffetes," said Bamalco gravely. "They hate each other. We're just beginning a whole year without anything being done while they scheme to get rid of one another."

"But you have good years to balance out. We just have bad centuries," Mauriz said, and then broke off. "Do I hear wheels?"

We moved forward a dozen yards, the closest we could get to the edge of the wood without being noticed, and waited. The sound of dripping water was all around me, and I could feel rivulets running down my cloak. The stream was dimpled and turbulent, and across from it there was the road. Still empty. We could see both of the side roads from here, but . . .

There it was. The clopping of hooves and the sound of wheels, going at quite a sedate pace from the sound of it. I saw two, four riders come into view, then the carriage horses and the carriage itself, nondescript and black, its wheels muddy. The only insignia was on the door, and I couldn't make it out at this distance.

"That's Alidrisi," Bamalco hissed. "No doubt of it."

Would he stop, though, or go on? I watched them pass the first turning, felt my heart almost knocking against my ribcage as they approached the second, slowed—and turned off. I closed my eyes and heaved a silent sigh of relief, watching the coach roll slowly up the gentle slope and around the corner, wondering how they would get it down again safely. Then it and the riders were hidden from sight, although I could still hear the horses' hooves and the wheels. Then they stopped and there was quiet again, except for the drumming of the rain.

"Presumably he leaves some people here with the coach," Tekraea said. "To keep an eye on it, while he rides up himself. You know we could be here for hours now."

"We will be," said Bamalco. "We know where they're going, now we wait while he rides five or ten miles up the valley, talks to Ravenna, and comes back down again."

"This valley's longer, it's Matrodo that's about ten miles."

"So after he leaves, we're going up that valley *in the dark*?" Mauriz asked incredulously. "You're mad. Heaven only knows how bad that path is—and how do you expect to find it, anyway?"

"Cathan's a Shadow mage, among his other talents," Palatine replied. "Something you never bothered to find out. He says he can find the house better in the dark."

"We'll all find our deaths better in the dark." Mauriz paused for a moment. "You know, if I was him and wanting to cover my tracks, I'd take as many precautions as I could. Including parking my carriage on one road and then taking the other. Wouldn't you?"

We stared at each other for a moment, all wondering why none of us had thought of it. Probably because none of us had minds as devious and suspicious as Mauriz's.

"That means we have to find out, and quite soon," Palatine said. "The forest suddenly doesn't look as good a place to be. They must have someone watching the road, so it'll be difficult to cross the stream without being seen."

"They can't conceal their hoof marks all the way up, can they?" I said. "Surely we just have to go a little way up each track to find out which is the right one."

"Unless he's being clever, in which case we're stuck."

"It's no use arguing," Mauriz said. "Now we wait."

Chapter XXX

In the end there was nothing to do but wait, and we did so for several hours, watching as the sky grew darker. Then the lightning began, great sheets of it that lit up even the forest and forced us to move back from the edge in case the watcher who had to be behind the hill saw us. It was hard even to hear each other talk as the rain hissed on the stream and claps of thunder resounded like an endless charge of colossal horses. It was a nightmarish vision, the mountains illuminated by each successive lightning flash, the jagged outlines of crags and cliffs vivid for a split second.

It was a storm worthy of home, and we were out here in the mountains, unprotected by walls, buildings or an aether shield; it was only the second time in my life I'd been out in a real storm. At least now I wasn't trying to swim in it, but once again it was Palatine's idea.

There were occasional bursts of conversation that didn't last long because of the effort of making oneself heard. It would be almost impossible to communicate later on, and not for the first time I wondered how on earth I was going to lead everybody miles up the road. It could be ten miles or more, and much of that over steep terrain. And how would the horses see? If we had to lead them even part of the way, it would take much longer. As daylight faded I felt less and less confident of the plan working, and increasingly anxious.

Bamalco was the first one to say that there was no sign of the rear party who were supposed to have followed us; they were supposed to have been around the last bend, sheltering wherever they could, but as the storm increased in fury they didn't arrive.

He beckoned us back into the relative dryness where the horses were, farther away from the stream and thus quieter, leaving the two guards to keep their eyes open. "Alidrisi has a long way to go still, and he'll be riding in the dark at this rate," he said, looking, as the rest of us did, like some primeval river-spirit, water streaming down his cloak. "Wouldn't it be more sensible for him to stay the night there with all his people and set off again in the morning? It wouldn't look suspicious if he arrived late at Kalessos, not in this weather."

"He'll be a whole day late getting there," Tekraea said.

"No one expected the storm to be this bad, so his clan will understand. Anyway, who's going to ask questions?"

"The Domain." Tekraea gave Mauriz another unfriendly glance. "Not now, but when they discover their men are missing."

"That might be put down to the storm as well," said Mauriz. "But—" There was a truly ear-splitting crack of thunder, and I jumped. "Thetis, I've never seen such appalling weather in the Archipelago. We really have to check whether Bamalco's right. If Alidrisi's people have gone on, it means we can start out earlier. If they haven't, we might have to do something drastic."

"That's a last resort," Palatine said firmly. "Better for Alidrisi not to know something's wrong if he's going on to Kalessos."

"What would he do with the carriage?" I asked. "And the horses? Just leave them there all night? Otherwise they've got an extra ten miles or more to and from the hideaway, which can't be an easy journey."

"They're well trained. I'm sure they can cope with a walk up a rocky valley in the middle of a storm," said Palatine. "He can't leave them. The carriage is all right on its own, but not the horses. Or the attendants. Cathan, I think you'll have to go around and have a look."

"I've got to cross the stream somewhere, which means taking the horse." I looked out at the rainswept rocks. "Can't we just all ride out and have a look? Do you think they can really still have someone watching? He'd be half-dead by now."

"Try your shadowsight, if it works."

"Fine." I went forward again, to where we'd been standing before. Shadowsight was the easiest magic, so ingrained into my mind that using it was second nature. I didn't use it even at night if I didn't have to, because it turned the world into a gray place, like the landscape of a bad dream, without color or life and inhabited by ghosts.

But it made things much clearer. I pushed back the hood a little, closed my eyes and concentrated hard for a second. I felt my eyes tingle slightly, then opened them to a stark, very different world. Everything else was the same—the noise of the rain, the thunder, the smell of wet woods and leaves and the dampness of all my clothes. Only what I could see had changed. The mountains were much clearer now, dark gray with black detail—then a dazzlingly painful light gray with white, and I screwed my eyes shut instinctively, feeling as if they'd been seared.

Why hadn't I thought of that? Shadowsight worked better the less light there was, but it was hard to find anything more intense than lightning. It would blind me every time there was a flash—and for how long? I risked opening my eyes again, dreading more lightning, and scanned across the ridge opposite as quickly as I could, not stopping until another strike blinded me again. That was the worst of it, that I couldn't predict the flashes and shut my eyes in time. How on earth was I going to find the hiding place like this?

My eyes were beginning to sting by the time I'd finished, confident enough that no one was watching. I returned to normal vision as quickly as I could and walked back to the others, not quite sure that my normal sight hadn't been affected too.

"Well?" Mauriz demanded, but Palatine must have seen me blinking.

"What's wrong?" she asked.

"Lightning," I said, shaking my head to try and clear my eyes, as if that would help. "It makes the shadowsight useless half the time."

"Wonderful," Mauriz said. "The blind leading the blind."

"Is that a request? Because I'll happily grant it," Tekraea said angrily. "For you, at least."

"Gentlemen, this is enough," Bamalco said, stepping between them. "Tekraea, we're not here to argue."

"He seems to be."

"Stop it," Palatine said. "Both of you. Mauriz is right in a way: this means we have to go now. Whether Alidrisi's coming back or not, if we wait until dark we won't be able to find our way up there. That means we have to go now, so what do we do if there are people guarding the carriage?"

"No killing," Tekraea said, in a rare moment of sense. "If they're there we have to try and capture them."

"How impractical." That was Mauriz.

"How sensible," said Bamalco, looking disgusted. "We can disarm them and tie them up—stops them coming after us or going for help. If we kill them it's an incident; you've killed enough people in the mountains today." He turned his back on Mauriz and went across to untether his horse. The rest of us followed.

"If we ride along here for a while then cross the stream farther down, they're less likely to hear the horses' hooves. The others should be waiting somewhere around the corner."

It was slow going, picking our way through the forest, avoiding roots and fallen branches. We led the horses rather than riding them; if one of us fell we were less likely to harm ourselves, and we couldn't afford to injure a single horse. The first time we headed back to the stream we hit a deep pool and had to go farther on, but the second time we had more luck. We rolled up the oiled blankets we'd put on the horses' backs to keep them as dry as we could, and mounted, not an easy job when we were standing knee-deep in mud.

After so long in the forest the sound of perpetual dripping had begun to get on our nerves, and so for a while I was glad to be out of the trees and in the open air again. The sense of relief lasted for about as long as it took to cross the stream, with rain beating endlessly down on my hood and the back of my cloak.

We were almost out of sight of the two roads, and it was the work of a few seconds to ride beyond another cliff that hid us from view. Somewhere around here should be the others, but where? There was no sign of anyone else on the road, and there didn't seem to be anywhere beside the road that they could be hiding. We rode on a little farther, and then I was relieved to see the undergrowth at the edge of the forest rustle as one of Telesta's guards coaxed his horse down the bank and out into the stream, followed closely by Persea, then the others. We joined them where they reached the road.

"What's happened?" Persea asked, as soon as we were within earshot. "Alidrisi's gone past, and he hasn't had long enough to have been to his place and come back."

"We've got problems," Palatine said, and explained when we were all safely on the same bank. Thankfully, Telesta didn't make any acid comment as Mauriz had done, but the others looked worried even when Palatine told them why we'd come back.

"It doesn't sound very good," said Persea doubtfully. "I mean, if Cathan's trying to scale the walls of the place, for example, and can't see what he's doing."

"We're out here now and it's too late to go back. The storm will help once we've got her out, because they'll be as much at a disadvantage as we are."

"And the extra guards, Alidrisi himself?" Persea asked. "Won't it be even more difficult now?"

"We'll deal with that when we get there," said Palatine. "Right now I think we need to deal with the carriage and its people."

We decided to risk the road rather than go back into the forest, and kept off the stone surface, riding in the mud at the side where the horses' hooves made less noise. The horses were all covered in mud to the withers, and Mauriz's stallion didn't look nearly so magnificent anymore.

It seemed to take far too long to ride the couple of hundred yards from the corner to the base of the second turn—surely any guards must have seen us if they'd kept a lookout that I'd missed. The Thetians unslung their bows and pulled the covers off the strings—Palatine had said the strings themselves were made out of a waterproof material, but they were covered to be on the safe side. The actual bows were recurved and composite; they were probably very expensive and definitely designed for use from the back of a horse or in other awkward positions.

"Right," Palatine said as we stopped at the bottom of that second road. The Thetians nocked arrows to their bows. "Fighting staves, everyone? We ride up to the top: if there are people there, they should see us. Mauriz and his people should keep them covered while we tell them to surrender. If any of them has a bow and tries to use it, shoot him in the arm. I'm sure you can manage that."

Everyone nodded. I unbuckled my fighting stave from my back. A length of hard wood with metal tips, it didn't look very impressive, but in the hands of a master it became a lethal weapon. Unfortunately it wasn't so good against swordsmen unless you *were* a master—which none of us were.

"Now!" Palatine said softly, and we spurred our horses up the slope. If any guards were there they'd hear us now, but there was no sound from over the hill as we crested the top of the ridge. "Spread out! Archers behind!"

But I only needed a single look to see there was no point. The carriage sat forlornly in its space, traces empty, windows curtained. There were no horses, not a sign of anyone. I risked switching to shadowsight the moment the next lightning flash had faded, looked quickly from left to right, behind the trees.

"Nothing," the scout said. "They must have gone."

"Still, watch out. We'll ride down. Mauriz, keep your eyes open."

We rode slowly down into the little dip where the coach had been left, glaring from side to side in case there was a hidden ambush. But we reached the coach without any unforeseen trouble.

I saw Palatine heave a sigh of relief. "Now, which way?"

It was as simple, after all that, as riding a little way up each valley. Mauriz and I found hoof marks in the mud a couple of hundred yards up the Matrodo path, while in the other valley they petered out.

"He must have doubled back behind that hill over there," Mauriz said, "and led his horse down through the rocks to the road here. Quite a few horses have been this way, some of them quite big."

"Carriage horses," I said. "Thank you, Mauriz." For once his tricky Thetian mind was of some use, otherwise we might have ridden out down the other valley, none the wiser. The valley was ideal for such a deception, Palatine said when we joined up again, because the path became stony again a little way up, and it would be impossible to follow the marks of hooves any farther.

"So, it's the Matrodo Valley," Persea said, looking up through the rain into the drifting clouds that covered the valley's higher reaches. "Can you see things from farther away with that sight of yours, Cathan?"

"Yes, but it'll take more magic."

"Try a telescope for now," Bamalco said, producing one from his saddlebag. "I thought it might come in handy. It's a proper Thetian one, not the inferior model the Tanethans make."

We took turns to scan what we could of the valley, looking for tell-tale traces—smoke, straight edges, lights—but found nothing. Nobody had thought we would, not this easily. The hideaway would be farther up, probably concealed behind a spur or in a little side valley, and as difficult to find as Alidrisi could make it.

"How far do you think we can see?" Persea asked the scout. "Or, more importantly, how far can they see, looking down at us?"

"Realistically, just a mile or two. They'll probably see us before we see them, unless we're careful."

"That was why we wanted to go at night," said Tekraea.

"There's no difference between day and night now, not with this lightning."

"Damn this wretched weather. Maybe Sarhaddon's right—Althana's certainly doing nothing to help us."

"Don't blame the storms on Althana," Palatine said. "We might still need Her help."

We rode in a ragged group up the dirt track, into the entrance of the valley. Matrodo was, if anything, more twisting and torturous than the route we'd already come, with jagged spurs thrusting out of the mountains on either side, and cliffs overhanging much of the road. Sometimes we were sheltered from the wind by the rock around us; sometimes we were riding into the teeth of it, our cloaks flying out almost horizontally behind us. That was the worst, because the path was too treacherous and changeable for us not to look ahead and see what was coming, and the rain drove directly into our faces. I felt as though a hundred little rivers were trickling down through my collar and soaking me to the skin.

It was even darker here than it had been in the main valley, with the mountains looming steadily higher on either side, and the lightning flashes were sometimes quite mesmerizing, illuminating rocks that seemed poised to fall and crush us. Thunder was rolling back and forth across the sky in an almost continuous barrage, and once or twice when I dared to look up I saw swirling clouds piled up on each other, gaps between them lit up by periodic flashes. As far as I could tell the wind wasn't moving with the climate band, which meant that this was one of the true winter tempests, probably raging from Thure to Taneth.

We climbed bend after bend, the road snaking always onward and upward. Mauriz and the scout were riding in front to follow Alidrisi's tracks, a difficult job made almost impossible by the rain and by the fact that the riders we were pursuing had been pulling branches behind them to try and obscure their hoof marks. There was some consolation in that, since it meant we were on the right track. Otherwise why would he go to all the trouble? Ravenna was in these mountains somewhere, and with her, I hoped, the key to the *Aeon*—maybe even, I dared to think, some way to put an end to the storms themselves one day.

Every so often, when we came to a place with a clear view, we stopped so that I could use my shadowsight to search the eerie grayness of the mountains. I saw three or four crag forts, one perched dizzingly on the top of an overhang, looking as if at any minute it would break loose and fall on to us in the valley below. But none were occupied, none had the peculiar difference that meant they were warmer than their surroundings.

"Why does nobody use those?" Palatine yelled at Persea as we trudged up an awkward slope beneath another one, more conventionally built on a smaller hill with its back to the side of a mountain.

"No idea," she shouted back. "Maybe they're haunted, or falling down."

Or maybe they had been left that way deliberately. I wasn't sure which clan technically owned these mountains—it could be Tandaris or Kalessos. Or perhaps this was Tehaman territory, although I doubted it.

I wasn't sure how high we were now, although it had to be quite far up—I couldn't recall us going downward at any point. It was certainly high enough for me to feel slightly short of breath as well as saddle-sore—not a good sign. The sea was supposed to be a few miles ahead, yet we had to be well above sea level and still climbing. Was there a series of precipices ahead? Although I did remember, from the oceanographers' map, that the inlet was surrounded by steep cliffs on all sides, except near the inner end by Tehama, where the now-ruined port had been built on the rim of a bowl-like crater. That was inaccessible from our side, and presumably from Tehama as well now.

But the tracks we were following didn't swerve, didn't change. So we went on and on until there wasn't a single inch of me or my clothes that wasn't completely sodden—the horse's mane had long been a drab wet tangle against its head. And the cold! Elements, it was as bad as swimming down that freezing stream in Lepidor.

There was a squelching sound every time the horse took a step: I didn't care anymore whether it was the mud or my boots. My legs were rubbing against the saddle in some places through the wet cloth, so I would be in agony in a few hours. Here and there we saw side valleys opening up, but there seemed to be no way to reach them unless you were one of the mountain goats who I heard bleating once or twice. There were tigers in Qalathar, lions too, but those sensible creatures were probably somewhere warm and dry, along with the mountain cats, the birds, and every other animal with a shred of common sense. Unlike us.

At one point we climbed to what seemed to us like the top of the valley, because we couldn't see anything beyond it. But when we actually reached it there was no change, except for a slight dip in the ground beyond and a vaguely flat patch of rocks off to one side. And, as I saw a moment later, a side path.

"Stop, get back!" Palatine said. "We're very exposed here."

It was almost dark, the sky somewhere between gray-blue and black between flashes, so I doubted anyone would be able to see us even if they tried; without shadowsight, I couldn't even make out the mountains on either side anymore. I had to use that sight now, though, my range of vision extending the moment I opened my eyes again. The cliffs were sheer to the right, but between two more hills to the left there was a gap, a cleft leading up to a very high, narrow opening. And to one side, almost hidden behind some rocks, was a building—one not in ruins. I could see the roof, but my senses were almost numbed by now, I couldn't tell if there was heat coming from the building or not. Nor could I see any light, but that might have been because the windows were shuttered.

"I can't tell," I said, returning to normal vision as quickly as I could, and feeling totally useless. I'd told them I could find the house in darkness: that was why we had come all this way at night. But here I was, half-blinded by the lightning and unable to tell them whether this was the place we'd been searching for.

"Doesn't matter," Palatine said. "It looks good."

Mauriz and the scout went on a little way and stopped at the turning. Neither of them dismounted, but I saw them bend down and look at the ground. Mauriz said something, and the scout shook his head, but the Thetian seemed to persist. After a moment they rode off in different directions—Mauriz up the side road, the scout up the main one.

"Why do I get the feeling someone's playing us for fools again?" Persea said.

"Who? Mauriz?"

"Him or Alidrisi, I don't know. He's probably been making false tracks."

"He should have been a Thetian," Bamalco commented. "Alidrisi, I mean. Mauriz is the only one devious enough to spot all this."

Sure enough, Mauriz and the scout rode back to report that for the second time Alidrisi and his followers had pretended to take a different road. It was a more subtle attempt this time, apparently, but essentially the same trick.

"Tried and tested, presumably," said Bamalco as we rode on again, the brief surge of hope I'd felt that I might have found our destination dying away. "Mauriz has probably used this one himself."

"Setting false trails to get out of clan meetings?" Telesta said, with a faint smile. She'd been almost totally silent the whole way, leaving Mauriz to do all the talking. Maybe she wasn't as blithely confident as him. "I think Alidrisi's being careless because of the weather. He doesn't believe that anyone would be following him in conditions like these. The journey might be easier in summer, but we'd find following him a lot trickier."

None of us said anything, concentrating as we were on keeping ourselves in the saddle and our gazes on the path. There was no end to the storm yet, and I hadn't expected one. It could go on for days. If only we'd been going somewhere we could rest eventually. Once we'd done what we'd come to do, there'd be another endless ride down this valley and Thetis only knew how far beyond that before we reached shelter.

The consensus when we next stopped was that we'd been riding for three hours. Even at a snail's pace, we had to be nearing the end of this valley. It was dark now, for all intents and purposes, and we were picking our way along a trail illuminated only by the lightning. The hoof marks were still there when the road was muddy enough for us to see them, and we passed another ruined crag fort with a trail leading up to it, definitely wide enough for horses. The thunder and the howling of the wind, almost a constant whenever we weren't in a gorge, seemed to have acquired an accompaniment. Something like a demonic percussionist running mad among his instruments, especially the cymbals.

"There's something wrong here," I shouted, peering ahead into the storm as the road took a slight downward turn. "Stop!"

We did, and I looked up just in time for the next flash of lightning.

"Thetis!"

"Holy Mother of the Sea!"

I stared ahead in shock, the image imprinted on my mind in a single strike: a panorama of rock, and water, and mountains. They loomed miles ahead, but they seemed so close, vast walls of rock beyond comprehension, dwarfing everything around us. Rampart on rampart, so high that there were no breaks before they disappeared into the clouds, a sight so awe-inspiring that it reduced everything else to pitiful insignificance.

And below them, at the bottom of a chasm so deep that it seemed to go on forever, its dark walls drenched by rain and spray, was the sea. The inlet, white waves crashing against the foot of the cliffs, huge even from this far away. A stretch of black water racked and encircled by the white of breakers, swirling and eddying ominously.

"Tehama," Persea said, the word almost drowned out by the din.

"The end of the road," Mauriz whispered. "Thetis, there is nothing like this in all your realm."

I stared again through another flash, and another, the scene always the same, always breathtaking in its immensity. Palatine shook my arm, almost pulling me and the horse down the track as far as we could go.

"Use shadowsight—there has to be something here."

Reluctantly, feeling the ache in my eyes, I did as she asked. It was even more terrible like this, even more like a landscape from the Hell of some insane artist's imagination. There was not a trace of human habitation here, nor any indication that humanity, except for us, even existed and we were standing in a place we surely weren't meant to be. The cliffs of Tehama loomed only a few miles away, stretching up through the clouds until even shadowsight lost them, thousands of feet above us.

On this shore, where the mountains had until a few seconds ago been so dominating and were now, by comparison, so puny, the track ran along to the right, up, parallel to the cliff's edge and a couple of dozen yards away from it. I covered my eyes with drenched hands as the lightning made everything white for a moment, then followed the track up and up, behind some more rock, disappearing from sight . . . and there it was. From a shelf set back from the cliff, between one rock face and another, the signature of heat was unmistakable, as were the tracks on the road in front of us.

Alidrisi's stronghold was totally hidden by the rocks except from here, as far as we could safely go, where even now I could make out little more than that it existed, and the edge of its foundations.

The others were still staring in wonder, eyes fixed almost blankly on the darkness, waiting for more light, when we rejoined them.

"It's there," Palatine said. "It's there."

"Truly," said Mauriz with a shudder, looking at us in the darkness, "this is Perdition's Shore."

Chapter XXXI

We pulled back a little behind the last ridge, out of sight of any watchers who might be on the rock. I didn't think there'd be any, because even if they were dry and out of the rain, they'd see nothing in the valley due to the endless lightning. We'd been spared the worst of its effects because we'd had to keep our gazes fixed on the ground anyway, but it ruined one's sight after a while. And who would be mad enough to follow Alidrisi all this way in such conditions?

"So here we are," Palatine said. "Incredible as it may seem, we've made it. Now, do we go with the original plan or simply try and attack?"

"They must have an escape route," Persea said. "If we attack they may have time to slip past us."

"I don't think Cathan's in a condition to do what we planned. Nor would any of us be," Palatine added quickly.

"I'd better go and have a proper look," I said, dismounting. I felt strange for a moment, almost dizzy, but it passed, and I was glad that it was too dark for them to see me stagger as I set foot on the ground. "If there's no way in except the main gate, it'll have to be an assault, but I'd rather not."

"How do we get through the gate?" Persea's friend asked. "If we do that."

"We blow it up," I said, "quietly." I left them there to go back to the top of the ridge and crouched down behind a small boulder. There had been small trees and grass farther back down the valley, but up here there was nothing—it was too exposed and desolate. The force of the wind was staggering, strong enough to knock me over if I wasn't careful.

The road went around a field of broken rocks that was directly between me and one side of the cliff that concealed the house. Slowly, as carefully as I could, I started picking my way down between them. Everything was wet and slippery; I lost my footing twice and bruised my hands on sharp pieces of rock when I tried to steady myself. It was worse than ice in a way, because at least ice was smooth while this was fractured and spiky. Some of the rocks were big enough to hide behind, and I moved from one to the next as quickly as I could. It was like wading on a rocky beach, trying to find the flat, smooth rocks to stand on between beds of evil little pebbles.

I tried to look down as often as I could, but every time I glanced to the left in the lightning I could see the apocalyptic vision of Tehama and the painful brightness of the sky. Boulder by boulder, step by uncertain step, I made my way across toward the cliff that hid one side of the house. I couldn't see any break or possible exit on this side, but I didn't expect to. An escape route would go the other way, around the back of the house and out of sight of anyone in the valley.

I finally reached the foot of the rock face, stopped to steady myself against it for a moment, and then followed it as closely as I could, under a steady stream of drips. The roar of the surf below, the sea's accompaniment to the thunder, was even louder here in the lee of the wind.

I paused when I found a ledge at about chest height, looked up the rock face and got a drop of water in the eye for my efforts. I wiped it away, stepped back to see if the cliff was climbable. Maybe, but . . . I touched the ledge with one gloved hand, felt my fingers slide. *No, too dangerous.*

Here, for a moment, I was out of sight of any watchers, but around the corner would be a different matter. The rock sloped outward, stopping below where it met the road. Once past it I'd have a perfect view of the front gate, but anyone looking out would be able to see me, and they would be bound to have somebody watching here, if nowhere else.

Dropping down to a crouch again, I looked around, using shadowsight this time. Ahead and above, about twenty or twenty-five feet away, the road met a wall and a stout gate—the front of the house. Not very houselike, I had to admit; the wall ran all the way along the ledge and out of sight to seaward, with arrow slits at intervals. It was twelve feet high at least, a proper defensive structure, and raised above the gate.

The house was far larger than I'd imagined, maybe built in a cleft rather than on a ledge—I could see buildings beyond the walls, with tiled roofs. Perhaps "castle" was a better word for it. There was a tower looming at one corner, and I felt my heart leap as I saw the faintest cracks of light in some of the otherwise blank windows.

It didn't look very encouraging. The road blocked any access to the other side of the gate, and ahead of me there was only a dark hole ending in the rock on which the castle was built. And there was another wall on the far side of the road, which I suspected was there to separate it from the cliff edge. Beyond that there was only the sea, hundreds of feet below.

So, if there was a way out at the back of the castle, it couldn't be reached from this valley. Was there a passage, or a tunnel, parallel to the cliff's edge, that led through some back way into the mountains on one side? Then Alidrisi and his people could slip away and be lost in the darkness. It was a strong enough place to defend successfully against a few, and a large force would be delayed long enough to give the defenders time to escape. Perfect for Alidrisi's purposes.

I drew back, out of sight of the gates, and made my way back to the others, through the rocks again and over the ridge to tell them what I'd found.

"It looks as if we haven't got much choice," Palatine said. "I don't want to do this openly, it's too difficult. We have to get in, which involves using magic, then we have to defeat maybe a dozen guards in a confined space, stop Alidrisi himself from getting away, and then delay any pursuit for long enough to escape ourselves, which means heading down this valley in the middle of the night. People will get hurt— probably us, because we've only got bows and fighting staves."

"If there are deaths tonight we'll create more problems than we solve," said Bamalco. "I personally would rather not bury any of you, and if we kill any of Alidrisi's men it could turn into a feud."

"It will in any case," the scout said. "It'll be a matter of honor for him to get the Pharaoh back and deal with us in the process."

"Are you sure there's no way to climb either of those cliffs?" Palatine asked. "If it's too dangerous, then say; if there's any way *you* could do it, even if you don't think *we* could, then suggest it."

"The walls are out of the question," I said. "As for the other cliff, it's too slippery. I might be able to do it in summer—or with a rope, though there's nothing there I can see to attach it to."

"Do you have a rope?" Telesta's voice; I couldn't see her expression.

"Yes, but still . . ." There was one in my saddlebag.

"Mauriz has a flamewood-tipped arrow. It carries a punch like a cannonball when it's lit; it can go right through wood. It might also lodge in rock. It's a long shot, but if he could tie a rope to it and hit the top of the cliff, you might have your way up."

"But will it hold?"

I heard a rustling noise, and a moment later felt something pressed into my hand. It was an arrow, but I was astonished at how heavy it was. The fletchings were very thick, and the strange odor of flamewood hung about it—like sandalwood, only more acrid.

"It has to be made of the strongest wood you can find," Bamalco said unexpectedly. "Otherwise it will snap with the force of impact and the heat of the flamewood."

"It might work," Palatine said, musingly. The Thetians were proving their worth, it seemed, their usual effortless superiority achieved mostly by having equipment to hand that anyone else would have to pay a king's ransom for. But they still weren't trustworthy. We'd be under even more of an obligation to them if this worked, and Mauriz and Telesta had too much at stake not to call in their debts whenever it suited them.

"What about getting down the other side?" Persea said. "There might be a drop there, too."

"Maybe not," Palatine said. "In their place I'd use the top of that cliff face as a rampart. No use tonight, too exposed, but in fine weather you could station archers there, maybe even a small catapult if there's enough room, and hold off a whole army. So there should be a way inside once you get to the top."

I stared doubtfully over at the cliff face in the grayness of shadowsight. There *were* hand- and footholds, just not reliable ones. But if I didn't try this our only option would be a full assault, during which I'd have to use a vast amount of magic. Enough for the Domain's mages to detect, even this far away from Tandaris.

"I'll try, then," I said, thinking how many things there were to go wrong, how easy it would be to slip and fall; then everything would have been in vain. "If I'm captured I'll use magic, probably water to scour the corridors. Watch from here and I'll give a signal of some kind. Ride to the bottom of the approach and wait for the gate to fall. As soon as it does, you'll just have to ride up and deal with Alidrisi's men as quickly as possible."

"Even if you use magic, the Domain will take a while to get out here and investigate, which gives us a few hours of leeway."

"If we have to attack, people will get hurt, so I'll try not to be captured. Don't worry if I take an hour or so, but any longer than that and something's gone wrong. Then it's up to you."

"It won't come to that," Palatine said. "Remember, whether it's a good thing or not, our family has the luck of the damned."

"Damnation was invented specially for the Tar'Conanturs," said Mauriz. "By the first Prime, to put Aetius in. You should be honored."

Neither of us said anything as Palatine and the scout helped Mauriz knot the rope around the arrow. It was as good a rope as I could find, one they'd given me in the Citadel, and I'd be sorry to leave it behind. Would there ever be a more worthwhile time to use it, though? I couldn't think of one. Persea held my cloak as I buckled on the light harness I'd brought.

Bamalco brought a tinderbox out of his waterproof bag and we clustered around Mauriz to form a windbreak as he struggled to light the arrow in the rain. It would certainly alert any watchers who saw it, but we'd moved around so that we'd be firing from a spot invisible from the rain wall. From everywhere except the rampart itself, in fact.

"It'll cool down as soon as it hits, so the rope won't catch fire," Mauriz said when he'd managed to light the arrow. It glowed a vibrant orange, the first warm color I'd seen for hours. Its incandescence was gone all too soon: as he fitted it to his bow, it shrank to no more than a point of burning light alone in the darkness with a circle of illumination around it.

Then he fired and the glowing arrow streaked across the field of broken stones, to be cut off abruptly, silently, as it hit the cliff on the other side about a foot below the top.

"I told you we were demon archers," Palatine said, when I confirmed that it had hit where it was supposed to. "Good luck—may Thetis go with you." She gave me a hug. "Remember why you're doing this."

Then I was setting off again through the rocks, more confidently this time because I was retracing a path I'd already taken twice. I didn't fall again, thankfully, or stumble more than once. Every moment I expected to hear a shout of alarm from the rampart, but there was nothing.

I reached the bottom of the cliff below where the arrow had struck, found the rope and looped it into the climbing rings I was wearing on my harness, muffled with thread so that they didn't clink together. Then, tentatively, I tugged on the rope; there was no give. I pulled harder, took a deep breath and began to climb.

It wasn't the normal way to climb, and I'd have preferred to use pitons, but I managed with the rope, pulling myself up hand over hand when the cliff face wasn't convenient, otherwise searching for the safest rather than the easiest holds. There were advantages to being small and slender that perhaps compensated for my lack of brute strength, and being in the Archipelago—especially around Mauriz and Telesta—had reminded me that I wasn't actually that short after all, except by the standards of northern Oceanus and Taneth.

I wasn't sure how Orosius managed to be taller than I was, since we were supposed to be identical twins. Perhaps he wasn't really, and that was just how his projection on to the agent looked.

An almost-missed handhold pulled my thoughts back to the here and now, and I concentrated on making my way up. Seventy feet or so, I'd estimated, probably about the limit Mauriz could have reached. Not a distance to be tackled by anyone sane at night in conditions as terrible as these. Thank Thetis, this wall was mostly protected from the wind, otherwise I'd have been slammed against the cliff or blown swinging from side to side. Climbing without a cloak was bad enough, although I'd already been more or less wet through before I took it off. It was the cold that was damaging here, every breath of wind making it worse. Ravenna would probably think I was some apparition when she saw me.

It seemed to take an eternity, hanging and climbing in the pouring rain with the endless thunder and lightning, the roar of the surf breaking far below on the cliffs of Perdition's Shore. It was surely one of the most dramatic places in the world, and here I was scaling its rocks during the worst storm for years. If I could make some of the Domain's collective nightmares come true, I told myself, this would all be worth it. If it could give the Emperor himself nightmares, even better.

Finally, my eyes streaming from the pain of using shadowsight amid all the lightning, even when I was only looking at the rock face, I saw the arrow just above me, and mustered enough energy to clamber the last few feet, grip it and then pull myself gingerly on to the top of the cliff.

I felt emptiness below me. Utter terror gripped me, making my muscles go totally rigid before I realized I was stable, and that there was rock only three feet below me on the other side. I swung myself over and felt relief as my feet touched solid ground. Unsure quite how I'd manage the descent, with the arrow stuck just below the outer edge, I unhooked the rope and coiled it hastily on the parapet.

Around me it was just as Palatine had predicted: an empty area of rampart with battlements hewn from the rock. It was quite narrow, only five or six yards across, and down on the other side was a courtyard with a wooden staircase leading down into it. The castle was spread out below me, towers, buildings and all. But there was no cleft in the rock at the back, no second way out. The cliff I was standing on went halfway around to meet a spur of the mountain above us; a walkway linked it to a similar platform on the opposite side, with the castle nesting safely in the hollow in between. There was even room for a small garden with a few orange and lemon trees on the far side where it would catch the sun.

Where was the escape route, then? A tunnel beneath the other side, I supposed. There wasn't time to investigate now. I had to find Ravenna, which would need only a little magic. She was here, I could feel it somehow. I shouldn't be able to—Ukmadorian had been most emphatic that a mage could only detect a fellow mage if they touched or if the other used magic. But the mind-link we'd done in Lepidor made things different, and there was a thin thread between us. Nothing to do with love, simply the fact that for a few moments our minds had been merged, had worked together without the need for words.

And if I could feel Ravenna's presence, then almost certainly she knew I was here now.

I concentrated, emptying my mind of all extraneous thought as I'd spent so many weary months practicing. Then I looked down, saw the presence of another's magic in a room overlooking the sea, across the castle from where I was standing. From there she'd be able to see Tehama, the homeland she seemed to love and hate at the same time, which had been supposedly cut off from the world for centuries.

Now came the difficult part. I drew on the shadows that were all around me, used the power that came from an absence of light, and wrapped the darkness around me, layer after layer, binding it close so that it wouldn't disperse for thunder, or flame, or anything else. I could only use shadowsight now, though thankfully my protection against prying eyes also shielded me from the lightning, and would continue to do so for a while.

Then, like a wraith, a being of the night whose only form was an absolute darkness, I held the handrail carefully and walked down the slippery steps, along a short passage between two buildings and into the courtyard. Even here the windows were shuttered or curtained, but I could see light around the edges of some of them. The question now was how to reach the seaward side through a maze of corridors that were certain to be occupied. It was still quite early in the evening, well before people would have gone to bed, and my cloak of shadows wouldn't work in bright light.

I crept over to a door in the front wall of the courtyard and put my ear to it. No sound came from inside. I searched for a keyhole to look through, but there wasn't one. It seemed a little strange that they wouldn't have internal locks, in case someone got over the ramparts, but I pushed the door tentatively.

It gave way, and I froze as it creaked slightly. The noise must have been swallowed up by the thunder, though, because no one stirred.

I opened it enough to slip through, then closed it behind me as gently as I could. There was a bolt on the inside, probably more than enough for defense, but it hadn't been drawn across.

A stone corridor led off at an angle, closed doors on either side. A single flamewood torch burned in a wall sconce, but there was no other light, thankfully.

I could hear the sound of voices dimly, indistinctly, from somewhere ahead. I was facing in the right direction, but how to get where I wanted to go was the problem. Ravenna was ahead of me and to the right.

The corridor ended in a circular hall, an aether candelabra hanging from the domed ceiling. There were columns around the walls, and the floor was decorated with a Qalathari-style mosaic; whoever had built or restored this place hadn't spared any expense. It looked almost like the front hall of an elegant house, except there was no door, just four corridors at the compass points. That was why the corridor was at such an awkward angle, so that it would meet this hall at the right point.

Ahead there were lights, and the sound of voices. Several of them, and talking freely; I heard the clash of crockery and a bellow of laughter. Supper, then. That simplified things. With any luck most of Alidrisi's people would be there, out of the way. But it ruled out the corridor leading in that direction. I could see a flight of stairs curving around just inside the right-hand exit from the hallway. The courtyard I'd come through was at the same level as the gate, but if I remembered rightly the buildings were two stories high at the front. That meant I needed to be upstairs.

I heard footsteps, drew back into the darkest part of the corridor and saw a man carrying a bottle of wine come up the staircase and walk across the hall toward the lighted, noisy part of the house. Not until there was a shout from the dining room did I dare to move out again, run across the hall and up a few steps. The staircase went down as well, presumably to the wine cellar.

I couldn't hear anything from upstairs, so I climbed the last few steps and risked a look out into the upper corridor. There was outside light here again, from windows at each end, and the glare of lightning lit up its length every few seconds. There were no lights on, though.

She was here, I could feel it, only a few yards away. A room at the end, perhaps, where an uncovered window looked out over the inlet and Tehama. The floor was wooden, irritatingly enough, and was therefore bound to creak, but fortunately there was a long rug running down the middle of the corridor. At least the walls were stone or plaster, to judge from the murals, so they wouldn't creak—as wood might—if I accidentally touched them.

I was in an agony of suspense as I made my way step by step toward the room, sometimes in total darkness and sometimes in intense light.

Even the slightest sound seemed painfully loud, as it always did when I was trying to be quiet.

Finally I reached the end, and saw two short recesses on either side with doors at the back of them. There was no question in my mind now—it was the one to the right that I wanted. I moved forward, held my hand to the door to knock gently, and hesitated, I wasn't sure why. Then I knocked, softly, three times.

There was no answer. Maybe Ravenna was asleep. I tried the handle and felt the door open to the left. A large room, no lights, with a few pieces of furniture, a rumpled bed—I took all that in in a split second, before I looked at the slight figure sitting in a chair facing the window, hooded for some reason. She was here.

"Ravenna?"

The hooded figure slowly got up and turned around, as my shadows evaporated and fled.

"Don't you recognize your own brother?"

Chapter XXXII

The door slammed shut behind me and I fell against it nervelessly, unable to move or say anything, paralyzed not by any magic or poison, but by total, disbelieving shock. A shock that turned in a second to despair as the figure threw back the hood and I saw his features clearly in the lightning. He gazed at me for a second, a smile playing faintly on his lips, then walked forward, took one of my wrists and slipped a bracelet on it, locking it before I had time to react.

"My apologies, brother," he said, "but I'm not very fond of shadows." His words jerked me out of my paralysis, and I looked down at the ornate silver bracelet, set with stones that looked like jets. My shadowsight had fled, and as hard as I tried I couldn't bring it back. There was a barrier over my mind similar to the one the mind-mage had put there, though subtly different.

"You did well to get so far. Not that I ever doubted you would, with such an incentive."

"How—?"

"Just a second." He raised his right hand and brought it toward me.

"No!" I cried, desperately.

"A safeguard. I'm afraid I don't trust you—something I seem to have in common with many."

The pain threw me to the floor as fast as my legs could give way, and I collapsed, my scream momentarily drowned out by a barrage of thunder. It ran through me as it had done last time, stripping away any control I had over myself, my muscles feeling as if they were being torn apart.

He stopped mercifully quickly, leaving me gasping for breaths that were agony when I took them and with enough sense of touch still to be able to move my hands. Just enough to feel crippled.

"You still have no defense against me. I thought you might have been ready this time. Not that it would have helped, of course." He turned his back on me and went to stare out of the window. "Beautiful sight, isn't it? Aptly named. Those monstrous cliffs, the sea, the prisoner in the castle . . . like something out of an opera, except no composer could ever have imagined anything as beautiful as this." He turned away abruptly, and my gaze followed him over to the bed with its rumpled cushions. "Or this." He pulled a blanket away in a single, fluid motion.

They weren't cushions.

"Your instincts didn't deceive you, brother. Just your naïveté, and your judgment." He bent over her, blocking my view for a moment, then moved back to the window. "Reunited at last."

I saw murder reflected in Ravenna's eyes as she stared at him, gasping for breath. She must have been gagged when I came in, so she couldn't have warned me, tied up and hidden under a blanket on the bed as she had been. Stricken, I didn't say anything, not even when she looked at me. Our gazes met uneasily for a moment, and there was a strange expression on her face.

"No words of devotion?" the Emperor said, sounding surprised. "Even I could do better than this. Or is it because I'm here, and you'd rather be alone?"

"You blight the world by your very existence," said Ravenna furiously. "It doesn't matter where you are."

"I thought it was the Domain that you hated," Orosius said, feigning surprise. "Or do you have enough hatred for all of us, for the nobles of your own land who have reared and protected you, the leaders of the heresy who taught you to be a Pharaoh, the people who would accomplish your dream only as part of their own?"

"And *you* reserve *your* hatred for those you know but see as strangers," she said, immediately. "Your cousin, your brother, those who should be closest to you."

"Those who seek to destroy me," Orosius replied. "Cathan has plotted with Palatine for my assassination. Is that the conduct of relatives or enemies?"

Ravenna didn't reply.

"Life is capricious, isn't it?" he went on. "Even the best-laid plans come to nothing, in the end. In the days of the Old Empire you two would have been my most powerful vassals. The Pharaoh of Qalathar, the Hierarch of Sanction. The three of us would have been able to change the world if we wanted to. Neither of you have ever worn your crowns, though, and you wander the world as vagrants, sucked into other people's schemes, used as puppets by this faction or that. Pawns—so helpless, it seems, that even the little people can move you where they will."

"Do you have any idea how absurd that sounds?" Ravenna said. "You, talking about *little* people? A little Emperor, his name never spoken except in derision?"

"Not even being the foremost of my subjects would excuse those words," he said, "but I don't have the time to argue. The time of this island and its dissidents is over. And a pathetic showing it is, too: after twenty-four years of occupation by the Domain they can't manage to muster more than seven people to rescue the Pharaoh. And three of those aren't even Qalathari! Ravenna, your downtrodden people came here tonight to rescue you from the late, unlamented President Kalessos. But is it an army of Qalatharis chanting your name, having planned this all by themselves? No, it's two Thetians, one Mons Ferratan and four of your own people trailing along. It wasn't even a Qalathari who had the idea, it was my cousin and my brother."

"So what happens now?" I asked, knowing that whatever he said we'd failed again, and that this time there would be no rescue.

"I'll leave you to find out. Oh, there'll be no death, not for any of you. To kill the only Archipelagan with any initiative at all would be wasteful, while to kill you would remove some of the joys of life. There are people waiting for us below, so, brother, do I have to tie you up or can you bow to the inevitable for once? My people are more than capable of dealing with you, and your friends will be disarmed and under guard by now."

"I'll come," I said, trying to pull myself up but not succeeding. The Emperor looked down for a moment, smiling, then extended a hand. I looked at it for a moment, then took it, meeting solid flesh, no illusion.

"I am not a projection this time," he said, opening the door. Two men emerged from the doorway opposite, wearing golden scale armor and royal blue cloaks, their faces covered by triton helmets. In the semi-darkness I could just make out the symbol *IX* embossed on their masks. Ninth Legion, then, the Imperial Guard. How had they got here? They must have been here even before Alidrisi.

"Untie the girl's feet and bring her," Orosius said, helping me through the door with the appearance of perfect courtesy; the guards would know better.

Girl. She was six months younger than the two of us.

Every step going along the hall and down the stairs was jarring agony, and Orosius made no effort to stop me falling or, after that first time, to help me up again. He wore no armor, just a white tunic and trousers under the heavy indigo cloak he'd used to deceive me for that split second.

He led us across the circular hall and down the corridor leading to the

front. There was no sign of the servants or any of the household staff I'd
seen a few minutes earlier. We went through the room where somebody
had been eating supper—the Imperial Guards, presumably—into the
front hall, and then out into the storm.

We were standing on the terrace below the room Ravenna had been
in, looking out over the sea. And in the far corner Mauriz, Telesta and
the four guards had drawn bows trained on Palatine and the others. So
that was how he'd known what was going on. We'd been betrayed as
well. Palatine's hood had slipped off but she hadn't bothered to put it
back on. She just stood there, ashen, in the pouring rain.

Orosius raised his hands dramatically, and I saw people jump. Then the
rain stopped falling, becoming instead a curtain of water around the edges
of the terrace, under which the Emperor could stay dry.

"So here we all are, finally," Orosius said. Imperial Guards holding
flamewood torches stood at all the exits from the terrace, the two who'd
been upstairs holding Ravenna between them, her hands still bound.
"Cousin Palatine, it's been too long."

"It's never too long, Orosius," she said, lifting a drenched head to stare
at him. There was such an intense pain in her eyes and she seemed about
to break down. But she kept her composure. "You offered them their
lives if they would betray us?"

I looked at Mauriz and Telesta, but both had their faces covered by
hoods. That was why Mauriz had been so clever; because he knew what
he was doing, he must have known all along where this place was. And
we'd trusted them. Had even that last hurdle of trust Mauriz leaped over
for us with his flamewood-arrow device been planned? Had the Emperor
even known where I'd come in?

"I offered them their lives to serve their Emperor. Only a fool or a
heretic chooses death when there is chance of a proper life. That's what
the problem you all have is, that you're too ready to die for this false Faith
of yours, but never to live." Orosius made a small signal with his hands
and the guards pushed Ravenna forward.

"Here is your Pharaoh, whom you've been awaiting all these years.
Being the only Archipelagans in all the world who made an effort for her,
however pathetic it was, you deserve this sight of her. And you deserve
this last sight of your native land before you leave its shores forever."

He waved an arm, taking in the whole vista of sky and mountains and
sea. "Remember this, cherish it. You too, Ravenna. Look at your true
homeland across the water. Even now they hide from you, and will they
come to your rescue? No, they will not! Tehama, like the rest of the

Archipelago, has had its day. A thousand years ago was the Archipelago's time, but you are unlucky enough to live in the present. There is only one god, only one religious authority on His world, and you will obey that.

"You might think that Thetia's time has come and gone too, but there you would be wrong. Palatine, Mauriz, Telesta, you are honored to be the first to hear this. That from now on the true faith will be enforced where for so long it has not, where its absence has corrupted the land, permitted you to grow soft and perverted.

"By my decree there will be a cleansing, a purging from the Empire of the ills that have infected it for so long. The Inquisition will bring a new life with it: an end to orgies, to banquets, to all the things for which we are despised! Isn't that what you've always hated about Thetia, Palatine?" Orosius asked, his voice taking on a tone of wonder, like an idealist or a visionary talking about their life's dream. "You will see it change before your very eyes, as the indolence, the decadence, is swept away. The dead wood of centuries, those who make my land a laughingstock . . . will be gone. There will be a new era, not of luxury and avarice, but of glory and prosperity. An end to heresy in the homeland and abroad. Isn't that so, Sarhaddon?"

I didn't dare turn because I knew I didn't have the strength or stability left after the day of riding, the climbing and the power Orosius had hurled at me, but I wasn't surprised. Sarhaddon and I were linked in some way, so that he always appeared at the moment of my defeat. And here he was again, with six Sacri and two mages flanking him. He looked unimpressive, fragile in his white and red habit, overshadowed by the veiled Sacri, the splendor of the Imperial Guard, and the Emperor's undeniable presence. But he was impossible to ignore.

"A harrowing," Sarhaddon said, leaving his Sacri's side to go and stand beside the triumphant Emperor. "One that even your sacred Citadels will not be proof against. There are purges going on in Oceanus, where the King cleanses his clans of their evils. A King who is doing his best to make his land utterly pure. Now that you have an Emperor of the true faith, the evil we have struggled against for so long will finally be suppressed." He sketched the sign of the flame over the Emperor, and Orosius inclined his head in acknowledgment.

"So what do you get from this devil's pact?" Palatine asked unsteadily.

"A true faith, a true Empire, and you." Orosius smiled. "By my and the Inquisitor-General's decree, you have all been condemned to death across Aquasilva. But I have suspended that sentence. There will be no restoration of the Pharaoh. All of you, including her, belong to me now. Tomorrow morning she will give her abdication speech in Tandaris, when I will announce the appointment of a Viceroy who will serve me instead of himself. But we wait here too long. Sarhaddon, do you have everything you came for?"

"Indeed," he said. "A moment, though, before we go our separate ways."

"Of course."

Sarhaddon came over to stand in front of me.

"I am a servant of the true faith only," he said softly. "I will not tolerate heresy of any kind. It is my duty to purge it from the world, along with all that goes with it. Ranthas will give you his own punishment, but I cannot think of anything more fitting than to deliver you into the hands of the brother who is everything you should have been. I am truly sorry that you missed your chance for redemption, but since you have, I am glad that you will suffer at the hands of one who is Ranthas's true servant. Oh, and I will spare your family in Lepidor the knowledge of your suffering. They will only learn of your death, erroneous though the reports might be."

He turned away again. "Your Majesty, our holy work is done for tonight. If you would care to embark first, I will follow you."

"My thanks, Sarhaddon," the Emperor said. "Bring the prisoners—we will leave now."

Two of the Imperial Guards opened a large, heavy door at the end of the terrace, and light spilled out from the passageway inside. The Emperor strode ahead, while two of the Guards seized me and more or less dragged me after him. It hurt, but not so much as walking would have done.

The corridor inside was wide, well lit, and ran a short distance through what had to be solid rock before it came to an open space with machinery in it, a wide, flat platform with drains around its edges and a complicated chain mechanism running through the middle.

Why on earth would anyone build a flamewood lift out here, I wondered as they pulled me on to the platform and held me upright. It was only large enough to take twelve or so of us, so some of the prisoners, Sarhaddon's people and the remaining Guards were left for a second trip.

Then we started our descent, into a shaft with the rock a few inches away on each side, down and down and down, until the top of the pit was little more than a tiny spot of light and I could hear the roar of the surf very close. The rock was damp down here, green with mold, and the air was very humid. No one said anything, and the only sound, apart from the sea, was the clanking of the mechanism as link after link of chain was paid out.

The lift finally stopped at a door cut in one side of the shaft, leading into a huge cavern that reminded me oddly of the one in Ral Tumar where Mauriz and Telesta had taken us to have our disguises done. What a waste that had all been, and now the man who only a few hours ago had been talking sadly with Palatine about their home and shared hatred for the Emperor, who had kidnapped me to destroy him, had betrayed us to him.

There were two sea-rays moored at a wooden quay, one so large that it had its own extension to reach the pier it was tied to. Its surface was smooth, unmarked by the ravages of the sea, and the Imperial dolphin crest was emblazoned on the roof. We were taken to it as the lift set off again.

"Can I walk for myself?" I asked Orosius, before the Guards pushed me in.

"If you're strong enough," he said, waving them off. I tottered for a moment, saw the expression on his face, and forced myself not to fall, grabbing the edge of the hatch for support.

"He's no weaker than you would be," said Ravenna. "Monster."

"Let her walk by herself too, then," he said offhandedly. "Follow me."

It was palatial inside, with a small, one-story well and a pilot's cabin large enough to be called a bridge. They took us into the cabin, huge and with rows of upholstered seats each with the dolphin symbol embroidered on the back. There were wider seats in the middle, ornately carved, on one of which the Emperor sat.

"Can I still trust you?" Orosius asked, pointing to one of the seats behind him.

"For what you think it's worth. Don't you trust her, though? Is she so much of a danger that with a dozen armed legionaries in the room you're afraid to untie her?"

"I choose to leave her that way."

"I kicked him in the stomach, that's why," Ravenna said defiantly. "About four hours ago. So, in his enlightened way, he's having his revenge." She sat down in the seat beside me, although because of her bound hands she couldn't sit back properly.

"Well done," Palatine said. "Orosius, I didn't believe you could regress any further, but obviously I was wrong. Is that the excuse on her death warrant?"

"I would advise against saying anything more, any of you," the Emperor said in a brittle voice. "You do not have immunity, whether you are members of my family or not."

I felt totally empty as I sat there in the Imperial launch, waiting for the rest of Orosius's escort to come down and close the hatch behind them. Things had gone too wrong too fast for my mind to take them in. Whatever the Emperor thought he would do to me, to any of us, we were alive and would stay alive; unless that had just been another empty promise, as it could well be, to get us to Selerian Alastre and then have us tried and executed as enemies of his new order.

All too soon the others came, Guards and prisoners taking up the rest of the seats, and someone pulled the gangway in. I heard the thump of the hatch closing, and the faint hum of the reactor changing its tone. In front of us Orosius had a clear view through the front windows, and although he partially blocked it for me, I could see enough to watch the Domain sea-ray with Sarhaddon on board pull away from the quay and dive.

Unnavigable in winter, Tamanes had said, yet the Emperor and Sarhaddon had come here from their ships and didn't expect any problems getting back. How much did they know that we didn't?

As the water covered the windows and the cavern disappeared, I stopped watching. There was nothing more to see ahead of us except blackness. We were passing below the cliffs of Perdition's Shore.

And for the first time, except for that brief moment in the room, I summoned up enough courage to catch Ravenna's gaze. She was in pain, too, more than she would ever show. There wasn't a trace of defeat or despair on her face, only pride and anger glistening in her dark brown eyes. And something else, I saw as she looked at me and smiled sadly. I held her stare for a moment as I managed a weak smile, shutting out the rest of the room, the Emperor's presence, everything. And for once, nothing was lacking for being left unsaid.

Then Ravenna lowered her head ever so slightly and glanced down at my left wrist, the one with the Emperor's bracelet around it, and on around and down as if trying to see behind her own back. I looked down at her hands and saw her shift one wrist in its ropes, enough to cross her thumbs and uncross them a second later.

I bit down on my lip to stop any expression showing, giving the barest acknowledgment that I understood what she meant. Despite all the Emperor's power, there were still some things he didn't know.

I avoided looking at her for a while, although there was nothing to be seen outside except blackness. I couldn't see the aether displays in the bridge to follow our course, but presumably we were heading up the inlet to join mantas waiting outside. At least two, a Domain and an Imperial, and probably some Imperial escorts as well. This had to be a secret journey, but the Emperor didn't seem the type to travel unescorted.

How had they managed it? Those ships had to be waiting somewhere on Perdition's Shore, and from what I'd heard, the weather underwater would be the same as on the surface. No one knew why the sea was so treacherous here, Tamanes had said, but the currents were an unchartable nightmare, unpredictable and very strong. Strong enough to destroy mantas, which usually had enough engine power to break free—perhaps it was the chaotic conditions, the fact that it wasn't just a matter of pulling against a single very strong current such as there were out in the ocean.

"How did your people get through Perdition's Shore in the old days?" I asked Ravenna softly, a while later. It had to be ten miles or more from the head of the Matrodo Valley to the inlet's mouth, so we were here for a while—or were the ships farther in? A genius of a pilot in a big ship, Tamanes had said, which would make sense. The smaller the ship, the more vulnerable it would be, so the Emperor's manta was waiting somewhere out in the inlet.

"Good pilots," she said, without questioning why I was asking. "And there was a safe channel, which everyone thought was blocked."

How the Emperor had discovered her ancestry I didn't know, but I suspected he'd got it from her in those hours before I arrived. Or maybe from Alidrisi.

We talked quietly for a while, a gesture of defiance and distraction, something Orosius would expect, until he threatened us again and we fell silent; there was no point provoking him now. He was very edgy tonight, more so than he'd been the previous times I'd met him, and his patience seemed to be only skin deep. If he hadn't believed we were completely in his power his calm wouldn't have been there at all, I thought.

"The *Valdur* is in sight, Your Majesty," came the navigator's reply, many long minutes of silence later. Nobody had said anything in the cabin except for us; there was no one for the Emperor to talk to except his prisoners, and we were beneath his dignity at the moment. "And the *Furnace*." Sarhaddon's ship, presumably.

"Good. Check their status."

"Aye, aye . . . Your Majesty, the captain's sending an urgent message. They've lost touch with the escorts outside."

Orosius stood up and went forward into the bridge. "What's this?" I heard another voice faintly, from an invisible communication screen. "Has the weather worsened? I ordered them to keep station, no matter what . . . I know this shore is dangerous . . . Well, keep on sending. Fools."

He came back to his seat without looking at any of us, and I pitied the flag captain he must have been talking to. He'd left the escorts outside, in the lee of Perdition's Shore? How callous could he be?

I couldn't see the *Valdur* until we were virtually on top of it, a huge bulk with lights dotted along its sides suddenly materializing out of the gloom. One, two . . . four decks? Elements, it was huge, and as we swooped below it the pale underside, lit up by aether lights set into the hill, seemed to go on forever. I'd thought the *Shadowstar* was large, with three decks, but this was bigger than I'd imagined was possible.

We came to a stop finally and began to rise. I saw the edges of the docking bay, then the sides as the launch gently pushed itself upward and into the clamps. Even the bay was opulent, I saw, looking out of the portholes at the bright lights and the immaculate, painted walls with the Imperial dolphin crest on them.

The ray shook as we made contact, and then I heard a hissing sound from outside, the thumps of gantries connecting and the door closing much more quietly than usual. Two crewmen in pressed black uniforms emerged from the bridge and opened the hatch. We were too high off the deck for me to see if there was a welcoming committee, but I doubted there'd be one.

"Bring them," Orosius commanded, getting up. "As before." He disappeared through the hatch and I heard the shrill notes of a boarding call.

The leader of the Guards, with a white crest on his helmet, waved his hand impatiently, and his men began hustling the others out of their seats. I was glad to stand up because my clothes were still wet; they'd managed to drip all over the seat, making it progressively more uncomfortable to sit in.

Ravenna stood up unsteadily, and I followed her out of the cabin, through the well and then down the staircase. There were three or four officers and ratings there, all wearing black rather than the Navy's royal blue, and two more were talking to Orosius. A captain and an admiral, from the stars on their shoulders.

"How can there still be no word?" the Emperor was asking, though not angrily, not yet. He sounded more puzzled than annoyed. "They should have been able to keep in place with the protection I put on the hulls."

"There's only a very narrow stretch of water that's safe," the admiral said. "If they left it for any reason, to respond to a distress call, for instance, they could be a while getting back against the currents."

"There's no one out here to be in distress. I'll come to the bridge." He started walking toward the door, then stopped and addressed the leader of the Guards. "Tribune, secure the prisoners in the brig. All except those three. Leave them in my quarters—I have some unfinished business with them. Mauriz and Telesta will accompany me." He frowned, pointed one hand at me, and I felt my skin tingle, steam rising from my clothes. When it stopped, they were dry again.

"Yes, Your Majesty," the Tribune said, as the Emperor left the bay. "Decurion, take three men and do as he ordered. Everyone else return to scheduled duty. You three—" he indicated Palatine, Ravenna and me "—follow."

I didn't like the tone of the Emperor's voice when he said *unfinished business*, but there was nothing I could do about it. We followed the Tribune out of the bay and forward along a wide high-roofed corridor. This would have been the cargo space on an ordinary manta, presumably used here for storing the Emperor's baggage train and accommodating extra weapons, so the *Valdur* effectively had five decks, not four. The walls were painted, the floor covered by the same matting that every manta had—to provide the best footing—here painted crimson. Silk banners hung on the walls; I supposed this was the way along which state guests would be conducted on board.

At the end we went up a wide staircase with banisters into a circular room oddly like the one in the castle, although it was decorated in Thetian style. Then up more steps, this time sweeping around the edges of the circle, into a truly huge well. I looked around in amazement at the opulent decoration, the gilding on all the woodwork, even the imitation mosaic pattern on the floor. I got a quick look into the bridge as we went past, only to realize that there was another, smaller well with rooms off it between us and the bridge—the front windows that I caught a glimpse of had to be twenty yards away.

"This is an Imperial flagship," the Tribune said, as if he was talking to a group of awestruck tribesmen. "The largest manta in the world; what do you expect?"

Little he knew about it: the *Aeon* was much bigger than this. But that didn't stop me admiring the interior of the *Valdur*, even though it was, for me, a prison.

We passed more splendid rooms on the next floor up, where perhaps guests were entertained, but the Emperor's quarters were on the top deck, where a flamewood chandelier, rigidly anchored, hung below a crystal-glass skylight.

Two guards outside a set of double doors facing aft jumped to attention as the Tribune came up the steps, then opened the doors.

"He doesn't stint himself, does he?" Palatine said, looking inside at the blue carpet, the Thetian murals, the passageway's arched roof.

"He is the Emperor," was all the Tribune said.

A short, wiry man in plain black stepped out of a door at the end. "Tribune."

"These three prisoners are to wait in the reception room and be left alone."

"Good. The Emperor will not appreciate mud on his fine rugs."

An extra precaution, I supposed, as we were led barefoot into a huge room lined with windows, the floor covered with thickly woven rugs. This was more like a palace than a ship, I thought, looking around at the chairs and sofas, the wine cabinets, the ivory-topped table at one end.

"You will not move," the Tribune said, stopping at the door on his way out, after he'd made us kneel on the carpet. "The Emperor will deal with you shortly." Then he closed the door behind him.

Chapter XXXIII

There was a moment of leaden silence, as if we were all holding our breath, while the Tribune's footsteps receded. Then, once we heard the faint click of the outer doors closing again, the tension was released.

"Orosius destroys everything he touches," said Palatine in a grief-stricken voice. "And he knows where to touch it. Everything we do, they are a step ahead of us. We handed ourselves to him on a plate: we might as well just have surrendered."

"Is this Palatine who's speaking?" Ravenna asked.

"Palatine was a friend of Mauriz," she replied. "Palatine could make a plan without it going wrong."

"Would you have chosen the other way?"

"Rather than serve that monster?" There was resignation in Palatine's eyes. "I never have the choice. Because they anticipate everything we do; every time we try to strike at them, they are the ones who win. We promised each other after Lepidor we'd never let this happen again, but it has, and this time it's not some jumped-up little Halettite."

"No, it's a twisted madman who would be nothing without his throne and his magic. He'll destroy himself, given a few years."

"We don't have a few years. Cathan knows what he did to me, and that was when he was at his least subtle and inventive. I can remember a few people, one or two of them friends, disappearing, and a few months later they came back as his creatures. That's where he gets most of his agents. The death sentence means that we have no protection anywhere on Aquasilva."

"This is his own death sentence," said Ravenna calmly. "He means to do to Thetia what the Domain have done to the Archipelago."

"There's nobody left who will kill him."

"Someone will, if he goes ahead with this. He doesn't have the power, you said."

"Even with Sarhaddon?"

"Sarhaddon's a kindred spirit." She sighed and flexed her arms slightly, pain showing on her face for a moment.

"Do you want me to loosen the ropes a bit?" I said. It seemed so strange, being in this magnificent room as captives, I thought, looking around at the plushness of the chairs, the delicately executed murals, the rug that I was kneeling on. A room fit for an Emperor indeed, but not this Emperor.

"No. It's bad as it is, but if you tamper with them it'll last longer. He won't untie me for another few hours at least, but it doesn't matter. I just remember that I managed to hurt him, not as much as I'd like, but I did it."

"We're moving," Palatine said suddenly. "How did you manage it?"

"He came too close. He enjoys inflicting pain, he's worse than the Inquisitors. They do it because they believe, however evil it may be, that they're doing Ranthas's work. It's different with him. He went raging mad when I kicked him. I was terrified. Like you are when you have nightmares of being chased by wild animals, or trapped in a room full of snakes."

"He didn't just tie you up, did he?"

"I was already tied up. He killed Alidrisi and his men without my even hearing it, and then came up. I thought he was you, Cathan, which gave him enough time to block out my magic. You're right, that wasn't all, but it will heal eventually."

The resentment that had been smoldering inside me blazed up into fury, but there was nothing I could do, no one to hit out at, however futilely. I had to . . . *we* had to make him pay somehow, and it would be a very long reckoning. My anger remained, though, bottled up without an outlet. I didn't care what he did in return, but I *would* hurt him. Somehow.

"And thank you both for trying to rescue me," Ravenna said gravely. "Don't say anything, Cathan. We will talk sometime, but not now."

I leaned closer to her ear, not sure if the steward would be listening in, and asked softly, "Did you get any nearer to finding the ship?" I didn't know whether this would be our last chance to talk for a while. I couldn't see Orosius leaving us together, whatever else he did. It was ten times worse knowing that she and Palatine were at his mercy too, that his cruelty wouldn't be confined to me.

"Only a little, I'm afraid," she whispered back, and I bent down a little so she could go on. "Some Imperial officers once wanted to find the Admiral's body and erect a memorial. Tanais said something like, 'He has his own memorial and the sea guards it from all who would defile it.' It was in a history of the Navy; Alidrisi gave me a whole heap of books from somewhere to keep me occupied."

" 'The sea guards it,' " I repeated musingly. Then I told her the gist of what I'd worked out, leaning back once I'd finished to give her a chance to take it in. She bit one side of her lower lip, an unconscious gesture that went with her thoughtful expression.

"Somewhere only you can get her—the ship, I mean," she said. "That makes sense. Carausius called himself a child of the sea, and you're the same, you understand it in a way nobody else can. You should know how to unlock its secrets, while others would try to use force, and magic. That's the difference between you and your . . . between you and Orosius: that he's much more powerful than you but he'll never understand how or why."

"He's not supposed to have power at all."

"Something went wrong, then. But if we're both right, then she should be in a place that only you could reach, that would defeat everyone else's attempts. Like those caves in Thetia that you mentioned. Deep under one of the islands, maybe. Do you remember, there was a battle there during the war? One side's fleet hid in them and ambushed their enemy."

"If you mean the Battle of Immuron," said Palatine softly, "our fleet was commanded by Admiral Cidelis. I remember it from the *History*."

"The scene of a great victory, but forgotten since then. That would make sense."

Could we have found the *Aeon* so quickly? So easily, just by putting our minds together? "But how is it guarded by the sea, in that case?" I asked, spotting the flaw in our reasoning.

"Carausius was with Cidelis, that's how we know about Immuron," Palatine said. "Carausius did the navigation, down there in the dark where they couldn't have relied on normal means."

"So even if someone else worked it out . . ."

"Even if they did, they wouldn't be able to find the ship. Not even Orosius."

"Unless he could force *me* to," I said, my elation draining away. Despite our whispering, we might still have been overheard, and if Orosius continued to be frustrated in his search, he might turn to other methods. He might even come to the same conclusions that I had.

"That's our weakness," Palatine said. "One of many. That's why we're together and not separated, because he can put more pressure on you this way. Neither of you two will do anything that hurts the other."

I stared at her for a moment, understanding what she was saying and sickened by the thought. But I remembered Sarhaddon's use of the hostages in Lepidor to coerce the sailors into calling off their attack, and the version of the story he'd told me in Sagantha's place. It was so easy once they no longer cared about life to use the threat of taking it against those of us who did.

"Sooner rather than later," Ravenna whispered. "But not too soon. Get him to let down his guard a bit, to think he's terrorized us. I'm not going to provoke him again unless we absolutely have to."

The Emperor might have neutralized our individual magic, but she thought—knew, probably—that we could still do something together, when he'd be least expecting it. But would it be enough? He might well be stronger than us together—he outmatched any of us acting alone—so it would have to be the way we attacked him, not the strength we used, that was unexpected.

We didn't get a chance to say anything more, because all of us heard soft footsteps outside and then the door opening. The Emperor looked down at us, smiling coldly.

"How gratifying to see you obeying me already. Quick studies."

"Have you found your lost escorts yet?" Palatine asked, not rudely but not submissively either.

"We're looking for them now. In a few minutes we'll pass through the entrance to the inlet and you'll get a chance to see Perdition's Shore at first hand. Sarhaddon has kindly agreed to help us look for them; his mages can detect flamewood a long way away, even under water."

"How are you allowed to be one of the corrupt, twisted elemental mages he talks about in his sermons?" I asked, hoping to keep Orosius occupied for as long as possible. With luck, the search for the escorts would distract him, although even if we managed to overcome him, what we'd do on the Imperial flagship and surrounded by guards was more of a problem. Would it be worth enduring whatever he did and waiting for him to let down his guard, I wondered, if Palatine was right and he meant to keep us together as hostages for each other?

"Because, unlike you, brother, I do not believe in false gods. My magic is used in the service of Ranthas, not in that of darkness and shadow. The Inquisition and I share many of the same goals, as well as the same contempt for you."

"I'll take that as a compliment."

"You may come to change your mind," he said, and strolled over to one of the wine cabinets to pour himself a glass of clear, sparkling Thetian blue. "To Sarhaddon." I watched him carefully to see how much he drank, wondering if he had the same inability to handle drink that I'd inherited. But he drank like any normal person would, draining the whole glass gradually as he talked to us. "My father despised anyone with a warlike disposition: to be held in contempt by him would have been a mark of esteem. As you've been frequently told, Cathan, you're very like him. Without the artistic abilities, of course. Your gifts lie more in the line of oceanography, talents possibly even more useless than those of our father. At least he left works of art and poetry behind that may be remembered." Orosius took on the demeanor of a connoisseur discussing art with his fellow critics. "Somewhat too conventional, perhaps, but nonetheless inspired. Especially his paintings of our mother, I'm told, from when he first met her. But those have, regrettably, been lost."

She probably took them with her so Orosius wouldn't be able to have them. He might genuinely be very fond of some kinds of Thetian painting, although I didn't know what my father's subject had usually been.

"If I'm so useless, why have you been so keen to capture me?"

"Because, as I said earlier, your worth relates more to what other people see in you than in anything you might accomplish for yourself. And it's not as if I needed to try very hard, is it? You fall so easily into people's hands. Even the tribesmen's."

I bit back the retort that came to my lips, not wanting to provoke him yet; thankfully he saw it as fear rather than control.

"You've heard how unwise it is to anger me?" Orosius said, sipping the wine. I felt very thirsty watching him; I hadn't drunk anything since before I'd scaled the cliff. It didn't feel like such a great achievement now that I knew he'd been waiting for me, that Mauriz had known the cliff would be scalable and unguarded. None of us had thought how suspiciously convenient the flamewood arrow had been.

"Is that why you claim to be served by fools?" Palatine burst out. "Because you go berserk so easily? Or because they have scruples and decency, both of which you lack totally?"

"Where have your scruples got you?"

"Lacking them does not make a successful Emperor. Maybe you think you have to use torture—but to enjoy it, and to inflict it yourself because of that?"

" 'If you think something unpleasant has to be done, do it yourself and see whether it's really necessary.' For all his faults, Aetius got a lot of things right."

"That only works for someone with a few morals. I don't know whether you treat your concubines in the same way, but you're a Thetian Emperor. Do you imagine people would have a shred of respect for you if they knew what you did to Ravenna?"

"I was within my rights to *execute* her for attacking me."

"No, you weren't!" Palatine snapped. "We have such a thing as a trial, you know, witnesses, law, a judge who isn't also the plaintiff. Do you remember that? Have you degenerated into a Halettite savage now?"

"Oh, a high-treason trial because she kicked me in the stomach. You and your remaining republican friends would find that very funny, wouldn't you? Don't you think my way was better?"

"What, to . . ." She broke off and glanced across at me. "There is a difference between revenge and torture, Orosius. Torture isn't a punishment in Thetia, it's a means to an end that only a few people resort to."

"How like a moralizer. You make Thetia sound so enlightened, Palatine, when all our laws and our mercy have done is to reduce us to a laughingstock. Did Aetius hesitate to torture people for information during the War? Don't the needs of the many outweigh the needs of the few?"

"I wasn't aware you were at war with Qalathar," Ravenna said.

I stayed silent throughout the exchange, fists clenched at my sides, trying not to react. Whatever he'd done to Ravenna, Palatine knew and wasn't telling me. It was bad enough to wash away the fragile self-control that I was trying so hard to maintain in the face of the Emperor's hideousness.

"We hold totally alien views, Palatine, you and I, but it is my way that has brought victory every time. Religious law now takes absolute precedence over the secular legal code throughout the Empire, so those accused of heresy will no longer be able to extricate themselves as Mauriz did. To hold that the Empire would be better without Ranthas's divinely appointed ruler, why, that is heresy. Those who still hold the same quaint beliefs as you will learn the error of their ways, unfortunately. It doesn't matter; most of them aren't worth saving. In a few weeks your beliefs should be extinct. And Thetia will be the richer for losing them."

"Why does everything you do have to bring blood and death?" Palatine asked, brokenly. "You admired my father—would he have done this?"

"Your father was able but misguided, a contrast to his daughter. Do you realize how little you've accomplished in your life, Palatine? Always the great leader among the little people, the one with the plans that might succeed when you're fighting mock battles in the training school or on a remote island. But every time you've tried to rise beyond that, you've failed. The republicans only respected you because you're Reinhardt's daughter, Tanais only tutored you because you're my cousin.

"Did you actually *do* anything in your time in Thetia? Were there any successes, any new converts to the cause?" Orosius shook his head, finishing the glass and putting it down on the large, ebony-topped low table between some of the chairs a few paces away—the table was clamped to the floor, I noticed, like the rest of the heavy furniture, so it wouldn't slide about in rough conditions. He pulled the nearest of the lighter chairs across and sat down in it, which I'd been expecting him to do for a while. It would reinforce his sense of superiority. "Have you done anything since then? It was some obscure Oceanian tribune who saved you from execution in Lepidor. Whatever you came here to do, you failed, and you didn't rescue Ravenna either. It's an abysmal record. You should have stayed in Oceanus to fight the tribesmen, who are on your level."

"I'd rather be forgotten by all the world than be remembered as you will!"

"As the restorer of Thetia? How small. Perhaps your name will occur once or twice in the histories, in a footnote somewhere. Cathan doesn't even want that much, does he? He'll get his wish to live and die in obscurity." Orosius laughed, a sound without any humor in it at all. "That's what you've been longing for during the past few months, isn't it, my brother? To lose that clan name that you've never admitted to having. I'll grant that wish for you, have the Exarch countersign a mundane decree stripping you of a royalty you so obviously don't deserve. And as for Ravenna—well, you're the Pharaoh who never was. The only time your people will see you is when you abdicate tomorrow and surrender your crown and yourself to me. A more glorious end than your dynasty deserves: a single upstart with a twenty-year reign and then a girl who rules for half an hour. All of you are failures."

"Then why are you taking the trouble?" I asked. "Why keep us alive, if we're so worthless? I thought you only wanted the best in your brave new world. Wouldn't that be the safest course, so that we can never threaten you again?"

"You will never be able to threaten me, or even be in a position to try. That is sufficient, and you might make good palace servants in time."

I wasn't convinced. Surely inflicting pain couldn't be Orosius's only aim here: there had to be something else he wanted from us, some other reason to keep us alive. He was intelligent enough to know that death would be the only way to stop us making trouble for him but for some reason he didn't want that. Why? I felt a chill run through me as I remembered the *Aeon*. Was that it? Not to be mentioned until he was sure he'd broken us? No, he didn't strike me as patient enough for that. If he wanted the *Aeon*, he'd want it soon, to give him more power and security while he carried out his purges.

"We were part of your price for letting the Domain in," said Palatine. "Do I see a merchant's mentality here, not wasting what you've bought?"

"Spoken like a good commodity. Yes, I have bought you, haven't I?" He gave an amused smile.

"I'm flattered that you think we were worth it. I'm sure the Inquisition wouldn't have thrown us in free."

"The Inquisition wanted you out of the way," he said, shrugging. "Either I took you or the sea did." He stood up again abruptly and walked around us toward the windows. There was silence for a minute.

"We're just passing the mouth of the inlet, although there's no way any of you could tell. Now our communications are no longer blocked the crew should be able to find our escorts, and we can be on our way. Always assuming they don't have to stop for repairs, which could delay things a little." Orosius started walking back to the door but paused behind us.

"Your fear of me is already stronger than your affection for her, isn't it, Cathan? No chivalric loosening of the ropes? I'm disappointed. Or maybe she just prefers it that way."

Thankfully we were saved from answering by a buzzing from the aether screen set unobtrusively into one wall, disguised as a painting. Orosius walked over and pressed something, and the painting was replaced by a view of the *Valdur's* huge bridge with the captain in the foreground.

"Your Majesty, we've received a distress call from *Wildcat*. She's been swept out to sea to the west, but she says she's got a fix on *Peleus* at long range. They can't communicate, and *Peleus* is being swept deeper and deeper into Perdition's Shore."

"Why?" the Emperor demanded. "Is it so hard to keep station?"

"The second Domain ship has gone as well, they think the same way as *Peleus*."

"We're going after them," Orosius said. "I'll not lose ships like this. Set course for *Peleus's* position, signal *Wildcat* to keep away from the shore. Tell Sarhaddon what we're doing."

"Yes, Your Majesty." The screen went blank, but a moment later the captain was back again. "*Domine* Sarhaddon is offering his help in finding your escort, although they warn that the sea is very treacherous."

"Thank him, and accept. I'll come down." Orosius cut the connection and turned back to us. "Remain as you are. You have wasted time with your talking." He left without ceremony, without even a parting remark.

"Obviously his magic isn't as strong as he thinks it is," Palatine said with grim satisfaction. "Perdition's Shore isn't obeying his commands."

I looked out of the windows and saw the Domain manta coming into view about a hundred yards off our starboard wing-tip and slightly below us. It was unimpressive by comparison with *Valdur*, but its firepower would be boosted by the mages. Not that there was anyone to fire on, or anyone within a few thousand miles who'd attack the Imperial flagship.

"Is there any point trying to kill or overpower him?" I whispered to Ravenna. "It's not as if we can get anywhere, with a whole shipful of Imperial Guards and that carrion crow of a steward over there."

"We'll be on this manta for weeks," she replied. "Anything can happen in that time. We should be more than able to deal with this crew between us, although the ship might not recover, and there are the others."

"Take over the Imperial flagship by ourselves? You're mad."

"Cathan, I'm not. *He's* mad." She closed her eyes and took a deep, shuddering breath, and I suddenly realized how pale and tense she was. "His mind is sick, demented, and I cannot bear the thought of being in his power for even a few more hours. I thought I could, but I've never hurt this much in my life. We have to think—now, while he's not here."

The hum of the reactor, ever present on a manta, had been almost imperceptible until now, more a slight vibration that I could feel through my knees on the carpet than an audible sound. But now it increased, just enough to be heard.

"We're picking up speed," Palatine said. "I think it must be a double reactor—she'd be a lumbering whale of a ship otherwise—so she's probably quite fast."

Outside the windows, I saw the wing-beats increase in frequency, and a moment later the Domain manta was doing the same. We were racing deeper and deeper into Perdition's Shore, into treacherous waters that had been swallowing up ships since long before the *Revelation* and would continue to do so well into the future.

But even though we suddenly had the time to talk for as long as Orosius didn't appear, none of us could suggest anything. We'd only have one chance, and we would have to kill him. No one wanted anything less. Maybe by his death we might even be able to reverse the Thetian edict, but we had to find a way to kill him first, using a technique that he wouldn't just be able to deflect with the sheer power of his own magic.

We knew it was murder—high treason, indeed—that we were planning, but none of us cared anymore. Maybe Orosius was my brother by birth, but I hated him now more than I'd hated the Domain. For what he'd done to me, to Palatine, would do to Thetia—and, most of all, for what he had done to Ravenna.

But the fact remained that he was more powerful than any of us individually or all of us together and all he had to do was physically separate us to render our magic useless. Unless we attracted his attention first by getting rid of the bracelets that locked our magic in. Ravenna wasn't sure we could.

The minutes went by, each one more tense than the last as we waited for the sound of Orosius's footsteps outside. But *Valdur* didn't slow or stop, hurtling farther and farther away from the safe channel, the Domain manta sticking to it like a kitten following its mother.

Even with the flagship's huge size, we began to feel irregularities in its motion, slight veering toward or away from the other ship, which seemed to be struggling to keep up. It was falling farther and farther behind.

"The other ship's going to lose us in a minute," Palatine said, interrupting the conversation. "I can hardly see it anymore."

"It's not big enough," said Ravenna. "The escort won't be either, unless it's another battle cruiser."

"Orosius must think *Peleus* is still out there, or we wouldn't still be going farther and farther in."

I craned my head around, trying to make out the dim shape of the other manta in the murk, only visible by the hazy dots of light from its portholes now. As I watched even those disappeared, and there was nothing except a faint redness that we watched for several minutes.

"Why is it red?" Palatine asked, her attention caught. "It wasn't red before, it must be three or four miles away now, so how can we see it?"

"I don't know."

A moment later I saw an expression of shock cross Ravenna's face. The glow was still there but, crimson on black, it was hardly visible.

"Cathan, untie me, quickly!"

"Why?"

"Don't ask, just do! Please, we've only got a few seconds."

I pushed myself backward, shaking my head frantically to ward off sudden dizziness, and fumbled with her ropes. Orosius hadn't left her any slack at all and there was no way that she could have freed herself, but I could see what I was doing. I found the knot and tore at it, more frantically than scientifically. "What's happening?" I asked, silently cursing my fingers for being too clumsy when they were most needed.

"Fire magic. Very strong—they're doing something. Please, come on!"

I jerked the loose end of the knot finally, pulled the ropes away from Ravenna as quickly as I could, and gently moved her hands down to her sides. She swayed, but Palatine was there to stop her falling forward. She cried out in pain as the blood rushed into her arms again.

"Cathan, mind-link, now!"

I shuffled around again and grabbed Ravenna's hands while Palatine kept her steady, and emptied my mind of everything. There was a wall in my mind, put there by the bracelet, that was similar to one I'd seen before, the one in Palatine's mind when she'd lost her memories.

Ravenna gripped my hands so tightly it hurt, but it was enough to remind me what I was trying to do, and suddenly everything opened up, the barrier dissolved, and we were both there, a combined consciousness floating in the void.

Destroy the bracelets. I reached out and felt our minds merge for the slightest fraction of a second, looking at ourselves as if from outside, gray forms in a total darkness. We nudged first my bracelet, then hers, watching them fall to the ground. Only then did I see the marks scoring Ravenna's whole body, black and livid against the insubstantial grayness, the ache in her arms paling into insignificance.

My own anger pulled us apart, breaking the link abruptly as I opened my eyes again and shouted the Emperor's name, looking around for him. I pulled shadows in from outside, hurled them against the room's door and watched it disintegrate in a black cloud, like a wounded fish attacked by piranhas.

"Don't waste your strength, please," Ravenna pleaded, still kneeling where I'd left her. I had no memory of having stood up.

"Thetis protect us," Palatine breathed, her eyes fixed on the windows.

I turned and saw a ball of flame racing through the water, bubbles streaming off in all directions, headed directly below *Valdur*. A blinding pain shot through my head, one that I knew from before I had to ignore if we were to survive this.

"Get underneath something!" I shouted. I grabbed Ravenna and almost threw her under the table, pushing myself in beside her as Palatine squeezed herself under the sofa, realizing what I meant. I banged my wrist and my leg, but I ignored the sharp pain and the agony in my skull. I was glad that Ravenna and I were thin enough for there to be just about room for both of us.

I didn't even have time to frame a prayer that *Valdur* would be strong enough to survive before the hammer-blow hit and we were slammed upward against the underside of the table.

As the aether conduits along the wall exploded, showering everything with sparks, and the lights cut out, I felt the manta lift and heard Ravenna's scream of pain.

Chapter XXXIV

It was a hundred times worse now than it had been on the *Lodestar*, a nightmare of chaos and noise as *Valdur* was flung upward. As the orange sparks died away the darkness was total, but I didn't have time to worry about that. The deck gave a sudden tilt and lurched sideways sickeningly fast. I fell again, hard, against the legs of the table on my side, the breath driven out of me as Ravenna slid down the deck and landed on top of me. Even moving a few inches was agony, and the eldritch screeching of tortured metal lanced through my head again.

"Brace!" I heard Palatine cry out as a faint red glow filled the room. We were still rising, heading up and listing at a crazy angle to starboard, when the second charge hit. I blindly grabbed hold of Ravenna to stop her falling farther, then another sickening blow drove the whole ship down. This time I screamed as my feet hit a leg of the table, sending a jolt up my whole body. There was a crack and I thought in a moment of hideous pain that my leg had broken, but it was only the wine cabinet coming away from the wall.

The deck was almost vertical now, and the cabinet plummeted down the length of the room, the wine bottles falling out in a welter of broken glass and cascading liquid. Another almighty crash sounded as the wooden wreck hit the far wall and then there was a deeper rumble as it went straight through. After that I couldn't distinguish any more individual noises in the cacophony around us. Seconds dragged on forever; we were falling impossibly fast, as if through air rather than water. Bubbles streamed past the windows, lit up now by the orange glow of flames from somewhere in the room.

I gulped air in ragged gasps, praying that the table would hold. Warm liquid was flowing down the deck, soaking my hair and my face. Blood? Who was bleeding? I couldn't raise my arm to see if I had a cut on my head, but a moment later I smelled alcohol, and realized that the "blood" was actually wine from the broken bottles.

The water outside the windows was becoming red again, casting a lurid light over the burning cabin. *Please don't let there be another one*, I prayed frantically, waiting for the impact that would surely snap the table and send us hurtling down the length of the deck. I moved my feet slightly to try to ease the pain. Then I felt us falling and reached out for the nearest leg—too late. Ravenna took the impact this time, on her shoulders, thankfully, not on her head, but I could feel blood, not wine this time, on her face. The table legs buckled but held, Thetis knew how.

No time to think as a massive sofa broke free from its clamps and fell through the far corner, bringing down what remained of the end wall and crashing out into the corridor. We were diving still faster now, the red glow remaining, only bubbles visible outside the window. Something heavy rolled down and landed on my legs as more of the room's furnishings flew over our heads, down toward the fore end of the ship.

The deck shook. There was another terrific crash, the floor buckled upward a few yards away, and something metallic ripped through planking and carpet as if they weren't there.

Then, from outside, a series of tremendous thumps sounded from right above us, and something huge and dark flashed past the window—the manta's tail, broken off and falling past us. Another surge of terror seized me, and I imagined the manta toppling over on to its spine, our fall reversing, and all the objects that had fallen rolling back to crush us.

More sounds, more blows. The noise of all the equipment that was either unsecured or had broken loose falling down the ship, crashing through bulkhead after bulkhead into the aft well, was thunderous. I shifted position slightly and felt another sharp pain as something stabbed into my side. I was still clinging on to Ravenna, trying to shield her from the heavy objects that were still moving, whispering entreaties for the table not to break, for Palatine's chair to stay where it was. The flames were dying down, but I could see more below us, glowing through shattered doors and walls. The acrid smell of flamewood smoke permeated the air, mingling with the fumes of the wine soaking into the carpet inches from our faces.

The manta was slowing, I could feel it. I was almost beyond caring what happened now; I only wished that the agony would end one way or another. The deck lurched yet again, throwing us against the top of the table, and I caught my breath, waiting for it to topple over, for the landslide of wreckage to reverse its course again and drown everything at the forward end of the ship.

For an endless second the manta hung like that. Then, gradually, somehow, the *Valdur*'s descent became a glide, flattening out as we slowed down, the red glow outside the windows entirely gone. How far had we come? I couldn't tell, but we had to be very deep by now.

A series of ominous groans sounded, the ship itself shuddering and creaking. There was another crash from beneath us, and the crackling of flames from farther up the deck, but the ship was suddenly quiet after the thunder of its headlong dive. I was lying on the carpet again, finally, after being jammed for so long against one surface or the other of the table. My body throbbed in a dozen places from cuts and bruises.

But I was alive, and so was Ravenna, although her breathing was very ragged and uneven. I pulled my hands up from my sides and pushed against the table. It gave way immediately, its buckled legs finally breaking. It was the work of a moment for me to push it up and over, so that it landed with a dull thump on the deck. For a moment I lay there, too battered to move, and did nothing except turn Ravenna's head to one side so she wasn't breathing wine fumes anymore.

"Palatine," I called, my voice sounding very small. There was no answer. "Palatine, where are you?"

"I'm here," she said from somewhere, in a voice that was little more than a croak. "I can get out, you look after Ravenna."

Ravenna's face looked very pale even in the glow of the flames inside as I pulled her away from the table, trying to find a spot that wasn't strewn with bits of glass and splintered wood. There were none; I turned her over as gently as I could, moving all the glass shards out of the way, but she still cried out.

I heard a clang a few feet away and looked up to see Palatine's bloodied face emerge from under one of the few heavier chairs left in position; its back had been snapped off like a twig. Her hair was disheveled, and there was an ugly bruise on her forehead. She dragged herself out very slowly, every movement an effort. I tried to get up to help her but I tottered unsteadily and she waved me away.

"I can cope. How is she?"

"I'm here," Ravenna said very faintly, her lips hardly moving. She screwed her eyes shut and opened them slowly, dancing flames reflected in them. "I'll live."

"We all owe you one this time, Cathan," Palatine said, extricating her foot from a jumble of broken wood and glass. "Ouch. It's everywhere, and we're all barefoot." She slumped into a half-sitting position, struggling to breathe.

"I think our shoes will have wandered off by themselves," said Ravenna weakly.

More creaks, and an alarming crack from somewhere in the ship, a hollow object falling against metal that sent echoes ringing around the empty space. The fires across the corridor seemed to be gaining ground.

"We don't have much time." My head was pounding as if a herd of wild bulls was running amok inside it, and every time I moved I discovered some new tender spot. "The reactors are either dead or unstable, so either we'll hit the Shore or blow up."

"Optimist," said Palatine. "But even if we could get out, a little sea-ray won't be able to deal with the currents."

"There are the others, too, in the brig," I said. "They wouldn't have seen anything coming, wouldn't have had anywhere to hide as we did."

"They might have survived," Palatine said, trying to smile but failing. "The brig will have proper walls, they'll only have been thrown about inside. Who knows, if they were chained up securely it might even have been better than it was for us. Then they wouldn't have been thrown around nearly as much."

"We don't leave without them," said Ravenna. "But we mustn't be trapped up here."

Flames were licking at the wooden walls forward, from one of the rooms on the other side of the corridor. Below them I could see the body of the steward, his head twisted around at a crazy angle. Dead, as the rest of the crew probably were. We wouldn't have survived without the protection of the table and chair.

"We need to reach one of the sea-rays, or the launch," I said, wondering how I was going to stand up, let alone walk, like this. "Preferably the launch. Do you think there's an aft stairwell?" I tried to point, but the fingers of my left hand were bruised and almost immobile, streaks of blood running down my palm and all of it hurting unbearably. I didn't even remember doing that. Surely no one else could have survived, or at least be in any condition to move. There was only the faint hope that the brig had shielded some of them. There must have been hundreds on the *Valdur* before the attack. Including the Emperor . . .

I looked over at Palatine. I felt strangely horror-stricken at the prospect of the death of a man I hated, as I realized for the first time what it meant.

"They betrayed him," I said, not believing it myself. "Sarhaddon betrayed him."

"If he's dead," Ravenna said, a catch in her voice, "then it's no more than he deserved."

I remembered the livid marks I'd seen all over the mind-image of her body, a reflection of life, just a few seconds before the Domain had attacked. "What did he do?"

Palatine looked away and tried again to pull herself to her feet—anything to avoid answering my question.

"Not telling Cathan won't help," Ravenna said. "He used a whip with aether. It feels like being burned, I've never felt so much pain in my life. No time now, though. Please help me get up."

I pictured the Emperor's shattered body lying in the darkness of the bridge, felt a savage rush of hatred, hoping that he'd died in as much pain as he'd enjoyed inflicting on others. That he'd known, before he died, that his life had been as much of a failure as he said mine was, that the credit for all the grand programs he'd launched would be taken by his successor . . .

"Who succeeds?" I said aloud, then repeated the question more urgently, light-headed with the wine fumes and not really knowing why I wasn't thinking about survival instead of the Imperial throne. But the Domain had turned against him, wanted him dead. Why? He was perfect, he supported them utterly. Where could they find another to fit their plans as well?

"Arcadius," Palatine said. "Or me."

"You're supposed to be dead. And why kill Orosius to put Arcadius in? He's a moderate."

"I don't know," she said.

"Please can you get me up?" Ravenna said, an edge of fear in her voice. "The fire's getting closer . . . I don't want to be burned again."

Aether whip, I thought, as I inched my good hand under her shoulders, and she put an arm around my back, clutching at my tunic. Palatine, finally on her feet, came over, trying to pick her way through the field of broken glass that was everywhere, and took Ravenna's other side. How could he have done that? Aether burned anything it touched . . . the sheer inhumanity of using it on anyone, let alone a bound and helpless woman—girl, he'd called her. Whatever trace of a link to my brother there once had been shriveled away and died. I would rather Lachazzar himself sat on that throne than Orosius. Even if we died down here in the abyss of Perdition's Shore, Sarhaddon would have done us a favor.

But we wouldn't perish here. As we heaved Ravenna to her feet, ignoring her cry of pain because we had to, I knew that there was no question of her dying. We would survive. We would survive because the Emperor had wanted to make us his slaves and I wanted to prove how wrong he was. Because the world deserved better from Orosius's death.

And because I was going to find the *Aeon*, and Sarhaddon would be proved wrong too, and I could watch the sunset from Sanction with Ravenna . . . so many things. Life went on. What was the point of being alive if there was nothing to look forward to?

"Palatine, do you have any idea where the brig might be?" I asked, gasping at the racking pain in my legs that came from being thrown against the table.

"It's usually on the cargo deck, but you're not supposed to be able to reach it except from the bridge deck. Remember the *Shadowstar*?"

"I wasn't looking for the brig on the *Shadowstar*."

"They used it for stores, and I had to go and get something from it a few times, while you were having sailing lessons."

"If you know where it is, go ahead. We'll go straight to the sea-ray bays and try to find one that's workable. We don't have much time." That was an understatement, I knew, but there was no point panicking.

"I'll go. But I won't be able to get the others out—I'll need you to break the door down."

"You can move faster than us," Ravenna said. "The rest of the ship's in bits, the brig should be at least dented."

"I'll go. Borrow a sword from someone who doesn't need it anymore. But you . . ."

"We will get out," I said firmly. "Go!"

Palatine went, feet crunching now and then on glass fragments, leaving bloody footprints on dry patches of the floor.

Leaning unsteadily on each other, Ravenna and I slowly made our way forward. It was impossible to avoid stepping on the glass, and it stabbed into our feet more with every step. Most of it was bottle glass, thankfully, which didn't usually break into slivers, but there were evil little shards here and there that sank into our skin like splinters.

We got ourselves through the space where the door had been but couldn't go on without sitting down and pulling as many of the splinters as we could find from our soles. It was hard to see them in the unsteady light of the flames, and one or two were still embedded when Ravenna called a stop and we went on again, limping.

There was still a very slight angle to the deck; the manta was descending slowly, probably pulled down by the currents now, as the *Revelation* had been. The *Revelation*, I thought. A downward current. Why should there be a cross-current at that depth? They'd been going a few miles past the edge of the continental bedrock, so why was a cross-current pulling them in?

We reached the forward well; by mutual consent we'd agreed to go down this way, if we could, because the aft stairwell would either be a ladder or very narrow, and neither of us wanted to risk that if it was possible to get down the main stairs.

"Some of it's left, at least," Ravenna said. "The forward bulkhead held." A dozen or more splintered pieces of equipment were piled up on the inside of it, though, including the remnants of the wine cabinet and the chairs. The double doors were gone, of course, the body of a Guard broken beneath one of them. If the Inquisition wanted to kill the Emperor, why did it have to be like this? Why all of his retinue too?

I breathed a sigh of relief as I saw that the port staircase was still relatively intact, although with no balustrade and a great chunk carved out of it halfway down. More flames were reflected in the skylight, from two or three scattered little fires down at the bottom of the well where mangled bodies were heaped in with wreckage. I felt sick.

"It wasn't just him they wanted to kill," Ravenna said, clutching my shoulder in a vicelike grip as we began edging our way down the stairs, step by painful step. There was a rumbling sound from deep below, and a high-pitched whine from somewhere that was intensely nerve-racking. "It was you and Palatine. Me too, I suppose. That's why they were so ready to hand us over, why Sarhaddon said that about announcing your death. All of us wiped out in one fell swoop, and our deaths blamed on the sea."

"But why the Emperor?"

"I don't know. Your Arcadius didn't seem very extreme, as you said, so why would they want to put him in when they'd got such a perfect Emperor?" Ravenna's voice developed a sob at the edge, and she clung to me suddenly, crying, her head buried in my shoulder. This was the woman who had never let herself show weakness, especially not to me, had endured those welts and the ropes for hours . . . what had Orosius done to her?

She stopped after a moment and looked at me worriedly through eyes still glistening with tears. "This I don't, can't . . . Cathan, what am I saying?" She shook her head, brushed her eyes and we went on, flattening ourselves against the wall to get around the gaping hole. There were more bodies here, too many to ignore. It was grotesque, a scene that burned itself into my mind and would never leave it as long as I lived. The worst of it was that they weren't mutilated, or even bloody, just twisted and shattered.

We went past and down as quickly as we could, still four decks above our goal. The next landing was the level of the bridge, and here it was worst. We skirted around the flames, unable to put them out. Twisted metal hung all around, and here the dead *were* mutilated, their faces scalded or melted when the aether conduits had exploded.

As we reached the bottom of the stairs Ravenna pointed at a body lying where it had fallen, her finger shaking. For a moment I didn't see why. Then I took in the black clothing without rank markings, the long hair, the body's shape. I stared at it for a moment, numbly. Then we stumbled over to it and kneeled down together beside it. Telesta's eyes stared sightlessly up at the skylight, a trickle of blood running down the side of her face.

"It gained her nothing at all," I said sadly. "They're both to blame for this, the Emperor and Sarhaddon. She didn't deserve it."

"*Not all omens are good, Mauriz. It's hard to tell at the moment which way this one will go,*" Ravenna said. "That's what she said in Ral Tumar, when we met her. I didn't agree with her, but you're right."

I reached out awkwardly with my right hand and closed Telesta's eyes, then saw movement at the corner of my vision. A Guardsman, moving feebly, his arm dislocated. I moved over to him; he was the first man we'd seen alive.

"*Imperatore mei,*" he said, with a cough that almost turned into a spasm. Something had hit him in the chest, driven his armor into his body. Ravenna shook her head slightly, helplessness and frustration written on her face. She looked close to tears again.

"*Te no adiuvi.*" His stare was fixed on me, but he obviously couldn't see properly. "*Cuite?*"

I paused for a moment, saw him take a ragged breath, his eyes clouding over.

"*Requiescete en Rantaso,*" I said softly, hoping it was in time for him to hear. Ravenna closed his eyes for me as I stared down, feeling my own eyes fill with tears. It should not have come to this. A dying man had mistaken me for my brother on a ship of the dead, a ship heading for oblivion because of the Domain's treachery. The *Peleus*, the escort, would be gone too, I realized, maybe the *Wildcat* as well. All for some twisted purpose of Sarhaddon's. How many more would die for the two of them?

"*Imperatore,*" Ravenna echoed, staring into the flames that were slowly creeping forward, their expansion inhibited by coolant water that had soaked everything. "He was sorry he couldn't help you."

I barely heard her words above the crackle of the flames and another drawn-out roar from aft. I could see fiercer flames along the corridor, toward Engineering, but from forward I heard a faint moan, the sound of someone crying not from pain but from despair.

"There's someone still alive in the bridge," I said.

"I can't hear anything."

"I can, just about."

"That's where the Emperor was. What if he's still . . ."

He was. That was why I could hear it, because it was my brother weeping. How? How had he survived where so many others had not? He didn't deserve to. I would finish the job Sarhaddon had begun.

I tugged at Ravenna's sleeve, pointing with my damaged hand, and after a moment she gave in. We hobbled together down the passage, over more bodies, through the little mini-well and into the cavernous darkness of the bridge. A single aether light, sputtering but somehow intact, cast an eerie white light over everything; otherwise the only illumination came from the ghostly images of flames from aft reflected on the windows.

It had been a magnificent ship half an hour ago, the bridge dwarfing any other I'd seen, a model of naval architecture. Now it was ruined beyond repair: the ceiling collapsed in places, every console dead, twisted metal, broken wood and chairs everywhere.

Most of the crew lay beneath the windows or trapped behind their stations around the edges. The air was unpleasantly warm, I noticed for the first time; it had been outside as well, but on the bridge it was mixed with steam, and felt clammy and oppressive.

Ravenna made a sound somewhere between a hiss and a snarl as we saw Orosius, buried by the wreckage of the captain's chair. Blood stained the white tunic, though I couldn't tell whether it was his own or not.

His face was twisted into a grimace of despair and sorrow, his lament punctuated by sobs and shrieks that sounded like the howling of a lost soul. It was unearthly, the inside of an abandoned madhouse where only one occupant was left.

"Is he dying?" Ravenna asked fiercely.

"He soon will be." I pointed to a tiny blinking red light on one side of the window that had somehow survived the devastation where its fellows elsewhere had not. It signified reactor overload, although it lacked the surrounding ring that would indicate imminent meltdown.

"Then why are we wasting time?"

"I don't know." In truth, I wasn't sure, but it was hard to believe that this crumpled figure, weeping inhumanly, was the Emperor who had been our captor, Ravenna's torturer. He was, though. I couldn't mistake the face.

I saw Orosius try to shy away at the sound of our voices; he stared directly at us with wild, dilated eyes. Eyes that were gray, not sea-blue, I could tell that even in this darkness. "No!" he cried. "No! Please! Don't come near me! I am unclean!"

"You are worse than unclean, creature," Ravenna said as we stood over him. Her fists were clenched, and for a moment I thought she would lash out at him, pathetic and defenseless though he was. "You are an abomination."

"I know," he said, in a voice that sounded more like a frightened child's than a grown man's. "Ranthas, no! You!" He tried to pull himself away, gave a racking cough and fell back again. "No . . ." His cry turned into a wail, and I looked away, avoiding the sight of the contorted face.

"How does it feel?" Ravenna said grimly. "You thought I hurt you, this must be ten, a hundred times worse. Worse than what you felt before, anyway."

"Then it wasn't a dream . . . I hoped . . . What is this?" He thrashed around, arms and legs flailing feebly, held one hand in front of his head as if to protect himself from us. "Mother, where are you? I need you!"

"He's gone completely mad," she said, her voice a mixture of distaste and something else. Maybe satisfaction, maybe not. "Insane now, not just twisted."

"Where are you? Why is it dark? I hate the darkness . . . but they come and close me in, they say the light hurts. It doesn't, Mother, please come and open the shutters for me!" The Emperor rambled on in his delirium.

"Mother?" Ravenna repeated. "*Mother?*"

"He sent her away," I said, quietly. "After he was ill, about seven or eight years ago." My father said that illness had changed him. Coming so soon after Reinhardt Canteni's death, it had been the end of the "Canteni Renaissance" that had seemed imminent during Perseus's last few years on the throne. Was that where Orosius had slipped back to, in his dying hallucinations?

"Kill me," he said, snapping back to lucidity, his limbs stilling. He fixed his stare on Ravenna. "Please? Won't you, you deserve to after what I did . . . Screaming, you were screaming, and I kept on. On and on and on and . . . and on. Hung you by the feet . . . no, not you that wasn't, someone else, red hair. Oh Ranthas, what did I do? How could I?"

I kneeled down beside him, grabbed the hand that was covering his head, and concentrated, sending my consciousness along it. I closed my eyes: the bridge vanished, and I floated in the darkness of my own mind, looking at Orosius's body lying there. One leg was crushed, bones fractured from thigh to foot, he was bleeding internally, and there was a dark, raised bruise on the side of his head as well as dozens of other abrasions, cuts and burn marks along his upper arm.

And, as with Palatine, there was the alien overlay of magic on it all, generations of it concentrated in every cell of his body. But it seemed like an afterglow here, as if there had been something more that was gone now, something that would not come back.

I slipped a layer below, careful to remain apart as I looked into his mind. The fury, the bitterness hit me like a wave, but there was so much sorrow there too, in a mind chaotic, twisted, scarred.

And there was a wall there, as there'd been with Palatine, in exactly the same place, the same way, only older, stronger. But it had been broken down, only the ruins remaining, his mind a whirlpool of emotions. I felt an awful sense of guilt and broke free in one go, ripping my hand away from him.

"Are you all right?" Ravenna said, concern showing in her voice. She kneeled down next to me and held my face for a moment like a healer looking for symptoms. Then she reached down to take the Emperor's hand, as I had. He pulled it away but she caught hold of his sleeve and pulled his hand back, ripping the cloth of his tunic as she did so.

It seemed to take an eternity before she broke the link, letting him move away.

"It's the mind of a madman, Cathan," she said, her eyes haunted again. "There's nothing anyone can do."

"He's lost his magic, hasn't he?"

"Yes. That's why his eyes have changed back to what they were originally. He'll die powerless, like all the people he hurt over the years. It's horrifying. I got off lightly—the things he did to them, the things he let others do . . . if this hadn't happened . . ." She closed her eyes and grabbed my arm to keep her balance as I wondered how I could maintain even the semblance of calm. But I couldn't feel fury, not looking down at the man who less than an hour ago had been Emperor of Thetia, and now raved as he lay slowly dying on the bridge of a ruined ship.

"Please kill me before you go," Orosius pleaded. "I'm sure you can grant me that favor, brother, even if she won't."

I shook my head mutely, not sure why.

"Why? Why, after everything I did to you, can neither of you kill me? Cathan, I don't deserve to live, I'm a monster, you said it yourself. Mother said it, everyone says it. They all know what I did."

"Life is a greater curse than death, say those who know not how to live."

"Cathan, no!" Ravenna said urgently. "Remember who you are, who he is."

I had told myself that a few months ago as I faced my own death in Lepidor. But I would not die tonight, and neither would the Emperor. I hated him for what he'd done to Ravenna, still, but in my mind there was the image of a thirteen-year-old lying in a darkened room, shaking with fever, crying out for his mother. I had been ill, desperately ill, when I was thirteen. So had he, but where my adoptive parents had always been there, his real ones had not. Perseus had been dead, his mother had been kept away . . . kept away—by the priests. I was seeing snatches of his memory, I realized. We were identical twins.

It seemed a stupid thing to do, to try and save someone who was my enemy. An act that would surely haunt me, because if he healed, he might return to what he had been, and I would have missed the chance I'd been so happy about only a few minutes ago, to rid the world of him.

But so would Sarhaddon. Orosius had served his purpose, been betrayed even by those who had shared his dreadful vision. The Domain wanted him dead. They wanted a new Emperor. And while I would never be anyone's savior, Thetia had once seen Orosius as a new hope, and he might still be what they wanted.

"He is my brother," I said. "And the Domain's enemy, since Sarhaddon's turned against him."

"And he is our enemy too!" Ravenna fumbled with the fastenings of her tunic, half-undid them and pulled the garment dramatically away from her shoulders, the Emperor's presence forgotten. "Can you see these marks, even in this light?" The savage welts I'd seen reflected in the mind-realm, livid and raw, the skin around them burned or blood-encrusted, striped her shoulders and arms, the tops of her breasts, even her throat where the collar of the tunic had covered it. "This is what he did, and you would spare him?"

Elements, the agony she must have been in all those hours while he'd crowed over us. How could I save the person who'd done that? The marks were all over Ravenna's body and I didn't even know if they would heal without scarring. Certainly not, if we didn't get her to a healer—and I had no idea where we could find one back on land. Not in a city—the Sacri would be there—and I didn't think a village crone would be enough.

"She's right, Cathan," the Emperor said. "I did that, I ignored her pleas for mercy, so don't you see why the world needs to be rid of me? I have done that to so many people over the last few years, tormented them, reduced them to husks . . . walking corpses, no spirit left in them, no life. All me, all me . . ." His voice trailed off again into a fresh frenzy of tears and howls.

Ravenna pulled her tunic back over her shoulders and hurriedly retied the fastenings. "For once in his miserable life I agree with him. Let him die here with the ship and all the people he condemned by his actions."

She had lost all reason where this was concerned; she was as single-minded as I knew she could be, and I didn't blame her. But if I went now and left Orosius here to wait for the *Valdur*'s end, it would haunt me for the rest of my life. I might regret taking him with me, but I knew I would regret leaving him more.

"Ravenna, he wants to die. You want to hurt him; if you must, do it by keeping him alive with the knowledge of what he has done. His magic has gone, and his crown has gone. We're all supposed to be dead, and after tonight there will be another Emperor, whoever it is."

"Then why not you?"

"Because I am not an Emperor!" I shouted, and saw her flinch. "I am not, nor will I be, ever! That crown belongs to someone else. Do you want me to do what Valdur did, to take the crown from a brother I killed? *I am the Hierarch.* I was born Hierarch, and if I must have any title that will be it. Better not to have anything. Let Orosius atone for his own mistakes. Punish him if you will, Ravenna, but for Thetis's sake think! He took a revenge on you that was beyond all proportion. You'll be doing the same if we leave him."

"Why do you want to save him?" Now she was shouting too. "Why? When you thought he was dead you were as glad as the rest of us."

"You lost a brother too!" I replied, and she fell backward on her heels as if I'd hit her. "They're the ones who take life meaninglessly, not us!"

"My brother was an innocent, a seven-year-old child. This . . . thing is not innocent of anything. Think of all the people he's destroyed, all the lives he's ruined."

"Think of the child who played with Palatine in the Imperial Palace while the old Emperor was still alive. My father loved him, so did my mother, while neither of them ever knew me. My father didn't even know I existed: for him, Orosius was the only son he had. He went mad, but there must be a way to cure that. I was ill too, Ravenna, when he was. Count Courtières sent my father . . . Elnibal . . . the best healers on all the Continents from his hospital to save me. They succeeded where the Imperial healers failed. A chance of fate, that was all. Don't you see? If the priests hadn't taken over when Orosius was ill, he'd never have become like this. Mauriz was wrong in Ral Tumar: Orosius is much closer to me than you think."

"You can't excuse what he's done because of an illness. He's had every opportunity to change since then, but did he ever take it?"

"Has he now?"

"I don't know, Cathan! Why should he survive when no one else on this whole ship has? Whoever becomes Emperor will destroy Thetia using *his* edict, an edict that he gave to the Domain. The price they paid was to sell us as if we were slaves. We *would* have become slaves in the end."

"That was what I wanted!" the Emperor said, as a series of ear-splitting cracks echoed through the bridge from somewhere aft, and I thought I heard a voice calling my name. "All of you, slaves—my own brother, the cousin who was my friend once, a girl I tortured for hours because she tried to stop herself being captured. Can I call myself a human being after that? There is so much more, so much worse."

"He will live," I said, trying desperately to convince Ravenna. "Remember what Palatine said earlier. If we leave him here we are no better than him! Who are we to set ourselves up as judges when we are the accusers too?"

"Who are we to deny his wish to die?" Ravenna said, tears running down her face over old stains. "He has judged himself."

"Then he is rational and worth saving. After all the luxury, the comfort that he has known, he will become a penniless exile with a group of ragged fugitives. Please, Ravenna, help me! I don't love you any the less for this, but *I can't leave him.*"

I couldn't move Orosius on my own, I couldn't even stand up on my own. I waited in suspense; I knew my face showed as much as my voice had before. Ravenna looked uncertainly from me to him, wavering, as more groans shook the ship, and the ring around the red light came on, a red-rimmed warning eye in the darkness. The *Valdur*'s end was only minutes away.

"On your head be it," she said. But at that moment the Emperor gave a strangled cough and a series of choking gasps. His face twisted with pain and blood almost cascaded from his mouth. Ravenna grabbed his hand again and held it for a moment. "He's dying. Please leave him—we'll never be able to heal him and we may kill ourselves."

She was right. We'd have to drag him all the way down, and who knew whether he'd survive, or whether we could even carry him. But we had to try.

"Who could save him?" I asked Ravenna, as a wild idea came into my head. "Suggest anyone, anywhere, who might be able to. Then it'll be out of our hands, it'll be their responsibility."

"Your hospital," she said, confused. "My people, your mother's people. But they're all too far away!"

"How do you make a rift?" I asked Orosius. Then I shouted, "Tell me!"

"No! I don't deserve to live. They have other patients, more deserving."

"Does your mother? Tell me how, and you'll see her again!"

"She'll reject me, just as I sent her away, away . . . She knows what I am now."

"Then if she rejects you, that is the end," I said. "Tell me, otherwise we will try to save you ourselves, which will be far worse."

"I have given so much pain," he said, gasping for breath, his face beaded with sweat. He was dying, I knew it for certain now: he had been all along. He would die now, if we tried to move him, but maybe others' arts, the powers of those who cared, would make a difference. "That . . . it is only right . . . to receive it in return."

"Your fate is in our hands now! You do not have power over your own life anymore and you will answer to those who can pass judgment one day. If penance is what you really want, they will give it to you. But not now."

Orosius stared up at me, his brother, his captive, his enemy, for a long moment. I looked down at his lower body, saw more blood seeping out from underneath the pile of wreckage, and noticed how pale he had become. His arm reached weakly up to his chest. He pointed and I saw the outline of a medallion beneath his tunic.

"Take that off me . . ." he ordered. "Quickly." I wondered if he was answering my wish, but I did as he asked and brought out a silver dolphin pendant set with a single flawed blue sapphire. I put it in his hand. His fingers closed around it and I saw it shimmer slightly as he placed it awkwardly on his chest.

"Cathan, my whole life has been a failure, a parody," he said, fighting for every breath now. "It is too late now, the Inquisition has killed me . . . Is Palatine still alive?"

Ravenna nodded, answering for me.

"Then she is my successor. Please make her see that she must accept it, because she will be better than . . . whoever else . . . they try to put in after me. She will be Empress now, and you will be her Hierarch. Drive the Domain from Thetia, from the Archipelago, with my blessing. Make Thetia great again, as I could have done but didn't. Let . . . one of us have been worth something, be everything that I was not." He turned his dimming gaze toward Ravenna, seemingly unable to move his head, and I knew our efforts to save him had come too late, that they had been in vain. "Ravenna, you are Pharaoh of Qalathar and so will all your descendants be for as long as the line lasts, second in authority only to the Emperor.

"Undo as much as you can of what I have done, please, save those of my victims you can . . ." Orosius broke off, going into another and more violent coughing spasm, his fingers scrabbling for my hand. I gave it to him and let him hold my fingers weakly. "Tell our mother that I'm sorry, so sorry, and that I love her . . . that I realized what I'd done before it was too late. It's dark, Cathan. Goodbye." He gave a last shuddering breath, and lay still. The medallion on his chest glowed suddenly, painfully bright, and then faded again, although the sapphire now had a luster that it had lacked before.

I didn't move, but stared down at the body, anything I might have said catching in my throat. For a moment there I had caught a glimpse of what might have been, of a boy who had played in the Palace Gardens in Selerian Alastre in a hopeful time all those years ago. Before his mind had been poisoned by his illness and the priests, and yet . . . by their betrayal they had nearly given him a second chance, a chance to live again and redress the wrongs he had done.

I reached out and closed the gray eyes.

"*Requiena el'la pace ii Thete atqui di immortae, nate'ine mare aeternale'elibri orbe,*" I whispered, the Thetian blessing for the dead that I couldn't remember learning. *Rest in peace with Thetis and the immortal gods, swim through the ocean free forever from the world.* "I will do as you have asked. Aquasilva itself will avenge your death." The Inquisition had no defense against what the storms could do in our hands. The planet itself would be turned against them, to ravage them, to destroy them, to scatter them beyond the ends of the earth.

Then I forgot everything—the *Valdur*'s impending destruction, Palatine, the others—as I gave in and wept over Orosius's body, the world shrinking to a blur through eyes full of tears. I didn't see Ravenna gently lift the medallion and slip it into the pocket of my tunic, barely felt her pull me around to cry on her shoulder. I didn't even see the single tear that she gave to the Emperor at the end.

I had hardly known him. My brother was dead.

Chapter XXXV

All too soon I felt Ravenna shake me slightly, calling my name, her voice urgent. Her fingers brushed gently across my eyes. "Cathan, there isn't much time. We have to go."

I wiped the tears away with the back of my good hand, stared at her blearily and blinked.

"Of course," I said, reason asserting itself again as unearthly screeches sounded from aft. "You're right."

We stood up, although my gaze never left the Emperor's body as we made our way around him. The flames were fiercer now: I could see them at the end of the corridors, advancing by leaps and bounds. How much time had we lost? We were supposed to have been finding an escape craft, not trying to save a dying man.

I couldn't stop myself from pausing and looking back as we left the bridge. A slight glow surrounded the Emperor's body, growing brighter as I watched until it was painful to look at. It happened to those who were part-elemental at death, I knew, and we watched in silence as something like a faint mist rose from the body and vanished through the windows, leaving the glow to fade away. I saw Mauriz's body out of the corner of my eyes as the glow rose to its height, but there was no more time.

"He has gone to the sea," Ravenna said, a valediction and a message that it was over. I didn't look behind again as we half-hobbled, half-ran through the little corridor and out into the well. A wall of roaring flames was advancing down the starboard corridor, while the fires in the well itself were gradually engulfing the port staircase, the only one leading downward that was still intact.

We pushed each other on, stepping over bodies and broken furniture, feeling the heat of the flames beating at us. The banisters were on fire, already dropping away in some places, and the carpet, smoldering here and there, was beginning to catch fire at the edges.

"Magic," I said, pausing to use water-magic to extinguish the fire.

"No time," said Ravenna. "There's still a path, and a little singeing won't be any worse than what we've already suffered."

Arms linked for support, we started down the steps, the carpet painfully hot against our bare feet. I could feel the skin of my ankles stinging as we stumbled past the small flames that were licking at the carpet, and I pulled my trousers as far up as I could as I stepped across the gap left by the one step that was too far gone, terrified that a stray spark would catch on my clothing.

But somehow, miraculously, it didn't, and we made it past the fire to the bottom of the stairs, the lower well.

"Palatine!" I shouted, wondering if the brig was somewhere on this level, but there was no answer. The stairs to the lower deck were, thankfully, still free, but there was water up to the third or fourth step. Freezing cold water, if it had come in from outside. A pinhole leak or two would be enough to flood the ship at this pressure and depth. Not a single light shone down there.

There was no answer, and I felt a stab of worry. What if Palatine had got trapped by the flames aft, or failed to get into the brig? There were so many things that could have happened to her while we were wasting time, and I was the one who'd sent her off on her own, just because she was in better shape than either of us, untouched by aether or the Emperor's magic.

"We'll have to go on," I said, pointing down into the darkness. "If it floods too much we won't be able to get into the sea-ray."

Always assuming that any of the sea-rays had survived being flung about inside their bays.

"Shadowsight," Ravenna said. "And we try the launch first, it's biggest."

I nodded in agreement, and we went down the steps. I put out a foot to test the water, jerked it back as if someone had stabbed a thousand needles of ice into me.

"I can make things a little better," I said, glad that my magic would be some use at last. "We need to soak ourselves."

"What?"

Steeling myself, I grabbed her hand and started walking down the steps, wishing a moment later I hadn't.

"Not the best way," Ravenna said, hesitating before going down another step. She pushed me in the back, and a moment later icy water engulfed me, the pain almost as bad as the Emperor's magic. There was a splash as Ravenna landed beside me and came up a moment later, shivering and drenched from head to toe. "Nnnnow?"

"Underwater," I said, through chattering teeth.

Submerging myself—after the initial shock it was better than being out in the air—I emptied my mind, purging it of everything extraneous as I'd been taught, and sucked in water to make a shell around each of our bodies, like a liquid suit of armor. I sealed it in place, as much as I could do for now. Freezing cold as it was at the moment, our body heat would warm the water, and the shield would function like a Thetian flipper suit.

Ravenna gestured to me impatiently and I pointed insistently down and along the corridor. We had to swim underwater for a while or the shield wouldn't work as well; nor, in fact, would we be able to breathe in air for a very long while we had it because the water covered our faces as well.

It seemed to take forever to propel ourselves along the corridor through the dark water, steering by shadowsight, trying to remember where we were from only the bottom of the doors. We went straight on at the junction, and I saw that the door at the end was open, leading into the massive darkness of the launch bay. The shadowsight wasn't very far-ranging or effective under water, so I couldn't see what was inside or even what was above the surface.

I went more slowly than I would have done on my own, waiting for Ravenna as we gradually warmed up again, the water around us keeping the heat in like a second skin. There had to be a water version of shadowsight, I realized, although I didn't know how to see that way. Maybe if I could find a water-mage they'd tell me, or perhaps I could work it out for myself.

Then we reached the bay, and I saw, incredibly, close to us now, the shadowy launch still held by its clamps, although the rest of the room was wrecked . . . and a light was shining out of the launch's open hatch and its front windows.

"Palatine!" I called again, surfacing. "Palatine, is that you?" Yellow lights were burning in the darkness, like those of a welcoming house seen through the rain; I'd never wanted to reach illumination so much. There was a splash beside me as Ravenna surfaced and looked around wildly, gasping for breath. "You can only breathe water like this! Act as though you were still submerged." She looked strange, with a halo of water around her head, almost as if she was trapped in glass, but no stranger than I probably did.

There was a moment's pause, and then someone wrapped in a heavy cloak leaned out of the hatch and held up an aether torch. "Cathan, thank Thetis! Where are you?"

"We're over here." I waved an arm. "By the door. We'll have to swim—can you let the gangway down?"

"Yes."

We didn't wait for more but ducked back underwater and kicked our legs harder, wanting more than anything to reach the light and warmth of the sea-ray. It was actually more comfortable swimming than it would have been walking, but still, I'd rather not have been moving or running around at all.

Those last strokes took forever, but then I saw the end of the gangway in the water ahead and pulled myself on to it. Too drained to do anything else, once I'd dissolved the suits we crawled up and collapsed on the carpet inside the hatch.

"Elements, you poor things," Bamalco's deep voice said. "Quickly, they need to keep warm." We were lifted up and bundled in heavy Guard cloaks that they'd found from somewhere. I looked around and saw Bamalco, Palatine, Persea . . . and Tekraea, lying unconscious on the floor, swathed in more cloaks.

"The others didn't make it," Persea said sadly. "Bamalco and I only survived because the bastards chained us against the forward wall. Tekraea's in a bad way but he'll survive."

Those deaths were on my hands. I was the one who'd come up with the plan, because I had wanted to rescue Ravenna.

"They knew they might not survive," Persea said, her face sad but composed. "For Qalathar. Are there no other survivors? We wondered where you'd gone."

"There were," I said. "I'll tell you later. But none of them made it."

"We don't have much *later*," Bamalco said. "The reactor's going critical, and there's no way to get out of here without flooding the ship."

It wasn't over yet. "Just check one last time that there's nobody else out there, then close the hatch. Is this thing intact?"

"As far as we can see," Persea said. She and Bamalco didn't seem as bruised as we were, except for livid marks on their wrists and ankles from the chains that had, ironically, saved their lives. "And hope," she added wryly.

Palatine called out into the darkness, but there was no answer except for a shudder that shook the whole ship. I felt awful, not knowing how many others might have survived in cramped corners of the ship but would soon be left behind. If we didn't get out now, though, there would be no survivors.

"No one," Palatine said, closing the hatch as I hobbled through into the bridge and sat down in the navigator's chair. The launch-bay doors had to be operable in a situation like this, with every other system on the ship destroyed. Or was this only an official craft, not designed for emergency use? I asked Bamalco whether he knew.

"Yes, it's properly kitted out for an escape, obviously for the chief thug himself to get away in. There're provisions and these Guard cloaks, a few other things, two little sleeping cabins, and a cubicle aft that's even got a shower in it. Orosius didn't believe in stinting himself."

"Good, because we'll need it. Who's the best pilot?"

"You are," Palatine said. "We're underwater, remember. None of us are anything like as good as you."

"Thank you, but I need to make sure the water doesn't come into the bay while we're getting out."

"I'll pilot, then," Palatine said. "Unless you're better, Bamalco, which you probably are."

"I'm an engineer, not a pilot. I'll sit at the side and give you a hand." The bridge area was large enough for four people to sit in, with extra chairs to the pilot's right and the navigator's left. Palatine slipped into the pilot's seat, while Persea helped Ravenna into the chair next to me and then, with Bamalco, went to put Tekraea in one of the berths aft.

"Engines ready?" Palatine said, looking, as we all did, very out of place, a ragged figure amid the surroundings of an Emperor's barge, although only her trousers were soaked while Ravenna and I were wet all over. That wasn't necessary, I realized, wondering how I could have forgotten such a basic piece of magic.

It should have been the work of a moment to dry out all our clothes as the Emperor had done, but I was reaching the limits of my energy. Magic was only there as long as the body could support it; battered, bruised and tired, I wasn't capable of much.

I managed it, though, and received grateful smiles from the others as a thanks. Now there was just one more thing I had to do, that I *would* have enough power for. As Bamalco came back and slipped into his seat, Persea sitting in the Emperor's chair behind us, Palatine started up the engines. The bay outside grew lighter, lit up by the flare of the exhaust.

"Ready to release clamps when you say so, Cathan."

"In a minute." The void again, harder now than it had been even a minute ago. I started gathering magic in from all around, felt my skin tingling, burning with the effort until Ravenna's consciousness suddenly joined me, passively standing by to let me draw on her energy. This was my magic entirely . . . or was it? I called her silently to join in and help me push the water away from below us, under control . . .

"Now!" I said, and heard, as if from a long way off, the thump of the clamps being released and the grind of the doors opening. Unsure how the water would behave at this depth, I simply kept a barrier across the gradually opening space, stopping it from going any farther. Maybe it was completely unnecessary, but I wasn't going to take that chance.

We held the barrier together as the launch sank down through the floor and out of the ship, until at last it was free of the *Valdur*'s hull. I let go of the water, of my magic, of everything except Ravenna's hand, and slumped back in the seat to watch Palatine fire up the engines and propel us as far as she could away from the stricken Imperial flagship.

The oval aether table between us and the front windows came on, showing the *Valdur* falling away above and behind us. A row of figures along its edge and the aether display screens showed, among other things, our depth.

"Eight and a half miles," Ravenna said, and we looked up at the hull. Would the launch be able to take the crushing force for very long? I'd have to use my magic again if it didn't.

"They've got some kind of a jet-stream mechanism," Palatine said. "Streamlines the ship, should help us a little . . . Elements, the currents!"

We were still far below Perdition's Shore, probably only a few miles from the *Revelation*'s final resting place. The cross-current. I sank my hands into the aether pad, zooming out on the sensor image until it was at its maximum.

A nightmarish landscape of canyons, little mountains, twisted rocks was all around us; we were even deeper than some of those submerged islets I'd seen from the safety of the oceanographic station in Tandaris. Only two days ago. It felt like a lifetime. I could see why it was so treacherous, but why the cross-currents? Why had . . .

Guarded by the sea. Caverns.

Palatine was fighting with the ship, trying to keep it under control but failing, the currents too strong for the engines. The *Valdur* was still drifting inexorably downward and inward, pulled into a gaping blackness on the aether display. A cavern mouth hundreds of yards across.

We were still not as deep as the *Revelation*'s last position, I realized. They had gone down past the edge of the shelf, not on to it . . . which meant there was another cavern entrance below us, probably a truly colossal one in the bedrock of Qalathar itself. Facing outward toward the open sea, miles down. Much more reachable in a huge ship than the Thetian caves, useful though they'd been for a fleet of mantas. Thetia was shallow-water territory mostly. I reached for the seat harness and strapped myself into the chair.

"Palatine, give me the controls," I said quietly. She looked at me as if she was about to protest, then I sank my hands into the pads and felt her transfer control to me. I veered around, pointing us deeper and deeper. The others hastily followed my example, strapping themselves in to stop themselves falling forward.

"What are you doing?" Bamalco asked. "We need to go up, not down, to get away."

"We're going somewhere safe," I said. "I'll get us through the currents."

And so began an endless, silent dive through the utter blackness, farther and farther from the world of light and air into the abyss. The abyss that, forty years ago, had swallowed up the most advanced ship in the world, and now would swallow us up too.

Or it would have, if I hadn't been what an accident of birth had made me. I was using my own senses as much as the aether sensors. This was my element, literally, and the shifting morass of currents and eddies all made perfect sense. It was like seeing a tangle of black threads, and then suddenly each one was a different color, so easy to disentangle.

I weaved the giant sea-ray in and out, riding the currents as if they were waves to surf on the shoreline of Oceanus in summer, slipping from one to another, following the thread I had chosen to lead us down. The currents went farther out to sea down here than anyone knew. The *Revelation* had been caught miles from the shelf, dragged in by one of a thousand eddies and currents. All of them led the same way, as if there was a giant whirlpool down here that had been tossed on to its side.

I heard someone gasp as we arched out over the edge of the abyss. I stared in awe myself at the monstrous cavern opening in the cliff below us, extending three or four miles in either direction, at least two miles deep. Only I could see the currents that guarded it on all sides, though, the twisted rocks, the hidden dangers, layer upon layer of them as far as my sight reached. Even the passage to the open sea, between two irregular promontories of rock, was criss-crossed by treacherous currents strong enough to dash in pieces anything smaller than the *Aeon*.

The launch jolted and jumped as I navigated it out and around in a huge circle, coming about to meet the center of the cave. The hull creaked alarmingly but didn't give way; it wouldn't, because in the last resort I could draw on Ravenna's magic again to relieve the pressure. But I wasn't sure we'd be able to survive the ascent if I'd been wrong. I could feel the *Aeon*. She was down here somewhere.

A tiny speck in a vast blackness, we sailed into the center of the cavern, the walls and the roof cutting us off from the open sea. Even in here the sea maintained its vigilance; there were side caverns, cracks in the walls and roof leading off or up to the base of the Shore. I felt a link with the ocean stronger than it had ever been before.

Nobody breathed a word. They stared, transfixed, at the image in the aether tank as the walls fell away again and we passed through a vast gallery, surrounded on all sides by utterly dead, black rock. Nothing could live down here: we were in a place where no one had been for two centuries. Perhaps no one had *ever* been here before.

It went on for miles, that gallery, or tunnel, now contracting, now expanding, sometimes enlarging into massive caves, but only curving very gently. There was still no sign of the *Aeon*, but even something so big would have been able to make its way along here.

And then, finally, eleven and a half miles below the surface of the ocean, directly beneath the colossal mountains of Tehama, the walls, the floor, the roof all fell away in a cavern so vast it defied imagination. The currents ended and I brought the sea-ray slowly to a halt, floating in the absolute blackness of a titanic underwater cathedral whose far walls we couldn't even see on the aether sensors.

And then, here in the darkest place in the whole world, the shadows in my mind were swept away as I saw, as we all saw, the awe-inspiring immensity of a ship as old as its name, hanging in the darkness. There was no way to describe it, no way the accounts could have prepared me for my first sight of her.

I had found the *Aeon*.

Epilogue

A Thetian officer appeared on the manta's screen, a gray-haired man in his early fifties with the calm bearing of a career officer, standing on his bridge. Officers and ratings around him were pretending to pay attention to their consoles while surreptitiously glancing at their own screen.

"I am Admiral Charidemus, Imperial Naval Commander of Eastern Thetia, on board the *Meridian*. Please state your nationality and business."

"Admiral, this is the *Naiad*."

Admiral Charidemus smiled broadly. "Then may my squadron and I have the honor of forming an extra escort for you?"

The *Naiad*'s captain turned around inquiringly to look at the man standing in the shadows at the back of the bridge. He nodded and walked forward into the light.

"Your Imperial Majesty," Charidemus said, bowing. "It is a true honor to be the first to welcome you. May your reign be long and glorious."

"I thank you, Admiral. And the honor is mine, in being escorted." He noted with satisfaction the gazes fixed on him from the *Meridian*'s bridge, the military discipline that not even their eagerness to be the first Thetians to set eyes on their new Emperor could conceal. There was hope, as he'd known there would be.

They had much to learn, but so did he. It was the first time he'd crossed any sea at all, but where those he'd known all his life would be uneasy, he felt as if he was returning to his element. He could command armies and, by the grace of Ranthas, he could command fleets as well or better. It was a challenge he relished.

"We will be home in a few hours, Your Majesty. Your empire awaits."

"May I request your company at lunch, Admiral? Before we arrive?"

"I gratefully accept, Sire."

"Until the second hour of noon, then, Admiral. I look forward to it."

"As do I, Your Majesty."

The image disappeared and the screen vanished, leaving only the view from the windows of sun-dappled blue waters. It was the first day of summer. He walked over to them and gazed out into the sea, watching the shapes of Charidemus's squadron form around his own small escort. The mantas were so graceful, such beautiful ships. Even the boats with their white sails on the mountain lakes didn't compare to them. They looked as if they were truly alive, and they were in the hands of a people—his own people now—for whom the sea was their element, who were as comfortable in the water as other men were on land.

He would never see things the same way again, he realized. He'd spent all his life in a place that was so limited, so enclosed, and had wondered why he never felt truly at peace. He had known the answer the first time he'd stepped on board the *Naiad*, and the following weeks had only made him more certain. There was more to be gained, a better life to be lived, out here in the green islands and the clear, sandy blue seas of Thetia and the Archipelago than in a thousand years in the land he'd known all his life.

The Emperor Aetius VI smiled contentedly to himself as he watched the ocean and his new fleet, the fleet that was bringing him home.